I0694533

INFINITA BOOK 1

OBLIVION AWAITS

INFINITA BOOK 1
OBLIVION AWAITS

CHRISTOPHER HOPPER

HOPPER CREATIVE GROUP

SOMNIUM PUBLISHING

NEW YORK

CONTENTS

INFINITA CODEX

For an even deeper experience, keep the Infinita Codex handy while you read. You'll find a vast glossary, organization histories, a character reference guide, timelines, and universe maps all at your fingertips. Proudly powered by World Anvil.

infinita.christopherhopper.com

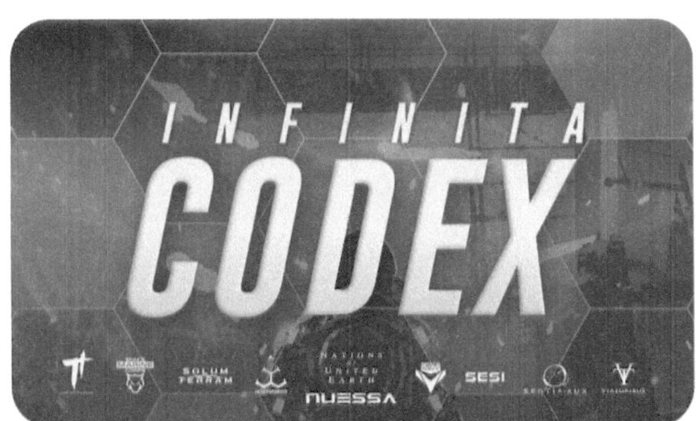

INFINITA
CODEX
SOLUM FERRAM
NATIONS OF UNITED EARTH
NUESSA
SESI

PROUDLY POWERED BY

WORLDANVIL

INFINITA
SYSTEM PLANETS
EUROPA
JUPITER
CALLISTO
GANYMEDE
SUN
MOON
EARTH
CERES
MARS
DEIMOS
CHRISTOPHER HOPPER

INFINITA
MOON
EARTH
EARTH

ASTRAEA STATION
INFINITA
NUESSA

To Carl and Stephen

"Our planet is a lonely speck in the great enveloping cosmic dark. In our obscurity, in all this vastness, there is no hint that help will come from elsewhere to save us from ourselves. The Earth is the only world known so far to harbor life. There is nowhere else, at least in the near future, to which our species could migrate."

—Carl Sagan
Pale Blue Dot: A Vision of the Human Future in Space
1994

"We believe that life arose spontaneously on Earth, so in an infinite universe, there must be other occurrences of life. Somewhere in the cosmos, perhaps intelligent life might be watching these lights of ours, aware of what they mean. There is no better question. It's time to commit to finding the answer, to search for life beyond Earth. We are alive. We are intelligent. We must know."

—Stephen Hawking
Royal Society, London
2015

PROLOGUE

Jack

You don't like killing people, do you, Jack?

No. Enjoyment is for the locker jockeys and stim ward rats. They get off on that sort of thing. Pay for it, in one way or another.

But not you.

You kill, if you must, because it's math. Everything's math. How many mouths can Earth's current crop yield feed? How much time before the population exceeds supply? None of it's hard to process. At least for you. But for them? What, with all their irrational sentimentality? It's downright paralyzing.

Which, you suppose, is why they sent you up here among the stars, isn't it, Jack. Because you do what needs doing. You have what it takes, they said. You've proven your allegiance to the cause, and now you've graduated. You work alone because you're capable, Jack. You're someone they believe in—someone *she* believes in. And you won't let her down. You're the man who will turn the tide and get the world's attention back to where it needs to be.

You down the rest of your bourbon and suck one of the ice cubes from under the lid. But then you remember your role and spit it into the glass. Mr. Samson wouldn't do that, so you don't do it. Instead, you flirt with the flight attendant at the end of the row. Her credentials will serve you later. You'll need to get close. Touch her skin. You could kill her and take it all. But the part she needs to play isn't that involved. You only need a sample. She'll have a headache tomorrow, nothing more.

You call her over and make casual conversation. Everyone else is cogged out, distracted by the verb's endless echo. A few still have their eyes open, but even they stare off in the distance. One man has his mouth agape and drools. They don't even notice you're talking with her. Because these people are sheep. They could never make the hard choices about what's good for humanity. But you can, Jack, can't you.

The attendant compliments you on your flight suit. She should. It's worth her year's salary. But it's not your suit anyway. It's Mr. Samson's. And why is he using public transport when he owns several shuttles? You lie and say you like changing things up, adding, "You never know when the planets will align." But really it's because your powers of impersonation can only take you so far, only gain you so much access until someone calls you out.

Still, she buys it. You compliment her eyes. It's a subtle remark, but a precision tool that you've honed. Because she needs to buy it. Despite the untold numbers of passengers who've flirted with her, your advance must stand out above theirs.

She looks away. Blushes. And you have her.

In a private crew compartment during her break, you sleep with Luna. You tell yourself you feel nothing. It's the role. Play the part long enough to skim some neuronanos from her skin. You press the extraction ring on your left middle finger against the small bald patch on the back of her head. Three seconds, and it's done. The architects tried explaining it. You called it a hack. They called it elegant infiltration. Either way, it's too easy.

You and Luna exhale as the Earth spreads out beneath you in your shared V-cog suite. Whatever you lack in physical attributes, you've learned to make up for virtually with neurohaptics. It's beautiful and tragic all at once. The Earth, that is. But you're doing something about the planet in ways you couldn't before. This. Her. And *Astraea*. It's all part of what you want.

You dress in zero gravity while she looks at you with something like hope. But you don't answer any of her questions, because Mr. Samson wouldn't. You, Jack? You might. But you're not you today. So you smooth your flight suit, give her Mr. Samson's public virtual record locator, because she asks, and then float back to your seat in First Class.

She'd loathe you for lying to her. For impersonating someone else, a man you unplugged less than eight hours ago. But that's the irony of it. If she knew why you were here and the importance of what you were doing, she'd hate you if you *hadn't* killed him. If she knew what was at stake, really understood the math, she'd have helped you with the yank and watched his body convulse.

That's why you don't feel guilty, isn't it, Jack. Because you believe in the greater good. This. Her. You.

It's all just numbers and fractions, ratios and probabilities. You do what needs doing. And you'll make Neon proud at last.

Fifteen minutes remain to docking. You decide to get your first glimpse of *Astraea* and slip back into V-cog. The ship's customer menu fills your VR lobby—a luxuriant Falkland Islands beach in sunny Southland, like that old poster that holds your wall of fame—and you select the nose camera. The pre-timed crossfade transforms the tropical landscape into a live view of the orbital legacy hab suspended in an endless sea of stars. Eight kilometers in diameter and thirty long, the cylinder gleams white in the sunlight, tattooed with the NUE's obnoxious orange filigree.

Your heart skips a beat.

So many people, so completely oblivious. And with each meter, each second that passes, their demise draws closer. And it will end, all of it. Sure, every attempt before this failed. But that's because they fought fire with fire. And those were short-lived battles with orbital defenses, cleaned up by Space Marine gunships. The paladins never stood a chance. But this? You, Jack? They won't even know you're there—don't even know you're here now. Because the hack? It's working.

You touch your lips and wonder if the three cargo cases have been discovered. But that's foolish thinking. Neon's architects saw to it, and you trust their work. Everything is going as planned. At the end of this, if no one impedes you, you'll have what you want, Jack. You'll have secured the survival of the entire human race. And all of the terrible things you're about to do and all the ones you've already done will be justified.

And if something gets in the way? The Tantum Terrae have no shortage of resources. Even now, incogs wait in the wings, watching you. They are nothing more than shadows who move in and out of the world, ready to step in should you fail. Which you won't, Jack. You can't fail. You trust the data too much. And that's what hardens your resolve.

In your mind, you reach out and touch *Astraea* with your fingertips. She's soft and clean like the flight attendant's body. But you have no more feelings for her than you do the legacy hab. They're both rank with the frontier's promise of immortality and guilty of all this… sterility. Of dustless crew rooms, white-walled corridors, and germless sex. All lies.

Like Luna, who would thank you if she knew what was at stake, you imagine the hab saying the same. She invites you forward. Beckons you through hard vacuum and wills you to do what you must. To sacrifice it on the altar of human survival. And then, just then, maybe the wasters will finally rethink their priorities.

"Another bourbon, Jack?"

It's Luna, the flight attendant again. Why do you commit her name to memory? Maybe because you do the same for yourself, changing only your last. They warned against such things, but you ignored them. Why, Jack? Because you don't like the rules? No. The rules are what drove you here. Probabilities that become certainties, and the infallibility of logic. You kept your first name so that you don't lose yourself in Mr. Lourde, Mr. Washington, Mr. Samson, and Mr. Faust. You keep Jack so you keep yourself in the midst of the madness.

"Jack?" Luna whispers, closer now.

You slide out of V-cog and smile at her inquisitive eyes. Would she really be this kind if she knew? Would she understand her own death as being a part of the cost?

You smile, and she serves you. Then she drops her V-rec in your public lobby. You didn't ask for it, like she did for yours, but you register this as more evidence that the plan—it's working. So you thank her, but you don't log the rec. You just stare at it in the corner of your consciousness as you promise her that you'll be in contact once your business is done.

Five seconds after she floats away, you find yourself sucking an ice cube again. But you shouldn't be. You're still Mr. Samson. Mistakes like this will get you noticed, and they'll see right through you, Jack. You can't afford that. Not with so much riding on you. But you only need to be Mr. Samson for a little bit longer. Because you do what needs doing.

The math demands it.

1

JERICHO

"Ya got some nerve drinking on this side of town, spacer," says a man who's had more than enough for the night.

I ignore the drunk leaning against the building and look for a grid car on V-cog. A lender would do too; it's not even midnight yet.

"You hear me, Viatoribus? You don't belong." The man pops off the side of the White Rabbit, an adequate watering hole for a quick beer before I crash back at the hotel, and ambles toward me. "Yeah, I see your ink. Shoulda covered it up in these parts."

I stuff my right hand in my leather jacket's pocket. I'm not interested in a brawl. New job starts in the morning, and this was just supposed to be a quick layover in Winnipeg with HR before heading south.

"Hey, I'm talking to you, asshole." The man grabs my arm.

But I'm about ten beers more sober than he is and jerk away. "Go back to your post, Mitch."

He looks surprised, like I just used some voodoo magic on him. Right. The ragged High Top Uranium patch and name tape are still mostly legible on his dark blue coveralls. Finally, in a stupefied epiphany, Mitch looks down at his chest and then thrusts a finger at me. "Nobody, not nobody uses my name but Solum Terram. You got that?"

"Whatever you say." I take a few steps away.

He grabs me again, harder this time. "Don't you walk away from me, boy!"

It takes everything in me not to swing. But I refuse to show up with bloody knuckles tomorrow.

A new figure pushes out of the bar, spots our growing altercation, and then steps around us.

"Listen," I say, squaring with my inebriated accuser and getting a good whiff of what he's been drinking for the last several hours. "I don't know who you think you are, but you're gonna take your hand off my arm and go back to—"

"Hey. You're… you're Fox, ain't ya? Hell." At least he lets go. But now he's making a scene. "Everybody! Would ya get a load of this? It's Jericho freaking Fox in the goddamn flesh." Good thing "everybody" is just Mitch, the new guy, and me. But the rant's not done yet. "He's decided to ascend"—*descend*—"from on high to grace us mere turtles"—*mortals*—"with his royal… royalish… -ness, 'ism presence."

"Don't hurt yourself."

"Well here's what I think of you, ya bastard." Mitch makes a well-practiced hand gesture over his loins and then spits at me. He misses. "Hope you rot in hell."

With that world shattering discovery made, I head across the street to meet some incoming headlights.

"I'm not done with you, Foxy," says the drunk and starts following me.

The new bystander comes alongside him and says, "Yeah, you are."

"Who the hell are you? Get off me, man."

"I don't take kindly to people messing with my caste." The newcomer holds up his palm. The overlapping letters V and T flash in the streetlamp's light. Then he curls his fingers into a fist. "You feel me?"

"What is it with all you spacers? Ya don't have enough room up there, so you gotta come down here and take more? Damn wasters."

"What'd you call me?"

Mitch eyes his quarry. "*Waster.*" He spits on the man's boots.

That's all it takes for both men to go at each other, hands swinging, beer bottle cracking, and glass flying. Somebody's gonna get hurt. Probably me. And I'm gonna regret everything tomorrow, I know it. But this kinda stuff makes me sick.

I choose my opening and jump in between the two men, turning into the other vee-tee to try reasoning with him. "Just let it go, man. It's all good." I push him back. "Hey. Hey! I said that's enough!"

The two men reluctantly back down, Mitch because he's too drunk to keep standing without the support of a wall, and my fellow politicast member because he's got a bad cut over his eye that's gonna need a nanopatch.

I pull out a wad of cocktail napkins I'd absently stuffed in my pants pocket and offer them up. "You okay?"

"Fine," he says, holding his head. "Just tired of all their BS, ya know?"

I nod, keeping an eye on Mitch to make sure he finds his wall again.

"Plus, I hate when people talk about you like that.

And here I am, getting to meet the man himself. Who woulda thought."

I nod at his eye. "You paid a high price for the meeting."

"It's worth it." His smile fades after a second, and he lowers his voice. "We know you weren't guilty, Fox. Everyone does. Solum's just out to spin whatever they can in the verb, know what I mean?"

I don't reply. Not because I disagree, it's just… well, I don't wanna talk about it anymore. That's why I'm here, trying to put some distance between me and the rest of the system. Trying to lay low until I can figure things out. But apparently that's too much to ask.

"I'm Ruben." He offers the hand not holding the wadded napkins against his head.

"Jericho. Nice to meet you."

He shakes my hand a few extra times as if savoring the action. "Nice to meet you too."

A grid car slows in the oncoming lane, and I ping it in V-cog. It's empty. Perfect.

"No one's ever gonna believe this," Ruben says as I walk toward the vehicle.

"That's probably for the best. And, if you wouldn't mind?"

"Sure. Anything."

"Don't tell anyone we met."

"WHO'D YOU PISS OFF?" the guy at the top of the ramp asks. He's probably not even old enough to stim. Legally, anyway.

I trudge toward the ship's port door but don't feel like replying.

"Strong silent type then. Okay, okay, I see you. Guessing you're good with the ladies, am I right?"

"Just a pilot."

"I knew it." He claps once. "Told my ma' I was getting a new cap today."

"Not a captain. Pilot," I clarify above the sound of the wind and send him my V-rec.

He acknowledges receipt by the time I reach the top and then steps aside so I can get out of the heat. "Name's Kit. I'll be your flight engineer and provider of stories and snacks. Welcome aboard, sir."

This is gonna be a long route. "Barometric pressure's falling. I wanna get underway."

"Aye-aye, sir." He hits the button for the ramp door —a physical button. Haven't seen that in a while. Which means this old bucket isn't fully integrated, and someone really doesn't like me. Kit points to a storage rack while the hydraulics whine in the background. "You can stow your pack there for now. I'll show you to your bunk later."

"Roger." I knock sand off my bag and pull out my flight helmet. Kit seems irritated by the mess I've made but looks away. I shove my belongings in the rack, strap them down, and then pause to enjoy the AC vent blowing cold air on the back of my neck.

"Uh, bridge is this way, Cap?"

I nod and follow him through the short corridor to the two-seater cockpit. It's tight, but everything looks in working order despite its age. He also uses bleach instead of ammonia, but that's personal preference. And how you're raised. "Someone's done a good job keeping this ship up."

"That'd be yours truly," Kit says as he wiggles in the copilot seat and starts strapping in.

Likewise, I slide into my chair, put on my helmet, and orient myself.

After a few seconds, Kit asks, "You, uh, new at this?"

"Come again?"

He nods at the flight hardware. "You fly much?"

"Not used to the physical controls." I tap the side of my helmet.

"Ah. Yeah, we get that a lot. But you get used to it. Nothing like going old school, you know what I mean? Couple times with your hands wrapped tight around the—"

"Pre-flight?"

"Oh. Yeah, roger. Sorry." Kit's fingers dance across the screens as I read off the checklist. He comes back in the affirmative with a sing-song tone for every item I call out. He's quick. Eager, maybe a little too much. But clearly on top of keeping sand out of this ship, which is a full time job, I'm sure.

After we're powered up and everything checks out, I say, "So, you've been at this a while then?"

He offers a proud smile. "One year, two months, and eleven days."

"That's a long time."

"I know. And with some luck and hard work, I might get promoted soon."

"Good for you." The guy's diligent, that's for sure, but he's long overdue for a promotion. Plus, he doesn't exactly fit the profile of a hardened miner. Skinny as a rail and probably one of the pastiest guys I've ever seen. Some higher-up clearly passed him over, he just doesn't know it yet. Poor kid.

"How about you, Cap? All I see on the roster is…" He pauses to slip into V-cog. "…Jericho Fox. Thirty-five. Pilot. Handle: Knight. And then a whole lot of empty space."

"Not exactly a long record, is it."

"Ha. My pug has more details on his chart."

"I don't doubt it." I nod toward the nav screen. "Set up contingencies for those first two waypoints. If that storm picks up speed, we'll want to adjust them east three klicks and then double back behind that ridge for cover until it passes."

Kit hesitates but then starts working the map. "You, uh, know your stuff, huh?"

"Once in a while." I double-check the flight systems and then nod out the port window to the ground crew. The chief gives me the all-clear.

Tower control comes over the flight crew V-cog lobby. "Happy flying, One Seven Niner."

"See you tomorrow, tower," I reply.

"Oh, and, Fox? Try not to blow it up, would ya?"

Normally, I'd respond. But I'm tired and, quite frankly, I don't even want to dignify the comment with a response. "It's a new day, Jericho," I tell myself.

"Say again?" Kit asks.

"Nothing. Hold on." I ease the throttle up, but we're not lifting off. So I push harder and play along the edge of capacitor charge-back.

"You gotta bump it," Kit says. "Bring it back down and then just—" He demonstrates the motion with the heel of his hand. "The old linear cores like the punch, even when we're empty."

I wink at him, do as he says, and feel the thrust jump by half, which gets us off the tarmac with a jolt. Sand washes over the ground crew, and I can hardly see the command building. But all sensors are nominal, and just like that, we're four meters off the deck. Then I ease the controls forward and feel the tail lift as we surge ahead. More thrust, more altitude, and we bank to starboard. The ship surges over the flight line and climbs away.

"Handles better unladen, right?" Kit asks.

I shoot him a sideways glance. "It might be a few years since I flew an LACH, but I know when someone's trying to hustle me."

"Ha. So you *are* rusty."

"Never said I wasn't. And no, they handle better at 90 percent load because that's where they spend the most of their time. The closer you get to their hundred-meter max ceiling, the more control you lose."

"Not bad." He points at me. "But you've still been out of the saddle for a while, right? I'm adding that to your file, Mr. Mysterious."

"Be my guest."

We climb out of Old Cheyenne to a cruising altitude of a whopping fifty meters, which is just fine with me because I'm still flying something. Plus, there's value in helping provide communities with power, right? So I can feel good about my work.

I point the ship north toward our first waypoint and then lock in the autopilot. Pretty sure we'll be activating the alternates since the horizon to the west doesn't look promising. But we've got time to kill until that decision has to be made. "How about you show me where my bunk is."

"You… want to leave the cockpit?"

I raise an eyebrow at him. "Is there something I need to know about the ship?"

"Uh, well, no, but—"

"Show me my bunk."

Kit doesn't move.

"Listen. The autopilot's on, and I'm assuming you have those alts set with threshold triggers, right?"

"Yeah."

"Then we're good. Nothing to see here but sand." I unstrap and pat his shoulder. "Bunk. Let's go."

KIT GETS me squared away in my quarters. One bed, a hand sink, and a storage locker. Everything's in good repair too. But it's smaller than I remember. Then again, I was a kid, so… yeah. It would look smaller now.

The head is behind the crew quarters to starboard. A stainless steel toilet, shower, and sink all in one stall. Efficient. And it's clean. I relieve myself and I make a reminder in my notes to recommend that Kit gets a raise, maybe even a promotion if he wants to pilot. They probably won't listen to me, but it's worth a shot.

When I'm done, I grab two bottles of water from the galley and return to the cockpit. "Here."

Kit takes the water and stares at it for a few seconds.

"You drink it."

He lets out a nervous laugh. "Ha. Yeah, I know, I just…"

"You just what?"

"Never had a captain"—he wags the bottle back and forth—"serve me a drink."

"I can take it back."

Kit flicks off the cap, takes a swig, and wipes his mouth. "You're the nicest one I've been assigned. Cap, I mean."

"Oh yeah? Who do you usually get?"

"The assholes."

I smile at him. "Who says I'm not?"

"Eh, I'm a good judge of character."

My smile fades.

I figured the suits would put me on a rough route. Sure, the northern Saskatchewan runs are paradise, but beggars can't be choosers. Plus, the Wyoming Territory badlands are quiet, and the lack of pilots means I can take as many runs as I want. Anonymity, unlimited flight time, *and* a steady coin stream flowing into my wallet? What more can a guy like me ask for? Well, actually I can think of a few things, but those aren't realities for me right now, and probably not ever again.

What I didn't figure was Command not only assigning me their least updated cargo hauler, as evidenced by the lack of V-cog integration, but they also gave me one of their least liked flight engineers. Though, I have to say, Kit's worked miracles with this ship; the thing should have been retired years ago. But that doesn't change the fact that he's been passed over for promotions. I understand why they wouldn't like me, of course. That's a no brainer. But Kit here? He's freaking harmless, aside from his wiry hair. Probably just got blackballed by the employees of a mining corporation who don't exactly enjoy do-gooders like him, except as a punchline for jokes.

I check the weather map. Storm's definitely getting more dense. "Go ahead and override the thresholds. I want the secondary waypoints."

"On it." Kit updates our heading. "You mind a question?"

"Only if you don't mind me not answering."

"Ha. That's fine. What was that about back there? The whole macho, ya know, 'Try not to blow it up' thing? Uh, uh, uh."

I stare at the dunes to the north and follow the horizon west to where it disappears into the storm. It's weird looking through glass. Makes me feel uneasy. Like the outside is gonna suck me out and swallow me whole.

I'm not gonna lie to this guy. He doesn't deserve it. But he's also not getting the whole truth because that defeats the purpose of why I'm out here—to try to get away from everyone who knows.

"I worked on a project. R&D. The prototype—"

"A ship?"

"—the *prototype* failed. Lost investors a lot of money, and I lost my job."

"Ouch. Sorry." He seems to think about something for a second. "There was probably a girl too, right? You have to have lost the girl. The one that got away, yeah? And now it's your life-long mission to track her down against all odds and win her heart back."

"It's my lifelong mission to eat, wear clothes, and sleep inside."

Kit sighs and looks out the windshield. "So you are an asshole."

"Hey."

"I'm just messin'." He gives me a stupid grin.

I like him. But now it's his turn. "So what did you do to get all the assholes like me?"

Kit's left knee starts bouncing up and down. "Long story."

I backhand his arm. "Nuh uh. This is a two-way street here."

He grimaces. "I got… I got in trouble with one of the execs."

"Of High Top?"

"Yeah. So, that wasn't great. They made me their

whipping boy. But I still have a job, and the pay is pretty good, so…"

"You're hauling uranium in a low-altitude cargo hauler, Kit. Of course the crypto stream is pretty good. It's not like we're doing this for the joy of changing the world or anything."

He's still wound tight.

"Alright. What'd you do?"

"I'd rather not say."

"Hey, you promised stories, and I'm the captain."

"You said you were just a pilot."

"Not when I need more data."

Kit blushes and takes a swig of water. "So, you know Mr. Ogilvie?"

I give him a sideways glance. "As in Chairman of the Board, Mr. Ogilvie?"

Kit nods. "I was at Lefty's one night. You know, downtown Winnipeg? May have had one too many beers. And me and the other FEs, we start talking shop and sharing stuff about our bosses. Lots of funny stuff all around, right? But I'm new enough that I don't have any good stories for myself yet. So I make up this whole thing about dating his daughter, Chloe. Who's super pretty, by the way. Wow. She's got these eyes that are just—*phew*. Anyway, in my story, I'm taking her for joyrides in his car and making out with her in the back seat. Until Mr. Ogilvie walks up behind me 'cause he happened to be at the bar that night and overheard us."

"Oh no."

"Oh yeah. And it gets worse."

I already feel bad for this kid. It's like watching a maglev wreck in slow mo.

"So my friends are giggling at me, and I think it's

because they're jealous or think I'm funny or whatever. So I keep going."

"No."

"By the time I'm done, me and Chloe have eloped and bought a house on Lake Manitoba using her dad's coin stream. That's when I feel a hand on my shoulder and look up."

"I'm so sorry, Kit."

"Oh, I'm not done."

"There's more?"

He nods. "I don't know Mr. Ogilvie. Never seen him before in my life. So I get in a fight with this old guy in a suit who I think's trying to mess with me. I even break his nose."

"You what?"

"He started it! Anyway, bouncers throw us both out, along with my friends."

I don't mean to laugh at him, but damn. "No offense, Kit, but how the hell are you still employed here?"

"That's the beautiful part of being a nobody, I guess, and him being a somebody. Turns out he was there to meet an escort. One of my pals recognized her."

"Because your pals have that kind of flow?"

"Nah. It was my buddy Johnny's sister."

"My god."

"Anyway, when I sober up and clock in the next day, I have an eject notice in my lobby."

"So you did get fired."

He grins. "I figured I had nothing left to lose. So I got all the way through to Ogilvie's personal secretary and delivered an ultimatum. I keep my job and the chairman keeps his secret."

This guy's got balls the size of the Yukon. "You… know they could have killed you, right, Kit?"

"Maybe. But I'm a flight engineer, Cap. A freaking nerd, right? I put a dead man's switch on a blockchain wallet containing the video we shot of us telling stories. And who's in the background?"

"Mr. Ogilvie and Johnny's sister."

Kit clicks in the side of his cheek and points a finger-gun at me. "Bingo. Nerds rule the world, baby. Of course I never considered the chairman might make the rest of my career a living hell…"

"Ya think?" No wonder he's been stuck in this ancient wreck for so long.

The drive core's hum fills the cockpit as the conversation fades away. Need to raise his spirits a little. "Listen, it won't last forever, ya know. How old are you? Twenty? Twenty-one?"

"Nineteen."

"Then see? You're a talented guy, and you've got a whole life in front of you. Things can't follow you around forever."

"Then how come the ATC knew your story?"

"Hey." I point at him. "We're talking about you here, not me."

He smiles out the window. "I know things will come around, eventually. I'll get my shot."

An alarm sounds on the console. Kit silences the audio and brings up the weather map. "Oh, man. That's a big one."

"And we're not gonna make it to the ridge in time."

"You wanna head back then?" The hopeful look in his eyes makes me wonder how many of his previous captains decided to keep flying in similar scenarios. His finger hovers over the Return to Home button.

I'm about to indulge him when I hear something. "Wait." I lean forward. "Something's on comms." I try boosting the signal in our flight crew lobby. "You hear that?"

Kit turns his head as if it will help. Hard to untrain a million years of evolution. "Sounds like... like someone in distress."

"Vector?"

Kit's fingers move fast as he works to triangulate the origin. "Bearing three three five. Range..." He looks up. "Six point four klicks. Holy biscuits, they're inside the storm."

"See if you can clean it up." I grab the controls, turn off autopilot, and then pull up the sat tracker in V-cog. I still have credentials for the global transponder system—they haven't revoked those yet—so I look for other vessels in the region. But there aren't any closer than we are.

Meanwhile, Kit clarifies the transmission as best he can.

The voice is male and intermittent. "Mayday, may-day. All stations, all sta... is High Top Papa Tango Eight Zer... immediate assist... any vessels in... we have twenty-five souls, four critic—"

"Sorry, Cap. Too much interference." He meets my eyes. "We'll need to get closer. We, uh... We doing this?"

"It's your call."

"Mine? But... you're the captain."

"Just a pilot."

He wrings his hands as turbulence jars the ship. "I'm... not sure. I..."

"Pros and cons."

"Huh?"

"What are your pros and cons? Quick."

"Uh, pros, we… save a lot of people. That's a personnel transport down there. Sounds like they crashed and need medical. 'Course they could just ride the storm out… but if things are bad, then, yeah, they'll need help."

"You'll also get a promotion."

He lets out a nervous laugh. "Didn't even think about that. Cons? Uh, we could bite it."

"We could die, yes."

Another gust of wind jostles us.

"What are yours, Cap? Pros, I mean. Guessing our cons are the same."

What *are* your pros, Jericho? Because if you save people—which, how can you not try?—word is gonna spread, and that will get you in trouble. Because Steiner, your new boss, told you to keep your head down. "We don't need any bad press, Fox." Your old man went to bat for you on this one too, said Steiner owed him a favor. So if your name hits the verb, you're fired and right back to square one: jobless in a politicast that doesn't want your services anymore. But hey, you got the chance to do something meaningful again. And that's what you're after, right? To matter? Shame it always bites you in the ass though.

"Those people sound like they're in trouble to you, Kit?"

He swallows. "Yeah."

"And if you were them, would you want assistance?"

"I… guess so? But we don't have enough room for—"

"A few tons of ore?" I wink at him. "Lotta people we can fit in that hold. A day of rad therapy, and they're good to go."

"Roger." He loosens the uniform around his neck. "But what if we don't make it?"

"Then we're not around for bullies to pick on us anymore."

He seems to weigh everything and then his eyes meet mine. "You'd get one too, I bet. A promotion, I mean. I'd put in a good word for you."

"For a man you just met? Kit, you've got a lot to learn."

"Like I said, I'm a good judge of character."

"And a lousy liar when you're drunk."

Kit laughs but avoids my glare. He seems to consider everything one last time and then tightens his straps. "I'm in."

And me? I'm so getting fired.

2

———

EVELYN

"Jesus. Just give up, Dr. Park," someone calls from outside the ring as they walk by.

"It is kinda hard to watch, Eves," Sam adds. She's hiding behind the ropes like they'll protect her from the hits I'm taking.

I've raised the combat level of the sparring excipion a few degrees higher than I normally would. But that's the only way a person learns, right? The white and grey bot pulls a left jab and commits to a right hook. The blow catches me in the side of the head, and those who hear it around the gym gasp. Or maybe that's just my lungs giving out. I can't tell.

My blood's on the mat, and there's another trail across the excipion's chest in a diagonal line. I swallow the iron taste in my mouth and collect my thoughts. Wish I could make this thing bleed like it's making me. So I jab twice at the boxy head, cover and lean away from a left hook, and then jab a third time to gain two points. I glance at the scoreboard overlaid in V-cog. Forty-three, eleven.

I drop back and shake my arms out, dancing lightly around the mechy. It tracks me with interest while I pause to catch my breath. I press one glove against my bare stomach and the other on my hip in an attempt to focus on breathing from my diaphragm and not my upper chest. But I exceed the sparring mode's quarter counter, and the bot comes at me. Fast.

I dodge a jab, block a hook, and come back on center just in time to take an uppercut to the head. Solid. Knocks me back into the ropes where Sam catches me.

"Evelyn, why do you torture yourself like this? You never beat this level."

"Not yet I haven't."

"Well maybe you should at least think about it."

I laugh and then move back toward the excipion.

I never was the best in a fight. There was always someone stronger, faster, and bigger—not that that's very hard. But I did have one thing a lot of street thugs didn't. Determination. Of course, a person can be determined all they want, but running into a brick wall over and over doesn't necessarily turn out for the best, so says my uncle. That's where my other skill comes in. Being clever. Or at least thinking I am.

My opponent charges my corner, guard up, looking like it's about to do its patterned right jab, left hook, right uppercut combo. The moment it throws the right jab, I drop low, pivot behind it, and then swing with all I've got at the side of its head. The blow lands true, earning me three points and one extra for impact velocity.

The bot's torso swivels. Too fast. Its right elbow drives into my sternum and throws me down on the mat. Head hits. Ears ringing. Migraine.

I can't breathe.

Feels like a rib is broken too.

"Eves, call it," Sam hollers.

"Not yet."

"No! *He's calling*," she repeats, and I realize I misheard her. "Lem wants us in the CEL."

"Tell him we'll be back after our break."

"He says the engineers are back. Two this time."

Dammit.

"He's locked them out for now," Sam adds. "But says we have fifteen minutes to shower and get there."

The excipion stands over me and makes a little "get up" gesture with its mitt. Thing's pissing me off.

"End session," I say as I rip my right glove off and flip it the bird.

The guy walking around the ring adds, "I told ya you couldn't beat this level."

I flip him the bird too.

"WHAT DO you mean they have to shut us down?"

I know none of this is Lemuel's fault. He's just doing his job. But he's also the only one who can deal with me when I'm mad. That's probably why I don't have many. Safe places, that is. Or friends.

We're standing in Lemuel's virtual suite, a spacious study with dark oak bookshelves interspaced with floor to ceiling windows that look onto a wide lawn. Leather furniture, some Tiffany lamps, and a brass telescope are the only notable fixtures he's chosen. Timeless, priceless, and reliable—just like Lemuel. Even the chain and medallion he wears around his neck speak to his love for the arcane despite my well-worn objections to his misappropriated faith. He could afford to render out a lot more than this, but that's not his style. Just another reason why I trust him.

"It's only for a few hours, Evelyn. Then you can get right back to your work."

"But we'll need to recalibrate. And I think we're tracking something that…"

"Shows real promise this time? Is going to change everything? Is the most important discovery in human history?"

I plop down in an armchair. "I hate when you do that."

"Your words, not mine."

"That's why I hate it." My face scrunches up. "But this check wasn't scheduled. I don't understand. We should have been notified at least—"

"A month in advance. Director Johnson agrees, but in this instance, they say it can't wait."

"It will be two weeks of work, *gone*."

He shrugs. "You know how they are with the scrubbers. No chances."

"I get that, in the main hab. But we have so many redundancies in the bubble. Who cares? Just one more day. Twenty-four hours. Then they can play engineer all they want."

Lemuel pushes his big lower lip toward his nose. It's his fatherly "I wish I could do more but my hands are tied" face.

"Try? For me? Please, Lem?"

His jaw juts out, and his shoulders stiffen. But it only lasts a second. "You know, sometimes I wonder who the boss is in this relationship."

"We both know it's you."

"Do we?" He holds my eyes and then looks down. "I'll call him one more time."

"Thank you, Lemuel."

He points at me. "But don't make trouble up there. We're already on thin ice."

"Promise."

He doesn't look convinced, so I give him my best acquiescent smile.

Lemuel's face softens. "You're a pain in my ass, Dr. Park."

"As are you in mine, Director Brown."

And with that, his room vanishes and I'm back in my own suite.

I slip out of V-cog. The two techs are still standing right in front of me as before, dressed in their black NUESSA work uniforms. The agency's orange logo and rank adorn their left shoulders, while the acronym's full description runs down their right sleeve: Nations of United Earth Space and Science Administration. I really wish the word Science had been put first in the name.

"And?" the senior most tech says with an arrogant glare.

"And Director Brown is still waiting for confirmation."

The tech pops into my virtual lobby—a space that I've made minimalistic and inhospitable on purpose— and holds up a data pad. "But we have a confirmed work order from Command. Shut 'em and read, Doc."

Doc? I don't bother closing my eyes to read the issuance; I can guess what it says. Plus, if I want to review it, there's no need to "shut 'em"—I worked hard to acquire the discipline of simultaneous visual perception when I was five. But this man's disrespect is what really irks me. Just because people don't understand what we're doing doesn't make it any less valuable to the greater good. SESI always has been the frontier's bastard child.

"I don't care if you have my dead mother's signature"—I squint at his right breast's nametape—"Senior Engineer *Hodges*. You aren't powering down this research lab until I hear back from Dr. Brown, and that's final. So we can either stand around and waste one another's time, or you can float off to your next job and keep on schedule."

"But—"

"No."

"They'll be—"

"Don't care."

"I'll have to—"

"And don't you just hate when that happens?"

Hodges fumes but finally seems to figure out that his efforts are pointless. "You'll be hearing from my section supervisor, ya know."

"And I'll be sure to tell them how good you were." At what? Trying to get an irritable and overtired scientist to comply with safety concerns in the hard vacuum of space?

He throws a finger in my face. "This isn't over, doc."

I consider batting his hand away but choose civility instead.

Hodges waves at the other tech, Del Toro, and they push toward the lab's main door.

When the bubble's exit seals shut, Collins floats beside me. "I think you made them piss their suits."

I tuck some strands of hair behind my ear. "Good."

"You know it's not Hodges's fault, right?"

"Why does everyone say that? Of course it's not. But he's the messenger, and contrary to popular belief, they do get shot."

"By a SESI scientist turned Space Marine? Got it."

"Sam. They're not taking us offline. Not when we're so close."

She shrugs. "No one ever faulted you for a lack of tenacity."

"And they'll thank us when it's over."

I expect her to confirm my statement, but she avoids eye contact.

"What?" I ask.

"Nothing."

"Come on. Spit it out, Dr. Collins."

She sighs. "We've been on this run for… how long? And you're willing to draw the ire of Station Command just to finish a sweep that will most likely—"

"Watch it."

"—end the same as hundreds before it?"

"Ouch."

"I just don't see it, Evelyn. I'm sorry. We can recalibrate tomorrow, start fresh, and no one loses their jobs."

"Losing jobs isn't on the table, Sam."

"Isn't it?" Her cheeks flush a little. "They'll do it. They'll shut it down, put money elsewhere. And you know it. The only thing keeping us up here is Brown. Not me. Not you. Not any of us. And I know you don't want to hear this, but they don't care about the *idea*. They care about *results*."

"But the ideas *are*—"

Sam raises a hand. "You don't have to sell me, Eves. I'm still here, remember? But if you don't ease off the way you've been acting lately, I won't be."

"Is that a threat?"

"No. It's a reality. Because if we're not fired from SESI outright, we'll be looking through double refractors in the Floridian wastes."

She's right. Not about the double refractors bit; that's a 200-year-old joke that astrophysicists still love to throw around. I mean about me being on edge lately. The last three weeks have been strange. *Astraea*'s coming up on her fortieth birthday. She's far from a midlife crisis, but you wouldn't guess that with the way the techs have been running around lately.

What I hate most is how much of my mental energy has been diverted from the project. I've had to monitor well-meaning hab engineers to keep them from tripping a breaker or clipping a signal path that would jeopardize my work. *Our* work—it's a public effort. Just feels personal when you seem to be the only one who believes in it.

But you're not the only one, Evelyn. Reality check.

"You're right, Sam. I'm sorry. I just…" I run a hand over my face.

"My opinion, here? You need to go out, relax a little. And then, ya know, get a good night's sleep." She winks at me.

I double-check the time and tap the end of my nose with a finger. Maybe I do need a nap. As for a date, I consider telling Sam that I haven't been on one in years and that the prospect kinda freaks me out at this point. But that would only motivate her more. If my mom were still here, I'm sure she'd side with Sam. Maybe they're both the cause of the ache in my neck. No matter how much I rub it, I just can't seem to—

"Evelyn?"

"What?"

She gives me a concerned smile. "You, uh… just tuned out for a second."

"Sorry." I take a deep breath and thumb toward the door. "You okay if I…?"

"Of course. Get outta here. And I'll keep Hodges on his toes if he comes back."

"Thanks, Sam."

She nods, then offers up our motto. "Forging paths?"

"Through the darkness," I answer. "See you at six tomorrow."

"Sleep in and make it eight."

"We'll see."

I EXIT THE BUBBLE—OUR pet name for the celestial exploration laboratory—and slide into the main legacy hab's constantly spinning central shaft. Due to our need for a non-rotating observation environment, the bubble is bearing-isolated from the main O'Neill-Oberth cylinder. It's also one of the only segments of the thirty-kilometer long environment that has windows, which is all the more reason to keep it stationary. The vertigo from spinning stars would be unbearable.

I love the bubble and everything it represents—the mission to find what I know is out there: extrasolar sentient intelligence. That said, my love for the main legacy hab is a close second. It stands as a bulwark against humanity's Earthly destruction, one that says we will not go gentle into that good night but instead lunge defiantly into the vacuum of space and survive among the stars. Forever. This is where humanity finds our next stage of evolution, meeting our destiny with those who will help us find the way through the darkness.

I float to the elevator bank, enter a pod, and order it to the surface four kilometers below. For the uninitiated, going from zero g's to one in a matter of two minutes can be an unsettling experience, as can the increase in centripetal acceleration. But my brain got used to the transition in the first six months—what is it, three years ago now?—and instead lets me focus on the spectacular view out the glass.

This never gets old.

As the lift leaves the power level, consisting of a light tube that runs *Astraea*'s length and is filled with the energy core and zero-gravity manufacturing, I marvel at the twenty-five kilometer circumference that encircles what has become my whole world. The soft curves and gleaming white surfaces of early twenty-third century architecture merge with forests, parks, and glistening blue streams. Clouds roll through the hab's fifteen-hundred cubic kilometers of humid atmosphere, and it looks like the south end is in for a summer rain burst.

But the most important thing in *Astraea* is her people. As of this morning, the population is 376,291—over a third of a million inhabitants who have pledged their lives so that humanity might live beyond where we began, so that we might dwell among the stars. They're busy proving to the whole system that we can do more than just survive beyond the dying planet we evolved from. We can thrive. Education, commerce, exploration, and so much more—it awaits us all. But it won't last forever.

When the lift doors part on section thirty, I step into the open air, slip off my shoes, and scrunch up my toes as my feet touch the smooth walkway. Then I close my eyes and dim the lights in my V-cog lobby. One deep breath later, I've completed my ritual. Silly, I know. But if I quiet myself and listen, bare feet on the deck... if I take a deep breath and hold the air just long enough for my heart to skip a beat, I feel it. Sense it. The vibration of life.

Of hope.

I open my eyes and look up to the far lands of quadrant C arching overhead in the majestic sweep of human ingenuity. And as the light tube starts to wane and plunge *Astraea* into night, I can't help but thank the stars that I'm alive to see such a sight.

"Good evening, Dr. Park," says a kind voice beside me as I collect my shoes.

"Hi, Julio."

"Was it a good day up there in your space cave?"

"I've had better. You?"

"It's always a good day when you're scooping out ice cream. Something for after dinner?"

I smile at the old man who's still in his prime thanks to his base editing. He's a testament to what science can do, if only the naysayers would listen. "No, but thank you."

"My *treat?*" He loves that pun. "I see that grin, Dr. Park. You can't fool me."

"Twist my arm, why don't you."

"Your usual?"

"Why mess with a good thing?"

"Coming up."

I FOLLOW one of my favorite wooded paths in the direction of section twenty-nine and sit on a bench that looks onto a park. Children organize a game with a ball, and I dip into the mint chocolate chip made in the agriculture and subsystems level below. I'm not sure if I needed the break or if mint chocolate chip just tastes better in space. Either way, this hits the spot.

Millions of people would give anything to be in my position right now, here in the twilight of a legacy hab as the streetlights come to life. The air temp cools, and crickets tune up for their evening serenade. There's no remnants of the Hundred Years Migration here, no bad memories or mass graves. Just tranquility, at least as much as humanity can manufacture. And therein lies one of the many ironies.

None of this is good enough because none of it answers the question of what we do next. Not sufficiently, anyway. Oh, sure, the legacy habs and dome settlements will get us through for a while. But anyone not looking at the big picture is just shoving their head deeper into the sand. Seems to be a recurring pattern for humanity. I don't believe in miracles, but it's a wonder we've evolved as far as we have.

In a sardonic way, the protesters are right. Whether those lobbying for the NUE to pass the lottery bill so "the commoners" will have a chance to replace the "beautiful ones," as we've been called—a strange name for scientists and their offspring—or those fighting to abandon space expansion altogether, claiming it to be the fatal distraction against Earth's renewal. All of this is a temporary solution to a much bigger problem. Even if few see the pending cataclysm for what it really is.

Extinction.

We must find another planet.

And here it is, the greatest irony of all. Many critics were reportedly surprised that our "space race," which started in the twentieth century, continued throughout the Hundred Years Migration in the twenty-first and -second centuries. Like those today, they claimed that our time and energy should have been spent elsewhere. But they all failed to recognize that the great driver of technological innovation was not the purist's love for all things bright and beautiful. It was war. That primal desire to stay alive against the face of overwhelming odds. That is what funded the Great Wall of China; Roman, German, and American roadways; the Apollo, Mars, Ceres Lander I, and Ganymede Explorer IV missions; and eventually every branch of the NUESSA and SESI program to settle the solar system and reach into the vast unknown.

"There's help for you still," I say to the children playing in the distance as I daydream about the generations yet to come. "If we fail, you must carry on." Such are the words of a pioneer mother to her children. "But, stars, I hope we don't."

There's a whoosh of air through the leaves, and then a ball smacks hard against a tree trunk. I lose the spoonful of ice cream to my lap. The kids shout for me to throw the ball back, clapping their hands and giggling. I give it my best throw and then watch them resume their play. Most of these are first-generation space farers. They've never touched Earth. Many never will. Their little bodies were engineered for zero-gravity, high-radiation living the moment they were conceived.

"We'll take you to the stars, lovelies," I whisper. "You'll have your home yet. Never fear."

I decide to save the rest of the ice cream for later, close the container, and carry on southbound toward section twenty-nine. The grass feels good between my toes, enough that I consider lying down to relax. But then I'd just fall asleep out here. Sam's right. I do need a break. And that's one of the problems about this place: there's nowhere else to go. Nowhere but further out into the big black.

That's why I'm doing this. All of it. Because the answer for humanity doesn't rest with us. It can't. We've seen what we can do, and at the end of the day, it's not enough. Exoplanets are too far, terraforming is too slow, and legacy habs are too small. For what must come next, we need help. We need those who are beyond us to reach back and teach us how they solved the same problems we're facing. We need guides—sages among the stars. I know they're out there. I am certain of it.

A chime sounds down the path toward the nearest public square. There's a commotion, and someone screams. Unlike old starships that use klaxons for emergencies, *Astraea* uses chimes—at least as far as I've experienced. Research shows that people respond better to less abrasive audio prompts, and I, for one, am grateful. I never understood the idea of creating more anxiety by telling an already uneasy crew to be more anxious. But there are enough people making a fuss about something ahead that I hurry along the path and emerge from the wooded park to see what's the matter.

A crowd has gathered in the smooth white curves of Webb Square. They're standing near one of the support columns for the elevated walkway. I jog to the group, push through the back row, and announce my credentials. If something's happened to the structure or someone's hurt, I might be able to help. Plus, I'm curious.

When I finally near the front, the crowd separates to reveal a human body splattered across the ground.

3

JERICHO

THE STORM'S THREATENING to rip the rivets from our hull. But that's if we manage to stay aloft. With the LACH's max altitude of a hundred meters, a sudden twenty-five-meter drop is not something I'm thrilled about, especially when we hit two in a row.

"Having second thoughts?" I ask Kit.

"No. No way. Those people need us, right?"

"Roger that. Divert the rest of our auxiliary power to stabilizers."

"Aye, sir." Kit's fingers slide across the screens. A moment later, I feel the understeer disappear from the controls. Not sure how long it will last, but I'll take any advantage we can get. "I'm rerouting some of the environmental system power too. It eats a lot, and we don't need it right now."

"Good thinking."

A moment later, he says, "I'm getting a more detailed fix on their location, Cap. Seems they're right on the edge of a... of a canyon."

We exchange looks. No wonder they weren't willing to ride the storm out—aside from any urgent medical issues, that is.

A slurry of sand and rain grinds against the windshield. Fortunately, we still have enough top speed to keep it from caking. But how long that lasts is anyone's guess. It still amazes me that glass was the preferred viewing medium for the first hundred years of flight.

The air traffic controller's static-laden voice tries to push through comms. "Foxtrot Char... Niner... off course. Be advised, you're—"

Kit replies but interjects his own version of static. "We barely—*kshhh*—read you—*kshhhhowwww*—Tower. Come back—*kshhhhhock*."

"Uh... What are you doing with the noises there, Kit?"

He smiles. "They're probably gonna try and call us home, right?"

"Rather than risk losing a ten-million-coin aircraft? You bet your wrench set they are."

"Right. So, we can't exactly *defy* orders that they don't think we heard. You catch my drift?"

Huh. Smart guy. "Defying orders?" I turn up the tower's channel in our V-cog lobby to emphasize the static. "I don't hear a thing."

"Yeah, that's too bad." Even when he's on edge, Kit's thinking outside the box and keeping it together. Duly noted. "The mayday transmission is clearing up, Cap. I'm also getting transponder data and..." He pauses to read it. "Wow. It's a new ship."

"How new?"

"Like, brand new. Two months."

"What?" I lean over to look at Kit's data console. Sure enough, the manufacturer's commission stamp reads May 21, 2251.

"You think it's a lemon?" he asks.

"I think someone spent a lot of money on a brand

new low-alt personnel transport when they could have saved a small fortune on a used one instead. Try to get through."

He tries the LAPT again. "Papa Tango Eight Zero Two, this is High Top Charlie Hotel One Seven Niner. We read you and are en route to your position. Over."

The pilot's voice on the other end comes through loud and clear. "Thank God. Good to hear you, One Seven Niner. How far out are you?"

Kit studies the nav console. "ETA in three mikes."

"Copy. How much room do you have?"

"Enough for your whole crew. Over."

There's a pause, and I already know what the other pilot's thinking. "But you're a cargo ship."

Kit smiles at me. "Yeah, but we're outbound and still empty. Your people will need radiation therapy, but that's a lot better than dying in a sandstorm in the lower reaches."

There's another short pause as the man on the other end considers this. I'm not sure why he's taking so long —it's a no-brainer as far as I'm concerned.

"Roger that, One Seven Niner. We'll be ready. Be advised, we are in a highly unstable position and at risk of overturning. Please approach at a minimum safe distance of two hundred meters."

Kit raises an eyebrow at me and then replies. "Copy, Eight Zero Two. Will comply."

The other captain thanks us and closes out the channel. Kit switches lobby comms to standby and cinches his real-life straps again.

The sky has darkened even more over the last minute. "It's gonna get worse before it gets better," I say. "Hold on."

I maneuver up and over several dunes that churn in

the low light and high winds. If lives weren't on the line and we were guaranteed a rescue boat if we fail, I might actually enjoy this. Reminds me of racing RDX-60s.

"You okay?" Kit asks.

"Why?'

"You're smiling."

"Just having some fun."

"This is fun to you?" He points out the window but then smiles. "I see. You're messing with me, aren't you."

I give him a shrug and try to keep our LACH under control as we descend.

"Hey, hey! I see it." Kit points out the window. Again, I hate having a glass windshield. But without V-cog integration and external cams, a seamless nano-comp hull is pointless. Still, he's spotted the downed Regent-class personnel transport with his naked eye, and that's what we need because sensors are going nuts. The dark blue-grey hull is half covered by a sand drift, as is the gold and white shield-shaped High Top Uranium logo on the windward side. But the leeward side? It's hanging off a drop that I can't see the bottom of.

"Overlaying proximity ring now," Kit says. "Should see it on your console."

I do, and it definitely helps. The last thing I want is us to blow that ship over the edge because of a clumsy rescue attempt. Of course this would all be a whole lot easier with virtual cognizance integration. I can't believe High Top's even been allowed to field a ship without it. Then again, our vessel probably isn't even on the books, and Ogilvie isn't exactly going to miss the guy who hypothetically ran off with his daughter. I get it.

The distance to the target ship creates another problem: walking the people through a storm that could just as easily blow them into the canyon as it might the ship. Normally, drones would serve as guides, but there's no way they're going out in this. Rovers couldn't handle these ground conditions either, and we're not important enough to carry excipions. Good thing I have something up my sleeve… just hope I don't die trying to pull it off.

"Kit. We need to point our aft bay toward their stern. Compass is squirrelly, so I need you back there guiding me."

"On it."

He unbuckles and dashes out of the cockpit. Fifteen seconds later, an incoming request to share Kit's POV pings in my suite. I accept and get his eyeball-view of the personnel transport as seen out our stern window as an overlay in my FOV. The sand and rain are getting worse, but I use the nav lights and Kit's coaching as we descend.

"A little to port," he says. "Okay, too much, Starboard. Starboard!"

"I got it."

"Good. Now straight down. Straight. A little lower annnnnd…"

The landing gear hits.

"We're down!"

"Good job."

"You too, Cap. Solid flying. Except for that one part where you started to slew too far to port and I had to—"

"Kit, I gotta hail the other captain."

"Oh, right. Totally. Sorry about that."

Over our ship-to-ship V-cog lobby, I say, "Eight Zero Two, this is…" I consider using a pseudonym, just to avoid delays. "…this is Lucky."

Kit mouths the word "Lucky?" to me.

I ignore him. "Who am I speaking with?"

"Captain Vern McCutcheon." The pilot steps into the lobby in a High Top flight suit. He's way too clean cut to be a hauler, assuming his avatar is real to life. He looks at Kit. "You're not the pilot. Everything okay here?"

"Oh, yeah. Cap's just—his patch needs some maintenance, you know? Voice only."

I make a note to thank Kit for covering for me. "I'm right here, McCutcheon. And we're parked two hundred meters from your stern now."

He sounds annoyed but gets his professionalism back fast. "Roger, Lucky. We see you. Be advised, our passengers aren't equipped for weathering this storm, and we're not carrying any robotics. So it might be a little slow going, especially with visibility decreasing."

Kit gives me a confused glance, but I ignore it. "Copy that, McCutcheon. We'll try and provide some guidance. Wait for our signal to proceed."

"Roger. See you soon, Lucky."

As soon as the connection closes, Kit asks, "What miners aren't equipped for this?"

"None that I know."

"Then who the hell does he have on that ship?"

I UNBUCKLE MY HARNESS, grab my leather coat, and book it to Kit's position in the aft. He's got his hand hovering over the cargo hold button, and he's watching the other ship like a hawk. When I start unclamping the deck hatch to the exterior ladder, he looks at me like I'm crazy.

"What, uh… whatcha doing there, Cap?"

"Going to lend a hand."

His eyes get big. "But it's dangerous out there."

"Which is exactly why they need a hand."

"But the… and then the radioactivity… and you'll need—"

"I'll be okay. Probably. But if I don't return, you make sure whoever's on board gets back to base. Got it?"

"As in, fly?"

"You know how, right?"

"Um… Well, yeah, but—"

"Good. I'm counting on you."

With the last manual lock released, I tap the Open button and the seal gives way. A gust of dirty air shoves the hatch up. I swing the cover to its locked position and drop my feet through the hole.

"Stay safe out there, Cap," Kit yells. "You're my favorite asshole so far."

A STANDARD ISSUE flight helmet's got powerful LEDs on each side, along with an IR patch for tracking. When well maintained, they provide adequate lighting in standard low- to no-light situations. Of course, this is not a standard situation, nor do I have well-maintained equipment. Why? Because the only person who seems to like me at present is Kit, and even his allegiance is newly pledged. Bottom line is that I should have checked my gear before sliding down the ladder. The left-side LED has a loose connection somewhere, and the right-side one isn't working at all. As for the IR patch, V-cog can't find it, which means it probably hasn't worked in a long time. Surprise, surprise.

I flip up my collar against the biting sand and use our ship's stern lights to scan the hull for the aft utility compartment. The door takes a few jerks to open, but I find what I need: a spool of nano-fiber line used for surveying. Standard length is 500 meters, and the faded stencil on the housing confirms I'm in business.

I maglock the line's socket end to our hull beside the cargo bay doors, orient myself toward the personnel transport's taillights, and then start walking with the spool case in my hands. The slurry of sand and rain is like sludge, and it's getting worse by the minute. Which is exactly why I'm dragging this depth line: no way passengers are making the transfer without one.

As I get closer to the LAPT, I spot the yawning black chasm to its leeward. There's no seeing the bottom from here, and I don't need my aerospace engineering degree to know the people inside won't survive a fall. But I also notice just how much of the ship seems to be hanging over the side. I pick up the pace.

By the time I reach the aft doors, my lungs and legs are burning. I smack the spool housing's magplate to the hull, hit the auto-tighten button to lock the line, and then jump into McCutcheon's lobby with audio. "Here for escort."

McCutcheon's avatar looks shocked. "You're… outside?"

"Roger."

He disappears from his lobby. The next thing I know, hydraulics lower the aft ramp, and I get a good view inside. Not only is this transport new, but it's also loaded. The rear service compartment has a kitchenette, a refrigerator, and a mess of plates, glasses, and bright silverware on the floor. I look past the wood trim and into the main passenger compartment to find some two dozen frightened faces staring back at me. Of *course* they're not prepared for this kind of weather: they're not miners at all. Not by a long shot. They look more like investors and politicast members in fancy clothes and tidy hairdos. Well, shit.

McCutcheon moves down the center aisle smoothly and reminds everyone to stay calm. When he gets to the service compartment and sees me, his face lights with recognition. "Ho-ly hell. You're—"

"Ready for you, Captain," I shout above the wind.

It takes a few seconds for him to regain his composure and probably to think through whether or not he wants to send his passengers to my ship. But he's not exactly overwhelmed with options right now. "Roger. Uh… You should know that we're, um… That the ship is…"

He's trying to choose his words carefully, and I'm guessing it has to do with a load balance issue and the rim that the ship's perched on. "We need to move smoothly?" I offer.

"Affirmative."

"Got it. Just remind everyone to take their time. No rush."

"Understood. And your rovers?"

"No go. You got me instead, and I've run a safety line."

He considers my less-than-optimal presentation of the facts, eventually nods, and then turns around to give instructions, taking special care to emphasize "Captain Lucky" when describing the pilot the passengers will see pointing them toward the rescue ship. It's not lost on me that maybe I should have picked a different pseudonym.

When he's finished, McCutcheon turns back and says, "Take care of them this time."

I nod, but that's all the recognition I'm giving to the jab.

One by one, I work with the ship's service crew to help passengers down the ramp and along the safety line. "Don't let go! Watch your step," I shout on repeat. The wind speed is picking up, making my choice to run the tether all the more important. But with each passenger who disembarks, I sense the ship listing to starboard. The stern is rising too.

A third of the passengers are off the ship when I halt the next person with my hand. "McCutcheon," I say over V-cog so as not to alarm anyone. "We're losing ballast. Any more, and I'm worried we'll lose the ship."

"Yeah. Ideas?"

Several go through my head, but none are good. Kit could tow us using the depth line, but this gauge of nano-fiber isn't rated for those kinds of loads. He could fly up underneath the leeward side, but that would take an expert pilot and a flawless approach. Not to mention the damage it would cause our ship if anything went wrong, and then we'd all be stranded in the open. Way too risky. I even think about having the remaining passengers hold onto the line and let the transport fall away like in the movies, but that's the only place for such fictions. Plus, it looks like there are still plenty of injured passengers left.

"Please, sir," a woman in a business suit yells above the storm. "I want to get off the ship!"

"You will, ma'am. We just need to…"

That's it.

The ship!

"McCutcheon. This Regent-class… what else is it used for?"

"We… transport high-profile clientele to—"

"I know that. I mean, when you're out giving tours, do the investors ask for core samples?"

"Of course. But I don't see—"

"So you've got a sample rig on the belly. Did it survive the crash?"

Understanding dawns on McCutcheon's face. "You want to try and use the drill to anchor us."

"Bingo."

"Yes, the system still looks operational. But the force will sheer the shaft. It won't hold long."

"Doesn't have to."

He starts nodding. "It's worth a shot. I'll get it online."

"But slowly, McCutcheon. We don't want the force adding to our situation. And keep it quiet. People might not get it, and we don't have time for questions."

"Roger. Stand by."

A well-dressed man with a wavy coif of hair looks over the woman's shoulder at me. "What's the hold up, Captain Lucky?" With the way he says my name, I can't tell if he's making fun of the moniker or if he's recognized me. He does look kinda familiar.

"We just need to let the ship balance out." It's enough of the truth to make us both feel okay. I hope. "A few more seconds and then you can proceed."

He eyes me skeptically but then disappears behind the woman again.

Barely audible amidst the sound of the storm, the drill spins beneath the ship and starts boring into the sand. Mr. Fabulous with the perfect hair looks around the woman again and eyes me.

I give a fake smile but keep my hand up. "Just another moment. Promise."

When the drill hits bedrock, the ship shudders and several passengers cry out.

"What the hell?" the business woman hollers.

"McCutcheon?" I say over comms.

"It's okay," he says in a reassuring tone. "I'm in. Closing on one meter. How far, you think?"

I don't have time to calculate what we need, so I go with my gut. "See if you can get three. And go easy, McCutcheon. Nice and easy."

"Roger. Stand by."

The drill tip burrows deeper, and the grinding sound gets softer. Soon, all that's left is a faint hum.

"Okay, three meters. But I'm already getting warning indicators that—"

"It'll hold, Captain." To the woman and the man with the perfect hair, I say, "Alright, let's get you outta here."

I help them down one at a time, but Mr. Fabulous grabs my hand. "That was your idea with the drill?"

I ignore the comment. "Hand on the line, sir. Don't stop."

He smiles and then plunges into the storm.

Kit calls over comms. "I see the first passengers now, Cap. Opening the hold."

"Good. Do your best to get them squared away."

"Copy that."

The last passengers to leave are those in the worst condition; this crew's priorities are a little back-asswards if you ask me. But then again, I'm not entirely sure Mc-Cutcheon is running this show based on all the suits and money that just walked by me. I help pairs of injured passengers and crew off the ramp until it's just Mc-Cutcheon and me.

"Last off," he yells.

"Roger."

The captain refrains from closing the ramp. If he's thinking it might unsettle the ship, I fully agree. He grabs the safety line ahead of me and starts moving away. Then I demag the spool housing from the transport and start the auto reel. The last thing I want is a snapped nano-line whipping through people's hands when the ship falls.

I can't see our hauler's running lights anymore. The storm is too strong. Even with my flight helmet and jacket on, sand is working its way into my hair and down my neck. My feet miss a step, but my hands are locked on the spool handle, and I stay upright.

At last, we reach the cargo bay and I follow Mc-Cutcheon out of the weather.

"Grab a seat, Captain," I say to him. "I'll be up top if you need me."

"Roger that."

I exit to find the ladder again, but McCutcheon grabs my arm. "Thanks, Knight. If you hadn't shown up, I..."

Right on cue, there's a loud *snap!* followed by the sound of metal grating over stone behind us. We look back to see the personnel transport's lights point straight up and then vanish over the side.

"Don't mention it," I reply. "To anyone."

"Not sure you're gonna have much choice there, Knight."

The abandoned ship crashes into the canyon floor. "Yeah. That's what I'm afraid of."

4

EVELYN

I MOVE CLOSER to examine the body while bystanders cup their mouths in horror. They keep their distance from the radial blood splatter like insects afraid of a pesticide spill. A woman reaches toward me as I pass, but the effort is half-hearted.

"Miss. What… What are you doing?"

I ignore her. I'm too focused on the victim's body—or what remains of it.

"He just… jumped," says some ignorant man behind me. "From the skywalk."

"No, he didn't." I kneel beside the mess.

"Excuse me?" He sounds irritated. Seems to be my superpower these days.

"He didn't jump off the skywalk," I reply.

"Like hell he didn't. And how would you know anyway? You just… showed up here a second ago."

I look over my shoulder. "And you saw him jump then? From up there?" I nod toward the elevated footpath.

The man swallows, and his pupils dilate as he considers lying to me. But I'm not blinking, nor am I letting him get away with such an irrational conclusion.

"That's what I thought."

I look back to the body and start talking through the problem, for my sake if no one else's. Maybe they'll learn something in the process. "Sure, to the non-physicists in the room, this looks like someone fell from the skywalk. Maybe it was an accident, or maybe the person jumped on purpose. We trust the investigators to deduce what happened. However, there are two problems with the elevated walkway theory. The first is that the bridge is only eight meters overhead."

"I don't understand why that's a…"

"Sure, you might break a bone, or even your neck if you dive headfirst. But there's no way you reach a velocity that causes your body to explode on impact. Not like this.

"The second problem with the jumper theory is that there's blood splatters on the support column."

"There are?" the man asks.

"Halfway up."

"But that's just from—"

"Noooo. Not from when the body hit down here: from when it first impacted the column."

My mind flashes back to the *whoosh* in the trees and the sound of the kids' ball hitting the trunk. *The sounds.* They were too pronounced for a child's toy passing through the air or hitting a tree. I should have picked that up. The timing was uncanny, yes, but still a product of chaos.

"There's only one way a human body suffers this level of catastrophic trauma. And you're half right, sir. He did fall."

"Ha! Ya see?"

"But not from the skywalk."

High above us, the power level is in night mode,

now a blackened cylinder emitting synthetic starlight. I squint and search the surface for some kind of small opening. It's a vain attempt, I know. The cylinder is four kilometers away, but there's a hole up there somewhere. It's the only possibility, one I'm going to attempt to explain to anyone who cares to listen.

"Whether by accident or by force, this person—yes, a man, if I had to guess, though he was traveling too fast for any bystanders to see his gender—was pushed out of the power level, and at a sufficient angle to counteract the hub's painfully slow rotational speed. From there, he flew sideways through space as if the hab wasn't even here, minus any wind resistance, of course. Meanwhile, the ground's angular velocity—that is, the rate of the hab's circumference and the speed necessary for *Astraea*'s population to experience one g—whipped by at 198 meters per second. So when the man flew above our heads, or, rather, when our heads flew beneath him and he smacked the support at four times Earth's terminal velocity, he bounced off the column and landed a few meters away with his body pulverized. Not the worst way to die—it's instantaneous—but certainly not the best."

Judging by everyone's silence behind me, I'm reasonably sure they didn't follow along. That, and a few seem downright appalled with me. Too direct?

I let out a sigh. "Does anyone remember the old drum-style tumble dryers? The ones that pushed the clothes around with baffles?"

Heads nod.

"Well, imagine I put a cherry on the end of a stick and hold the fruit inside the spinning drum in the center."

"With the door open?" someone asks.

"Yes, with the door open. Then I slowly move it toward the wall. The cherry is barely moving relative to the air space inside the drum. But relative to the baffles? It's whizzing past. If the drum spins fast enough and I move the cherry within range, the next incoming baffle is gonna hit it hard enough to pop."

To my astonishment, there's still a general sense of confusion.

I run a hand over my face. "The victim is the cherry. The column is the baffle. Human meets a hard thing, gets pulverized."

"Oh my god," says one woman. "That's terrible."

It *is* terrible. But god has nothing to do with it. And, yeah, I probably could've been more tactful in how I shared all that. But I'm impatient because something's bothering me. Something big.

The victim didn't scream.

Which means that he wasn't conscious. Or if he was, he was gagged and his V-cog was shut down. But that's hard to do.

And then there's the conundrum of being knocked out. V-cog has emergency alert protocols for that, especially for engineers, which the victim's uniform says he was. Security would have been notified instantly. And where the hell are they anyway?

Someone vomits behind me.

I stare at the pulpy flesh for a few more seconds. That noun won't go away. *V-cog.* Whatever the scenario, accident or murder, conscious or unconscious, this man's virtual cognizance system was offline. And that's impossible to do without being very intentional. He either wanted to die or someone else wanted him dead. Someone with serious skills and lots of access.

"Please move aside," voices say from far back in the crowd. "Coming through."

It's security. Finally.

There's one more thing I'm curious about before they cordon off the area and detain everyone for questioning. While remaining focused on the scene, I slide my hand down my thigh, feel the pouch that I keep strapped to my leg, and remove the multitool inside. Then I use it to reach toward the fabric folds in the corpse's chest.

"You're gonna touch it?" a woman says. "Are you crazy?"

"Depends who you ask," I say under my breath. Then I use the pliers to pull up the uniform. The movement makes several onlookers squeamish. A second person vomits.

That's when I see it.

As if remembering a dream I'd forgotten moments after waking, it all comes back to me. I know this man. I was with him no more than thirty minutes ago.

It's Hodges.

"Listen, Officer—"

"Inspector," says one of a few dozen investigators who've been paired off with witnesses of the "unfortunate accident," as they're calling it. He's muscled his way into my V-cog lobby to keep this "confidential," and I'm counting the seconds until he's gone. The man's singled me out and already seems to have drawn his conclusions about me.

I start again. "Inspector Stamos, I already told you

everything I know, and I have an urgent matter to attend to. May I?"

But Stamos doesn't seem all that concerned with my priorities. "You certainly do seem to know a lot about the specifics of Mr. Hodges death. A lot of… technical details."

I fold my arms. "I'm Chief Astrophysicist on station."

"So you've said. You're also very familiar with his whereabouts before he died. In fact"—his eyes close and he holds up a paper notepad in my lobby—"records show you were the last person to see him alive."

I shake my head. "Check your log again. He had another tech with him."

Stamos frowns in V-cog and then writes something down in his notepad. "Seems awfully convenient that we haven't found this mystery tech. You got a name?"

"What? No. He was a nobody. Just—"

"*A nobody*. Got it."

"No, you don't write that down. I'm saying that—"

"Anyone else see this *nobody*, Dr. Park?"

"Of course. Dr. Samantha Collins. And his name was Del… Del Toro."

"You hesitated."

"Because I was trying to remember! Stars. And I don't like your tone, Inspector."

"I'm sure you don't."

I need to calm down. This guy's pushing my buttons. I'm tired, and I want my ice cream. After a steadying breath, I jut my chin toward the section one precinct tab on his collar. "A little far from home, aren't you?"

"I'm on loan."

"How convenient."

He cocks an eyebrow at me. "I don't think I like *your* tone, Dr. Park."

"Then we're even."

He flips his notebook closed and exits my V-cog lobby. "You're sure you didn't push him out of the power level?"

I blow some hair out of my eye. "You know what? Now that you mention, I think that was me, yes."

His eyes grow wide, but I stop him before he mistakes my sarcasm for a confession. "No, Inspector *Stamos*. I did not push a human out of the power level, cross back to the hub, travel four kilometers down the elevator, purchase an ice cream—"

"You said it was gratis."

Bastard. "—and then arrive faster than humanly possible to see the man die down here. Now, unless you're arresting me and making a formal accusation— and keep in mind that I don't take veiled threats or implications lightly—I need to get back to my office. There's important work that needs attending to."

"The same work that Morgan Hodges threatened to shut down by following his orders?"

"That... has nothing to do with this."

"I'll be the judge of that."

I spot the sharp VT logo on his palm. "Never figured a Viatoribus would understand our science anyway."

He bristles at the slight. "What's to understand? Your laboratory has been shut down on account of—"

"What did you say?" The words come out louder than I mean them to, but I'm not about to apologize. I'm upset, I'm overtired, and I just saw what happens to the human body when it meets a solid object of greater mass traveling just shy of 200 meters per second. And I still want my damn ice cream. "If you people even so much as touch my lab—"

"*Touched*, Dr. Park. As in, it's done. And it's not yours anyway. It's the people's, as I recall."

Being orphaned in Seoul by age ten comes with certain… *perks*, ones unique to the painful experience. Of them, a heightened survival instinct doesn't pair well with the role of famed scientist and award-winning researcher. That, and most people don't expect a woman of my stature to know how to throw a punch, much less possess the moxie to deliver it. But there were a few years between Bukjeong Village and the University of Canterbury, Christchurch that I learned to take care of myself when others could not. And while I've kept the often-times boiling water from throwing off the lid for over twenty years, right now I sense that I'm losing the battle. All it's going to take is…

"It's not like you were going to discover anything of importance up there anyway, Dr. Park. We did you a favor, if you think about it."

THERE'S a knock on my door. Physical, I mean. The sound is both unusual and endearing, bringing back old memories from before I could afford things like virtual technologies. I brace myself for whoever's about to read me the riot act next. "Come in."

The two bruisers stationed outside my door activate the lock and peer in at me as if I've used the last hour to construct some sort of weapon that I might use against them.

"Yeah, I fished two mag rifles out of my toilet and

built a flame thrower from my stove, guys. Better come get 'em."

The friendly bloke smiles at me, satisfied that I'm no threat, while the frumpy one just sneers. Then a familiar face appears between them.

Sam.

"Hey, Eves."

I set the ice pack aside, rise off my couch, and embrace her. "Nice of you to drop by."

"I didn't really have a choice." She taps my temple with a finger. "They've locked down your lobby hard."

"Think I can keep it that way when this is over?"

"Recluse." Sam smiles. "How's the hand?"

"Fine."

"Liar." She moves to the couch and takes a seat. "So what does it take to get a drink around here? Or did they lock down the tequila too?"

"Hardly. Lime?"

"Not today."

"Neat it is." I enter my kitchen and pull my best añejo bottle from the auto-slide. The service cabinet pushes two small snifters to the tabletop, and I fill them each a finger high.

"Make mine a double," Sam calls back.

I walk out and hand her a glass, then we clink.

Sam adds, "To pissing off security like a rock star."

I tip my glass to that, sip the faded yellow liquid, and then sit. "So. How bad is it?"

"His nose? Or what they want to do to you?"

"Yes."

Sam half smiles. "They say it took the inspector twenty minutes to remember his name once he came to. Concussion. And a splint."

I smile and take another sip. I'm not proud of hitting him. But I'm not sorry either. "He was trying to pin Hodges on me."

"That's what everyone figured. Serves him right anyway. Heard that one can be a real prick if he wants to."

"Or it's just an unavoidable character trait."

Sam lets out a small laugh and sips again. "As for consequences, they want you off station."

"What? But they—"

"Won't get it, of course. We both know Lemuel and Eric won't go for it." She looks into her glass. "But they at least have to act like they're deliberating about it. I'd say you have another day up here before NUESSA makes the call. Two at most."

I lean back and take in the news. Granted, I expected they'd keep me locked up for a little bit, but one never knows, especially with the recent tensions over expansion funding. In the meantime, I do have two questions for Sam. "They have any leads?"

She puts her elbows on her knees. "You really think he was murdered?"

"Come on, Sam. Look at the evidence."

"Yeah, I know. It's just... *Astraea*."

In her forty-year history, there's never been a murder on the station. Of course, that fact has been spun by every politicast since it was first reported. On one hand, the Sentia Aux, Viatoribus, and even some of the Preservationists hail it as what's possible when humanity is relieved of pressures that threaten survival and, instead, given the very best opportunities to thrive. On the other hand, the Solum Terram says it's because NUESSA only selects Earth's most elite candidates. I always argue that the rich are just as capable of murder as the poor. The only difference is the resources to hide the bodies. But that's not something they want me saying on the verb, which is why I don't get any camera time.

And then there's the Tantum Terrae who go further, claiming we use mind control with V-cog and engineer malevolence out of the population. That, and we don't faithfully report what goes on up here at 40,422 kilometers, hiding the truth behind mountains of money. If we had that ability—engineering the moral compass of the species—we would have done that a long time ago. This, *Astraea*, and every hab that's come since are the alternatives. And yes, they cost a lot of money.

"Anyway, no," Sam says after a moment. "No leads. But they suspect the other tech."

"So they listened to me?"

"Of course. Stamos was just being a dick."

"Serves him right." The tequila is starting to loosen me up.

"At least you finally landed a jab on someone," Sam says.

"You saw it?"

"Who didn't see it? Spread through the verb fast thanks to all the witnesses and their pixies."

I tap my nose with my index finger. "Guess I forgot about that."

"You do kinda tune everything else out when you get laser-focused, ya know."

I take another sip and pose my second question. "They really unplugged the CEL?"

Sam looks back into her glass. "There was nothing we could do."

"And the scan?"

"Aborted with nineteen hours remaining."

"Dammit." I set my drink down. "Was any of it…?"

"Salvageable? No. Parallax hadn't validated any-thing yet. Not enough to go on."

"Of course not. Why would it?" I fold my arms and lean back hard. "Bastards."

"We'll get another chance, Evelyn. They've already restored power. Once they let us back in, we'll fire things up and restart the sweep."

I look out the window and across the hab. Aside from the artificial stars, the only other light comes from thousands of homes and pathways stretching up the curved background. I let out a deep breath, buoyed by hope but marred by despondency. "I think people as-sume I love it up here."

Sam doesn't answer.

"I do, of course. I mean, look at what we've been able to accomplish. But it's not the end. It's not how we'll live for another millennium. Stars, I doubt we can for another hundred years." I swipe my glass off the table and point at her. "This is the one, Sam. I feel it."

"Says the woman who doesn't feel anything."

"I'm serious, Sam. They're out there."

"Then they'll still be there when they let you out."

I take a deep breath and down the rest of my tequila. "'Nother round?"

She shakes her head and finishes her glass. "I need to send a report to Lemuel."

"About me?"

She looks away for a second. "I didn't want you to—"

I reach over and touch her arm. "Don't worry about it. You tell the truth, and we'll get through this."

"Right. Just… don't do anything to raise eyebrows while you're up here, okay? Maybe you can use the time to actually relax a little."

I laugh. "Right."

Sam hands me the empty snifter, says goodnight, and then knocks on the door to be let out. The guards eye me suspiciously after she leaves. I'm about to offer them something to drink when I remember Sam's warning not to raise eyebrows. So I opt for the sarcastic route instead.

"You boys better be careful," I say and lift the two glasses. "I might use these to kill you."

Only the one seems to get my dark sense of humor and gives me a smirk, while the other offers me a deep scowl.

"Sleep tight, Dr. Park," the nicer one says.

I wink and watch the door slide shut. And then, just like that, I'm alone again. I set the glasses in the auto-cleaner and settle back on the couch. I consider pouring myself a second drink; there are enough reasons to. So much wasted time, and a life snuffed out violently. Who knows how many more lives the delays will cost in the long run.

And for what?

That's the question gnawing at the back of my mind. All of these happenings—the increased safety breaches, the CEL shutdown, and Hodges's murder— they all point to something, I just can't see it yet. And I don't trust the station investigators to find it. Which means one thing…

It's time to get to work.

5

JERICHO

"Nice flying out there, Fox," a voice yells across the locker room as I dry off. "Least ya saved somebody's ass besides your own this time."

"Ignore them," Kit says next to me as he dresses. "They're just jealous."

He's kind. But the attempt to console me is pointless. Not because Kit isn't genuine—far from it. I actually appreciate that he's trying to encourage me without having any clue what I was involved in. One more reason to like the guy. Consoling me is pointless because the comments from the other flight crews are coming in fast, which means word has spread, and my attempt to remain incognito has vaporized. It won't be long now before the final nail is in my coffin. Any minute now, admin will call me in.

I'm pulling up my pants when an official sounding voice shouts from the adjoined office entrance. "Leslie Christopher Smith?"

I don't bother looking up until Kit says, "Uh, I guess they want me, so… I'll see you in a little bit, okay?"

I slip on one of my boots. "Leslie?"

"That's why I go by Kit. It's short for Chris, and nobody likes to say Christopher. So when I was like seven, my mom—"

"Don't wanna leave them waiting," I interject.

"Oh, right. Yeah." He holds a hand to the side of his mouth. "Be right there!" Then back to me, he asks, "You think, uh, they'll call you in next?"

"I'm counting on it."

"Cool. Okay. Meet back here then? Beers later maybe?"

I'm not sure how to break the news to Kit that this is where we part ways. He's happy, and I don't want to ruin his day. In fact, the further he stays away from me, the better—for his sake. I pull my shirt over my head and then grab my coat and backpack. "Kit, you're getting promoted."

"We're *both* getting promoted."

I take his misguided assumption and work with it. "Which means two people who won't get assigned to the same hauler."

He frowns. "Huh. Didn't even think about that. But I'll request a transfer."

I pat his arm. "I wouldn't. But listen, if they at least put us in the same neighborhood, you bet: beer's on me. But for your sake? I wouldn't mention my name in your official report."

"But it was your—"

"*Your* idea, Kit. I was just along for the ride. Remember?"

"I don't understand."

"Then I'll make it easy. You made the call."

He thinks for a second, and then some amount of understanding dawns on his face. "Because you were 'just a pilot.'" Kit's face gets all sorts of melancholy. "You don't think you're getting promoted, do ya."

"I knew you were sharp."

The voice yells again. "Smith? Leslie Christopher?"

"I'd better go. Don't wanna miss that." He swallows. "Thanks, Jericho. For… ya know."

"Being your favorite asshole?"

He nods and can't seem to find any words.

"Same, Kit. I'll see ya around."

"HAVE A SEAT," says the secretary—a dour looking man who's losing the combover competition to middle age. "They'll be with you momentarily."

I do as he says and make myself comfortable. Kit's nowhere to be found. It's a miserable little room, a relic of another age. The vinyl covers on all the chairs have split from years of service, and the plastic on the corporate posters has yellowed. Even the drop ceiling sags from all the sweat and cigarette smoke—the latter being an artifact from when the habit was commonplace and not an off-book indulgence of elitists who viewed stimming tobacco a cheap counterfeit to the real thing. And if you have the coin to cure second-wave cancer, why not? Those same people have enough to fix this room ten times over, but I can't imagine the higher-ups make it this far south very often, so why waste the crypto?

This whole thing—whatever happens next—is just a formality. A virtual rubber termination stamp on a day-long employment contract. Part of me debated leaving the shower and walking straight out the back doors without following through. Clothed, of course. But that's not my style—leaving before things are seen to their rightful conclusions, I mean. And I'm curious who's been assigned to drop the axe on me. Last gig, I got the director himself. But we were friends. At least back then.

The door to the inner offices slides open, and a woman in a business suit steps through. "Mr. Fox?" There's neither sarcasm nor disdain in her tone, just professionalism. "This way, please."

I follow her down a hallway that, like the waiting room, has seen better decades. No doubt this facility was kept in the company's holdings from before the migration. They knew uranium would still be a valuable commodity once the planet settled down—no sense spending money to build something new when you've already got a foothold in the wastes. Anyway, the weather would make all but subterranean builds impossible to construct, and who has time for that? Especially when all that hardware gets shipped off planet faster than the verb's hourly news cycle?

The woman stops next to a glass partition with a swinging door that leads into a conference room. She holds it open for me and nods.

There are just two people behind the wide table: a man on the left, and a woman on the right. Neither of whom I recognize. This was a waste of time. And why's that, Jericho? Because you thought maybe they'd send Steiner himself? Come on.

The secretary steps out and closes the door behind me.

"Mr. Fox," says the left-hand suit in a thick old African accent. He gestures to the only chair on my side of the table. His skin's dark—that kind of purplish ebony like dad's. He's also pushing the limits of his business suit's integrity with his chest, arms, and shoulders. "Please, take a seat. It will be worth your while, we assure you."

I set my backpack on the floor and sit. The room's shutters are closed to the morning light, which, given how little I've slept and the headache I'm trying to fend off, is appreciated.

"It's been a busy night for you," says the woman. She has an athletic build under her business attire, and despite her counterpart's dominant physical presence, I get the feeling she's the one in charge here.

"Busy night for a lot of people."

"Mmm. The powers that be thought you'd like to know that all souls have been accounted for and are expected to make a full recovery once they receive medical care."

"I'm happy to hear that. Thank you."

She nods and then offers nothing more. We all just sit there. I can't tell if the two of them are reviewing something in V-cog or intentionally trying to fill the space with a long awkward silence. Either way, I feel it's my job to break it up, so I clear my throat and ask, "We doing this?"

"Doing what?" asks the woman.

"Termination."

The two exchange looks, and then the man says, "We are not terminating you, Mr. Fox."

"Oh?"

"That was done shortly after you landed, from what we understand."

The woman's eyes stutter as she steps into her V-cog. "According to company records, it appears you ceased being an employee of High Top Uranium Corporation three hours ago. Likewise, your severance has been added to the blockchain. You may collect it at your leisure."

"So you're not with High Top then?"

"No."

Those damn bastards didn't even bother telling me to my face. Instead, I get these suits, and they're not even with the company. "Then what's this about?"

"Your next job," the woman says.

I blink at her and then glance over my shoulder, half expecting to see Steiner or some other exec laughing at me from behind the glass wall. But not even the secretary who escorted me here is around. "I'm sorry. Is this some sort of prank?"

Again, they exchange looks.

"No prank, Mr. Fox," says the woman. "In light of your recent *availability*, our employer would like to make you an offer."

Nothing like one door closing so a window can open. "I'm listening."

She steps into my virtual lobby holding one of those old fashioned leather briefcases. They're worth a small fortune if you can find one in the real. Seems a little pretentious to ply one here, but appearances mean something, or else people wouldn't spend coin to stylize their virtual spaces. My own public lobby is a good example. We're standing below decks in a perfect replica of a 2071 Berret-Racoupeau-inspired Amel 60 sailboat. Not that I expect anyone to know what the ship was, but I can always spot a fellow seafarer when they do. The woman before me? Not a sailor. She pays my carefully crafted environment no mind whatsoever; to her, this is just one more V-cog lobby to tolerate before she moves on.

She sets the case on the galley table, activates the spring-loaded latches, and raises the lid. Inside is a single sheet of pressed linen paper.

"What's this?" I ask as she hands it to me.

"The offer."

Before I can read the short paragraph of text, my eyes stop on the header: From the Desk of Sir Nigel Sallsworth. My face flushes—from embarrassment or anger, it's too soon to tell. I wish I could control it more, but I can't. Family trait.

"You lied," I say to both of them back in the conference room.

"We beg your pardon?" the man asks.

"I asked if it was a prank, a joke, and you said no." I don't like being so critical, so skeptical. It's not like me. But a few major disappointments in a row will do that to an otherwise optimistic guy. Some call it being jaded, others call it maturity. Jury's still out on what I think it is —probably a little of both.

The man places a hand on his chest as if to exude some heartfelt sentiment and then raises a finger. "Mr. Fox, we can assure you that Mr. Sallsworth's desire to employ you is legitimate."

"And he wants me to be"—I skim the text further—"his personal pilot and a chief technical director of one thing or another? Forgive me if I don't sound enthusiastic."

"The details of the job description will be ironed out later," he adds.

I hand the paper back to the woman and step out of my lobby. "Why?"

The man begins to reply, but the woman holds up a hand instead. I think she senses the real meaning behind my question. "Because you saved his life, Mr. Fox."

All at once, I see a memory of the man in the back of the LACH: Mr. Fabulous and his perfect looking hair. Of course. *That's* why he looked familiar. "He was on the ship we rescued."

"Correct. And he's rather grateful—something that works to your favor, given your current situation."

My memory of the encounter rushes back. All the passengers looked like they had money, and I figured there must've been some powerful people on board, but I didn't expect this. "Mind if I ask some questions?"

"Within reason," she replies.

"What was the leader of the Solum Terram doing in the Wyoming Territory badlands? Unaccompanied?"

"He was not without security," the man interjects. "You helped save them too."

My mind flicks back to any number of people who could have been part of a plain clothes security detail. "Still doesn't answer my question."

The woman nods once. "A routine investigation of the politicast's mining interests within the American Heights."

"He doesn't have people for that?"

"Plenty," she replies without batting an eye. "But sometimes he prefers to do things himself."

"Fair. But why here? He can make a much bigger show by visiting Cigar Lake."

"And he's scheduled to. But not all visits are meant for the public eye."

"You mean for ratings," I correct.

She smiles. "For votes."

"And he's got no qualms over my…" I roll my hand through the air. "You know."

"Your what?" she asks.

This lady's either naive or playing me. I can't decide which yet. "My accident?"

She gives a half-smile of understanding. "He believes you know how to handle yourself under pressure."

"That's not exactly what I meant, Miss…?"

She sidesteps her name. "What then?"

"You don't see it, do you." But they're not stupid. They're just not allowed to say, right? Because this is what it really comes down to and why I felt flustered moments ago. The job offer isn't about me saving Sir Nigel Sallsworth's life.

It's about politics.

"Come on," I say at last. "The head of Solum Terram—the man charged with championing nothing short of, what? The pro-Earth causes of all three nation states? And he hires *me*? I don't think I need to spell out the kind of negative implications that would have for the spacers, or even the Preservationists. But it sure would look good for Mr. Sallsworth. The headline practically sells itself, doesn't it? 'Ill-Fated NUESSA Captain Changes Tune, Condemns System Expansion, Joins Solum Terram.'"

The man shifts in his seat, whereas the woman doesn't so much as blink. "Mr. Fox, while I cannot speak to all of Mr. Sallsworth's political motives, I can assure you that his gratitude toward you is genuine."

"I'm sure it is."

While Sallsworth isn't as bad as the Tantum Terrae extremists, he still actively lobbies against everything I stand for, and I'm not about to get sucker punched all because of an easy paycheck. Not after what his politicast did. What *he* did.

"How can he prove it to you?" she asks.

"He can't."

"Name your terms."

The man gives her an uneasy look and shifts again. Apparently this wasn't in the playbook.

"My terms?"

She gives me a single intentional nod, all business.

I let out a soft chuckle and lean forward. "Alright. *If* I was ever desperate enough and couldn't find work anywhere else in the Heights, *and* I was stimmed out of my goddamn mind, then I *might* consider Mr. Sallsworth's offer, assuming he could unilaterally change my politicast"—which, privately, I have no doubts that he could, such is his power and wealth. The 100,000-coin fee wouldn't even be noticed in his ledger. "But with several conditions, and I'm just making these up as we go here, so bear with me.

"Number one, he contractually promises never to divulge my name or reveal my face. Number two, he keeps all payments confidential. And number three— and this one's the real clincher—he agrees never to publicly speak ill of my mission or its crew again. As in, for all time. If he's good with all that? Then… I might be willing to talk pay and benefits. But until said time, I not so respectfully decline."

The woman's eyes stutter. Two seconds later, she says, "Done. If you ever find yourself in the first part of your hypothetical scenario, then Mr. Sallsworth accepts all three points of the second."

A flame of anger lights in my throat. "He's observing."

"Of course."

I bite the inside of my cheek, thinking of what to say. Despite all my experience in high intensity situations, I've never been the best with witty comebacks under pressure. I wish I was. Instead, I just say a bunch of words and then spend the next two weeks thinking of what I would've said differently while lamenting how I sounded. But I can still fly the ship and repair the engine, and that's what matters at the end of the day.

The woman produces something from inside her blazer pocket and slides it across the table. It's a blockchain coin the size of a poker chip—a real one with a digital display. I've only seen the cold storage marker in V-cog, never in the real.

"A token of Mr. Sallsworth's goodwill," she says.

"I don't need his money."

"You might." She stands, which prompts the man to get up too. "Thank you for your time, Mr. Fox. Have a good life."

I want to tell them to stop walking and take the chip back, that leaving it here is a waste of money, and that I'll never use it out of principle. But I'm also curious how much is on it because, if I'm really jobless, *again*, then I could use a cushion to fall on. The only question is how far do I need to fall before I choose to use it.

The door closes behind me. Now it's just me and the chip staring each other down. It's matte black surface and slow-pulsing pixels beckon me to pick it up. But I can't. Sallsworth believes system expansion is a threat, that the mission has doomed Earth with how it consumes time and resources, ones better spent on restoring the planet. As such, Sallsworth stands against everything I've tried to help champion.

Well, not everything, Jericho. You both want to save people. Save humanity. And you're both men of conviction, believing that your own way is right. That's laudable, isn't it? Even if you disagree with his premise, you can at least find virtue in his larger motive… in his desire to save lives.

"Mr. Fox?" It's the secretary who escorted me. "I'll see you out now."

I stare at the chip and its stupid pulsing light, then grab my backpack and walk toward the woman. But with each step, I can't help feeling that I'm walking away from a valuable opportunity in a season that few will present themselves. That damn marker is magnetic. Even as I press toward the lady holding the door open, my legs feel like they're trudging through rain-soaked sand.

"Mr. Fox?" Her eyes dart back to the table. "I think you forgot something?"

6

EVELYN

"Hold," Sam mouths from the ground four stories below. With my V-cog access to the network locked down, traditional mouth and hand signaling is all I have to go on. But it's working. Sam's sitting on a bench and doing her best to act casual between frantic spats of pantomime. It's another perfect evening on *Astraea* Station with crickets chirping, streetlamps glowing, and couples on after dinner walks. I'd wait until after station curfew, but we need all the time we can get for what I have planned.

"Clear," Sam mouths.

I nod and continue side-stepping along my neighbor's balcony. Mr. and Mrs. Gibbons turn off their living room light and retire to the bedroom. I accidentally bump a planter they've placed on a way-too-narrow stand but catch before it gives me away. With balance restored, I press on and climb over the far railing.

Breaking out of my Fairmont Valley apartment and hopping onto adjacent balconies isn't something my minders have noticed so far, and probably won't, allowing me to get back the same way before the scheduled check in. Sam and I won't encounter anything we can't handle. Why am I getting away with such a daring escape and return? Because no one expects the station's chief astrophysicists to try her hand at multi-story acrobatics.

There are other perks to being a former street rat besides learning how to throw a jab. Yeah, pickpocketing is one, but I never liked it. I got too much of my dad's work ethic and mom's moral compass to resort to taking what wasn't mine. I'm talking about the perk of learning how to break out of places meant to keep you in.

It started with other kids trying to trap me in lockers or alley crates. At first, I just felt sorry for myself. But I learned pretty quickly that no one wanted invites to my pity parties, so if I was gonna survive, I needed to "use my thinker"—a favorite line of my father's.

So I did.

I began carrying a small multitool that let me knock pins from doors hinges or pry open old locks. I also packed a lighter to set fire to wooden crate lids—not enough to burn me up with them, but enough to send out smoke that forced even the meanest of kids to concede defeat, or at least open the box out of curiosity. A jab was always waiting for them when they did.

I also learned who my friends were in the process. Good ones came to help me escape once the bullies had gotten bored; the best ones took on the bullies outright. And that was the real secret to survival in Bukjeong: sticking together. In fact, the hardest part of my uncle taking me to the Southlands was saying goodbye to my friends—the ones who hadn't betrayed me.

I leap a half meter onto the next balcony and roll to a crouch. Hip and elbow hurt. Leg too. But nothing serious, and I have to keep moving. This was easier when I was younger.

It took me a day to coordinate this escape with Sam, mostly because she wasn't permitted to visit me again for another twelve hours. But a few whispered exchanges with music playing and our backs turned to my apartment guards got the job done. Another twelve hours after that, she's here, and I'm almost in the clear.

I make it as far as the Kapoor's bay window when Sam shakes her head. I stop just as she smiles at a wealthy couple with a dog, then looks back at the apartment. She holds her hand up for a three count and then gives me the all clear. I slide past the window and head for the escape ladder built into the building's curvy exterior. The handholds are made to look like part of the architecture, but they're really recesses for emergency descent. I check one more time with Sam before she gives the go-ahead to climb down.

When I finally emerge from the bushes and greet her on the path, she says, "You're nuts. You know that?"

"Hadn't noticed."

"You know we're getting in so much hot water for this."

We both wave at another couple on an evening stroll.

Through a tight-lipped smile, I say, "I told you I'll take the heat."

"Even bystanders get burned."

I shrug. "Fire retardant clothes?"

"Speaking of which, you tore your pants, and you're bleeding."

"What? Where?"

Sam casually points to my calf.

"Shoot. When did that happen?"

"When you were busy playing spider girl and leaping between balconies."

I kneel down, trying to act like I'm re-cinching my shoe, and tear away the pants leg at the knee with several jerking yanks. Then I used the extra fabric to wipe up the blood.

"Like you're not gonna stand out now, Miss Random Fashion Show," Sam adds.

I pull out my multitool and hack away the other pants leg.

"What are you doing?"

I stand and examine my lower half. "Shorts."

"They're… two different lengths."

"New style. Let's go."

We move down the walkway, acting as nonchalant as we can, and eventually arrive at the hab's endcap elevator bank that rises to the power level. This is our first test: to try and board the lift with only one of us having active credentials. I've never done it before because I've never had V-cog severed from the grid. But I'm hoping that the blackout comes with some benefits, like a lack of auto-alert tracking. Which, so far, seems to be panning out. No one's sounded the alarm, and we're not being followed.

Sam calls a lift up from the ag level using V-cog overlay. A moment later, the doors open and we step inside. She inputs the floor, goes through the required credential check, and then waits. The pause is longer than normal, which we expected.

"It's asking for my cargo manifest," she says. The lift senses the extra weight, and without a second V-cog sig, it assumes she's carrying supplies. Again, neither of us has ever spoofed the system before—there's been no need. But all of this is worth the risk if we can re-initiate our terminated scan while also getting a jump on Hodges's killer.

"What other options does it give you?" I ask.

"Nothing. Just cargo manifest entry and… Hold on. There's an exceptions tab."

"What's it say?"

She pauses, then adds, "Bingo. Says 'Request manifest from secondary reference holder' and then asks for a V-rec locator."

"Use Lemuel."

"What?"

"If he sees your name attached, he'll be less likely to raise the alarm. He'll figure it out."

"We're so screwed." She waits a moment, and I peek out the doors to make sure we're not being followed. "Accepted." The word is barely out of her mouth when the lift starts its four-kilometer ascent.

I ask her for the time as I grab hold of a safety bar.

"Nineteen forty-six," she says and then smiles. "That's weird."

"Me asking you what time it is?"

"Yeah."

"It's weirder not having access to the grid, trust me. Reminds me of…"

"Being a kid in Australia?"

"School was New Zealand. Street life was South Korea."

"Right. Forgot about that. Sorry."

"I try to forget about it too."

"That bad?" She waves a hand in the air. "Never mind. I shouldn't have asked."

I stare through the transparent ceiling and up the tube. "Dad died when I was nine. Mom, when I was ten. Spent three years on my own before an uncle from Christchurch found me."

Sam seems suspicious, then catches me giving her a stern look. "No, no," she says with a wave. "I'm not complaining. I'm just… well, you've never wanted to talk about your past before, is all."

"I guess punching someone and breaking out is bringing up old memories."

"Yeah, I could see that. Not that I relate, I mean. That's not something most people have had to live through." Sam reaches out and touches my arm. "Sorry, Evelyn."

"There are still plenty of people who have it a lot worse."

"Sure, but *no* one should have to have *any* of it, right?" Sam eventually pulls her hand away when the silence gets awkward. "So, this family. They got you back to school?"

I nod.

"God bless them for that."

"God had nothing to do with it."

Sam holds her mouth open for a second and then closes it.

I exhale. "Wasn't very religious growing up."

"Okay. Got it."

Gravity's been losing its hold on us as we ascend to where we're almost free of the floor.

"I admire you, ya know," Sam says with one minute left.

"For what?"

"How much you've been able to accomplish. How you say exactly what you're thinking. And then do stuff like this." She gestures to the elevator. "Wish I was more like that."

I pull my head back. "You see where you are right now, don't you?"

"Yeah, but it was your idea. I'm just along for the ride."

"Well, passenger or wheelwoman, you're still a culprit. As for me saying what I'm thinking, it's not always my best attribute."

"It's badass."

I smile at her. "Thanks. But you've accomplished just as much as I have or you wouldn't be here."

She pinches the air with her thumb and index finger. "Little less."

We ride out the remainder of the trip in silence, and I think about what's coming next—gaining access to our lab, powering everything back up, and then two objectives: one, to restart the Cygnus constellation scan, and two, investigate Hodges's murder. And all of this before 0300.

When the lift finally stops, Sam exits right first while I float behind a bulkhead in the seven-meter wide tunnel leading to the CEL's main door. The security sensor will scan the entrance area to verify V-cog signatures and life signs, which I need to be clear of.

While she's busy there, I double-check the lift to make sure it's not being recalled to the main hab level. I consider blocking the doors with something, but that would raise suspicions, or at least summon a repair team. Best to leave it as is.

"I'm in," Sam announces. "All clear."

I push away from the bulkhead and glide through the corridor, eventually catching myself on safety rungs around the opening. As soon as I'm inside, Sam orders the doors shut and turns on the lights.

"Better to use workstation lights," I say.

"Right. Sorry. Kinda new at all this sneaking around stuff."

The main lights dim, allowing a noiseless view of the starscape outside. Our celestial exploration laboratory is a massive sphere stuck on the hab's sunless end. Its carbon nanotube reinforced glass walls provide the best show around; only a spacewalk can beat it. Clusters of workstations dot the inside surface at the six axes, while a central spherical command station floats in the middle, held in place by six support arms. The bubble can hold thirty working scientists comfortably, but we've had as many as sixty observers when making presentations.

I float to the central station and join Sam.

"So?" she asks. "Where do you want to start?"

This is where things could become tedious. While having my V-cog suspended has given me some unexpected mobility void of the station's passive surveillance, it's also cut me out of the ship's virtual system access interfaces, including the proprietary systems in the CEL. In other words, any work I'm doing will be the old fashioned way—mechanical and slow.

I tap the end of my nose. "Let's restart the Kepler-1649c sweep first. Then we'll tackle Hodges. We're gonna be able to move fastest if you navigate the root menus and I initialize the calibration sequences. Then we'll access the security files on the main network to retrace Hodges's steps. Sound like a plan?"

She nods but then asks, "You really think we're gonna find something on Hodges that the station inspectors haven't?"

I cast her a mischievous grin. "Sam. We hunt stardust in space for a living."

She smiles back and then cracks her knuckles. "Let's get to it then."

WITH THE CLOCK running out for when I need to be back inside my apartment—the check in is less than an hour away—we've just now completed the calibration and positioning of the station's multi-spectrum telescopic array. It took longer than I wanted, but that's what we get for having two operators working a five-person job and me using an old fashioned mechanical keyboard pulled from under the workstation.

"Annnnd… Parallax is online," Sam confirms. "Now we hurry up and wait." She casts me an inquisitive look from her terminal across the bubble. "You still have that good feeling about it?"

"I do."

"Cool. Me too." She lets out a nervous laugh. "Then again, it might just be the adrenaline from all this excitement."

"Might be." Her optimism makes me smile. Stars know we can use all we can get. Optimism, that is. But smiles are welcome too. I'm just thankful to have a friend right now. "Alright, time to snoop."

Sam joins me at the central command sphere and starts calling up the station's security menus. A perk of being heads of the science division is having unfettered access to every system on station—well, except those you're locked out of for being under house arrest. Unlike municipalities legislated by bureaucrats, watched by lawyers, and enforced by police, the Space and Science Administration's orbital legacy habs fall under special jurisdiction—that of the nerds. It's still a democracy with checks and balances, of course, thus why I couldn't unilaterally extricate myself from my apartment. But every democracy has its loopholes, including the ones we're exploiting now, thanks to Sam.

"Where do you want to start?" she asks as she brings up the security search bars on the main console's glass for me.

I tap the end of my nose. "Logic says we review all footage from inside the power level, working backward from the time and location of the impact."

"But won't the inspectors have already scrubbed it for clues?"

"Definitely. But we know this station differently than they do, so I'm hoping we'll see things from a different angle. They may have missed something."

She pauses, long enough for me to guess what she's thinking. "They're smart people, Eves. Maybe we should just stick to being astrophysicists and let them stick to being investigators. Plus, I still don't see what this has to do with us."

Sam's not wrong, about the authorities being smart people, I mean. They are. Well, mostly; verdict is still out on Stamos.

"It's not their intellect I'm worried about, Sam. It's that we have a responsibility to all of this." I tip my chin at the bubble.

Her eyes narrow. "You think they're trying to stop us from making a discovery?"

I know it sounds crazy; even hearing her say it out loud makes me second guess myself. But I know what my gut is telling me. "If *I'm* their primary suspect? That can't be arbitrary, can it? Or they're just completely inept."

"Orrr they've just never had a murder to investigate, ya know, as in, *ever*?"

She has a point.

"Plus," she continues. "If they're really trying to stop us—stop you—then why kill Hodges since he was the one who was tasked with turning off the power? That doesn't make sense."

Another good point.

Still, this whole thing isn't something I feel like leaving to the authorities, at least not entirely. I touch the back of her shoulder and nod at the glass displays as if they're already showing us what we want to see. "You're right, Sam. I *don't* have it all figured out. But something feels wrong with all of this. And for the sake of our mission and the safety of this station, we need to look into it. We have to. If this was murder, and I'm confident it was, then I'm guessing the culprit tried covering their tracks."

She sighs. "You're probably right as usual. Although, I hope you're not on this one. I hope it really was just an accident. I'll start double-checking everyone's work and look for clues."

"Good. And trying running a search on any anomalous sensor data for crew activity in the power level. I'll go over the roster again."

She nods, and then we both get to work. However, Sam isn't more than a minute into her task when something stops her. "We have a problem."

"What is it?"

"More like what it isn't." She takes over my glass so I can follow her work as she moves through V-cog controls. A few seconds later, a multi-stage index window appears on the display. Sam points to a security folder. "It's empty."

I do a double-take and feel my pulse spike. "Someone deleted the security data?"

"No. That would leave a system event log."

"Let me guess: there isn't one."

"Bingo."

"So… what?" I examine the empty file's metadata. "They weren't recorded to begin with?"

Sam nods. "That's the only good explanation."

"And a bad one?"

"Someone breached the station's operating system kernel and disabled the OPI bus to prevent data capture in the first place. And that's not happening. Ever. We'd lose the entire hab."

"So, since we're still alive, you think someone compromised the sensor stream?"

She shrugs. "It would be a whole lot easier than forging the super user credentials required for that kind of root level operation."

"You sure know your computer science, Dr. Collins."

She smiles proudly. "Eh, ya know."

"So if a person wanted to prevent data capture, where would they do it from?"

Sam grabs her lower lip. "Easiest place would be the camera modules."

"Which we can investigate?"

"Sure. If you have a week." When I raise an eyebrow, Sam continues. "There are over five hundred class A units in section thirty alone. That doesn't even count secondary sensors without video. Granted, the generator core doesn't look like it was affected, but we're still talking almost 63,000 square meters on the power level cylinder's perimeter."

"You're saying that none of them captured data?"

"For almost five whole minutes, yeah." Her face takes on a grim look. "A little far-fetched, I know. But the logs don't lie. Someone did not want eyes or ears in there."

Just then, my search query chimes. I scan the results. "Nothing out of the ordinary with staffing."

"So it was one of the scheduled crew members," Sam says.

"Unless someone breached the system."

She shakes her head. "That'd be pretty much impossible."

I point to my temple. "Like locking out someone's V-cog?"

"Okay, *almost* impossible. With you, that's a standard grid mute. But this? I dunno. We're taking top-level luxury code writing, Eves." She eyes me for a few seconds. "But you don't seem convinced."

"Nah, it's just… None of this adds up."

"What do you mean?"

"Why go to all the trouble of blocking the sensor data with your lux code in an entire section just to kill one person? That's a lot of hardware to sabotage, isn't it?"

Sam nods but doesn't add anything.

"And why not just focus on the exact area where your victim's gonna be and then sabotage one or two units as a diversion? You get away clean with plenty of time to keep the authorities busy."

"You sure you haven't done this before?"

I smile, but it's half-hearted. "All I'm trying to say is why compromise an entire section? If you know who you're targeting, why waste the time?"

"Fair point," Sam replies.

"We need to see one of those cameras."

Sam hesitates. "Wait, you mean, right now?" Her eyes flick into her V-cog, and I know she's checking the time. "Evelyn, you've only got twenty-five minutes."

"That's plenty. Come on." I push toward the exit.

"No, it's not plenty, Evelyn."

I reach the safety bars and wait for her to open the hatch. "Any day now."

"Don't you want to change?"

I look down at my bare legs but shake my head. "No time. Let's go, Collins."

She lets out a reluctant sounding sigh, and finally the hatch's metal leaves spiral open. I exit the bubble, look over my shoulder, and give Sam a wink.

"You coming or what?"

"I'm so getting demoted."

JERICHO

Physically, I'm sitting in my studio apartment in Ottawa. It's home, for now. And it's a good part of town, a good building. I'd planned on relocating to Winnipeg after my first month commuting for High Top. So much for that. My savings will get me another month—two if I ration my food. I can sell my pixie, maybe some other hardware, but I'd rather not part with my tools. For anyone else, a month is plenty of time to find work in their field. But High Top was my last option. Well, my last good one anyway.

Virtually, in my private suite, I'm overlooking the Mediterranean Sea from my balcony apartment. Supposedly, this is what the Amalfi Coast looked like 200 years ago. Stunning blue waters littered with boats, plunging mountainsides dotted with villas, and eighty-five-degree heat abated by a westerly sea-salt breeze. Listen to me: I sound like a damn poet. The setup cost me half a year's salary when I originally joined NUESSA. But I was young and didn't know that smart people save for when they get fired from their jobs, as evidenced by where the Mediterranean meets a solid blue wall. Sold that part of the sea to pay for an attorney. The first causality and probably not the last. So I'm enjoying the view while I can.

A floating call window pops up next to my reclining deck chair. I was expecting this. I take one more sip of my beer and answer. "Hey, dad."

"Steiner called me."

"Nice to see you too. How's your day?"

"I told you to lay low, son."

"Yeah? But did he tell you why we did it?"

"It doesn't matter why you did it. You just screwed yourself."

I shake my head. "Unreal."

"All you needed to do was stay low and—"

"We saved their lives, dad."

"Lives that were going to be saved anyway."

I cock an eyebrow at him. "We were the closest ship."

"They scrambled a quick response team. Would have been there—"

"Not in time. Ship was perched on a ledge. Those people—"

"Would have been fine, and you'd still have your job. I called in my last favor for you too, ya know. Steiner wasn't happy."

"Always about you, isn't it."

"Me? I did this for *you*!"

"I'm thirty-five, dad. I don't need you to—"

"I did it to get you out of space!" He takes a breath and shakes his head. "I still can't believe those bastards and their idiotic ideas. They kill people, Jericho!"

I rub my face once and take another pull on my beer. He wasn't always like this. But people change. "Anything else you wanna talk about?"

"This was your chance," he continues. "To earn your way out of the damn Viatoribus. You had it!"

"My god. How many times have we been over this? Just because *you* left doesn't mean that—"

"I put my neck out for you, Jericho! And you know what? Never again." He sniffs and raises his chin. "That was the last time."

"Finally."

He gives me his trademarked black scowl. "What's that supposed to mean?"

"I never asked you for help, dad. I'm not saying I'm not grateful. But you can't just—"

"So now I'm the bad guy?"

"I never said that." I attempt to take another sip, but the bottle's empty.

"So what are you gonna do now?"

"I'll figure something out."

A few seconds of silence pass, and his face softens, like the old days. "They called me."

"Who?"

"Sallsworth's people."

Dammit. I lower my head.

"It sounds like a good opportunity, son."

"I'm not taking it."

"Probably pays more than—"

"I said, I'm not taking it."

Another few seconds of silence pass between us. Of *course* it's the thought of my working for the Solum Terram that would make my father calm down. No doubt he praised me to Sallsworth's people even before they finished asking the first question. Can't fault him for believing in me—at least in word.

"You saved his life," dad says after a moment.

"But you just said it was stupid."

"I said you were foolish to go after them, but I didn't say there weren't benefits. Fate doesn't knock twice in the same day, Jericho."

"I already said, I'm not taking it."

"Why?"

I pinch the bridge of my nose. "Dad. I was their piñata, for crying out loud."

"Can you blame them?"

I widen my eyes. "Yes! I can!"

"You were simply the latest example of how NUESSA policies and Viatoribus spending jeopardized lives. We would have done it to anyone."

"Annnnnd there it is."

His face registers the misstep. "What I meant to say was that the politicast—"

"You said what you meant, dad. You're one of them, and I get that."

"Because I believe in what they stand for."

"And I don't."

"If you'd only—"

"I don't have time for this, dad."

"Wait. Wait. Just"—he holds a hand up—"please consider the offer."

"They put you up to this?"

"No." The hand goes to his chest. "It's just me. And I want what's best for you."

"I'll talk to you later, pops."

"Jericho, wait. I—"

I close the window, sit back, and look down at the bay. My Amel 60 is anchored there. Too far away to hit, but I hurl the bottle at it anyway.

⁂

THEY SAY Bordeleau Park used to be beautiful—where my apartment is in Lower Town. That there was once grassy lawn, meandering footpaths, and some trees. Today, it's high rises. What remains of the Rideau joins the Ottawa River one klick northwest of my twentieth-story overlook, which is about the only good thing I can say of my residence. If I have to live inland, I'll take any water I can get.

I walk southeast along King Edward Ave. Sure, I could call a grid car, but right now, I feel like going on foot. I need to save coin. Plus, the late July heat is punishingly harsh and serves as some sort of penance for not hearing my dad out. He pisses me off though. But whose old man doesn't from time to time?

By the time I reach Rideau Street, the heat is unbearable. I figure my penance is paid, so I leave the street level and take the escalator to the skywalk. Some people love Ottawa's heat. A tropical paradise, they say. They haven't traveled enough. And they certainly haven't left the city's center.

The AC feels good inside the closed skywalk. I even treat myself to a rest on the people mover and watch the buildings of Byward Market pass by. Through gaps to the west, I spot a few boats bobbing in their slips and people walking the shaded promenade. It's all colored hats and cotton clothes for the few city citizens who've found the good life this far south. Planetside, that is. What I wouldn't give to be back in space.

Maybe that's what's pissing me off the most. It's not High Top's lack of decency to fire me to my face, or Sallsworth's underhanded job offer, or even dad's semi-narcissistic attempts to get me to earn my way between politicasts. It's that I can't get back up *there*—a few thousand klicks straight up. Starships and space stations.

And even if I could, I wonder how many of them would accept me.

My melodrama gets interrupted by a news story on the public glass ten meters ahead: "...update on the dramatic rescue in the Wyoming Territory Badlands that took place late last night. In a public statement made this morning from their southern headquarters in Winnipeg, High Top Uranium Corporation said that one of their low-altitude personnel transports suffered critical damage during a storm and was unavoidably stranded in dangerous conditions."

I feel a lump in my throat as I prepare to see my face on the glass. It's something I thought I'd get used to, but I haven't. Suppose I never will at this point. So I hold my chin up and watch as... *not me* appears on the screen.

Instead, it's a pasty, scrawny-ass kid with wiry hair who steps behind a podium surrounded by pixies. The fleet hovers a meter from his face like a flock of hummingbirds expecting to find sugar water.

"Kit?" I say aloud. I feel questioning looks from those beside me, so I stand and move away.

The reporter continues as the people mover carries me past the double-sided glass wall. "...claim that a young flight engineer from Old Cheyenne, Leslie Smith, is responsible for the daring rescue."

The pre-recorded interview captured by the micro drones jumps to a quote from Kit. "Um, so, yeah, when we got there, the ship was on the edge of the cliff, right? And if we flew too close, we risked blowing it over. Instead, we ran a line that the people—the passengers, I mean—could use to follow. And then we just flew outta there like our lives depended on it, you know?"

The anchor picks up the thread. "Smith is being

hailed as a hero by many"—footage shows him walking out High Top's southern HQ to a small fanfare of people, excipions, and pixies—"and is expected to receive a promotion. While the company hasn't provided any more details about those passengers aboard the vessel or their well-being, our sources indicate that all were employees of High Top, with only a few suffering minor injuries. Up next, Phil Thompson has a recap of last night's game against the Rebels, and Minerva Tanner talks shop with a Wellington Village brewer who's making waves with their latest ales."

I'm not sure whether to feel relieved or angry by the total omission of my name in the story. No, I don't mean angry because of the lack of credit. You don't do good things to get recognized; you do them because they need doing. If the spotlight comes? Sure, it feels good. But it's not the motive.

No, I'm considering being upset because my absence from the headlines means that High Top doesn't want the heat. Sure, there's a feel-good comeback story in there somewhere if they want it, but they don't. Because no matter how someone slices it, I'm a pilot and engineer who got people killed and will bear that mark to my grave.

Today, I celebrate Kit and his ten seconds of fame. "Good for you," I say as the commercial break starts with a slow-mo shot of him waving to his public. "Hope it stays rosy for you, my friend."

Because God knows it didn't for me.

RIDEAU STREET TURNS into Wellington as the people mover carries me into the Downtown District, from one good part of town to the next. I exit the skywalk at O'-Connor and suffer my penance once again, though the heat is the least of my worries now. My destination is the monolithic building on Queen Street, home of Ottawa's division of the NUE Department of Politicast Employment Services.

Things were crazy in the wake of the Hundred Years Migration—not that I remember it, obviously. But the politicast system, despite its many opponents, was one of the things that helped maintain a sense of normalcy after so much death and displacement. By the late twenty-first century, advances in virtual cognizance allowed people to unite without regard for national borders. Since neo-tribalism had already proliferated faster than governments could legislate by the time the Migration stopped, it made sense to let people continue segregating themselves ideologically rather than nationalistically in order to preserve the delicate peace. All that was left was to automatically ink offspring into their parents' tracts and then create policy around the politicasts, and we had the makings of a "new system to ensure peace." Until it came time for children to question their parents' ideology or, as is my case, someone's record blackballed them from finding work in their politicast. Seventy-two years removed from the resettlement and its supposed "endless possibilities for stability" and I wonder if we're really any better off. That's why I want to do this meeting in person. Why I *have* to. I need to push the boundaries, and I'm relying on someone's humanity and reason to see past the bureaucracy of it all.

Back in the sweltering heat and humidity, I spot the skyscraper's main entrance and make a beeline for the doors. Once in the safety of the AC, I pass through the security checkpoint, and V-cog lets me know that I've waived all rights to everything about myself for the rest of time. Then I'm sent across a marbled floor and toward an allocation terminal along the far wall. Once I'm within arm's reach of a hip-height pylon, I get prompted to enter V-cog and join the building's virtual lobby. It's an endless white expanse, probably to both save crypto and keep people off balance at the sensation of being in the proverbial afterlife.

"Hello, Mr. Fox," says a woman in a white uniform with a purple NUE seal over her left chest. She's not real, of course. Just a service construct. But she's realistic enough to fool a few million years of evolution. "My name is Alice. What is the nature of your business today?"

"Employment Discovery Division, please."

She nods slowly. "Are you looking for a new position?"

"Yes."

"My records indicate that you were terminated from High Top Uranium Corporation eleven hours and sixteen minutes ago. Is that correct?"

"Yes."

"And are you in agreement with your reasons for termination? Or do you wish to appeal?"

I'm about to say "agree" when I think twice. "Can I see the termination registration?"

"You may." The woman withdraws a small tablet from a hip holster and hands it to me. The text heading lists the company name, my name, a bunch of metadata, and then "Reason for Termination."

I find myself reading aloud—for whose benefit, I'm not sure. Force of habit maybe. "...does hereby release Mr. Fox, Jericho B. for failure to execute duties in a satisfactory manner." The account goes on, but that's the meat and potatoes. It could be better, but it also could be a lot worse. At least they did me *that* small favor.

"It seems your performance was less than satisfactory," the construct says.

"That's a first."

"On the contrary, your file seems to indicate that—"

"I'm in agreement with High Top's reasons for termination."

"Acknowledged. I have updated your record and closed your employment history with the company. A copy of my work is available in your virtual record system."

"Got it."

"Would you like to browse your next exciting employment opportunities?"

"Can't wait."

Her head twitches once to the left. That's a bug. "Your next exciting employment opportunities include *zero* chances to better the members of your politicast with your unique skills. Would you like to review them now?"

I was expecting this, of course, but can't help the sarcastic tone that sneaks out of my mouth. "Absolutely."

Her head twitches again. "I'm sorry. My records show that there are currently *zero* opportunities for you to review. Would you like to schedule an appointment to speak to a DPES specialist?"

"Yup."

A translucent calendar appears between us. "Please select from the following dates and times for your convenience."

The earliest date is six weeks from now—time I

don't have. If I were any other person, I'd suck it up and register for the appointment. But this is where being a torque rat helps you get ahead in the world— one of the many ways. "I'd like all of the meetings that will discuss my zero opportunities."

Her head twitches twice. "I'm unable to complete your request."

"Why?"

Again, her head twitches, and her very human voice says things that a normal human would not say, which means her interface protocols are being overridden by her logic processes. That's good. It's essentially a V-cog version of a brain fart, only a lot worse. "Query parameters invalid. Unable to complete action."

"Alice, I request management verification of your inability to service me." Yeah, the innuendo is for my benefit.

"Management verification request confirmed." Then her face and body freeze.

It takes less than sixty seconds for a real person to appear in the building's massive marble-floored vestibule. He's about my age and height but twenty kilos heavier and with a crazy mop of hair. He's also squinting at the sunlight pouring in through the glass windows—all signs that point to him being sedentary and cooped up in a V-cog pod for hours if not days at a time.

I flash him my most innocent smile as he approaches the allocation pylon. "Seems to be a problem with it."

He doesn't reply, just closes his eyes and gets to work. I watch his eyeballs jitter beneath his pale folds of skin for all of fifteen seconds before he opens them and looks at me.

"You broke her."

I shrug. "Whoops."

The hint of a smile creeps into the corner of his mouth. "Respect." He takes a deep breath, pulls himself up to full height, and then rattles out a string of legalese that he's clearly not excited about. "On behalf of the NUE Department of Politicast Employment Services of the American Heights and the Employment Discovery Division of the Greater Ottawa Region, I do hereby act as your legal liaison until such time as you are delivered into the hands of a certified NUE DPES agent capable of handling your case."

"Does this mean we're dating now?"

"Basically. This way, please."

HER NAME IS ETHYL, and I'm pretty sure she's as old as the building. She sits across from me behind a translucent white desk with her wrinkly hands flat on the tabletop. The office smells of old people covered by botanical perfume.

In the slowest, most uninterested of ways, she says, "Please state your name and virtual cognizance record locator ID for the record."

I hesitate. "In V-cog or—"

"Name."

"Jericho Fox. V-rec 204-6659-8371-19."

"Confirming Jericho Fox, currently residing at 320 Cathcart Street, Apartment 208. How can I help you today, Mr. Fox?"

"Well, first off all, let me just say that I think your—"

"My hair is amazing, and I have the gorgeous body

of a twenty-year-old sports model slash actress slash billionaire heiress, I know."

"I was just trying to—"

"Please, Mr. Fox. Base editing was never in my cards. Best to leave your smarmy compliments for your fellow spacers."

"Smarmy?"

She casts me a wry look.

So, in the most sincere tone I can manage, I say, "I still like your perfume."

The corner of her mouth creeps up, but barely. It's progress.

"I'm here because… well, I need help finding employment. And before you send me to the back of the line in V-cog, yes, I've already tried that. You'll see it in my record that I have no—"

"Opportunities for employment. I still have eyes, Mr. Fox, despite what you might think. My suggestion is that you return to school and develop skills suited for a new industry within the Viatoribus."

That's the line I was expecting—the one every service construct in the system would feed me in V-cog. Which is why I'm here with Ethyl. If only she wasn't immune to my charms. Or maybe I'm just losing my touch.

I lean in. "Listen. I was hoping that maybe you might be able to look for another splitcast position."

One bushy eyebrow goes up.

Before she can counter, I add, "You can already see that High Top accepted me. And I hear that Lucid Transportation might have some new openings for—"

"Mr. Fox," she says with her gravely drawn out cadence built over what must be centuries of government employment. "Just because a company opens employment opportunities to multiple politicasts does not mean you are eligible to entertain them."

"I know that. But you can see that High Top—"

"Accepted you on probation and terminated you within twenty-four hours."

I look down, take a breath, and raise my head. "It's bad."

"Very bad."

"And I'm stuck."

"Very stuck. You won't be eligible for review for another ninety days."

I hear my father's voice creeping back into my head. His disappointment that I didn't follow him to the Solum Terram. That I didn't denounce the NUE's space program when they hung me out to dry like they did to him. "I don't have that long, ma'am."

"That must be very upsetting. Unless you have some savings or family to fall back on, as I said, I suggest that you return to school and develop skills suited for a new industry within the Viatoribus. Is there anything else I can help you with today, Mr. Fox?"

My mind is racing. I was assuming that there'd at least be something—that whoever I got might be persuaded to bend the rules for me a little. Instead, I got Ethyl. And she's got…

Me.

"Ethyl, do you have children?"

Her eyebrow goes up again. "I have *great* grandchildren, Mr. Fox. Seven of them."

Damn. She is old. "And if one of them were here in front of you right now, asking for help, desperate for work, what would you tell them?"

"The same thing I'm telling you. Is there anything else that I—?"

"But you wouldn't at least look for… *anything* that might help them get situated before closing the door on them?"

"No."

Old and heartless. Double damn.

"Ethyl, please. I—"

"Thank you for visiting the NUE's Ottawa Department of Politicast Employment Services. Have a good day, Mr. Fox."

Dejected and dreading the heat, I stand and move toward the office exit. The motion sensor activates the door, and I'm about to step out when Ethyl says, "There's a small avionics company in Riverside Park South that has an opening for—"

"I'll take it." I spin around and cast her a wide smile.

"—for a disposal maintenance technician. Your engineering degree over-qualifies you for the position, but I will add a note to your application."

"Ethyl, you're as sexy as a billionaire heiress to me right now."

"Flattery gets you nowhere in life, Mr. Fox." But she's starting to smile.

"Does that mean you don't want me to kiss you?"

"Have a good life, Mr. Fox. I hope never to see you again."

"I'll take that as a maybe."

8

EVELYN

WITH LESS THAN twenty minutes to go before my check in, Sam and I float down the transparent tunnel that leaves the CEL, serves the elevator banks, and connects to the power level's endcap. The 200-meter-diameter face, supported by the station's massive end-plate arms, marks the beginning of the free-flying cylinder that spans the hab's entire thirty-kilometer length. A centrally located armor-plated door awaits us, sealed with advanced security measures equal to those needed to access the station's other most secure area: the bridge. These critical locations are off limits to everyone except high level techs, the engineers who run zero-g manufacturing, and science officers—which means us. Well, Sam. I'm just on probation.

Sam pauses at the security console. "You really like this adventure stuff, don't you."

"I'm a sucker for a good mystery. Suits the job description too, don't you think?"

"That or maybe you missed your calling."

I tap the back of my hand to mark a make-believe wristwatch. "Time's ticking, Sam."

She nods, faces the door, and opens it via V-cog.

The power level is something of a marvel. Granted, all of *Astraea* is incredible, but this place is unique for many reasons. Down in the cylinder's southern end at section three lies the legacy hab's heart: a pulsed non-ignition thermonuclear field reversed configuration deuterium aneutronic plasma fusion generator. Nothing simple about that one. Its 100-million-degree reaction chamber sustains all critical systems on the station, including the electromagnetic field that helps shield *Astraea*'s biological inhabitants from the sun's and cosmic microwave background radiation.

And it's not alone.

The reactor's clone, the backup generator, is here in section thirty, and it takes up most of the inner core. But our interests lie in the surrounding shielded cavities that act as passthroughs to twenty-eight kilometers of zero-g manufacturing service corridors for the power level's light emissions system, or LES for short. It's here that all biological life on the station gets the synthetic sunlight and heat needed to carry out metabolic functions. Without it, the flora and fauna would be plunged into darkness and eventually die.

Upon entering the power level, we're presented with the glass security doors that lead to the backup generator's admin offices. Our business isn't in there, but we still need to move past the security office, which is bounded by smooth white walls lit in soft purple and branded with the NUESSA mark.

A single guard strapped into a crash couch snaps out of V-cog and waves. I look away, and Sam smiles back for the both of us. While she's got the white science officer uniform with red SESI logo on, I'm still in my t-shirt and hack-job shorts and beginning to regret not changing back in the lab. Seeing a science officer in passages normally frequented by techs and engineers is a little conspicuous, but it's not illegal. Sam has her charms, and the guard lets us pass without incident.

Four possible routes lead to the cylinder's perimeter and correspond to each of *Astraea*'s quadrants, numbered QA through QD in silver paint along the walls. We choose QA since, according to my limited calculations, Hodges was most likely ejected from the power level in that area.

"Hey," says a voice behind us. It's the security guard.

Sam spins around, careful to block me. "Yes?"

"I don't remember seeing you here before."

I sense Sam tense. "Uh. I'm Dr. Samantha Collins, with SESI."

"I can see your name just fine, doctor. And I remember you. I mean…" He jabs a finger our way.

Sam glances down at her uniform's logo. "You… never heard of Search for Extrasolar Sentient Intelligence?"

Oh, Sam. You sweet child.

The guard gives her an annoyed look. "Your friend, doc. The one behind you there? Her V-cog doesn't seem to be online either."

"Oh, right." She laughs. "Just an old colleague who wanted a tour. And yeah, her V-cog's been acting up. Scheduled for maintenance tomorrow."

"You and your friend interested in, ya know, hanging out later? Maybe a couple of drinks? Plus, there's no need to wait for repairs for that hardware. I know a thing or two about V-cog."

I catch Sam raising an eyebrow at me, then she says, "Uh, you know what? Thanks, but we're all set."

"You sure? 'Cause I promise that—"

"We're a couple," I blurt, grabbing Sam's hand and arm but careful to keep most of my face hidden behind her shoulder.

"Even better," he says.

I roll my eyes. "And not into that."

"Eh. Suit yourself." The guard pushes back through the security chamber doors, but just before they close, he adds, "Make sure you get that V-cog looked at tomorrow. You're gonna have a lot of trouble gettin' around the station without it."

"Will do," I say and send the well-meaning guy back into his cave with a tight smile.

"We're a couple?" Sam asks me.

"It was the only thing I could think of. Plus, you're cute."

She laughs. "Right."

By the time we reach the power level's perimeter corridors, we can already sense the slow moving effects of *Astraea*'s rotation. It's not enough to produce any meaningful gravity, but free floating is made more difficult.

Sam opens the QA hatch that runs south toward section one and then backs away. "After you."

I enter the well-lit shaft and start examining the LES access chamber doors. There's a hundred of them in this quadrant alone, and each looks the same as the next. Most people use these conduits to bypass the generator and get through to manufacturing—I can't even recall the last time I was up here. A year, maybe?

"Any place in particular you'd like to start, Eves?" Sam asks.

I hold up a fist. "Throw for a total?"

She raises her fist and pumps it twice, then we both

hold out digits for a sum. "Lucky number seven it is," she says.

I push forward and hunt for the stencil that reads S30-PL-LES-QA-B7, which happens to be twenty meters ahead. Once again, Sam activates the door from V-cog and allows me in first. The large chamber is dark and much warmer than the corridor. The only light comes from the thin gaps between LES radiant panels that cover the far wall in a gentle curve.

"Never been in here," Sam offers. "Like being inside the belfry of one of those old clock towers. Inner workings and all."

"Only those don't put out enough energy to sustain photosynthesis and warm a third of a million humans."

"Right. Where to?"

I look behind us to a camera fixed on the inside wall. Its multiple lenses and integrated software creates a 200-degree image of the space and links to the other cameras in the area so that the entire quadrant gets covered.

"Over there." I push off the nearest bulkhead and approach the device cautiously. It's the next piece of the puzzle. Sam joins me, and we get up close and personal with the unit, examining its multiple black wide-angle lenses.

"I feel bad for anyone monitoring this feed right now," Sam says with a level of mirth in her voice. "My nose has gotta be the size of Europa."

"Good thing I shaved this morning," I add.

Sam chuckles, but it fades fast. "I don't see anything out of the ordinary."

"Me neither."

"What were you hoping for?"

"I dunno." I tap my nose with a finger. "Some sort

of bypass harness or something? But…" I feel around the unit's base. "It doesn't look like it's been damaged at all."

"Same. Which means it has to be software related."

I squint at her. "I thought you said there wasn't any record of that."

"I did, yeah. Doesn't add up."

I thumb toward the bulkhead that divides us from the next chamber. "Let's check another one."

Sam nods, and we push south toward bay eight. The radiant panels hum to our left, and I sense my cheek warming from the ambient heat. They're pretty efficient considering that the opposite side could melt my face off in three seconds.

We arrive at a second camera and reach the same conclusion as the first. No sign of foul play.

Sam runs a hand over her hair. "I have a feeling they're all like this."

"Me too."

"We'd better get you back to your apartment."

I nod, but I don't mean it. I hate leaving this puzzle unsolved just to kowtow to some ignorant inspector and his bad call. Stamos should be the one sequestered in his apartment, not me.

"Evelyn?"

"What?"

"You… did it again."

"Sorry. Just thinking." I glance at the outer wall and float toward one of the curved support beams that holds the panels in place.

"Careful," she says.

"Yeah, yeah. I know." I grab the insulated safety bar and admire the LES craftsmanship. People down below take the ingenuity for granted. Then again, that's how most things are, I suppose. We just expect the sun to rise and the sky to be there each morning, never thinking for a second that they won't exist forever. The sun? Sure, it still has a few billion good years left. But not the Earth. We took her stability for granted for far too long.

"How do you think Hodges's murderer did it?" Sam says next to me, eyeing the nearest LES panel.

"Never took you for the morbid kind."

"I don't mean it like that. Just, curious, ya know?"

"The panels have exterior access hatches. See there?" I point to some hinges and a handle in the middle of a giant hexagonal section. "Once the handles are cool enough, you can open the panels."

"Which is why they did it at night. And there wouldn't be signs of tampering."

"Exactly. As long as you have tech credentials and everything's cool to the touch, the hatches are an easy open."

Sam mumbles something.

"Say again?"

"Tech credentials." Her eyes look scared.

It only takes me a second to pick where she's going. "You're thinking V-cog theft?"

She nods almost imperceptibly. "It's not possible though."

I shake my head. "Just because it hasn't been done doesn't mean it's impossible. Just highly improbable."

"Because there's no precedent."

"Correct." I have that uneasy flutter in my stomach. "If it's never been done, the inspectors won't be looking for it. No one would. And for someone to impersonate in V-cog, they would either need to replicate someone's credentials—"

"Which are quantum locked," she points out.

"—or remove the nanos directly."

"Right." Sam swallows. "And to do that, you'd need—"

"A lot of talent."

She laughs.

"What?"

"And here I was thinking you'd need to be really, really evil."

"Well, that too."

The combination of talent and evil genius really does seem unlikely all the way up here. Sure, every single person on this station is talented in one way or another. Even Julio is a xenobiologist when he's not moonlighting as Fairmont Valley's cheery-faced ice cream peddler.

But evil?

The psych evals alone on every person in *Astraea* fill multiple servers. Even the children go through quarterly reviews to ensure their mental health. Of course, any human can snap, especially under the duress of long-term space occupation. But that kind of degradation is well documented; we know what to look for and how to treat it before it becomes a problem. All station doctors are trained to catch anomalies during routine physicals.

The malevolence needed to pull someone's V-cog nano system right out of their brain while still connected is… well, it's unthinkable. The victim would be a human vegetable, stripped of everything but involuntary muscle contraction. Though, I suppose the mercy is that they wouldn't be aware of the violence.

"It's genius," I say at last.

Sam winces but eventually seems to agree. "The movies never explain how it's done. They just wave their magic wand and, *poof*, you have incogs. But I suppose if the criminal had some sort of stasis tissue to keep the V-cog nanos in, the grid would continue to register the victim's credentials indefinitely. Then to use them, you'd need some hefty splice code to allow yours and your victim's nanos to coexist. Like you said, it's hypothetically possible. But it's also"—she puts a hand around her neck and the other on the small shaved spot on the back of her head—"sickening." After a moment she looks at me. "There are safeguards in place to prevent that though, right?"

"Don't look at me, Sam. You're the computer scientist."

"Right." She swallows again.

I glance behind us. "It still doesn't explain the cameras though."

"Or what they were after to begin with," Sam adds as she comes out of her mini episode. "You don't kill someone like that just because you're angry, do you?"

"Not without tripping a whole lot of hostility indicators first." People planetside still fear "invasion of privacy" like the plague even though they gave it up hundreds of years ago. But on *Astraea*? We volunteered for this.

Absently, Sam reaches for her neck again, then snaps out of it. "We need to—"

The sound of a seal unlatching stops her. We look to the nearest door as it opens to the lateral access corridors. Five security officers push themselves through, weapons drawn, followed by...

"Inspector Stamos. I didn't expect to see you up here."

"I was about to say the same to you, Dr. Park. But then again, criminals do have a tendency to come back and review their crime scenes, don't they."

"Try asking the culprit when you catch them."

"I'm pretty sure I just did." He glances left. "Take them both into custody."

"Both?" I look at Sam and then back to Stamos. "Dr. Collins has nothing to do with this."

Stamos smiles. "Have you seen who she's keeping company with?"

His officers surround us, and I start putting up a fight against the PlastiCuffs they're trying to put on me. "You leave her out of this. I'm the one who—*Ouch! Easy*—manipulated her into coming up here."

"Manipulation doesn't exonerate anyone."

I grit my teeth and think of something harsher. "I extorted her."

"Evelyn, stop," Sam yells.

"Interesting confession," Stamos says to me. "I'll add to your list of charges."

"You son of a—"

"Under the Nations of United Earth's Legacy Habitation Charter, I do hereby place you under arrest for the murders of Senior Engineer Lewis Hodges and Second Engineer Marcus Del Toro."

"Del Toro?" I glance at Sam for some sort of help, but she looks like she's going to be sick. "You found his body too?"

"Don't sound so surprised, Doctor. You of all people should know that there are only so many places you can hide things on an O'Neill-Oberth cylinder. You have the right to remain silent. Anything you say can and will be used against you in an NUE court of law. You have—"

"I want probable cause. You have no evidence."

"Don't I?" He gives me a half-smile and a subtle shake of his head. "I took your suggestion, Dr. Park.

Fairly cavalier of you too. But that does tend to be most criminals' undoing. Turns out your math worked. And when your home turned up empty, and there was blood on the Gibbons's balcony, we figured we knew where your V-cog sig would point us when we turned it back on." He points down. "Right here. Add that to your command authorization on the camera software moments before a conveniently deleted portion of data at the estimated time of Hodges's ejection from the light emissions system, and we secured the warrant for your arrest from Captain Mombawe shortly after you were reported missing."

I glance at Sam. She's as pale as a bed sheet. Anyone could have figured out trigonometry for Hodges's fall eventually. Even Stamos. But Sam knows as well as I do that someone planted my V-rec sig and hid it from her latest search.

"You're making a mistake," I say.

"We'll see about that. You have the right to an attorney. If you can't—"

"Why're you staying so far away, Stamos?"

"If you can't afford legal counsel, then—"

"I've got cuffs on now." I shrug to show off my new jewelry.

"—then counsel will be provided for you."

"You afraid I'm gonna bite you?"

"You are a bitch." He waves at his officers. "Get them both out of here."

As the security team pushes us past Stamos, I whip my forehead into his nose and hear a crunch.

Over the top? Maybe.

Get me in more trouble? Definitely.

The inspector's eyes roll as he pulls back, swearing.

Mission accomplished.

9

JERICHO

IT'S BEEN three days since I started working at LMC Avionics Inc. in Riverside Park South. Three. Days. And already I hate my life. Which is unlike me, because I feel like I can get along just about anywhere.

But not here.

I'm partly to blame for all this too. Okay, maybe a lot to blame. When Ethyl said there weren't any openings, what she really meant was that all respectable ones were unavailable. I.e., they didn't want a maglev train wreck like me. Therefore, any company willing to take on *the* Jericho Fox was most likely shady as shit. Which, as it turns out, LMC Avionics is.

In the last few hours alone, I've noted three patent infringements, five manufacturing safety violations, rubber stamp approval on a parts batch that shouldn't have ever passed a quality control inspection, three counts of hazing, two blatant instances of sexual harassment, and an episode of professional misconduct that I can't decide if it's favoritism or nepotism—I guess it all depends on if the boss just slept with and promoted his mistress or his sister. I guess that would also make it incest. None of it would surprise me at this point.

But it all makes sense. Because LMC doesn't get the majority of their revenue from selling repackaged aftermarket hardware to desperate aviation developers looking to increase their margins—God only knows how many lawsuits they're holding at bay. I spotted a dark room behind the circuit board division that smacks of illegal stim coding and batch tweaks. People will pay a premium for good slicing on the lateral hypothalamus and medial forebrain bundle, as will they for instantly teaching their muscles how to bash someone's head in with kung-fu despite whatever havoc uncertified code will do to their own bodies if they bought a bad batch. Enough to keep a company like this covered from NUE investigations by a gaggle of heavy-handed attorneys and held afloat in the public eye by constant PR spin.

If the business itself isn't socially carcinogenic enough, the commute makes up for it. Public transport doesn't run this far out, and good luck securing a lender —the owner conveniently makes the fee for "potential damages caused by unexpected environmental incidents" the same price as a day's wages. So I've been walking and, hell yeah, using my PXSEE for surveillance further up the street—that's personal exo-sensory environment experience drone, or pixie for short. My aerial bot is a tantalizing target for any slummers in this particular stim ward still awake enough to notice it. Even broken, the drone parts and V-cog integration hardware could fetch them half a day's escape to pleasures untold. But they can't hit it with stones and bottles any more than a drunk can hit a dartboard with cotton balls.

And then there's the other half of the cognizant slummers who would throw something at my aerial scout but can't get their arms to work. Whether from broken bones or torn muscles, they've found their way into this ward from bad batch tweaks they can't afford to wipe out of their heads. They wander the shadows like zombies, hunched over with their heads cocked sideways, wrists bent in, and feet pigeon-toed.

The whole set is a wretched spectacle, one I've seen played out in cities across the nation states. It's why we have to find greener pastures as a species. Whether it's for fatigue from systems perpetually pitted against them or pain from demons gnawing at the soul, these are desperate people, and not unlike my distant ancestors. There's stim code for anything these days. You just don't know where it's come from until it's too late.

Any tweaked out threats I encounter along my surveilled path through the shadows of Riverside Park South are kept at bay by the five-shot Taurus 605 on my hip. Sure, I wouldn't normally brandish a revolver so brazenly; I'm an engineer and pilot at heart. But I'm also not stupid. The people who see it aren't stupid either and keep their distance. Everybody wins, and I get to my dead-end job in one piece.

"New guy! What's the holdup?"

I stick the toilet brush in the bowl and square with my foreman, Blanderson, as he enters the bathroom. He's a dick and a half who never saw the inside of an engineering school despite his fancy title.

"Just stretching my back, sir," I say, giving it a genuine twist.

"Oh yeah? 'Cause it looks like you cogged out for some titties. And we ain't paying you for titties, you feel me, Foxy?"

"I feel you. Quick question, what did you say your degree was in again?"

"I didn't." The smell of booze and unlaundered clothing bites me harder than his tone. He's also been tweaking; there's no way anyone gets muscles this big without way too much dedication to a gym—the time and discipline for which he doesn't have. He jabs my chest with a finger. "Less talking, more cleaning."

I pick up my trusty toilet brush and the ammonia bottle. "Copy that."

"And eyes off the titties!"

Blanderson storms out the bathroom and hauls off toward someone else who needs professional motivation.

Three days. And how many more, Jericho?

The trouble with being even somewhat smart is that you outthink yourself more often than not. You know the end from the beginning. And, for some people, that's okay. In fact, it's comforting because you recognize that you're never getting above a certain pay grade, which means you know what kind of apartment you can afford, what kind of things you can buy—private car, shared car, grid car, no car—and how long it will be until you retire. Or until you die with your bare hands on the toilet brush.

"This was a mistake." I say it out loud because I need to hear it—need to know that I'm admitting it for real and not just thinking it over and over and over again. Of course, right behind it comes, "So what are you gonna do about it, Jericho?"

The option of not working is out of the question. I have too much self-respect for that. Plus, my father, God bless him, taught me better. But more than those things, I want to contribute, to make a difference. I want to help humanity extend itself into the cosmos and secure its next thousand years of survival just like my ancestors did for me. The big question is if humanity will let me. And right now, the answer seems to be, "Hell, no. Take your toilet brush and leave us alone."

The other option is going off the books. There's plenty of under the table work—shoot, I could make a fortune in that dark room, if not learning to slice, at least repairing their neuronano protocols. I can do that in my sleep. But I'd also be selling my soul to the devil and reneging on everything I've believed in since… well, since I was a kid. Take care of yourself, do right by people, and use your gifts to better the world.

But going off the books means trouble with the NUE. If not now, certainly later. It means a lot of running. Of course, I could just suckle the system's tit, but we already covered why that won't work, plus Blanderson would be right in his accusations then.

An invite pops up in V-cog. It's dad. And I'm really not in the mood to talk to him, so I hit Dismiss and go back to my toilet scrubbing.

"Son?" Dammit, he's in my lobby. "Can you talk?"

I lower my head, let the toilet brush go again, and enter my Amel 60's galley. "What's up, pops."

He looks surprised to see me, like he knew I'd be avoiding him. No shocker there. "I, uh… just wanted to see how you're doing. At the new job."

"Fine."

He swallows and looks around the boat's interior. His face reflects an old sense of nostalgia. For the ship. Or maybe me—can't tell. "Anything I can help with?"

Weird question. Completely impractical. "Nope."

"Listen, I was doing some research on LMC, and I'm not so sure that they're—"

"Dad, I don't need or want you sticking your nose in my business."

"I know that, son. I was just concerned that—"

"Don't be. I'll contact you if I feel I need something, okay?"

He nods but seems to want to say something else. "Have you thought more about Sallsworth's job offer?"

"No. And I won't either."

I expect him to press me, but he doesn't. He just nods once, stuffs his hands in his pants pockets, and relaxes his shoulders. "Well, uh… Thanks for seeing me."

I step out of V-cog and go back to my toilet with that name on my lips.

Sallsworth.

That's the option I hate the most. Why? Because of what the man said on the verb about me. Or was it just his criticisms of expansion in general? Doesn't matter. They're one and the same anyway.

And then there's the issue of money. The fact that he would give me a cold blockchain chip to, what, buy my allegiance? To manipulate me into working for him through some twisted illusion of generosity like he does with all his minions? No thanks. I should've left that chip on the table.

Another incoming call. I accept without looking. "Dad, I'm not—"

"Hey, asshole." It's Kit.

I smile at his address. Probably took some balls for him to lead with that. Then again, I imagine he's gotta be feeling pretty large at the moment. "Hey, Kit. How you doing?"

"Good. Am I… interrupting anything?"

"Negative. What's up with you, Mr. Famous Rescuer?"

His cheeks flush. "You saw that?"

"Pretty sure the whole planet did."

"Yeah. Ha! Crazy, right? But I, um… that's kinda why I wanted to call, now that I'm settled in and the pixies have stopped hounding me. A little, anyway."

"Shoot."

"I wanted to— This is secure, right?"

I lift an eyebrow at him. "It's a quantum-locked V-cog lobby, Kit. Yeah, it's secure."

"Okay, okay. Just making sure." He lowers his voice nonetheless. "I wanted to apologize. They said that, well, when I was giving my statement, the High Top execs said that I, um, shouldn't—"

"Mention me in any way." I save him the effort.

His eyes get big. "Yes! Yeah, that's it exactly. How'd you—"

"And that you'd jeopardize your promotion if you did."

"Holy cow, yeah. Are you…" He studies my face. "You don't seem upset."

"Kit, I'm the one who told you to keep my name out of it, remember?"

"Yeah, yeah. I know, but I just didn't feel right about it."

"You did what I asked, and you were owed that bump in pay, buddy. I'd have been pissed if you *didn't* listen."

"Oh man." He wipes his forehead. "And here I was so worried that you'd be upset with me. I felt guilty, you know?"

"We both know the truth of what really happened. And I'll sleep a little better tonight knowing you have a good future lined up."

He licks his lips as if to say something but hesitates.

After a few awkward seconds, I ask, "You do have a good future lined up, right?"

"Um, I guess that depends."

"Oh, Kit. What did you do?"

He wrings his hands several times. "I felt so guilty about taking all the credit that I couldn't live with myself—"

"Kit—"

"—so I recorded a statement and put it on the verb."

"No. Why?"

"So I could sleep at night, Cap. You understand, right?"

God, this guy is too good for the world he was born into. I squint and rub my forehead with one hand. "They terminated you, didn't they."

"So hard."

"Dammit, Kit."

"I'm sorry, Cap. Worst part is, my upload only got a handful of views. I wanted the whole world seeing twenties, you know?"

I nod, feeling more sorry for this kid than I do for myself. A toilet brush in his hand would be an improvement.

He looks between his feet. "Worst part is that it was Ogilvie who came to fire me. Said it was the best part of his day."

"Talk about an asshole."

"That's what I called him too."

"Shut up."

"No, I did."

I let out a laugh in real and virtual life. "You have balls, Kit."

"Or I'm just stupid."

"You're not stupid. Maybe a little too… *thoughtful* for your own good at times, but definitely not stupid."

He blushes. "Thanks, Cap. I appreciate it."

I shake my head at him and put a hand on his shoulder. "So, what're you gonna do now?"

"Well, that's the other reason I called."

I feel a pit form in my stomach. "They blackballed you."

"Yeah. I tried making an appointment with DPES in Winnipeg, but they said that I'd need to wait at least—"

"Ninety days to schedule an appointment."

"Yeah. How'd you know?"

I wince, trying to get the image of Ethyl out of my head. "Long story."

"Anyway, I figured that of all people who might, ya know, be able to put in a good word for me, what with your new boss and all, you could see if your new boss could maybe squeeze me in somewhere? And I don't care what the job description is. You know I can handle hard work. Heck, I'll scrub toilets if I have to."

"Funny you should say that."

"Oh yeah? Why?"

Now it's my turn to open my mouth but not say anything. I already got this kid in trouble once; I won't do it again by inviting him into this hellhole. But I don't want to leave him high and dry either. He just lost his best shot at a real career because of me. Granted, I didn't ask him to. But I still feel responsible. Christ. Having a conscience really sucks sometimes.

"I might have something for you," I say at last.

"Really?"

"But don't get your hopes up."

"Oh, man, Cap! I won't let you down. Promise."

I hold my hands up to slow him down. "I said I *might* have something. I need time to sort it all out. But I'll be in touch."

"In touch, sure. Right-right. I'm not going anywhere. Ya know? Just let me know."

"I will."

"I'll be right here."

"Got it."

"Waiting on Captain Jericho Fox to save the day again."

I run a hand down my face. "Can you go now?"

"Absolutely." Just before his avatar blinks out, he adds, "Thank you. I was… kinda worried about what I was gonna do next, ya know?" Then he flashes me a stupid smile and vanishes, leaving me no other choice but to sell my soul to the devil.

10

JACK

How ARE you handling the pressure, Jack? Is it getting to you yet?

Do you feel the icy hand walking its fingers down your spine, willing you to back out? Or are you in so deep that there's no other way but forward? Because, contrary to what you might think, it's not too late. There's always an exit. Always a way out.

But you don't feel pressure like everyone else does, do you, Jack. And why would you? The only provocation that math asserts is the demand for a solution. The yearning for a problem to be solved. To reach an equilibrium that satisfies both sides of the equation. Like a vacuum yearning to equalize an atmosphere.

Your desire is to stop the wasters from spending trillions on a fraction of the world and release the resources for the good of all, to rectify the misalignment, and to reconcile the gross misappropriations that have caused so much suffering.

The first task, after clearing security and immigration, was having Mr. Samson check into his stateroom in section one's elite hotel, the Somnium Lux: Astraea. Leaving the zero-g transportation hub and sliding into gravity over four kilometers was a strange feeling. But you'd practiced for it and come off as the seasoned veteran of inertial transition that Samson is. Or was. Then you used the hotel's virtual check-in system and made it your room without incident. Well, almost. Twice, humans were sent to see if you needed anything. While the cheaper resorts used excipions, the elite still preferred the higher paid human touch. Fortunately, they took your dismissal to heart and left you alone.

For the curious, the billionaire recluse won't move for a week, as is his custom, if anyone cares to cross-check, which they won't. And if they do decide to check up on him and knock on his door? Well, they can only blame themselves for what's to follow, if you haven't detonated it before then.

Mr. Samson doesn't get off on endless parades through fancy parties or posing for photo ops that grace the "buy me now or feel left out" gossip racks. Which suits you just fine, doesn't it, Jack. Because few people know his face, and those who do won't find his body in the tropical Saunders Island mansion. Last they knew, he was taking another extended lap through the stars and enjoying the dividends of his shrewd investments. The Falklands won't miss him either. Nor will the rest of the suffering masses. They're too busy begging for reprieve, one you'll deliver to them, won't you, Jack. Because the math demands it. The equation must be satisfied.

With Samson's nanos removed from your brain and safely injected into the tissue stasis cube, you're a shadow again, a free agent walking the concourse of section one, quadrant C, trying not to look overwhelmed by *Astraea*'s magnificence. And it is magnificent, isn't it?—a magnificent mistake, one of eight legacy habs scattered from here to Ganymede. Its lines sweep overhead and stretch down the cylinder to the far end, wrapping around you like a mesmerizing city of miracles. Or nightmares, depending on whether you're Jack or Mr. Samson.

But *Astraea*? She's special. The first and the crown jewel of the NUE's space expansion initiative. The one that tells the rest of the world that they are inferior, that they aren't a part of the equation. The wasters claim to believe otherwise—of course they do. It's the only way they can sell it. But it's lies! All lies. Humanity's greatest resources and minds are being spent on creating things that could never help *every*one, only specific *some*ones. The *beautiful ones*. And no one balked. None but the Tantum, that is. And a few loyalists within the Solum Terram, weak as they are. No one bothered to ask why hundreds of trillions were spent on ventures to preserve the lives of a few when it could have been spent to preserve the lives of all.

But you tire of the argument. It has been made, it went unheard, and the deaf left you no other choice.

Now, here, is your moment. Neon inked your new tattoo herself, gave you the kiss, and bound you in blood, ironic as it is. You've been chosen, Jack. And you can't fail. Doing so would mean dooming the fates of billions. Plus, you know you have help. You don't know their faces or their names, but you do know they're out there, somewhere, sent by the architects, each having their roles to play. And right now, yours counts the most, Jack.

THE NEURONANO SAMPLE you skimmed from the flight attendant—no, from *Luna*. That was her name. Names are important. You're doing this for people, not just integers. The sample gives you access to the crew files. You stand at the terminal, hoping the hack works. They said it would. You doubted them because they're people and not as reliable as the equations. They err.

But the system sees the trace of Luna's ID in you as an anomaly and clears it. She can't possibly be on a flight back to the space elevator *and* be on Astraea, can she? So you smile once for the code slicers in Vancouver. Their insights have just made you invisible, a ghost walking among the living, a reject not worthy of being tracked, an exploit on the loose. The fatal flaw is everyone's assumption that virtual cognizance is an all or nothing system. But Neon's slicers figured it out—discovered that there are varying degrees of cognizance based on partial nano removal. It cost lives, yes. But it will save so many more.

You're about to scroll through the crew roster when a name near the top stops your eye. She—the one responsible for so much of the waste, for convincing so many of the powerful that hope lies beyond the Earth's atmosphere—is here, just as she is tacked to your poster. You would eliminate her if you could, but she's insignificant now, just one small pixel in a larger picture. And you can't afford to be distracted, Jack. Can't afford to let your rage overpower your logic. You must stay focused. You must remain rational.

You pull up a list of the lowest ranking engineers, the ones no one takes seriously but still have access to all the important parts of the station. Ironically, it's not the bridge you're after. Terrorists seek pain. Seek revenge. But you're not one of them, are you, Jack. Some might call you a hero one day; you won't rob them of that choice. But you're no hero. You're simply doing your part. And they'll all be so proud of you—*her* the most.

If anything, you're a pragmatist, aren't you, Jack. And this is not a terrorist attack, despite how the verb heads will spin it. This is a correction, one that opens the eyes of the blind and makes humanity wake up. Makes them question the frivolous pursuit of their backward dreams. Makes them realize that these—*Astraea, Calypso, Arete*, and all the other stations, sub-stations, dome settlements, and outposts—were steps too far. The monoliths represent humanity's misguided focus. And it would continue into oblivion were you not there to abort the progression, Jack.

The network presents you with a list of good candidates. It doesn't know that, of course. It's merely fulfilling its obligation to you as the phantom of a shuttle flight attendant who's initiated an untraceable query. But you see the name. Leach, Jared, first engineer, not three months into his commission, and his dimensions are a close enough match. He's on break in the dining facility six hundred meters from your present location in Kantree Atrium, which is named after a twenty-second century physicist, if you're not mistaken, and you rarely are.

JARED EXCUSES himself from the table—whether filled with peers or friends, you can't tell—and moves to the bathroom. He's feeling ill. Intestinal pressure, which will eventually lead to a fever, shaking, and then unconsciousness. He'll live. For a little while anyway. But that's none of your concern, Jack.

You join him in the bathroom, lock the main door behind you, and seek out his stall where he's moments away from blacking out.

"Someone there?" he asks with a trembling voice. "Can you hand me a towel? I don't… shit. I don't feel so hot."

"Of course." You take one of the folded towels from the linens conveyor and pass it over the frosted glass partition. "Here you are."

"Man. Thanks so much. I… I think I'm gonna… Oh shit, I…"

There's a *smack*, a squeaking of skin against glass, and then a heavy *thud*. You override the partition's locking mechanism with a quick V-cog command and find Mr. Leach facedown with his pants around his ankles. You press your ring against the back of his head and take just enough neuronanos to leave his mind intact but not enough for him to remember who he is—at least for a little while. He'll register in the grid as the anomaly, and you will be Leach. Smooth. Efficient. Textbook. Just like you were taught.

You take his pants the rest of the way off and put them on. Sizes match, as you knew they would. You don his jacket, boots, and watch too. Then you prop him on the toilet, naked, send your clothes down the chute, and check yourself over in the mirror. You're now Leach— Jack Leach. But the only thing you need to fool is *Astraea*, and she's already been duped.

You navigate to the guest cargo hold near the docking level and slip through security without raising a single eyebrow. And why wouldn't you, Jack? Leach has access to this area, so you do. You're one of them now. A spacer with their hopes on the stars. It sickens you to play the part, but the reward is worth the trial.

You use Mr. Samson's record locator to find the section, aisle, bay, and shelf that your—*his* suitcases are secured in. Three high-end bulletproof Shoreline cases that scream, "Tamper with these and my people will haunt you for the rest of your life." Two excipions arrive and place the cases on the maglev sled for you. One asks if you would like assistance to your destination, but you decline. Then the guest delivery system grants you temporary transportation privileges to ferry the items to Mr. Samson's stateroom. They'll never make it, of course. But the deed will be done before the timer locks out your permissions.

You push the sled toward the exit and approach four techs on break standing just beside the main hangar door. For a moment, your gut tightens, and you wonder if they suspect you. But given the rest of your camouflage, why would they? You're one of them now, hidden in plain sight.

"You ever wonder what's inside?" one of the middle-aged men asks you. Again, you wonder if he knows, if he's somehow managed to see through you. But the statistical likelihood of such a feat is infinitesimal.

"Do I ever wonder what's inside?" you match with the psychological precision of a master subliminalist. "Every damn day. Imagine how much sooner we could all retire."

This gets a round of self-pitied nods from the group.

"Never too late to try," says another.

"Who says I didn't?" You let your body sag into the lazy hunch of a man who's wasted the best years of his life doing other peoples' bidding. "Almost got pinched."

"Woulda been worth it though, I bet," says the first.

"Woulda been. See you on the rote."

"On the rote," a few reply—short for "rotation," a bit of slang gifted to you by Neon's people. And with that, you're free to wander *Astraea*'s labyrinthian corridors carrying the cure that will rid humanity of the abomination.

YOUR FIRST STOP was easy enough: a simple return trip up to the transportation hub, using a crew-only freight lift, from which you ducked into an unused utility room. Your second stop, however, is not as straightforward, and neither is the last.

You return to the main level on section one and descend further into the agriculture and subsystems level. It's the last deck that forms the hab's exterior hull and endures slightly more than one g, which you feel in your knees, hips, and subtle increase in pulse. But, like everything else, you're prepared, Jack. The months of extra physical training, the stress tests, the gene therapy and strategy sessions—they count right now. All you need to do is stay focused.

This package will be the first to detonate. It's the most unique as well, designed to breach the hull but not supersede the crew's ability to handle the emergency. "We train for these sorts of situations," they'll say for the verb pixies. "Our crew did an excellent job today, just as expected." Some funerals will be held, posthumous awards for heroism bestowed, and the general anxieties of all those far and wide will be coaxed back into manageable levels. New headlines will replace the old, and life will go on within the hour. Which will make the next blow all the more devastating, whenever it comes. Yes, you've injected a small element of chance into the second bomb's timing, but it's needed in order to place some of the responsibility on them. Some of the blame. However, it's all a calculated risk, Jack. If they fail to set it off, you always have triggers. Plenty of triggers.

You navigate the magsled into the utility lift that conducts you laterally along the hab's outer spine toward the station's midpoint. Even through the conduit's glass lining, you pick up the distinctly Earthen smells of dirt, manure, and animal sweat. You pass section after section of ten-meter high chambers that sweep up and away, filled with cows grazing in pastures, wheat fields rippling in artificial wind, or herds of sheep running up sloped walls, all under the same light emissions technology that radiates in the main hab level.

You feel sick, don't you, Jack.

Not only have they augmented themselves, but the creators of this demonic experiment have subjected the Earth's fauna and flora to their twisted genetic machinations. And then to imprison their subjects in the vacuum of space for the sole purpose of nourishing the beautiful ones? At least on Earth, these creatures would have lived lives under open heavens before yielding their energy to the circle of life. And at what cost? How much is spent keeping this perverse ecosystem sustained when so many more are being defunded on Earth?

You will end this, Jack. You will keep it from ever happening again. You will ensure that creatures are kept where they belong.

The utility lift stops at section sixteen, one floor beyond *Astraea*'s mathematical middle, because that would be too perfect. You push the magsled down a hallway that bisects two hydroponic greenhouses, one for tomatoes and the other for citrus fruits. Everything is so vibrant and luscious, good enough to eat. But, just like cutting into *Astraea* at the center would be, all of this is too perfect, and therein lies the flaw. None of this is real, merely synthetic—iterations and shadows. Attempts to be what it can never achieve: the authentic. The sublime. The world the way God intended it. And for all its attempts to be picturesque, the opposite is true: this place is sterile, utterly devoid of what makes life organic. It's the mess. The stench. The mark of a life born from the dust and sure to return there when its time has finished that makes life truly beautiful. Fragility is the essence of beauty, and destruction the temple of the sacred.

As you pass your fellow technicians, ranging from botanists and veterinarians to xenobiologists—all space farmers, you call them—you find yourself averting your eyes at their virulent creations the way an innocent soul might in Oslo's red-light district, and eventually come upon a sub-system cross corridor and then a man-sized utility conduit that runs the length of the station.

Leach, not you, opens the utility door with V-cog and steps through bearing the second case. You hesitate leaving the magsled unattended with the third, but why? You're a tech, Jack. This equipment is all normal, inconsequential, and benign. You care no more for these cases than you would for any other. Still, you can't afford to take chances now, so you deploy your pixie and set it to loiter out of sight. Then you leave the gear and plunge into the dimly lit tunnel that smells of metal, ozone, and processed sewer—traces of how this world ought to smell. Of course they would tuck it away, out of sight. Of course they would try to hide their true nature and leave the rest of humanity behind. How fitting that their demise should start here, blowing a gaping hole in part of the liquid barrier that shields them from so much cosmic radiation.

You don't use V-cog for navigating this last part, only pure biological memories partitioned from the nanos in your brain. Overlap was a risk neither you nor Neon's architects were willing to take. Data can be ripped from V-cog—even the dead have secrets to tell, a truth lamented by technology corporations as security councils sue them for criminals' credentials. And the human brain? Even in the quantum age, it still has its secrets, ones it can take to the grave. So you follow the path as rehearsed a hundred times, one foot in front of the other. You could do it blindfolded, couldn't you, Jack. Right up to the resonant target point that will let the math do its work. Frequency, harmony, volume—tools of the maestros, malcontents, and miscreants the world over. And you are no exception, Jack.

There aren't any cameras here. No sensors either. The only ones in the section are those you passed minutes ago, and it will be weeks before investigators think to look this far down—not that they have that much time to live. You're a nobody, Jack, doing nobody things. Cameras at your final destination? Yes, many of them. But Neon's architects have seen to those for you, and they won't let you down.

You open the latches and examine the payload, the redundant triggers, the interface—it's all there, all still in working order. You power up the cure, arm the device, and double-check the fail-safes. Satisfied, you give the final input: an audio command of your own selection. Neon left it up to you. You felt flattered. And you didn't hesitate. You programmed in the project name that started all of this… this insane pursuit of expanding beyond Earth's atmosphere and then seeking help from alien life in star systems light-years from your own. Poetic that it should end the way it began.

The word of hope becomes the curse.

You lean into the device, press the physical input key, and whisper the word that will eventually send *Astraea* hurtling back through the atmosphere in fire and taking thousands of souls with her.

"Infinita."

11

EVELYN

"You got any new tricks up your sleeve?" Sam asks me across the hallway in the detention cell block. It's both a sarcastic and rhetorical question because the last bright idea I had for breaking us out not only resulted in different cell assignments, but it also gave us a high-voltage, lower-amperage jolt of electricity that caused both of us to soil ourselves. Not the worst experience I've ever had, but certainly not one either of us would like to repeat.

I finally answer her with a defeated tone. "Not unless you want the guards to power spike you again."

"I'll pass." She lies down on the bed molded into the wall. There's an integrated foam mattress with a small mound to serve as a pillow that Sam's resting her head on. The accommodations aren't half bad. I've never been to section fifteen's security station, but it's a relative palace compared to jails I've seen on Earth.

I try lightening the mood. "At least they let us shower for the first time in two days."

Sam doesn't bother looking at me through our transparent safety glass walls. "Yeah, 'cause our pants were full of shit, Evelyn." She grunts once and then softens her tone. "Haven't done that since I was in launch training."

"You and everyone else. On the bright side, we have these snazzy new orange jumpsuits."

She casts me an emotionless smile and then drops her head back down.

I really don't mean to piss Sam off. She's my only real friend up here, even though we don't know one another much beyond our professional relationship. Maybe it's better to say she's the person I've spent the most time with on station. I can hear my mother saying I should have made more friends by now. "Go outside. Introduce yourself to people. Try new things, it might surprise you." Well, I have introduced myself to people, and I inevitably offended them because I said what I was thinking. Didn't know that was a crime.

Sam at least seems to tolerate me—even likes me, and I her. We share a similar passion for our work with NUESSA's Search for Extrasolar Sentient Intelligence division, no small thanks to our mutual Sentia Aux birthright. We both enjoy a good tequila, and we both have the intestinal fortitude to try to break the rules. Okay, so I exceed her on all points by some margin. But so far, she hasn't unfriended me. Not yet.

"So, as for any more tricks up my sleeve, I was thinking that maybe we could—"

"My god. I was kidding, Evelyn."

I close my mouth and nod once. Maybe unfriending is closer than I thought.

Following her lead, I fold my arms behind my head and lie back on the bed. The bright white ceiling could use some dimming, but at least the room is clean.

Over a minute of awkward silence passes between

us. Normally, I'd be fine with it, but I can sense she's upset, and I need to say something. "I'm sorry, Sam."

"It is your fault, you know." She doesn't bother lifting her head up.

"That's why I'm apologizing."

"If you had just stayed in your room, they probably would have let you out in a few more hours, and we wouldn't be here."

I sit up. Something's telling me not to open my mouth, but I ignore it. "Sam, you found evidence vital to the investigation."

"Evidence that makes it look like I'm the one who arranged it since I'm the only one who knew where to look!"

"They would have found it eventually."

She props herself up. "Okay, Miss Let's Go Help the Inept Investigators Do Their Job."

"And if you'd been given more time, you probably could have found out what was going on with the V-rec trace linking me to the cameras."

"And so could they, Eves. Only, *they* wouldn't have confirmation bias to contend with—*like they do now*."

Again, I open my mouth to say something, but this time I opt out.

Another minute passes. When Sam speaks again, her voice has lost its edge. "What happens next?"

"Hopefully not more power spiking."

She chortles. That's good.

I take a deep breath and let it out with my words. "We'll be detained until they can finish their investigation. Any direct charges will be dropped once they realize we're not guilty, and we'll be reprimanded for breaking out."

Sam sits fully upright. "Reassigned?"

"Well… I think it's too soon to tell, but—"

"Planetside?"

I keep my mouth shut.

"Dammit, Evelyn."

"They'll come down harder on me than you, don't worry."

Sam throws her hands up. "That's the whole problem!"

"I don't follow."

"You, Evelyn! *You* can't afford to *not* be here."

That's a curious way to put it. I sit and squint at her. "Whadda ya mean?"

"I'm not upset with you for… what's happened to me. I mean, sure, yes, I am. But what really bothers me is that you don't see the significance of your role here."

"I don't understand."

"And that's what I'm talking about! You don't see it because sometimes you're just so… stubborn, and that infuriates me. I get this, *ugh* inside, and then I'm like *arrrgh*, and you're like—"

"Sam?"

She shakes her head once as if to collect her thoughts. "You, Evelyn. *You're* the mission. I don't know if your whole conspiracy theory about someone trying to stop the Infinita program is real or not, but if it is, then it makes sense to involve you."

"I'm still not—"

"*You* are the heartbeat, Eves. You've accelerated SESI's work more than anyone else before you. God, your V-cog wall has all the proof we need. The reason Lemuel fights so hard on our behalf with Johnson isn't because he thinks we're close, it's because he thinks *you're* close. He believes in *you*. We all do."

As if having said the meat of what she wanted,

Sam's face relaxes, and she lies back down. "So when you put yourself in jeopardy, you put the whole damn mission there too."

Another long silence fills the space between us. I'm honestly not sure what to say. I've never considered myself as a reckless person. Maybe driven. Okay, *very* driven. But I didn't mean to put the project at risk, if what she's saying has any merit. But now I understand why she's mad at me. I'd be mad at me too if the roles were reversed. This isn't about her, or even me. She wants us to succeed—knows we must. This is about finding us answers. Hope. And if we're extremely lucky, a new home. For everyone.

"I'm sorry I jeopardized the mission, Sam."

"Me too." Then she adds, "But you're also trying to save it, I know that. And that's what pisses me off about you sometimes."

"I don't follow."

"You're so damn dedicated, Evelyn. Makes me sick." At least she adds a smile at the end and forces a puff of air out her nose. "You're a crazy bitch sometimes, you know that?"

"Thanks?"

"Yeah." She laughs. "Totally crazy."

We lie there on our beds for several more minutes, disconnected from V-cog, from the outside, from Earth and all the other legacy habs. Just two high-ranking scientists unfairly charged with conspiracy to commit murder—charges that will no doubt grow unless something is found to exonerate us.

"He'll figure something out," I say after some time. "Lemuel. He always does."

"Let's hope so. For the program's sake. The Solum Terram is going to have a field day with this."

"And the Sentiamus Auxiliumm will be there to challenge it."

Sam takes another deep breath. "That's the hard part of fighting from the place of no evidence, isn't it? You have nothing to show you're right."

"Not yet, Sam. But we will. Because we're right."

Having spoken her mind, the silence spans out over several minutes where we lie here, with me dwelling on the past and wondering about the future. I can't imagine being re-tasked to one of the other habs or, worse, sent back down to St. Johns. Maybe Sam's right. Maybe I should have stayed out of the investigation.

I'm just about to ask Sam a hypothetical occupational question when something shakes the floor. Hard.

"What was that?" we both say in unison.

Sam's eyebrows climb her forehead. "Felt like a…"

"Like an explosion," I finish.

She nods.

A beat later, the ceiling lights turn red and a klaxon starts sounding. So much for peaceful chimes.

"That's not good," I say as I roll out of my bed and move toward the cell door. Officers scramble at the end of the hall. "That's a breach alert."

"How can you tell?" Sam asks.

"Because they're grabbing face masks."

Sam follows my attention to the end of the hall. "Oh my god."

As if to confirm my suspicions, the stations's automated notification system chimes in with *Astraea*'s smooth female voice. "Warning. Warning. Hull breach detected in section sixteen, quadrant B. All personnel to nearest safety zones. This is a station-wide priority one alert." As soon as *Astraea* is done with the first of her indefinitely repeated monologues, two security guards decked out in full vac gear open our cells' safety glass.

"Where are you taking us?" I ask.

"Central containment. Move." But he's pointing us deeper into the station.

"Shouldn't we be heading *away* from the breached section?"

"We are." They hustle us forward with the non-electrified ends of two stun batons.

"Easy! Watch it." I shove one of them aside and receive a quick bat to the knee. It doesn't break anything, but I'll feel it until I get treatment. I collapse to the ground and wait for the guard to hoist me back up.

"Stay on your feet! And no more funny business."

Three lefts and two rights later, Sam and I find ourselves in a small gymnasium. It's an upgrade in spaciousness from our cells, but it still seems like a redundant move given the severity of the ship-wide alert. We should be relocated to another section, not another part of the precinct. Bureaucratic oversight.

"Stay here," the other guard says. "You'll be escorted back to your cells when the zone alert is cleared."

"Can't wait," I reply and watch as they close the glass partitions and run down the hall and out of sight.

"Your knee okay?" she asks.

"Fine."

"That was stupid."

"Maybe."

She folds her arms, then looks back down the hallway in lament. "Out of the frying pan, into the fire."

"Maybe," I say again.

She casts me a curious glance, then something like understanding dawns on her face. "Oh no, you didn't."

"Oh yes." I pull out a translucent keycard from behind my back. They serve as V-cog backups in cases of emergency, just like this.

"When you fell?"

"Yup."

"I thought you didn't pickpocket?"

"I said I didn't like it, not that I wasn't good at it." I waltz up to the manual override panel, wincing once on account of my bad knee, and then open the doors.

Sam casts me a surprised look. "After you."

We retrace our steps down the corridor, checking corners before committing. By the time we reach the security office's main room, the staff has cleared out. We strip out of our orange jumpsuits and grab fresh station security uniforms from the newly laundered cart outside the barracks. There's an overstock of masks in the fast deployment lockers, but I don't bother grabbing one. The time needed to drain all of *Astraea*'s fifteen-hundred cubic kilometers of atmosphere resulting from all but a total structural failure is measured in weeks, not minutes. The only reason the security forces have them is because they have stricter standard operating procedures than everyone else. Plus, I always viewed the breathability protocol a moot point when compared to the more robust proposition of sudden decompression. Either way, humans don't last long in hard vacuum, and that's the least of our worries—at least for the time being.

Sam and I exit the security station and immediately look north to section sixteen. High on the curved wall to the east is the aftermath of an explosion complete with black smoke being whisked away by high-powered emergency ventilators along the ground. With each second that passes, we get a better look at a hole that's bloomed open.

"Oh my god," Sam whispers with a hand reaching for her mouth.

Tens of thousands of bystanders echo Sam's response as they look across the expanse to the accident scene. We're all trained annually in emergency protocols, with new measures implemented as research provides better evaluations. Astraeans know what to do, but until the worst actually happens—which it never has— no one really knows *if* anyone will do what they're supposed to. At the moment, the whole hab stops and stares.

All but the emergency response crews, that is. Flashing lights from utility vehicles speed toward the epicenter while *Astraea* continues to voice her warning. In the back of my mind, I wonder if we'll get the message to abandon the station, but that's absurd. She was built for this scenario. What's best for Sam and me is to take advantage of the opportunity.

"Looks like it came from below in the agriculture level." I point to the breach. "See the trussing bent outward?"

Sam nods. "Some sort of gas rupture?"

"Probably."

"Maybe we should go back and get masks."

"No." I nod at the breach again. "The ground vents are drawing the smoke in. If there was a true threat, the gases would be going right through the hole. Emergency containment systems are doing their jobs."

"So we're safe?"

"For now."

Sam nods and then turns for the detention block.

"Where are you going?" I ask.

"Um… back to holding?"

I give her an annoyed look. "No, you're not. Come on."

"Where?"

"The lab. I wanna see where the scan is before they ship us back to the Heights." I change my mind and nod toward the office. "But first we need to get back into V-cog."

"You're insufferable, Evelyn. You know that?"

"You're the one who just said that *I'm* the mission."

"And I regret every word."

FROM INSIDE THE emptied security office, Sam manages, "through no small feat," she insists, to remove the lock on our virtual cognizance profiles and lift all restrictions. Our presence on the grid means we'll be traceable again for people with high enough clearance, but we have nothing to hide. We never did. And if the authorities really want to know where to find us, they don't need network tracking for that. We'll be in the place we never wanted to leave in the first place: the bubble.

With the rest of the hab focused on the explosion, Sam and I ride a lateral elevator to section thirty without delay. From there, it's a short walk to the vertical lift that rises toward the power level and then the tunnel connection to the CEL. We enter the elevator and start our ascent, adjusting to the slow reduction of gravity. Even from fourteen kilometers away, we can see the explosion's aftermath as a black stain on *Astraea*'s inner cylinder.

"How many people do you think died?" Sam asks.

"Too many." I dismiss her question, however, since,

for one thing, *Astraea* will tabulate that in due course, and two, I have to reach Lemuel. "I need a minute, okay?"

"Sure, yeah."

I call up Lemuel's V-rec and prepare to leave him a message. I'm sure he'll be busy. Instead, I'm accepted into his personal suite—the shelf-lined study.

"Evelyn," he exclaims from behind his wooden desk, then rises to cross the room. "Where are you?"

"I thought you'd be in meetings."

"I am!"

"You're aware of the explosion?"

"We are. And you're okay?"

"I'm fine. I'm here with Sam."

"I take it you both capitalized on the emergency then."

"We did, yes. I'm sorry if I—"

He waves me off. "They're assholes for thinking you'd be involved."

"Thank you, sir."

"But you didn't make our job any easier with that escape stunt."

"Sorry. Anyway, you can track us again; Sam's got us back online."

"I'm just glad you're okay." He gets a twinkle in his eye. "You find anything?"

"Nothing conclusive. But whoever killed Hodges went to a lot of trouble to cover their tracks and to try to frame me somehow. This explosion feels related too, but I can't prove it."

"Let me worry about that," Lemuel replies. "I need you and the rest of the team back in the lab."

"Sam and I are headed there now," I reply. However, his tone suggests something more. "Why? What's the concern?"

His face takes on an air of shock and wonder all at once. "It's Parallax. We have… positive confirmation from Kepler-1649c, Evelyn. You… you were right."

12

———

JERICHO

THE PRIVATE CHARTER from Ottawa to Helsinki probably cost half my year's salary at NUESSA, and it was definitely more than Kit made in a year at High Top. Not that I'm complaining. The chance to ride in an Embraer Legacy E-1200 is a once in a lifetime opportunity, let alone a custom one made for Sir Nigel Sallsworth. The reclining chairs were more comfortable than any bed I've ever slept in. And showering in a jet? Come on. But I took one. The bathroom was even stocked with Shade & Estuary moisturizing lotion. Stuff's like liquid gold. And why not indulge? If I'm selling my soul to the devil, then I'm getting my money's worth. Plus, there's no sense being ashy first day on the job.

Before the Hundred Years Migration, Embraer was based out of old São Paulo. Now, their headquarters are in the sprawl of Despedida, Argentina Territory, and damn if they still don't make some of the best aircraft available. Why wouldn't they? The Solum Terram endorses them as one of the only aerospace manufacturers *not* to double dip and develop for space too. In return, the company seems more than grateful, as evidenced by this custom aircraft, complete with Sallsworth's monogrammed initials on everything from seat pillows to toilet paper. Yeah, toilet paper. It gives me some small satisfaction knowing I wiped my ass with Sallsworth—perhaps a small oversight on his part.

Given our royal treatment, I thought maybe the man himself would greet us upon landing at the private airstrip just north of Länsi-Pakila—Helsinki's new geographic center. I hear there are some incredible dive sites in the old city. Bucket list updated. But when the flight crew escorts us into the blistering heat, Sallsworth is nowhere to be seen. And why would he be, really? Guess I just saw that going differently in my head. Instead, we take a gleaming silver Mercedes-Benz EQ-GLL Prestige limousine with gull-wing doors, leather seats, and an inside temperature of a cool twenty degrees Celsius.

"Champagne?" says a steward from the rear-facing attendant's seat.

"Uh, is it free?" Kit asks.

The man nods ever so slightly.

"Well then, heck yeah! It's five o'clock somewhere, right?"

I stifle a laugh. "It's five o'clock here, Kit."

"Oh. Totally." He accepts the flute of bubbling liquid. "All the more reason then, right?"

"Sure."

Part of this is Sallsworth trying to butter me up, I know that. He's playing the long game, hoping that one day I'll renege on my ultimatums about never releasing my employment profile or the fact that I agreed to leave the Viatoribus. But that's never happening, Embraer or not. As far as I'm concerned, this is all for Kit. Okay, and maybe a little for me since I never have to smell

Blanderson's bad breath again. If I'm cleaning a toilet, it's gonna be my own, thank you very much.

As the car weaves through the clean streets of Helsinki, I'm reminded of just how much crypto the Solum Terram has. A lot of people in the pro-expansion sectors play that element down. Even I've been guilty of imagining them as the struggling fighter clawing their way to being heard. That's how their PR spins the verb. While the Viatoribus and the Sentia Aux are painted as elitists—even the moderate Preservationists get that from time to time—the Solum Terram, "Earth Alone," are the people's champion. "For those who will never see the stars," is one of their more famous if melodramatic slogans. They act as though Earth's scientific community wishes to leave them in the dust, which is false. If anything, the pro-expansion politicasts are trying to find ways to get humanity off the planet as well as discover ways to rectify Earth's climate issues. But that's where politics gets in the way. Imagine that.

Contrary to popular belief, the Solum Terram is the wealthiest politicast of all. And why wouldn't it be? They have lobbyists for every enterprise on the planet, from biotech research and transportation to energy development and food chain supply. While our species may have several million spacefarers aloft, the source of life for them all is still the blue planet, and the Solum Terram will keep it that way as long as they can.

"Sorry you had to change your ink," Kit says after downing his first glass of champagne. "Sucks, I bet. Turning your back on everything you've ever believed in."

I look at my palm and then close my fingers over the new Solum Terram tattoo. "No one said I turned my back."

"Sure. Totally not." He faces the steward seemingly oblivious to what I said. "Can I have some more please?"

I look out the window and catch the sun's afternoon glare in passing skyscraper glass. Kit's right, of course. When you get your palm marker swapped out, you take an oath. Did I feel dirty doing it? God, yes. But I would have felt dirtier letting Kit down and being a slummer in Riverside Park South. Everyone has their price. The real question is, did I mean the words I said? "Earth alone holds the keys to humanity's prosperity," and "I pledge to resist all efforts that seek to draw humanity away from its planet of origin." No. Was I lying to myself? Not for a second. Lying to them? Hell, yeah. But the way I see it, I'm never going back to space anyway, so who cares? It's just an empty oath, and Kit gets free champagne. I can live with that—live with myself.

I also know this is just temporary. With the coin I'm about to rake in, it won't take long for me to accrue a nice nest egg to start my own courier company with. Maybe even a small aerospace firm. Consulting, specialized builds, stuff like that. If I play this right, I'll have Kit and me back to the Northern Heights before the year's out, complete with new palm ink and an LLC in the works. Just gotta bide my time and keep my head down.

"Pour me a glass too," I say to the steward.

"Alright," Kit exclaims. "Now it's a party."

"And cut him off, would you?"

The steward nods.

Kit gives me a disappointed look, but before he can protest, I add, "We all know how you get with CFO's daughters when you drink too much."

"That was one time! One time, Cap."

FOR TWO DAYS, we've been living the life of luxury. Kit and I have a brand new apartment in a prime spot overlooking the harbor. Makes my studio in Ottawa look like a closet. No, I mean, my old place is actually the size of my new walk-in closet. I don't even own enough clothes to make a dent at filling it out. Sallsworth had all my personal items flown in; he would have been better off spending that money on a new wardrobe... *which* is apparently included in my new stipend too.

"One thousand coins a day for clothing?" Kit asks in an astonished tone as he reviews the details of our new employment contract. Now that we're officially in Norasia, we get to see the details of what we signed on for.

"Just for the first month," I reply.

He laughs at my attempt to qualify the situation. "That's more than I've spent on clothes in my whole life!"

I cast him a half smile and then go back to reviewing my own contract obligations in V-cog. He doesn't know that our living arrangement was part of my negotiations with the Solum Terram. I would have preferred to have my own place, but the only way they would allow him to come on board was if I split my housing and my salary. He won't know that part either. But it's hardly a sacrifice. Even with half pay, I'm making more than twice what I made with NUESSA. Can't say that doesn't feel good.

"Says here I'm gonna be trained as a pilot," Kit says as he snaps out of V-cog to catch my eye. "A real pilot, Cap! Can you believe that? Flight school and everything. All paid."

"Congrats, bro. You deserve it."

He kicks his heels up on the coffee table and interlocks his fingers behind his head. "Captain Kit Smith. Stick jockey for the stars. Has a nice ring to it, don't you think?"

"First officer," I remind him.

"Well, eventually captain."

"Sure."

He sits up. "What about you?"

I shrug. "More flying."

"Come on. I want deets."

"He… wants me as his personal pilot—"

"Shut up!"

"—and when I'm not flying for him, working with his public transit aerospace engineering division."

Kit's mouth hangs open. "That's. So. Awesome!"

"Yeah. Not a bad gig."

"Cap, I…" He scratches the side of his cheek. "I don't know how to thank you for all this."

"You risked your life for those people just as much as I did. So you deserve just as much of the reward."

"Yeah, but, you didn't have to, ya know?"

I nod. "It was the right thing to do, pal. You just pay it forward to someone in your future. Copy?"

"Roger, Cap." He puts his hands behind his head again. "Pay it forward." But then his face takes on a wistful look. Not sad. Just… melancholy. Shoot, is that a tear in his eye?

"You okay, Kit?"

"Oh, sure, sure. Yeah."

"What's the matter?"

"I, uh… My mom, she only had me. One kid, right? Always wanted more, but restrictions didn't lift in Old Cheyenne until after she was… well, couldn't have any more kids. Maybe it's weird to say, but I wanted a brother, ya know? Someone I could go on adventures with. Get into trouble. Stuff like that. So… I kinda think of you that way, Cap. Like the big brother I never had. And you doing all this for me? Mom said the same thing when I told her the good news."

I give him a side smile. "I'm honored, Kit. Thanks. And it's my pleasure. Tell your mom that too when you talk to her next."

"I will." After a few seconds of silence, he changes direction. "So you think I'll get to meet him? Mr. Sallsworth, I mean?"

I shrug and sit back. "Probably. Just not sure when."

"Yeah. Busy guy, right?"

"I imagine so."

"Heard rumors that a lot of people want him to run for secretary-general."

"Wouldn't surprise me if he got the nomination."

"You'd vote for him, wouldn't you, Cap?"

I frown. Despite the intensity of what we've been through together, his statement reminds me that we still don't know each other the way close friends do, or will. As he said, Kit's like my younger brother by sixteen years, not a peer. Not only is he somehow still unaware of my past, but he also clearly doesn't know how deep my love for system-wide expansion runs. I won't go so far as the Sentia Aux does with their belief that aliens will save the day, but I wouldn't rule it out either.

"If he gets the nomination, we'll circle back and talk about his positions," I say at last.

"Making him work for your vote. I see how you are. I like it. So, you wanna get some breakfast or—"

A news notification pings in V-cog. Based on Kit's

interrupted thought, I'm guessing he's getting the same, which means this is a profile override alert. A big one.

"You seeing this?" he asks.

"Yeah." I send him an invite to join me in my sailboat suite. He accepts, and I open a live coverage feed in a floating window. The right hand sidebar streams the pertinent developing data, while the lower overlay reads "Explosion on *Astraea* Station." On the left hand sidebar, three stoic-faced reporters read from V-cog prompts and offer commentary on "what we know at present." But I'm hardly listening. Instead, I'm analyzing the footage that fills the window's center: a live feed of *Astraea* Station with a gash in her side.

The menu bar across the top offers several viewing options that I switch through in real time, ranging from external cams on cargo vessels around the hab to interior cams that are a part of NUESSA's twenty-four/seven public monitoring policy.

Kit's knees are bopping up and down underneath the galley's main table.

"Hey, cool it. I'm trying to focus here."

"Sorry." He stops fidgeting, but three seconds later his nervous energy resumes the banging.

"Kit!"

"Dammit. I'm so sorry, Cap. Can't help it." This time he slides off the bench seat and starts pacing. "You think… You think people died?"

I cast him a raised eyebrow as if to say, "Really?"

He nods a few times. "Yeah, okay. Me too. Um—"

"Shut up for a second, copy?"

"Right. Copy that, Cap. Copy so hard."

"Kit."

He draws his fingers across his lips like he's closing a zipper.

I resume my look at the footage and opt to fill my whole visual cortex with the main feature window and the camera control bar. I don't need the commentary either, so I mute the verb heads. The only other information I want is *Astraea*'s top metadata. It won't reveal too much about the station, but the stream does provide some helpful diagnostics.

Kit sees that I've gone full-cortex. "You got something?"

"Exterior rupture, section sixteen, B quadrant," I reply, talking aloud as I go for Kit's benefit. "But EPSS looks solid."

"EP—?"

"Emergency pressure seal system."

"Oh, sure. Yeah. That's good, right?"

"Yes." I cycle through a few of the exterior cams offered by both private and NUE vessels, zooming in for a close up of the blast radius. "Strange."

"What? What is it?"

I send an invite to my full-cortex feed.

Kit joins right away.

"You see the blast marks and hull damage?"

"Uh, well, I see hull damage, but no blast marks."

"Exactly."

Kit pauses a second. "What's that supposed to mean?"

"Shhh."

"Oh... okay, sure."

I switch to interior cams. The first few views are shots from the main hab—cams above skywalks or buildings. It's all from generic hardware aimed toward the blast. Any smoke has already been sucked out of the atmosphere, and emergency response units are responding fast. That's good. But those teams still aren't ready for this; none of them have actual experience in a hull-breach crisis simply because there's never been one. Dry rehearsals only get you so far.

I want a closer look, but none of the cameras will allow me to zoom in past the media's 100-meter restriction radius—viewer protection and all. I'm guessing ground zero is pretty graphic. Doesn't matter anyway: there's too much chaos on this level to confirm the growing suspicion in my gut. But even with the radial media wall, there's plenty for Kit to see.

"Look at all the bodies," he breathes. "Oh my god. They're… they're all dead, Cap."

"Yes, they are."

"So many people. Oh god. I think I'm gonna be sick. Do you think that—?"

"Kit, if you wanna be in here with me, I need you to be quiet."

"Right." He swallows in real life, loudly. "Sorry, Cap. I was just—"

"Kit!"

"I got it. Shutting up." Then I imagine him doing the zippered lips thing again.

I search the submenus for a few seconds and find what I'm looking for: the ag level cams in section sixteen, quad B. Interestingly, they're all locked down.

"Interesting."

"What is?" Kit asks.

"The ag level cams are restricted."

"Makes sense. Probably more verb lock, yeah?"

"Probably." But something isn't sitting right with me. While there could be some human casualties, the largest death toll here would be on animals and crops— not the sort of thing to get tagged for a media blackout.

"So, I really don't mean to interrupt your train of

thought or whatever, Cap. Just trying to figure out what it is you're looking for."

He's right. Plus, Kit's smart, so it's worth bringing him into my train of thought in case he has something to add. "At first glance, this looks like it could be a catastrophic system failure."

"Cascading?"

"Definitely. For anything to reach a point where that much energy is released at once, you've gotta have several systematic in-line failures."

"Makes sense. But… doesn't that bear out in the metadata? I see you got the diagnostics up."

"It does. It's the rupture itself that bothers me."

"How do you mean?"

"Well, you see here?" I bring up a few of the exterior shots again. "What shape would you say that breach is?"

"Umm… like, is this a trick question?"

"No."

"Round then."

"Perfectly?"

"I mean, just about, yeah."

I bring up one of the inside shots. "And here?"

"Still round. Does that matter?"

I nod, zoom out from one of the exterior images, and grab a stylus in my drawing application. Then I start sketching quick vertical lines around *Astraea*'s hull. "Critical systems near the outer hull—the kind that are capable of detonating—run concentrically in order to minimize any catastrophic failures from spreading to neighboring sections. It's a design fail-safe. Likewise"—I switch back to the interior shot again and draw on it—"inside the main level, critical systems run the station's length like veins in a tree. That way, if anything fails in one area—"

"There are redundancies built in," he interjects. "Not just systematically but structurally, right?"

"Bingo. So?"

He puzzles for a second, and then his face starts to light with understanding. "So you'd expect an explosion in susceptible systems to rupture along predetermined pathways! Holy biscuits, that means… oh man. Oh man! This wasn't a naturally occurring event. It was, it was…" His expressions go flat. "You think this was sabotage?"

"Too soon to tell. But the explosion should have at least detonated along failing system lines before *Astraea*'s emergency systems caught it. Another thing that doesn't add up is the lack of residue." I circle a grainy close-up of the blossomed seam. "See where the metal has blown out along the edge? Looks clean."

"Not following."

"In this section, you have pressurized reclamation systems, scrubbers, sewer treatment—a lot of things that could go boom, yeah. But if those elements were catalysts, you'd have a lot more—"

"Crap."

"Among other materials. And I bet if we go back, replay the footage, and run even a limited spectral analysis on the light, we'd find there was something much stronger in the mix."

"So it wasn't them. Those systems, I mean."

I nod at Kit but forgot that he's sharing my visual cortex in full.

"How do you know so much about *Astraea*, Cap?"

I take a deep breath and exit V-cog. My brain needs

a second to reorient in the apartment. Kits snaps out too and waits for me to answer his question.

"Up until a few months ago, I was an aero engineer."

Kit squints at me but isn't connecting the dots, until something clicks. "Wait, for them? You were... a NUESSA engineer?"

I nod once. "And pilot. Well, test pilot mostly."

"You?"

"Yup."

"You are—I mean, *were* a NUESSA engineer and pilot?"

"Yes."

"Holy biscuits." Then he smacks his forehead as *it* dawns on him. His eyes go wide as if he's seeing me for the first time. "*Ho-ly biscuits*! You're... you're..." His mouth goes slacked-jawed, then: "The *Perseverant*, you... You were on board." Kit goes pale. "You were the only survivor." He pushes himself away from me on the couch. "*You're* Lieutenant Fox?"

Annnd there it is.

I push my lips together and give a small nod.

But Kit is still reeling. "How did I miss this? I'm so stupid! You're Lieutenant Fox."

"Yeah."

"You're Fox."

"Yes."

"*The* Lieutenant Fox."

"Kit, we have a major crisis here."

He blinks twice. "Right. Sure, sure. I just thought..."

"That I'm a murderer?"

"Well, no, I... Okay, maybe a little. They just said that you, ya know..."

"Ohhh, I know."

Kit laughs nervously. "Ha ha. Yeah." His knees are bouncing like his feet are on fire. Then they stop, and he swallows so loudly I think his throat's gonna break. "You didn't… you didn't do it, did you?"

It's a vague question, but I know what he means. "No."

"'Cause we heard culpable homicide."

"That's because you're Solum Terram."

He grunts and gives his head a tilt. "You can say that again." Then back to me: "So it wasn't a homicide?"

"Am I in prison?"

His eyes dart back and forth. "No. Of course not. But…" Suddenly, his shoulders relax and his face softens. It seems as if he's just accepted my one word answer as gospel. That's a first. "Yeah. 'Cause you don't seem like the kind of person who would kill your own crew."

"If I am, you're in trouble."

He grabs his throat absentmindedly. "I suppose I am, yes."

"Relax, Kit. If they'd found me guilty, I wouldn't be here now, would I."

"No, I suppose not."

I nod and look down at my hands, remembering the PlastiCuffs. "It's all how the verb decides to cover it. They write the narrative, for better or worse. Like for *Astraea* right now. They've already made their assumptions, and once an idea takes hold, it's hard to uproot it."

"Confirmation bias."

I nod again. "Because we like buying what we already believe. And in the end, most news comes down to entertainment, not facts. But we have more pressing concerns right now."

"*Astraea?*"

"Yeah."

"But… we don't work for them. NUESSA, I mean. Why is this any concern of ours?"

Yeah, Jericho? Why is it any concern of yours? NUESSA's got sharper minds than you. Plenty of them. They'll figure this one out.

Just like they figured out the Perseverant?

"Cap?"

I glance over at Kit. "Spaced out, sorry."

"*Astraea* concerns us because…?"

"I'm not sure they're going to figure it out in time."

"In time?" Kit wrinkles his brow. "But you just did it in like two seconds. No offense, but aren't there a bunch of specialists on this as we speak? Ya know, piecing it all together?"

Yeah, Jericho, ya know: *specialists*. People who are experts and whose word can be trusted. Individuals who can be counted on to arrive at logical conclusions that suppress illogical premises and exonerate the wrongfully accused. Those kinds of people.

I clear my throat. "There are a lot of talented people working this problem right now. And they'll get to the bottom of it."

"You… don't sound convinced."

I run a hand over my hair and stand up. "They're gonna follow procedures, and that's gonna take time. They'll share data, eventually, with other investigators, compare notes—it's tedious, but they're not wrong. They're just…"

"Just what?"

"Just not fast enough."

"For what?"

"To stop whoever did that from doing it again." Before I can convince myself otherwise, I tell Kit to stand by, slip into V-cog, and pull up a name I never thought I'd make a call to again. I doubt he'll answer, but I have to try, no matter the embarrassment. No matter the ridicule that might come. I gave up believing that the agency had my back, but I still believe in saving people.

"Fox?" says the familiar figure surrounded by a frantic control room.

I wasn't ready to see him so soon. "Hi, Eric."

He opens his mouth to speak but then seems to change his mind. "You got something?"

"It wasn't an accident," I reply.

"I'm listening."

"You've got a killer on board, and I don't think they're done."

13

EVELYN

I can't respond to Lem.

I want to. Of course, I want to. But my mouth can't catch up with my thoughts. Until my inner devil's advocate takes over, and all I can think to say to Lemuel is, "Are you sure it's not a false positive?"

SESI's highly esteemed director shakes his head at me and can't seem to wipe the smile from his face. "Not according to what we saw."

"Lemuel, if this is some sort of joke—"

"It's not a joke. Parallax had positive ID on a one nanometer wavelength, three second pulse."

"X-ray?"

He dips his head, still smiling. "Hawking-Belmont window, just like you predicted."

My knees give out, but there's not enough gravity to pull me down. "Lemuel, this is… It's…"

"You still need to verify the vectors…"

"Of course."

"…then there's causality, authorial intent—"

"Yes, yes. Of course, but…"

"It's big," he concludes.

"So big." It's a dumb response, but I don't know what

else to say. This moment—what is potentially humanity's first contact with extra-solar sentient life—is the greatest discovery of… well, of *ever*. And it's happening right now, in real time… while there's a killer on the loose and a gaping hole in *Astraea*'s side. The coincidences are absurd. Yet here they are, all happening at once.

But this discovery? It's… everything. It's what I've worked for and I've believed in and… and, oh my stars, it's happening right now. How is this my life?

I smile at Lemuel because I can't help myself. Because I've never felt this happy. But then a new thought stops me. "You just said *had*. Parallax *had* positive ID."

"We lost connection with the lab. I'm guessing the explosion damaged a comms relay or created some EM distortion."

"You mean to say… the signal still might be coming in?"

He nods. "I don't see why not. It was certainly strong enough. Could have been a microburst, yes, but that's why we need you back in the lab ASAP."

Tears well in Sam's eyes as she holds my arm.

"Get everyone," I tell her. "We need them now."

She wipes the back of her hand across her eyes. "I… Yes, of course. On it."

Back to Lemuel. "I'm still a fugitive—"

"Me too," Sam interjects.

"We'll need help in case the authorities—"

Lemuel waves me off. "I think they have more pressing issues to deal with, but I'll make sure Eric is apprised of the situation's magnitude."

"Good." I put both hands over my mouth as a surge of emotion wells up in me. "Is this really happening, Lem?"

"Ha. You're the only one in the human race who can answer that with any certainty. But, yes, I think so, Evelyn. Damn, I think so."

I EMERGE from the elevator with Sam feeling grateful for our zero g glide toward the bubble's security door. I'm so amped up with excitement that I'm not sure I could walk straight. Plus, my knee is still pretty tender from the pickpocket incident.

For centuries, humanity has imagined contact with alien species. NASA and the Search for Extra Terrestrial Intelligence Institute led that mission well into the twenty-first century. And they did indeed discover life beyond Earth. Just not the intelligent kind—or at least not as smart as we daydreamed it would be. Intelligence is relative. Like all things to be quantified, we measure against known values. So, while the microbiotic methanogens on Saturn's moon Enceladus that employ chemosynthesis to digest dihydrogen and produce methane were, in fact, smarter than mycoplasma genitalium as found in primate waste organs, they didn't exactly raise the eyebrows of those who were waiting for little green people from Mars—not that Mars had any of those either.

But this? A distinct light value from a predicted target exoplanet in the habitable zone of a red dwarf star? This is no microbe.

"Are you okay, Evelyn?" I snap out of whatever trance I'm in to find Sam holding my hand. "You're shaking."

"Yeah, yeah. I'm good. I'm just—" A nervous laugh

erupts from somewhere inside me like a burp. "Ha-ha! I just… I can't believe this is happening."

She beams back and then pulls me into a mid-flight hug. "Same."

We gently collide outside the hatch and untangle ourselves before I slip into V-cog and release the security lock.

"Access denied," says *Astraea*'s smooth voice.

My natural high is cut down at the knees. "What?" I try again at the virtual access terminal in the bubble's command suite.

"Access denied."

"Let me," Sam says as she appears next to me in lab's V-cog lobby. She enters her credentials.

"Access denied."

"Elaborate," Sam demands in a frustrated tone.

"Unauthorized users detected."

"Unauthorized?" she asks. "On whose authority?"

"Section One Security Chief Inspector, Stamos, Alexander Paul."

Sam shoots me an angry glare. "Bastard."

"Can he even do that?" I ask.

"Dunno. But he has. I'm guessing it's some sort of emergency lockdown fail-safe… a loophole that overrides your override."

"Can *you* override it?"

"Trying." Even though her avatar is using a projected keyboard to interface with *Astraea*'s system, I know it's just a visual representation of what Sam's doing with her mind. I believe coders when they say we still need one foot in reality when using virtual systems, even if the actions are just placeholders. "Dammit," she says after a few seconds of work. "I don't think I can get around it, Eves. I'm sorry."

"That's why we have friends in *low* places," I reply and then ping Lemuel again.

"Communication privileges revoked," *Astraea* says.

"What?"

"Communication privileges revoked."

"It was rhetorical," I say with a sneer. I've never seen this before. "Override on my authority."

"Override denied."

"*Astraea*, who removed my comm privileges?"

"Section One Security Chief—"

I say the rest with her: "—Inspector, Stamos, Alexander Paul." Now it's my turn. "Bastard!" I would ask Sam to try reaching Lemuel, but without my security clearance, she'd just get stonewalled by a low-level aid in St. Johns.

A third person appears in the lab's V-cog lobby. "My, my, my, what do we have here?"

"Don't look so surprised," I say to the smug-faced inspector. Apparently he forgot to render out his nose splint.

"But I am surprised. I thought you were still in holding. Then I see this little indicator that says you've left the backyard and ventured into the woods again. Guess I should have known you wouldn't stay put."

"Stamos, listen. We've made contact with—"

"I don't care, Dr. Park. You've broken the law, and I have enough evidence to put you and your colleague—"

"You don't know what you're talking about, Stamos. Release the overrides."

He raises an eyebrow at me.

"You let us into the lab right now or—"

"Or what?"

"Or I'm going to recommend your termination immediately."

He chuckles and then waves a hand nonchalantly. "Go ahead. Make the call."

"Funny." *The fool.* "Don't you have better things to be doing right now anyway? You know, like investigating a breach?"

"Who says I'm not? Anything you'd like to contribute to make my job easier?"

"What? No!"

"Sabotage?"

"Are you out of your mind?"

But he's not budging.

"Why would I ever jeopardize my own research?"

"You tell me. As for calling your boss, I'll be happy to share what I know with any director who you—"

Stamos's avatar blinks out.

"Whoops," Sam says with a coy smile.

"Thanks."

"He was annoying me."

"Ditto." I put my hands on my hips—virtual and real—and let out a long sigh. "At least he hasn't completely booted us offline again."

"Not yet, anyway."

"Any bright ideas?" I ask.

"Do you have any more of the explosives?"

I shoot her a puzzled glance. "What?"

She laughs. "What he was implying—that you, ya know, sabotaged *Astraea.*"

"Oh. Right. Nope. Seems I'm fresh out."

She shrugs. "Same."

The elevator hub chimes behind us. Two sets of doors open to reveal four more of my mission team members.

"Got here as soon as we could," says Jose Ramirez, our dynamicist and astronautical engineer, who is accompanied by digital and electrical engineer Cheng Liu.

"Thank you." I nod at the two Southland natives. "Cheng, we're unable to gain access to the lab, and I'm worried we're not the only ones. Can you look into it?"

He nods and glances at Sam, who appears a little peeved. "Yes," Cheng replies. "I will see what I can do. And nice station security outfits."

"They were on sale," I reply and then swallow before saying what's coming next. "Everyone else? Parallax has a positive ID coming out of Kepler-1649."

The news has the desired effect. All four faces take a moment to register the intel. Natalie Mason, our linguist and cryptographer with a minor in astroarchaeology, is first to get her words straight.

"Positive ID? As in… we have a signal?"

I can't help but smile at her utter bewilderment. "Hawking-Belmont, three times ten to the sixteen, one nanometer, three second pulse."

Igor Kalashnik, our astrobiologist and resident medical doctor, is a blubbering mess. "You are being certain? Like, for very much real?"

"For very much real. SESI Actual confirmed the alpha signature but lost connection during the explosion."

He throws his hands up. "Crapholes! Is just perfect."

"But the sooner we can get in there, the sooner we can pick it back up," I add.

"Wait. They think it's still transmitting?" Ramirez asks.

"Unless it was a microburst, Lemuel couldn't think of a reason why it wouldn't be. Neither can I."

"Saints, Park. This is…" Ramirez's eyes dart back and forth wildly. "This is it!"

Mason grabs my shoulder. "You did it, Evelyn."

"Let's not jump to any conclusions just yet," I say. "We still have a lot of work ahead, and I need you at your best. As I'm sure you all know, the authorities aren't exactly happy with me right now, and there's a high likelihood that we get shut down over it."

Heads start nodding as each specialist registers the stakes.

"Bottom line, we need to work fast, work smart, and gather as much data as we can until Brown and Johnson come through for us. As more team members arrive, I'll need you to fill them in. And in the event that I'm detained, you must promise me that you'll fight this one through. No matter what."

"We are behind back, Dr. Park," Kalashnik says as he drives a fist into his hand. "If we see pissholes who are needing persuasion to stay back, we make sure to give message, clear and loud."

"Thank you, Igor. But I don't want any violence."

"Is no violence. Is small pressure on nerve bundle around soft tissue parts, yes?"

Ramirez puts a hand around his throat and then slips the other toward his groin. "Why does that sound really painful?"

"Because all doctors lie when they say you're going to feel some pressure," Natalie Mason replies. "Especially when they're former S.M.S.F."

Kalashnik shrugs. "Eh."

"We're in," Cheng says.

I spin around. Cheng and Sam watch the hatch leaves iris open. Beyond them, the lab is alive with audio and visual notifications. Everything we set up to register "the big one" is awake and squawking. If I believed in Santa, this would be Christmas.

I'm first through the entryway and glide toward the main command module in the middle. Ten different alerts vie for my attention on the single screen. I slip into V-cog—still operational for me so far—and activate the lab's augmented reality overlay as my team takes their positions around the lab. Instead of wasting time, money, and weight with dozens of old-fashioned hardware displays and interfaces, we all have software equivalents in V-cog. Sadly, humanity has the space program to thank for their verb addictions. But the tech allows us to do our tasks faster than any generation before us.

I bring up the main command interface and start working from top to bottom. The first item is the positive ID alert. Sure enough, whatever Parallax picked up, it ticks all the boxes. The second item is the initial coordinate verification lock. The data will have to be cross-referenced against the NUE stellar charts, but that's more of a formality. As it stands, the system pre-confirms:

Constellation: Cygnus

Star: Kepler-1649

Exoplanet: C

And then lists the elliptical coordinates.

I know what the fourth and fifth items in the list will contain: mission-critical data on the signal's nature. I'm beyond eager to get into all that, but it will take days to process—stars, it could take years! But none of that matters because it's incomplete, aborted mid record. Moreover, my eyes are stuck on the third item in the list.

"We have a problem," I say, but not loud enough; everyone's talking over me. "We're off axis!"

Heads swivel and conversations stop.

I nod toward the vast starscape beyond our bubble's walls. "I don't know how, but *Astraea*'s turned."

"The explosion," Cheng says with a soft tone. He studies a more detailed readout than I have. "It must have knocked us off course. Wouldn't take much."

"Shit," I yell and then palm my face. I pull my hand away and see a magnetic drink thermos on the desk in front of me that needs to be struck. I swing and miss. I swing again and hit it, but the base re-magnetizes on the desk, leaving me with a stinging hand. "Dammit!"

"We'll get back, Eves," Sam says in a consoling tone. "We just—"

"How far?" I demand from Cheng.

"Uh, well, I think if we—"

"How far?"

"Three mark six one degrees ecliptic longitude, two mark two four degrees ecliptic latitude."

This time I swing at the thermos and rip it off the desk. It flies toward Igor, who catches it one-handed. "We might as well be pointed at Centaurus," I shout, trying and failing to control my anger. "How long before we can move *Astraea*?"

Cheng hesitates and then grimaces.

"What?" I ask.

"The emergency protocols have locked us out of the flight systems."

"You've got to be kidding me."

He shakes his head, not realizing it was a rhetorical question. I grab the command desk with both hands and squeeze.

Rein it in, Eves. Deep breaths. You've waited this long, what's a little longer? You just need to coordinate with Captain Mombawe, explain the situation with Stamos, return elliptical command authority to

Cheng, and do it while *Astraea* recovers from her first-ever hull breach. With any luck, we'll be back on target in, what, a day? Two if things are slow? No problem.

"Evelyn?"

"What?" I snap.

It's Sam. She looks scared… of me? "It's not looking good."

"No shit."

Sam winces.

"Sorry." I fold one arm across my chest and tap the end of my nose, trying to think. To stay clear-headed. "Does anyone here have clearance to reach Director Brown directly besides me?" I already know the answer, but maybe they'll think of a work around.

Heads shake, and no one offers anything.

I chew on my lower lip, then throw my arms up. "How are we this close, people? And still so far away?" I thrust a hand toward the starscape. "They're right there! Right in front of us, and we can't even turn our damn heads to listen."

Silence fills the lab again, and I wait for the universe to inspire someone with a bright idea. None come. Because we all know the resources at our disposal and the limitations of our systems. We're at an impasse.

Then everything goes dark—the V-cog displays, the bubble's running lights—everything.

"I've lost power," Cheng says.

"Scopes, sensors, trig too," Ramirez adds.

"No, no, no!" With V-cog down, I start tapping the only hard screen in the room. "The data!" But the display isn't responding. I roar at the desk and try ripping off its supports, but it doesn't budge. Then one word seethes from between my lips. "*Stamos.*"

"Evelyn?" Sam asks. "I… I think we need to be rational here."

"Rational?"

She pulls back. "All I'm saying is that if you—"

"You want *me* to be *rational* right now? Okay." I cross my arms and feel frustration giving birth to anger in my chest. I'm not mad at Sam. She's just the one who happened to push the button. "Here's rational. We've all waited our entire careers—our whole *lives* for this moment. Right here. First contact with extra-solar sentient life."

"Evelyn, all I'm saying is—"

"No, no. You asked me to be rational. So I'm explaining myself. Rational is that the space station we're on right now has just received *the* most important transmission of all time, one that could lead to our entire planet's salvation if we're lucky. Billions of lives are in the balance. Our entire civilization is perched on this moment. And now we've been thrown off course by the first damn hull breach in hab history, and my team is being locked out by a fucking troll?"

No one moves.

No one answers.

We all just hang in zero g for a few seconds bathed in starlight.

Finally, Sam pushes away from me and floats toward Mason.

I rub the back of my neck. "Sam. I just…"

"It's okay."

"No. I apologize."

She reaches Mason's station, lowers her head for a second, and then turns toward me. "You want this?"

I nod at the understatement but don't say anything more.

Sam motions to the rest of the crew. "We want it too, Evelyn. We all do. But sometimes... things are just... out of our control. So we adjust and—"

"Carry on. I know." I swallow the bile in the back of my throat and take a deep breath. "I know."

"Do you? Because if you keep pushing, if you keep breaking the rules like you have been, then *none* of us will get to see that transmission again. Maybe that's already a foregone conclusion, I don't know. But it's not us I'm scared about." She swallows. "We can't jeopardize the futures of those who'll come behind us to finish the job just because we got impatient. I know you're pissed off, Evelyn. We all are. But don't risk everything simply because it isn't going the way you dreamed it would."

That stings. But there's truth in her words, even if I don't like them. Still, all I can say is, "I need to speak with the captain."

I push off from the command desk and get halfway to the door when it opens. I expect to see more members of my team. Instead, I see a nose splint, a stun baton, and several NUE Space Marines with weapons drawn.

NIGEL

Sɪʀ Nɪɢᴇʟ Sᴀʟʟsᴡᴏʀᴛʜ didn't trust her. But he couldn't exactly ignore her either. Not when there was an outstanding debt. Granted, the assassination had yet to take place, but that didn't stop her from calling in "partial payment," as she'd tactfully put it, and demanding he drop everything to meet her in person.

He knew they needed each other. And, as far as he could tell, the feelings were mutual. The Solum Terram and the Tantum Terrae were sibling politicasts, though that's probably being too generous—more like a divorced couple with a violent past. But life has a funny way of reuniting conflicted and distanced lovers.

No, Nigel didn't trust her at all. If she didn't extract everything she wanted, he suspected she'd either try to kill him or make him her puppet. Maybe both—marionettes are easier to move when they're limp. But if he played his cards right, he might get a puppet of his own.

Conducting their meetings over V-cog was always out of the question. Nigel knew the system could be hacked; half the coders probably came from the Tantum anyway. So they always met in person. This time, however, Nigel brought ten bodyguards instead of his usual three. Since she seemed to be sticking her finger in the frosting before the cake was cut, he needed to be ready for anything, especially since he was on her home turf.

He'd flown to Vancouver. He reasoned, if only for his own dignity, that it was easier for him to hide the flight plan in the mix of his busy schedule then explain why a gaudy black and hot pink Lynx-class Hyperion shuttle with overlapping double T's spray painted on each side had touched down in the sterile white space of Helsinki-Malmi Airport.

Neon was every bit as loud as her name, and those among the Earth's poorest loved her for it. The Scourge of the Elite. The Liberator of the Forgotten. The Witch of Calvert Isle. She put her money where her mouth was and refused to live in any home that her followers couldn't also squat in; extra expenses were justified by her need for security and, perhaps, her irrepressible and ironic love for the extravagant.

The ceiling of her office in the vast cement warehouse was three stories high, wrapped with bulletproof windows. Drapes of red, green, and purple plunged over railings and pooled on a floor littered with plush rugs. And in the center of it all was a massive oak desk surrounded by four bodyguards with automatic legacy weapons.

"You look scared, Nigel. Rough flight?" The woman named Neon sat back in a leather chair with her spray painted combat boots propped on the desk.

Nigel ignored the question and strode toward one of her low-backed chairs. He needed to maintain control —to be on guard against her barbs and bangalores. He passed his coat to his PA, who held the seat as Nigel made himself comfortable. "The flight was fine. Let's get down to business, shall we?"

"Business?" Her left eyebrow rose ever so slightly. "Always so to the point, this one."

"Is there another way?"

She pulled her boots down, spread her arms across her desk, and rose, willing him to look at her. Which he did—up and down once. She was stunning, if not terrifying, clothed in Norasian orbital fatigues with a zipper that had given up fighting gravity midway up her chest. "Nigel, there are infinite ways, all depending on what kind of *affairs* you're conducting."

"Then let's focus on payment."

"Partial payment."

"So you've said. But we already settled on terms."

She turned her head slightly and cast him a shadowy look. "Then perhaps you aren't suited for the game."

"It suits me fine. I just don't like surprises."

"Think of it more like a spontaneous opportunity."

"Nor do I like the spontaneous. You know this."

She feigned a look of surprised disappointment. "Then I suppose you have other suitors who are willing to do your wet work?"

He sniffed in an effort to regain the scent of his elusive prey. At the same time, she strolled around her desk and approached him from the side.

Nigel tracked her. "I believe that our relationship can and will remain mutually beneficial so long—"

"As it's a win-win?" she said, drawing her finger over his shoulder as she passed behind him.

"So long as we both get what we want and keep things quiet."

"Which is exactly what I want, love, and the reason I've called you here."

He resisted the urge to bite and let the silence draw her out.

Neon took a seat opposite him in a beaten-up leather chair. "I need you to do an errand for me."

Puzzling. "What kind?"

"I have an asset on *Astraea* Station who needs a return trip."

"A pickup?"

She nodded.

"Don't you have people for this sort of thing?"

Neon rested her elbows on the chair arms and steepled her fingers. "Nigel, love, there's nothing I ever do for one reason alone, and had I the need to explain them all to you, it would make you an employee, not a partner. Unless, of course, that's what you want?"

He despised her leading questions—her suggestive advances and constantly shifting subtext. Traversing the minefield that was her intellect was as dangerous as it was fatiguing. But Nigel hadn't risen to his power and fortune by being a pushover.

"If this is indeed payment for services rendered, I will at least know why and for how much of the total sum. Since you have yet to even fulfill your end of the agreement, I see no reason to stay here if my terms aren't met."

"Nigel, please. No need to get your feathers ruffled. It's only a small thing I ask. And as for our agreement, the pieces are already moving into place. So, were you to back out now, well, I'm afraid that would end very poorly for you."

"I don't appreciate being threatened."

"And I have no tolerance for people who go back on their word."

"You just—"

"I'm doing you a favor, love. As for the why, let's just say that the situation is delicate and that my normal means of extraction are not viable options."

"And the balance?"

"You do this, and I'll halve the price."

He tried not to balk. "Fifty million."

She nodded, nonplussed.

It was a dramatic reduction, one he couldn't ignore. But there must be some catch. "Military? Defector?"

"A man with a place to be. No baggage. No drama. Clean V-rec."

"What is it you're doing up there? I can't afford to have this come back on me."

"And you can't afford to fail." She removed a **cylinder** from her pocket, applied a fresh coat of her bright lipstick, and then **twisted the tube** shut. "What'll it be, love?"

Nigel didn't like that she avoided his question about the asset's purpose on *Astraea*. He ran his tongue across the front of his teeth, looked from his assistant to his bodyguards to her bodyguards and then back to Neon. She was as sly as a minx in that blistered old chair. Such a small errand for such a substantial discount. There was a catch coming, he could feel it. He just didn't know where it was sneaking up on him from, and that unnerved him.

"Fine. Send me the details, and I'll ensure that your asset is picked up on time and delivered where you say."

"You see?" she said to her four guards. "Negotiating with all business partners should be this easy." She looked like she was going to stand but then stopped. "There's just one more thing I want."

Here it was. Nigel sensed her words closing around his neck like a boa constrictor. This woman could sense fear. Smell it in his sweat, he was certain. But he must remain in control.

"I want a special pilot doing the errand."

Nigel eyed her narrowly. "All of my pilots are of the highest quality."

"No, no, no. I mean a specific pilot, love." She licked her lower lip. "I understand that you've recently come into acquisition of a Viatoribus legend, albeit a disgraced one. I want him."

Nigel's throat tightened. How did she know? The whole premise of Fox's employment hinged on secrecy as part of the arrangement—a term Nigel was only too happy to comply with. For a time, anyway. He'd suspected others would pester him for Fox initially were they to find out, so the condition suited him only too well. He would eventually win the pilot over with the finest luxuries the Solum Terram had to offer, and then secrecy would evaporate at Fox's request. But now all that was in jeopardy because the Scourge of the Elite had wriggled her fingers into the cake somehow.

Denying it would only make him look weak, so Nigel charged ahead unblinking. "Jericho Fox is a gifted pilot, but he's unavailable. I'll have another pilot pick up your man."

The corners of her loud lips twitched. "I'm sure you'll find a way to open his schedule."

"Why do you want him so badly?"

Neon's head tilted slowly as she ignored his question. "What's it worth to you?"

"Alright. What's your angle here?"

But she still didn't bite on his questions. "Seventy-five percent."

Nigel balked. He couldn't help it. "You'll do the job for twenty-five million?"

She nodded once.

"If I have Jericho Fox fly this pickup run?"

She nodded again.

Nigel felt like he was losing leverage fast. This was a bowl he'd not seen coming, and his wickets were un-guarded. The only way to get leverage back was to swing. "No."

Neon's face flattened.

"We're done here."

She didn't rise to meet, an act that rankled his sensi-bilities. Or was it that her cool and calm demeanor sig-naled some other power she had yet to wield?

Nigel snapped his fingers for his coat, and his PA spread the shoulders. The sooner he was out of here, the better.

"Leaving so soon, love?"

Had she not heard him? He spun around and spoke bitterly this time. "I said, we're done here."

The words were barely out of his mouth when Neon stood, drew a revolver, and leveled at his chest. A beat later, the mechanical clatter of safeties, cocking hammers, drivers, and bolts rippled around the room as both teams of bodyguards squared off with each other. If this mad appointment was to end in a bloodbath, at least his side outnumbered hers two to one.

"What is the meaning of this?" Nigel said louder than he meant to.

"Insurance, future Secretary-General Sallsworth."

Nigel's face flushed. Was she really willing to kill him over Jericho Fox? It was obscene. The man was valuable, yes, but not worth all this, not worth the future of their politicasts. Neon needed Nigel at the top of the NUE to advance her agenda, and he needed her to do the things that his office couldn't. Nigel was right not to trust her, but he'd seen this moment coming far too late—a mistake he would never make again if he survived.

"So you'd kill me over this?"

"If I must. But I'd much rather take you alive."

"Take me?"

She tilted her head the other way. "What did you think I meant by insurance, love? Jericho Fox brings me my asset, and we write this off as nothing more than growing pains."

"And if he doesn't?"

She started counting Nigel's guards under her breath. "Then I have to dig eleven graves behind my vineyard." She noticed the PA behind him. "Twelve. Forgot you, dear."

"Call them off. This is ridiculous. You're out-numbered."

"Am I?" The way she said those two simple words let Nigel know that there were probably additional sol-diers out of sight. "Oh, and there's just one more thing." She sauntered closer, pressed the gun into his chest, and whispered in his ear. "I will have Jericho Fox."

He backed away. "What?"

"I'll even lower the fee. I get to keep Fox, and you get your assassination gift wrapped gratis. I'll even throw in a big red bow for you."

"Have you gone mad?"

"That's relative. But you'll want to call off your dogs, Nigel."

"Because you have to win?"

"Because I *always* get what I want. Last chance."

Nigel stiffened his upper lip. "No."

Neon's head dropped a fraction of a centimeter, as if her chin were the pin on the back of a brass shell, igniting the primer and detonating the gel propellant. There wasn't the rattle of five Tantum and ten Solum weapons exchanging automatic fire, but rather a singular all-consuming burst of twenty-one weapons hidden behind the drapes shooting at the same time. A concise simultaneous event that placed two rounds in every one of Nigel's security detail—head and heart. Several bullets passed through their targets to strike other victims, including Nigel. One bullet punctured his calf, while a second punched through his suit at the shoulder. He caught himself on the chair and refused to go down. He'd been shot before, but that didn't make the pain any less severe, nor the anger at losing his team any less infuriating. All ten bodyguards fell to the rugs, plus his unarmed PA who was alive enough to be writhing in agony.

Neon stepped to the PA, pointed her revolver at his head, and squeezed the trigger. Blood splattered Nigel's pants. He grimaced and looked away. Then the room was still again, almost. Even riddled with bullets, it took a minute for his guards' bodies to shut down.

Neon holstered her weapon and reached for Nigel's face. He winced, but she insisted. His skin trembled under her touch as she wiped her thumb across his cheek like a mother might do to erase a smudge on her child's face. Blood. Nigel's assistant's, most likely. Nigel thought of grabbing the woman's throat and ending her. But he'd never make it. He'd have a bullet in his brain before his hand reached her neck.

Neon licked her thumb and looked him up and

down once. "Cheer up, Nigel. You made it through. And let's get you patched up, shall we? You can make your calls on the way."

Assuming she would monitor every call he made moving forward, Nigel took a chance and sent one line of coded text to Jones and Afumba on *Astraea* Station:

TT PLAY FOR JERICHO. PROTECT AT ALL COSTS.

As FOR THE fate of his own life, he could handle Neon. Nigel had dealt with worse. It was all a matter of biding one's time. *Slow and steady*, he reminded himself. *Slow and steady wins the war.*

JERICHO

I CLOSE the connection with Eric and step out of V-cog.

"Was that the director of NUESSA?" Kit asks me.

I nod, still processing the call.

After a few seconds of dead air, Kit asks, "What? What is it?"

"He… wants me on station."

"On *Astraea*?"

Again, I nod and then lean forward with my elbows on my knees. "To help substantiate my claim."

"Whoa, Cap. Isn't that like…? That's a big deal."

"Yeah."

"So he believes you then."

"Enough to call me out of forced retirement anyway. Said he needs all eyes on the problem."

Kit leans across and hits my bicep. "Congratulations, Cap. Like, for real."

"I'm not going."

He gives me a confused look. "I don't understand."

I hold up my palm. It's inked with the silvery mark of the Solum Terram—my "never getting off the planet again" card.

"Oh, damn." Kit looks at his own palm. "I… forgot

about that." Then his head pops up. "Why don't you just talk to Sallsworth?"

"Right. Because securing a meeting with him is easy."

"Oh. Sure, sure. I see. But he owes you."

"*Owed*," I correct and then motion around our apartment. "A debt he's clearly satisfied." I cast a stern look at Kit. "And then some."

He puts a hand on his chest. "Me?"

"You were extra."

He gulps. "Thanks, Cap."

I stand and walk toward the kitchen. "You want a beer?"

"Why not. It's five o'clock"—he checks the time—"somewhere else."

I smile, open the fridge, and retrieve the two bottles that the AI has already prepped when it heard me. With the lids popped, I walk back and offer one to Kit. "To being grounded."

"To being grounded," he replies.

We sip, and I sit back down.

"You have access to his private shuttle, you know."

"Kit, I'm not stealing a billionaire's shuttle to rendezvous with a legacy hab under lockdown."

"Yeah, but, if you really wanted to you—"

"If I really wanted to, I'd ask to arrange a meeting and request exemption."

Kit sips and then wipes his mouth with his sleeve. "So?"

"So what?"

"So, do you really want to get up there and help the investigation?"

That is the question, isn't it, Jericho. How badly do you want to get back into hard vacuum and be a part of the dance? Of Exploration. Settlement. Expansion.

"What's so funny?" Kit asks.

I didn't even realize I was chuckling. I switch my beer to the opposite hand and look at my open palm. "Where was the invite two days ago?"

"Ironic, isn't it?"

"More like tragic."

Kit takes a long sip. "Nothing's stopping you from making the call, though. Least you can do is try."

I puzzle over the prospect for a few seconds and then set my bottle down. "Alright. Try, it is. And if it doesn't work—"

"We steal his shuttle!"

"Oh my god."

I'm not ready when Nigel Sallsworth invites me into his private V-cog suite.

The staff listing I searched moments before making the call to his office showed that his executive secretary had three assistants, all listed in order of priority with restricted access protocols in place. So I started with the first one and crossed my fingers. I barely finished my request when the woman said, "Mr. Sallsworth will see you."

And now, here I am, standing on a wooden deck looking out at what I believe are the Swiss Alps. The chalet-style mountainside home helps sell it too. Based on all the snow, I'd say early twenty-first century. The level of detail is amazing. He even has a light snow falling. I can't imagine what this environment cost him, but he's not exactly hurting for money.

"Do you like it?"

I turn to see Sallsworth in a navy blue sweater and chinos. He looks like a movie star with his ridiculously perfect hair.

"It's impressive," I reply. Not what I wanted my first words to be for the man who helped smear my reputation and scorn the mission. But he caught me off guard, probably on purpose. Best get to it then. "Mr. Sallsworth, I'd like permission to help NUESSA investigate the developing situation on *Astraea* Station."

He raises one eyebrow but then turns away to rest both hands on the wooden railing. I can't tell if he's stressed out or just annoyed with my question. Finally, he says, "Can you imagine what it must've been like? To ski here two hundred years ago?"

I glance back to the mountains, but I need this conversation to stay on task. "Director Johnson has requested my assistance personally."

If this surprises him, he doesn't show it. Instead, he pulls a piece of cardstock from his pants pocket and hands it to me. I hesitate, but he insists. "Go on. It won't bite you."

I take it. "It's a photograph."

"Of my eighth-great-grandfather and grandmother on their honeymoon. Here. In Davos."

I offer it back, but he ignores the gesture. "Mr. Sallsworth, I'd like to—"

"I often wonder if they knew that they'd be the last generation to ski here. If they had any idea, that in just one generation, everything they knew would change forever." He sighs, takes the image back, and smiles at it. "They look happy, don't they?"

"I'm sure they were."

"They also were a part of the problem."

He takes the picture between his index and middle fingers and flicks it off the deck. The tiny photograph spins through turbulent air before disappearing beneath the overhang.

"People don't think long term, Mr. Fox. Not that I blame them. It's in our nature, our lizard brain, to act in our own best interests for the moment. To survive. It's why very few of us ever invest in anything beyond our immediate needs. The above average will invest in things that might benefit them in, oh, a few months maybe. Smarter people will make decisions that have outcomes over several years. But the truly intelligent? They understand that delaying what you want today for the thing you need tomorrow is no mere matter of years. It's a matter of lifetimes."

He turns to face me. There's something behind his eyes that I can't place—something... nervous. Why?

"I suppose you're mad at me. Harbor bitterness, even? For the things I said against you and all those involved with the Infinita program. But I think you fail to understand my critique."

"That we're bumbling idiots not fit to lead."

He raises a finger. "I never said idiots."

"Right. *Buffoons*."

He winces. "I consider those in the Viatoribus and Sentia Aux to be among the most intelligent."

"Didn't feel that way when you dragged us through the verb like corpses on parade."

"Morbid."

"But true."

"It is not your intelligence that I fault, Mr. Fox. If anything, you exemplify my premise that the truly wise are concerned with the generations they will never meet. Is this not what drives you? To secure safety for your children and your children's children?"

I try to think of a smartass comeback but run out of time.

"No, Mr. Fox. It's not that you and your people— your *former* people—lack vision. It's that they lack perception."

"Is this going somewhere?"

"Reality, Mr. Fox. You champion the cause of spending trillions upon trillions for salvation in space, when those same coins could be spent here, solving real problems, bettering the world we evolved on. Our home."

I've spent so much time on this argument with others that I don't have the desire to pick it up again with Sallsworth. But he's made it too easy. "You just said that your great grandparents were the last to ski here. So you admit the damage is irreversible."

The corner of his lip twitches. "I admit that they had a chance to help rectify the problems that they were a part of creating and did nothing. You at least have the insight to think ahead, but you fail to see that it's not too late for Earth."

"But the science shows—"

He drops a fist on the railing. "The science is flawed."

"Then that's where we agree to disagree."

"Only because you are conditioned to believe it's too late."

"By my politicast?" I chuckle once. "I could say the same about you. Leopards never change their spots."

"Your father did."

That hits me like a gut punch. "You leave him out of this."

"I'd be curious to know why he changed his mind."

I shake my head. I won't be baited; it's bad enough that I have to ask his permission to help NUESSA keep a killer from murdering more innocent people. "Will you allow me to assist in the investigation or not?"

He rests his forearms on the railing and studies the falling snow. The relaxed way he eases into his stance compels me to look out at the snow with him. The modelers did an amazing job rendering the fractal precipitation. Not that I've ever seen any, but the archivists have lots of sample footage, and Sallsworth has lots of money.

"You puzzle me, Mr. Fox. Why didn't you just cash in that cold storage chip I gave you? It would have saved you a lot of trouble."

"Because I'm not for sale."

"But you work for me now."

"Work. I *work* for you. It does not mean that I believe—"

"Careful."

I check my speech, knowing this conversation is being recorded. Everything's recorded when you're near the world's wealthiest politicast leader. Someone would check the footage against my oath eventually. "It means that I give honest labor for honest pay. Nothing more."

"Well then. If you have an honest interest in saving lives and bringing criminals to justice, who am I to stop you?"

This is a surprise. "Then you're okay with me going?"

"Of course. Do you think me a monster?" Suspecting I might answer in the affirmative, Nigel quickly adds, "I know you don't care for me, Mr. Fox. And that's well and good. But I do hope that over time you will see that the Solum Terram has humanity's best interests at heart. We are not the extremists that other politicasts peddle. Rather, we are cautious. Calculative. And, when needed, clever."

That's one way to spin it.

Sallsworth wipes a snowflake from his nose and stares at it. If this was in nature, the flake would melt, but here it stays perfectly formed on the tip of his finger. "Your first job as my pilot, Mr. Fox, is to rendezvous with *Astraea*. There's a pickup I need you to make. You'll find the flight plan and instructions in your suite; the client will make contact with you at the appointed time. I have a shuttle docked with *Elpis* on Ascender 1. *If* you so happen to depart early, what is it to me if you use your free time to play Sherlock Holmes? I'll touch base with you upon your return."

"You're not coming?"

"Why would you assume that?"

"I… I'm your pilot, aren't I?"

"Who flies at my pleasure, yes. It does not always mean I am the cargo."

I don't like this. Not the part about being his errand boy. I mean the part about him acting like he already knew I was going to ask, about having this trip prearranged, whatever it is, and then all the small talk and propaganda leading up to now. "So what's the cargo?"

"More like who. As I said, he'll make contact." So it's a male. Noted.

Sallsworth is still studying the snowflake, admiring it like someone looking at a very tiny painting, only this time, his finger is trembling. "Our researchers say that our great grandchildren will see snow again. Do you believe that?"

"Sure. Just not on Earth."

"Hmmm." He inhales and then blows the little flake away. "Have a safe trip, Mr. Fox."

Before I can say another word, I'm kicked out of his suite and right back to my couch beside Kit. It takes me a second to let the sudden transfer wear off.

"Well?"

"Pack your bags, Kit. We've got our first job."

"What? Really?" His left knee starts bopping. "Where?"

I point straight up. "*Astraea*."

"God, is there like… anything you can't do?" He sits back and folds his arms. "One day? I'm gonna be like you. Freaking impregnate mermaids with just my good looks."

"Whuh?"

"Yeah. Must be nice gettin' paid to be stag. Hovin' with the hotties all through the—"

"Okay, lady killer. Grab a shower and then get your suit on. Skids up for Ascender 1 in thirty."

"Copy that, Cap." As he walks toward his en suite bathroom, I hear him say, "Hey. I'm Captain Kit Smith. Why, yes, I'd love to give you a tour of my ship."

Funny guy. But while he's getting prepped, I have a call to make. I reestablish the connection to NUESSA Mission Control in St. Johns, Newfoundland Territory, and see Director Johnson's face surrounded by glowing screens.

"Eric? I'm in."

EVELYN

"Marines, Stamos?" I say as two of the gray and black armored brutes walk me across a quad and toward section thirty's cargo hold entrance amidst a growing crowd of spectators. I want to jab him about not being able to handle the job himself, but he speaks up too soon.

"Your status has just been elevated to suspected terrorist, Dr. Park."

I struggle to face him, but the Marines are immovable. "I've done nothing wrong, you asshat."

"Language, please. There are children present."

Appealing to this man's sense of logic seems to be a pointless endeavor, which means I need to reach Captain Mombawe all the more. While a NUESSA captain is obligated to abide by the Nations of United Earth Military Charter, it doesn't mean he necessarily agrees with the terrorism charges against me. He's just following procedure. That said, speaking with him can only help my situation as his word will carry weight with whoever authorized the Space Marine intervention—I'm guessing Director Johnson under pressure from the NUE Security Council.

"Is this because I broke your nose?"

Stamos comes even with me and my Marine handlers but still keeps his distance. "It's because I suspect you're guilty, Dr. Park."

"Of what? Blowing up the hab? Are you out of your mind?"

"If I am, it seems NUESSA is too."

"What's that supposed to mean?"

Stamos waves a hand dismissively, the one with his crisp VT tat as if his centrist pedigree aligns him more closely with the NUESSA's cause. "I think this makes for three arrests in a row, if I'm not mistaken—a station-wide record—which also makes you a royal pain in my ass."

So much for the children's ears.

I make to interject, but he holds up a finger.

"And I advise you to choose your words carefully, Doctor. You are, as I think you'd expect, being monitored."

I grind my teeth to help hold my tongue. Few battles were ever won by those who lost their cool, and I can't afford any more mistakes. "I'd expect to at least be shown what damning evidence there is to justify terrorism. Isn't that how it's supposed to work, inspector?"

If Stamos wants to play, he's not showing it. Instead, he crosses the rest of the quad in silence. I cast him a few sideways glances. That's when I notice something unusual about his posture. He looks... disappointed. No, that's not it. *Defeated*. Like he's lost our contest to powers above his pay grade. The look surprises me and, for the briefest of moments, makes him somewhat more human—but barely.

Finally, we reach the imposing cargo hall entry. "After you," he says with a mocking tone.

The armored doors separate, and we leave the bright hab curve of summer for the dismal grey of utility. A standard ten-meter cargo container is centered in a bay to my left, but this one bears the scarlet and gold NUE Space Marine logo against its black exterior. Two more armor-clad Marines open the doors to reveal a glorified prison carriage, complete with a bed, shower, toilet, small kitchenette, backup control interface, and life support system. A security wall separates a pilot house in the far end. If this is going to be my home for the next few days, it could be worse.

"You really shouldn't have," I say to Stamos.

He ignores the remark and gestures to a new Marine in matte-black and gray armor, this one bearing a gold and scarlet shoulder insignia with three chevrons above and below a pair of crossed rail gun rifles. The man, somewhere in his mid-thirties, looks lean and lethal just standing still.

"Dr. Evelyn Park, my name is Master Sergeant Ishaq al Farooq, Squad Leader with Special Space Naval Operations. Under the NUE Military Charter's provisions for suspected terrorist activities, both foreign and domestic, I hereby relieve you of your duties and responsibilities, professional and private, aboard the NUESSA *Astraea* and remand you into Space Marine Corps custody until such time as your case may be heard by a military tribunal sanctioned by the NUE or—"

"A tribunal? On what grounds?"

"—or your guilt is absolved by an *apparent judicas*. If you have no legal representation, a court-ordered Judge Advocate General will be provided for you."

"On what grounds?" I say more forcefully, but Master Sergeant Farooq isn't budging.

"From this point forward, you are the property of the Nations of United Earth Space Marines. Anything you say or do, in real or virtual life, can and will be used against you. You are hereby guilty until proven innocent."

I shoot a look at Stamos. "You can't be serious."

He shrugs. "You played a dangerous game and got caught. Maybe next time, you'll think differently."

I wrestle against the two Marines holding my arms. It does nothing more than cinch their tweaked-out grip tighter, but it's the only aggression I allow myself since shouting is the enterprise of the powerless. "You're making a mistake, Stamos."

"We'll let the tribunal decide. See you on the verb, Dr. Park."

I'm sick of being arrested, and even more fed up with being cooped up inside holding cells. How long has it been—a couple of hours maybe?—but I've paced enough in my cargo cell to log a few kilometers. I'm not hungry, not that the MREs in the galley cupboard are the least bit appetizing even if I were, and I've forced myself to stay hydrated knowing that I need the water to keep my thoughts clear. V-cog has been shut off, of course, and I haven't heard so much as a peep from any of my minders outside.

The fact that I was the only one removed from the lab bodes well for the rest of the team, especially Sam. Whatever evidence Stamos gathered and NUESSA reviewed, she seems to be in the clear. For now. And since Sam's been closest with me on the project, I feel confident that she'll lead the team in doing all they can to preserve whatever information Parallax captured and work with the captain to realign on Kepler-1649c at the earliest.

I need to get back to the bubble, and to do that I have to connect with both Captain Mombawe and Lemuel. This whole thing has escalated far too quickly. Time to draw some attention. I don't know where they've put the cameras, but I'm guessing they're built into the room's corners. So I pick a side and start talking. "I'd like to make a confession to Sergeant Farooq."

I don't bother repeating myself. They heard me, and they'll respond if they're interested. If not, I have a few more tricks up my—

The security door unlocks and pivots open.

"That was fast."

"You called, Dr. Park?" says Farooq standing in front of two other Marines.

"I'd like to make a confession."

He doesn't seem impressed. "Go on."

I take a breath and lift my chin. "I confess that I have no idea why I'm being detained and the charges against me—"

"Close it up."

"Farooq, wait. Please."

"It's Master Sergeant to you."

"*Master* Sergeant Farooq, if you know, would you at least tell me? Please?"

He holds the guards back with an upraised fist but doesn't move beyond that. He just looks at me. I feel like I'm a kid back in Seongbuk-gu District being sized up by a bully. Only Farooq doesn't seem like he wants to hurt me; he's just doing his job.

He's too smart for charm, not that I have much. Plus I'm not exactly looking my best right now anyway, contrary to whatever Sam tries to sell me about my "natural beauty." So I play to the greatest asset I have…

The truth.

Always the truth.

"Sergeant, I've given my life to trying to save humanity. If I'm guilty of hurting anyone, it's those who've suffered because of my single-mindedness. And I tell you the truth when I say that I've had nothing to do with the deaths of the engineers nor the explosion. I know you can't let me go—that's not what I'm asking. But if I am going to stand trial, I would at least like to see what evidence has been found to condemn me before I arrive. Surely, that's something you can provide."

Farooq studies my face.

Stars, I hope he has more balls than Stamos.

We hold each other's stare for several seconds. But when he fails to budge, I lower my eyes and step away.

"They have V-cog access records of you entering the ag level five minutes before the explosion."

I stare at him slack-jawed for a moment but quickly regain my composure. "That's impossible. My own V-rec will show I was in holding."

"Not according to them."

"But they're the ones who arrested me!" This is infuriating. Then again, if someone is trying to frame me, it makes sense. "Stamos."

"Say again?"

I meet his eyes. "Stamos is trying to frame me. I can't be in two places at once. Have your people cross-check the detention logs. Dr. Samantha Collins can attest to—"

"I'm sorry, Dr. Park. This is outside of my control."

"Bullshit."

He arches an eyebrow, but then his face relaxes.

"Listen. If you are innocent, as you suggest, then trust the system to work it out on your behalf."

"I don't have time for that. Do you know what we've discovered up there? Sentient extrasolar life, Sergeant. Alien intelligence, one that's communicating with us as we speak." My brain accuses my mouth of inaccuracy, but I don't have the time to explain the physics of a 300-year-old light transmission finally arriving in our star system. "There might be circumstantial evidence to detain me, but there's one thing they don't have."

"What's that?"

"Motive." I point straight up in the bubble's general direction. "My whole world is up there. Everything I believe in. You have Allah, unit, corps, right? Well, I have *that*, Sergeant. Up there. It's my religion, this whole thing"—I gesture around the cell but mean the hab—"and I would sooner hurt myself than our work, believe you me. Our planet has been waiting 300 years to catch that signal, and there's no guarantee it will last more than a few seconds. Stars, it may already be gone forever. But I won't know until I get out of here and back up there."

There it is, in a nutshell. My best case. I only hope it's enough.

The sergeant thinks for a moment and then straightens his back. "Even if I believed you, Doctor, NUESSA is sending specialists as we speak. If your beloved work has any lasting merit, I imagine it will continue long after you're dismissed, and they'll get to the bottom of the attack against *Astraea*."

"What kind of specialists?"

"That's outside of my purview, ma'am. But he'll be the acting *apparent judicas* in the matter."

"Meaning?"

"He'll have the power to set you free if his investigation warrants it." Seemingly satisfied with the conversation, Farooq takes a step back and orders the door shut.

"Wait. Can you at least get a message to the captain for me?"

Farooq pauses. "That depends on what you want to say."

"Ask him if he'll permit me to resume my work in the lab under Marine oversight—you and a whole damn division if you want."

He raises an eyebrow again. "You're not familiar with military force allotments, are you."

"Just… would you tell him? I'm happy to comply with whatever the law demands. I only ask to resume my work. Please. For humanity?" Stars, I sound desperate. And grandiose, I know. If I were him, I'm not sure I would believe me. But it's the truth. I only hope he can sense it.

"I'll see what I can do."

A minor wave of relief hits me. It's a small victory, but a victory nonetheless. "Thank you, Sergeant."

"But no promises."

"Of course."

He orders the hatch closed, but just before it shuts all the way he stops it with a hand. "You really think they're out there? Like, Fermi Paradox level importance? This it?"

The sudden shift in the man's demeanor catches me off guard. For the briefest of moments, he's transformed from a stone-faced Marine to an inquisitive searcher. And then I see why. Barely visible between his fingers is his palm's politicast tattoo: the flaming offset concentric rings of the Sentiamus Auxiliumm.

He notices my eyes and smiles. "Forging paths…"

"…through the darkness," I answer in wonder. "Yes, Sergeant. And I don't think so. I know."

He gets a twinkle in eyes. "I'll get your request to the captain, but I suggest you get comfortable. It'll be hurry up and wait."

"Of course, yes. Thank you, Sergeant."

He smiles. "Call me Rook in private. And it's you who we should be thanking."

17

JERICHO

THE SOFT HUM of Ascender 1's number two passenger module serves as background noise to the conversations scattered around Kit and me. No matter how many times I maglift off the planet like this, I'm still captivated by the view, even if Earth is a shadow of its former glory. The wraparound windows on all three decks of Donut Two, as it's affectionately called, give unobstructed panoramas of the planet, interrupted only by the space elevator's second cable some 200 meters to the west.

We have first-class accommodations, care of the Solum Terram, which comes with unlimited drinks, something Kit has been all too eager to take advantage of. He hands me another beer while he keeps a flowery Mai Tai complete with a toothpick umbrella for himself. Kit does his best not to spill his drink by sipping as he sits.

"Last one of those for you, okay?" I say.

He pulls the maraschino cherry off its stem with his teeth and then chomps down, mouth open. "Relax, Cap. We've still got eight hours to go."

"Which is not nearly long enough for you to metabolize all that."

He sips again and tries to hold back a burp with a fist. "Please. I'll be—fine. *Burp*."

I take a pull on my beer and then stretch my other arm out on the couch back. I love the view, even if I have my misgivings about the last time I was headed this way. Kit seems to like the scenery too. The only time he's taken his eyes away from the window was to order more drinks or hit the head.

"So this is really your first trip up?" I ask.

"Yup. Hopefully not my last either. All you Viatoribus"—he realizes what he's said aloud and lowers his voice—"you guys get all the fun."

"Something like that." I drink some more and study the planet as it races away from us. "You ever wonder what it was like? The Earth?"

It takes him a second. "You mean, before?"

I nod.

"We have plenty of digital, Cap."

"Not like that. I mean to actually see it, ya know? From right here?"

Kit still looks confused. "I don't understand."

"You've seen this view a hundred times in V-cog, right?"

He nods.

"But this feels different, doesn't it?"

"Yeah. Because I know it's not a render."

"So wouldn't it be amazing to see 'not a render' from before the migration?"

With his speech getting worse, Kit says, "I see where you're going. You mean without all the—*burp*—brown parts."

I take the Mai Tai from his hand.

"Hey! That's my drink."

"Not anymore."

He crosses his arms and throws himself back into the couch. The fact that a passenger can get inebriated at 2,000 klicks per hour during a 33,000 klick journey into space proves we really haven't come that far as a species. Do we ever?

A server swings by and takes the upraised glass from my hand. Mai Tais creep up on a person fast; I should know. I nod my thanks to the server, order a round of waters, and then look back at Kit. "You see Old Cheyenne?"

He eventually plays along and squints toward the Northern Heights. "Yeah. In the middle somewhere. Wondering if my mom's looking."

I almost suggest he call her, but no one wants to see their son drunk during their first ride on the planet's space elevator. The server returns and hands Kit a glass of water.

"Hey, thanks." He looks at me. "Jeez. Great service around here. I don't even remember ordering." He takes a sip and then whispers to me. "I think they put something in this."

"Yeah."

He drinks again. "How many of your family died?"

I hold short of sipping my beer. "Wanna run that by me again?"

"How many of your family died?"

"When?"

"The Migration. When. *Pffft*. Please."

I take a deep breath and look back to the panorama of a world and its inhabitants ravaged by a four-degree rise in Celsius. Part of me resists the notion of talking about four billion deaths when my counterpart is drunk.

Then again, that seems to be the coping mechanism of most people when they reflect on the planet's greatest tragedy.

"My ancestors originated in Old Chicago before it was even named that. Some of the family claim Jean Baptiste Point du Sable is an umpteenth great grandfather."

"Who?"

"Exactly. Anyway, they stayed as long as they could until the upswell became too much. Started moving north to follow food production. When it finished, my paternal grandfather was a boy in northern Ontario. Lost both of his siblings. Then his father. His mother died a year after it all settled, 2180."

Kit nods and stares into his glass, but I'm not sure he's all there. "You know what I just realized?"

"What's that?"

"I think this is just water."

I shake my head and look away.

"I also just realized that you had the Great Migration and then the Hundred Years Migration, know what I mean?"

Huh. Kit knows some history, even drunk. Not bad. 'Course, I'm not sure how much of this he'll remember, but he can review V-cog later if he wants to.

Looking down on the massive swaths of brown continents and swollen oceans, it seems fitting to honor those who came before me from up here like this. Those who paid so many unspeakable prices so that I could live this life now. I wonder if they ever imagined where our people would end up... imagined that one day the war would be over, and that someone like me would be at the head of my class and a leader in frontier aerospace. They dreamed.

They fought. And it happened. Damn, did it happen.

"Maternal grandmother lost three siblings but kept both parents," I add in case Kit's still listening. "They never had any more after her. Couldn't justify bringing children into such a harsh world."

"So you were a single-path survivor?"

"Two generations worth."

His eyebrows hike up his forehead. "Who? Your father?"

"Both. Mom was an only child. So was dad."

"Holy biscuits. You, you—"

"You almost never met me."

"Yeah. That's what I was going to say, but then you said it. Thanks."

"No problem."

Riding into orbit and talking about my family history reminds me of how lucky I am, and not just to be the last Fox in my family line. I mean to be going back into the big black at all. Granted, I'd rather be headed up with a different politicast, but space is space no matter how you get there. The void doesn't care whose ink you rep. And if I play my cards right and ignore the past when it tries to raise its head, who knows, maybe there's a new horizon for me at the end of all this.

"How about you?" I ask. I'm not sure if Kit's sober enough to recite his family history, but it's worth trying.

"Me what?"

"The Migration."

"I didn't die in it."

Annnd not very sober.

"I meant your grandparents, Kit."

"Oh. Great grandparents then."

"There you go."

He sniffs and takes another drink of water. "We Smiths breed like pasty white wasteland rabbits. Like all sorts of pent up sexual energy and stuff, ya know?" He's gyrating in his seat like it's a freaking dance floor. "Probably an evolutionary survival trait. Like wasteland rabbits."

"You… mentioned that."

"Oh. Right." He calms down. "So, yeah, some of us died off somewhere. I can't keep track. But those who survived all stayed in the wastes."

"Really?"

He nods in an overexaggerated way. "'Smiths don't abandon their posts,' my granddad used to say. So my dad said it. Now I say it. See?" He holds his water aloft and some sloshes out of the glass. "Smiths don't abandon their posts."

I help his arm down gently.

"Anyway, we stayed put. Hunkered down in cellars. Built connection tunnels to each other's houses. Like wasted rabbits."

His mix-up makes me chuckle. "You sound pretty resourceful."

"We were. Up until we weren't."

"Ran out of coin?"

He nods. "And food. The older generation didn't believe in the blockchain when it resurfaced. Everything else became worthless, and by the time I came of age, we needed to get real jobs 'in the system,' as they said."

"High Top."

"Yupper-scupper."

I know Kit's not in his right mind recounting all this, but the fact that he and his ancestors survived in the old Wyoming Territory is nothing short of heroic. And idiotic. But hey, who am I to judge what people want to die for? He's still here, isn't he? Explains why he never left High Top, and why he has such an amazing work ethic. He's loyal, duty-bound, and a survivor. Like a damn pasty white wasteland rabbit. He also can't handle his liquor for shit.

Kit suddenly takes on a sober air and pulls his eyes away from the view. "You think it'll go up again?"

I lower my voice. "The temp?"

He stifles a burp. "Yeah."

"Well. It's anyone's guess." I'm lying, of course. I know the science, at least in part. But I don't want to scare him, or anyone for that matter. After all, I'm just a pilot with an engineering degree, not a climatologist. "Plenty of reasons why it could."

"Which means plenty more why you wanna get off for good, right?"

In an intentionally loud voice, I say, "Don't be silly. We've gotten the planet under control."

It takes a few seconds for Kit to register what I'm doing as well as the mistake he made. "Riiiight. Totally. Nothing to see here folks. Nothing to see."

Hopefully everyone within earshot chalks his babbling up to too many Mai Tais. But I can't afford for him to blow my standing with my new benefactor, not unless I want to take up desert living in Old Cheyenne. "Why don't you go get some sleep, Kit."

"But I'm not tired."

"You will be. Give it a few minutes."

In heavily slurred speech, he says, "You're just trying to ditch me. But I can be a very persuasive wingman."

I help him stand. At the same instant, a warning chime sounds. It's the midway point where Donut One passes us on its return trip to the surface. I glance toward the black of space and see it racing along its ever narrowing carbon nanotube cable. Contrary to popular belief, the forces acting on a space elevator require the widest diameter of ten meters to be at the orbital station's altitude, while the smallest, just thirty centimeters, is at Quito Station in Old Ecuador. Fitting that our equatorial step into space would be in a deserted nation whose name actually means "equator" in Spanish.

The two donut-shaped models, or three-toruses if we're being engineers, slow to accommodate the crossing. At a distance of less than 200 meters, a full-speed pass-by would mean a 4,000 klick-per-hour differential —not something paying customers would enjoy. I hold onto Kit as we decelerate to keep him from falling. "Easy there."

He points up. "Wow. There's a halo coming down from heaven on a string."

"Yeah." I ease him back to the couch as the other donut's glowing center gets closer. The quantum locked magnets in the middle are designed to resist the cable's magnets in sequence, regardless of the tether's diameter. Likewise, the two-cable transfer system minimizes the effects of harmonic vibration as well as doubles the elevator's cargo capacity. It was built and designed long before I was born. I'm just glad the migration didn't keep us from pioneering new tech because it'd be a shame to have missed this. Which is also how I feel about where we get to go next, even with all the emotional baggage it carries for me.

Kit lets out an audible gasp as Donut One rushes past us. "Wow. Did you see that?"

"I did. Pretty cool."

"The coolest."

"Alright, let's get you back to the room." I help him

stand again as we accelerate. The inertia shift is almost imperceptible, but we're regaining speed as we continue on toward the orbital station *Elpis*. Just eight more hours, and then it's on to *Astraea*, the one place in our solar system that holds some of the worst and best memories of my life.

Worst part is, I still want to go back. I have to. Not for the past, but for the future… for what I know awaits humanity. And for what I know I can still contribute if they'll let me. All I need to do is convince Eric that I'm competent—that I can save lives, not just lose them. And then maybe NUESSA will take me back. I just need this one mission to prove it.

"Um, Cap?"

"Yeah?"

"I don't feel so good."

"Alright. Just hold on for—"

Kit turns and pukes down the length of my uniform while holding my shoulders for stability. The vomit sends a wave of warmth down to my knees.

"Hey, Cap?"

"Yeah?"

"I feel way better now, thanks. And guess what else?"

"What's that?"

He giggles and then yawns. "I'm tired too."

Perfect.

WHILE FAR FROM the scale of a legacy hab, *Elpis* is nothing to ignore. And why would anyone want to? The station is legendary, enough that it's been designated an NUE world heritage site and one of the seven wonders of the modern world. Built ten years before *Astraea*, it became humanity's stepping-stone into the big black. Without it, we'd still be using conventional rockets and aircraft to ferry materials, supplies, and personnel into space, making our progress a fraction of what we've maintained for the last fifty years.

With over twenty decks to explore in its fat pancake-like structure, I've spent my share of time reading the plaques and studying the models in the museum dedicated to the station's creation and ongoing development. If all goes well, two more space elevators will be operational by the end of the year, one in Singapore and the other in Nairobi. Together, all three will ensure faster space settlement and eventual surface evacuation. We'll save humanity, if we're lucky.

There's no time for a museum stop today. We have a mission to get to, and Kit's late. I'm seated in the *Star Shadow*, a Venture-class PST 40 shuttle stuck to *Elpis*'s side by an airlock tunnel and two gantry arms. All systems are powered up and ready to go. I just need my flight engineer.

Kit finally floats into the cockpit looking a little worse for wear. He's managed to clean up his flight suit well enough. Mine had to be laundered by *Elpis*'s service department—charged to Sallsworth's account, of course.

"Sorry I'm late, Cap."

"I appreciate the apology. You okay?"

"Remind me never to have a Mai Tai again, would ya?"

He sits down and orients himself with the limited hardware. Unlike the LACH we met in, this bird is all state-of-the-art tech. No manual controls other than redundant emergency backups, and no glass windshield.

Once the main hatch is closed, the hull is a seamless nano-comp shell.

"You, uh, new at this?" I ask, repeating one of the first things he said to me when the roles were reversed. Skipping ahead, I add, "Yeah, we get a lot of that. But you get used to it. Couple times with virtual cognizance piloting and you'll have it down pat."

"Funny," he says, still rubbing his head. A beat later, he appears in *Shadow*'s lobby seated beside me in a replica of the cockpit, but one completely decked out in flight controls and instrumentation. In addition to the glass windshield and display screens filled with standard exterior views are several layers of internal and external cameras listed on side menus. The luxury shuttle's layout is enough to draw a solid "Wow" from Kit's lips. "I've never seen anything like this."

"Money can't buy love. But it sure can make you jealous."

"You can say that again." He moves his hands just above the panels and control screens. "Hello, *Abigail*."

I cast him a strange look. "Ship's called the *Star Shadow*."

"Not anymore." He lets out a sigh. "And aren't you beautiful."

"You… gonna be okay over there?"

"I just need another second."

I shake my head and let out a small laugh. "Alright, lover boy. Let's run pre-flight."

"Aye-aye, Cap."

I HONESTLY CAN'T BELIEVE I'm back behind the stick of a shuttle in space. What's more, I can't believe I'm headed toward *Astraea*. It feels too good to be true. Of course, I know it won't all be smooth sailing. As soon as someone makes my face, and all it takes is one person to recognize me, then word spreads fast and conversations get really uncomfortable. So I'll keep my public V-cog sig on privacy mode and wear a NUESSA cap to hide my face. There's no dodging serious scrutiny, however, nor will it go well if someone spots the Solum Terram insignia on my hand and uniform—which they probably will—but I'll weather that storm when it comes. And it will come.

A flight traffic controller's voice hails us over comms when we're 100 klicks out. "*Star Shadow*, *Star Shadow*, this is *Astraea Actual*. Come in."

"*Astraea Actual*, this is *Star Shadow*. We have you loud and clear."

"Hull ID and flight log are confirmed. You are clear to approach docking bay Bravo One Four."

"Docking bay Bravo One Four confirmed. See you shortly, *Astraea*."

"Safe flight. *Astraea Actual* out."

Kit pats the virtual console with a hand. "He means you, Abby. Don't worry."

I activate the ship's docking approach sequence and then turn to Kit. "Alright, spill."

"Spill what?"

"Who was Abigail?"

Kit folds his arms behind his head. "The one that got away."

"Really."

"Yup."

I wait a few seconds. "And?"

"Man, was she smart. Aced everything in school. And had the looks to back it up. The perfect woman."

"So what happened?"

He lowers his arms and shrugs. "Eh. She graduated and got a scholarship to St. Johns."

"Yeah, but before that. How'd it end?"

He looks at me confused.

When he doesn't add anything more, I say, "Wait. Did you ever actually *date* her?"

"No way, Cap. Way out of my league."

I laugh. "Kit, for one to get away, you had to have dated her."

"Says who?"

"Well, that's… kinda the nature of the expression."

He passes it off. "Semantics."

"Sure."

I glance over the *Shadow*'s—I mean *Abigail*'s status screens. Docking approach is nominal. Ten minutes out.

"Your turn," Kits says.

"My girl who got away?"

He shakes his head. "Your big sin. Your accident. What really happened?" Kit finally has the nerve to ask the question everyone wants to know but few have the courage to pose—mostly because I think they're disgusted with me. Or just afraid of the answer they might get. Nah, if Kit's gonna be with me on *Astraea*, then he needs to know. Better now than later.

Here goes.

18

JERICHO

"TEN YEARS AGO, I got my big break right out of school. Stellar Dynamics joined forces with NUESSA to begin work on a new exploration starship, and they needed brains and bodies."

"Marquis-class," Kit says.

I nod. "I get picked up by Stellar Dynamics as an engineering apprentice, but two years in, NUESSA makes me an offer: junior engineer and test pilot. Two years after that, SD comes back and wants me for special projects. And finally NUESSA plays a government trump card and secures me for project manager, indefinitely."

Kit blinks at me. "That's good, right?"

I chuckle. "Yeah, Kit."

"Cool, cool."

"The Marquis-class is all about distance and covering it as fast as possible."

"Because we need answers," he adds.

"A lot of them." I take another deep breath and lean back in my chair. Talking about this with him doesn't hurt. Not yet, anyway. Come to think of it, he's the first person I've broached the subject with since the trial. Shoot, he's even Solum Terram. But he's also becoming someone I trust, and I suppose that has a way of trumping ink.

Just in case the background isn't fresh for him, I offer a bit of a review. "While the Sentia Aux has always been about reaching out to aliens for help, the Viatoribus decided long ago that humanity couldn't wait for whatever alien-seekers they were hoping to find, if any. So we set our sights on interstellar travel. Or at least the first stages of it, anyway."

"This is all so cool to me, ya know? You were actually part of building the first crewed mission beyond the heliosphere," Kit says.

"You know a lot for an ST."

"Tats don't mean stats."

"True enough. Anyway, the X-10 ES *Perseverant* was our proof of concept for the engine systems before we installed them in the full-sized Marquis-class."

"The *Hope Futura*." He smiles to himself. "I built a model. It's still hanging in my room."

"I built a real one."

Kit stares at me like I'm god. Finally, he manages, "I still can't believe I'm talking to you. I feel like an idiot for not putting it all together when we met."

"Don't sweat it. Honestly, it was a nice change of pace not being recognized. Anyway, it's the maiden of the *Perseverant*. Flight test, run the engines through their paces, get a feel for the power. I asked to be on board instead of on *Astraea*'s command bridge; if those specialists were putting their lives on the line, then so was I. We pushed back from *Astraea*, all systems nominal. Then it comes time to test the Ebrahimi Drive. A five minute burn at six point eight g's."

"What was the max speed after that, like eighteen klicks per second?"

"Try twenty."

He whistles and gives an appreciative shake of his head. "Plasmoids, man."

"Christ, you know your physics." Then again, he did build a model of our ship as a kid. The experimental drive, named after the twenty-first-century physicist who first theorized it, Fatima Ebrahimi, harnesses the power of plasma bubbles that travel at twenty kilometers per second. But that's just the first stage of it.

"The burn was textbook. We covered the expected 3,000 klicks in 300 seconds. So we flipped the ship, slowed on the same burn, and then rinse and repeat to come home."

"And that's when it happened," Kit states.

"No, actually. We still needed to fire up the SPD."

Kit scrunches his brow. "I'm… not familiar with that."

"Because nobody is. Besides those in the program. Stands for super plasmoid drive."

"Super plasmoids?"

"Take the properties of the former and square them."

Kit just stares at me. "It sounded like you just said to square plasmoids."

"I did."

"But that's… that's…"

"Impossible?"

"I was thinking more like insane. Anything's possible."

"Yeah, well, that's pretty much what we all thought too when NUESSA's physics lab brought us the research. But it checked out. Moreover, it worked, at least in the lab. Took them five years to develop a modified containment field to handle all the energy. And even then, we couldn't let the plasma reach max levels." I pause long enough to make sure Kit's listening and to see if he'll connect the dots himself.

"You mean, the X-10 wasn't outfitted to handle a full reaction?" His brain works for a second. "Is that what happened?"

I rub the back of my neck, my real neck—the virtual one doesn't ache when I think about whiplash. "It's… complicated."

"Well un-complicate it, Cap!"

Yeah, Jericho. Do what hundreds of specialists and untold millions of armchair critics couldn't: explain what went wrong in the worst moment of your life.

I take a deep breath. Annnd the story is about to start hurting. "We'd arrived back at *Astraea* following the primary burn sequence. Finished uploading all the results and got the green light from Command to continue to the second phase."

"Super plasmoids."

I nod. "Only 1 percent thrust. We were cleared up to 3, but I didn't want to take any chances. Always leave plenty of safety margin."

"Right. Sure, sure."

"So I decide to pass the controls to Captain Mc-Cormick. She was the better pilot anyway, and I wanted to be in engineering to watch the reaction mass."

"But I thought you were at the helm?"

He's perceptive. "We'll get to that."

Kit nods at me nervously. If he had popcorn right now, he'd hardly have time to chew the handfuls stuffed in his mouth. I hope he remembers that people died on this flight. "And then?"

"Well, we're all strapped in, and I'm back with Lieutenant Hasan Khaled as close to the containment shielding and diagnostics as I can get. If anything goes wrong, I'm the one who makes the call to abort."

"Totally."

"If we were to perform the same six point eight g burn with max super plasmoid thrust, we'd experience over 136 g's. You know what that would do to a human, right?"

"Splat, man! Like a soggy pancake dropped on a rock and then hit by an iron pan so hard that—"

"Okay. Just relax." His enthusiasm's starting to wear on me.

"Sure, sorry, Cap. Keep going."

"We reduced the acceleration time to something more manageable."

"Sixty seconds?"

"Exactly."

Kit seems pleased with himself.

"Our bodies had already taken a pretty punishing twenty minute ride out and back, so we needed to stay below eight g's, but even that would be tough with the SPD—like trying to retrain a raging bull. The drive is designed to run hot by nature. Wants to go…"

Memories flash in my head. I squeeze my eyes shut and then blink them away.

"Cap? You okay?"

"Fine. Anyway, restricting acceleration and keeping it within one minute equates to just 1.1 percent of the system's power—well within safety margins, and we'd still be able to see the super plasmoids in action."

The memories come back again, faster this time— so quick that I almost want to stop telling the story. I also recognize that some of the data is missing, like my brain has already started to selectively delete chunks of time, synthesizing what I heard, saw, and felt down to the bare necessities. The shrinks said it was to be expected with PTSD. But then I'm also getting flashbacks of stuff that others tried to push on me. All the cross examiners and their false recreation models. The verb interviewers and their echo chamber of baited questions dangling like hooks for the watching masses. Hell, even my own father had his understanding of what went down. All the pseudo facts try puffing up their chests again, attempting to make me believe that they're real. But they're not. I know. I was there, even if some of the truth is growing foggy.

"If you need to stop," Kit says with a hand on my shoulder.

But I shake my head. I need to do this. He needs to know.

"Everything was fine at first. Khaled sat across from me, monitoring in V-cog while I stayed in the real, watching the backup monitors. McCormick and Kasongo were clear up front. Yang in nav, Müller in comms—everything was green. Even though we were just above the previous six point eight g's, you could feel the energy in the ship… like it just wanted to go, you know?"

Kit's knees bounce up and down.

Here comes the pain.

"I first noticed something was wrong twenty-four seconds into our outbound run. The acceleration rate crept over 1.1363 percent of max. At those speeds, you calculate to the ten-thousandth of a percent; we built the tolerances that fine." A shiver goes up my spine. "So alarm bells are going off in my head, and the value starts growing logarithmically. It happened so fast…

Next thing I know, the Ebra-Drive is pushing eight g's. Then nine. The mass reaction reducers aren't kicking in."

"So you abort."

I take a deep breath. "Yeah. In V-cog, I order a reaction shutdown and verify with Khaled. Practiced it a hundred times. But he's shouting in Arabic, then English. The drive isn't responding to abort protocols. I switch over to manual and order reaction termination, but the drive still isn't responding. By this point, we're pushing ten g's, which is more than you ever want to feel. We're trained for it, and we have base edits to account for some of that pressure, but that doesn't make it a picnic."

Kit's stopped fidgeting. His eyes are glued to my face, just like the jury's were. The swarms of pixies. The floods of spectators outside the courthouse in Oslo. I can't handle the attention, so I look ahead at *Astraea*, but even she seems to stare back at me with unwavering eyes.

"It's a strange thing to have your finger on the eject button of a fifty-billion coin project. A decade of work. More if you count the theoretical research. And then there's the thousands of people who've made this their life, and you have it all right there under your finger. You're about to destroy the investment, wondering if you've done enough to justify the action you're taking.

"The crazy part is that I remember processing that. Time really did slow down, at least for me, and there I was rationalizing if this was the right thing to do. But in the end, none of our physicists or engineers or project managers were in jeopardy. They were all back on *Astraea* or in Mission Control. They'd recover. The people whose lives were on the line were my crew. So I did it. I pushed the button."

When Kit grabs my arm, I recoil and almost punch him in the head.

"Christ, Kit!"

"Sorry. You just… spaced out there."

My heart rate has spiked. Maybe this wasn't such a good idea after all.

Several seconds pass with me trying to get my pulse under control.

Kit lowers his voice and asks, "What happened after that?"

I run a hand across my face. "The ship's ejection system blew all corresponding crew hatches, at least that's what the logs initially recorded. The X-10 had additional pressure in order to launch the team away from the engine exhaust as the ship continued accelerating beyond us. Most people don't consider the engine's heat output."

Tears are welling up in my eyes, but I don't care. I've come this far, and I want Kit to know it all, at least from my point of view.

"Every system on that ship had been designed, peer-reviewed, and then built with redundancies. Checked, cross-checked… But every system has possible points of failure. Because we're human. And, ultimately, so are our systems. It just so happened that we had two failures that day: the mass reaction regulators and the ejection system.

"I didn't know anything was wrong until well after I came to. I'm strapped to my chair with only my visor between me and forever, still carrying the *Perseverant*'s speed along with the ejection thrust vector away from the ship. The chair had auto-rotated and just started applying reverse thrust when Command hailed me. They said the rescue vessel was on the way and would intercept me in twenty-six hours. When I asked about the others, they didn't respond. At least not right away.

"Müller's beacon was vaporized when he couldn't get clear of the burn radius. His chair failed to engage the pressure booster. Yang's hatch released a split second after his chair fired, crushing his head and neck. Sensors later reported that Kosango and McCormick's chairs never fired. They sat there as the *Perseverant* just kept… kept accelerating."

"And Hasan Khaled?" Kit asks in a reverent tone.

"He got out. We even had a lock on his beacon. But his reverse thrusters never engaged, and no one was able to catch up with him. That's the problem when you're flying the fastest vessel ever made." I choke on something and clear my throat. "I talked to Hasan as long as IR would let me. Said I was sorry so many times that he swore at me and threatened to shut down comms. Said it was all worth it though, especially if we were one step closer to saving our species. I told him we were, and that I'd spend the rest of my life making sure of it. Then… his signal just… faded out. And he was gone."

"I'm so sorry, Cap." Kit's body shudders once, and then he looks up. "About the trial, I don't understand what you did wrong."

"According to the attorneys for the families who sued me and NUESSA, leaving the helm to my second officer was gross negligence."

"But you were mission commander."

It was the same line my defense attorneys used. It had kept me from being sued in the civil case and from jail in the criminal trial, but not from being fired. I smile sadly at Kit. "Their attorneys argued that had I been where I was supposed to be, none of this would have happened. Some even went so far as to accuse me of sabotaging the ejection system to ensure that I was the only survivor."

"Why on Earth would you do that?"

"To grandstand, they said. To secure my name in lights."

"That's completely insane!"

I nod and take a breath. "But people don't think straight when their family members die. And attorneys? Well, we all know about them. Everyone knew the trial was a sham, of course, all backed by the Solum Terram. No offense."

"None taken."

"You're talking about the wealthiest politicast on the planet, and they had no problem dragging my name through the mud."

Kit's eyes grow wide. "Sallsworth?"

"Sallsworth," I repeat. "When it looked like the judge was going to dismiss the case, he surprised everyone by blaming the crew for incompetence, not just me, and then used the accident as his poster child for why humanity is wrong for continuing system settlement and looking for an exoplanet."

"I remember that now." Kit stares at me. "The victim's families didn't respond?"

"They tried. Probably felt pretty betrayed, I imagine. But Sallsworth has inroads with enough verb pirates that those complaints never reached the public. And neither the Preservationists nor the Viatoribus would play the families against another politicast like Sallsworth had done, so there was no backfire. It all just went away."

"But you still got banned from returning to space."

I nod. "While the criminal trial was thrown out, the public outcry required that NUESSA make concessions. They were already under a lot of pressure, and every cause needs their sacrificial lamb."

"You."

"Yeah. It was a matter of convenience." I let out a sigh, but it doesn't lift the weight. "Truth be told, I didn't want to go back into space then anyway. I think that made Eric Johnson's job even easier. They got to take a stand, and I got to put distance between me and the accident. But I didn't expect the public to be so cruel, nor the politicasts. That's naiveté for you."

"Cruel?"

I give him a soft chuckle. "'Who'd you piss off?' Remember that?" It was the first thing Kit asked me when I boarded his ship.

He laughs. "I guess the answer was a lot of people."

"When you're a hero, everyone wants you. But the world always needs a new whipping boy, and public opinion turns faster than you can imagine. Anyway, after the investigation, there wasn't enough evidence to convict me. But there was a loud call for me to be banned from space. NUESSA eventually agreed. So I was a Viatoribus with nowhere to go."

"Except High Top."

"My dad pulled some strings."

"How?"

"Believe it or not, he was a LACH pilot."

He snaps his fingers. "Which is how you learned to fly so young! *That's* why you seemed a bit rusty. You cut your teeth on low-altitude cargo haulers for High Top Uranium Corporation."

"That and racing RDX-60s on the weekends."

A smirk creeps across his face. "Coulda' fooled me with how you tried to take off though."

"It'd been a while."

"Surrre." He thinks for a second. "But if your pops was a captain—presumably journeyman?"

"Master."

Kit's eyes widen. "Then how'd you get stuck with me? No offense."

"He still had a son who was a Viatoribus."

"Wait. He wasn't?"

"He inked out."

"No!"

I nod. "About a year before the accident. Said he didn't like where things were headed, and he wanted to focus on Earth's recovery. Told me I should do the same before I got hurt, or worse."

Kit runs a hand through his hair. "Holy biscuits."

"Yeah."

After a few moments, Kit asks, "Then why all this? Why come back up here and offer to help Johnson and the people who betrayed you?"

"I don't feel like they betrayed me. They did what they thought was best, and so did I. If anything, it was Sallsworth and the Solum Terram. Nah. Coming back up here is about Hasan and the promise I made to him."

"To spend the rest of your life saving humanity."

"That's the one."

Kit lays a hand on my shoulder again. "You're a good man, Captain Fox."

"I'm not so sure."

"Your crew wouldn't have flown with you if they didn't believe the same as me."

That puts a lump back in my throat. I barely manage a thank you and then tip my chin toward *Astraea*. "Wanna get our first look of the hull before we dock?"

"Totally, Cap. For Hasan."

"For Hasan."

OUR BRIEF CIRCUIT of *Astraea*'s outer hull reveals nothing beyond what we'd already seen on the public coverage. So we dock as instructed along the second transport circumference, known as the bravo ring, two kilometers up from section one's massive zero-g transportation hub with its central tower and hundreds of docking legs.

The explosion has created higher-than-normal ship traffic as vessels ferry people, supplies, and security on and off the station. I even spot a Space Marine vessel, which looks out of place on the civilian station. The increased activity forces us to the secondary docking location, but truth be told, I don't mind the hassle of landing on the one-g position. It keeps us out of *Astraea*'s main transport lanes and ensures that we stay away from the crowds, which is fine by me.

After climbing out *Abigail*'s top hatch and up the airlock ladder, Kit and I find ourselves in a cargo bay on the ag level. Various crews are coming and going, but only one person is paying us any attention. A man in his mid-forties, I'm guessing, unless base editing has kept him from showing his age, waves at us. He's wearing the black and orange Station Command uniform and NUESSA hat. "Captain Jericho Fox?"

"Let's just keep it to Knight," I say as we shake hands.

"My name is Lieutenant Lance Forsythe, and I'll be your escort for the duration of your stay aboard the *Astraea*. How was your trip up?"

"Smooth and uneventful." I cast Kit a sarcastic smile.

"Excellent. Under Director Johnson's orders and Captain Mombawe's supervision, I have been assigned to help you in your investigation however you deem necessary for the duration of your stay. This includes any and all access to the station's systems, archives, and personnel. Is there anything I can do for you immediately?"

"Any chance you have another cap?"

"Of course." He pulls the one off his head and hands it to me.

I adjust the band and put the hat on, making sure the brim covers as much of my eyes as I can without looking too suspicious. "Thanks."

"My pleasure. Where would you prefer to begin? Your options include the data center, blast damage on the main and ag levels, the suspected culprit currently in custody, and the—"

"Suspected culprit? You already have someone?"

"Yes. As soon as word came from Director Johnson's office that NUESSA suspected foul play, a station scientist was transferred from our possession to Space Marine custody on account of alleged terrorism."

That certainly escalated quickly. I'm feeling a bit over my head with what to do next since this is my first official investigation. I'm no cop. But I do know logic and experimentation, and Eric has put his trust in me—something I don't take lightly, because god only knows how long that will last. In the blink of an eye, I could be back in Helsinki doing Sallsworth's bidding until I save enough to get out. Time to make this opportunity count.

"Well, my orders are to get to the root of the accident. This certainly seems like it's fast becoming a bombing. So, if you all have a suspect, then let's start there. We can look at the site after that."

"As you wish, Knight." But Forsythe hesitates and looks at my uniform.

"Something I can help you with?" I ask.

"Are you certain both of you wouldn't like to change into the station's apparel?"

I don't have to look down at the Solum Terram logo on my shoulder to know what he's insinuating. I also can't commiserate with him on just how much I want to be free of the filigree on my suit and the ink on my palm—the NUE would have me arrested before my work here even began.

"I would like to remain in my politicast's uniform," I say, not meaning a word of it.

"Understood. I will attempt to deflect for you as much as I can, if that's desirable. And, given your particular history with the station and NUESSA as a whole, I'll do my best to help keep you from the public eye."

"I'm grateful. Thanks."

Forsythe straightens his uniform. "I'll request for the suspect to be transferred to an interrogation room now. We'll be there in about fifteen minutes. Shall we, gentlemen?"

"Lead the way."

EVELYN

Rook came through. I don't know how, and I'm not gonna ask. But I am grateful.

We exit the lateral lift at section fifteen and start heading for the command complex that contains *Astraea*'s bridge. There are two security checkpoints before we make it to the main building—a glossy white ten-story structure bearing the NUESSA logo in a barely discernible matte finish. Flags of all three nation-states sway at half mast in the gentle morning breeze on the roof while a pair of oversized flags for the legacy hab skirt either side of the entrance.

The final set of guards waves Rook, me, and my two armed escorts into the building after V-recs clear. Then the sergeant leads us across the vaulted lobby, drawing looks from passersby, and continues on to the elevator bank.

Once we're inside the lift, he orders my shackles removed. "You're not planning on escaping anymore, right, Dr. Park?"

"I wouldn't dream of it."

He winks at me as my two minders stow the binders

on their kit. Feels good to have my wrists and ankles free again.

"So who are we meeting with? The XO?"

"I got you three mikes with Captain Mombawe."

"Three what?"

"Minutes."

"Really?"

"I told you I'd get your request sent upstairs. Apparently he was eager to see you too but said we had to make it fast."

"Three mikes," I repeat to myself. No pressure, Evelyn. You got this. "Thank you, Sergeant."

"Thank me if it gets you what you need."

We ride the rest of the way in silence. I'm grateful to Rook for what he's done. I can't imagine it was easy either, and I'm not about to jeopardize his career by making a scene or trying to escape. Thanks to our shared birthright, I owe him. As does the whole of the Sentia Aux.

I've often thought that the politicasts do more harm than good, working to foment unrest in the guise of ensuring peace. All the segregation and ideological isolation seems backward to me. Then again, I've seen what immature humanity does when they disagree. Maybe that's why I like being up here—too much, probably. And yet, I want to save our species… just not their polemics. However, the system is too deeply entrenched to change now, not without major unrest again, and we haven't recovered from the last bout yet. Plus, if we do push the frontiers, humanity can segregate and isolate itself to its heart's content. The philosophers have long-theorized that half our problems would be solved if everyone just spread out.

Inside the command complex, the lift doors part

and we step into a dimly lit security lobby. Two station guards stiffen when they see the Marines.

"Master Sergeant Farooq reporting to Captain Abraham Mombawe as ordered," Rook says.

The lead guard's eyes blink as he checks V-cog without taking his attention off me and the three suits of armor. "You're clear to enter."

Rook nods and leads the way. We travel through two more sets of security doors and finally step onto *Astraea*'s bridge.

I'm a science officer—an astrophysicist through and through. What impresses me are supernovas and black holes, and supernovas being shredded apart by black holes in stellar tidal disruptions and spaghettification. I've never been one to get wrapped up in command centers and hardware. But being on *Astraea*'s bridge? Even I have to admit it's awe inspiring.

While most control rooms of any vessel in space are primarily driven by virtual cognizance, all legacy habitation cylinders utilize holographic and physical interfaces in conjunction with V-cog for redundancy. Every officer in the command center is put through rigorous testing and monthly reviews to ensure that they're at peak performance mentally, emotionally, and physically. With the welfare of over a third of a million people at stake, it's no wonder.

The number of holo screens, control interfaces, and glass display monitors is dizzying. Rook leads us to the edge of the split-level balcony-style room. It's kept dimly lit, making the sea of colors all the more vibrant. My previous visits here found a quiet and calm crew. But now the space is a beehive of activity directed by an unseen conductor who sustains the constant thrum of station life following an explosion.

On the main floor below, I spot the XO who nods at Rook, says something to the captain, and then points our way. In turn, Mombawe sees me and tilts his head for us to join him in his quarters. We move down a curved staircase to the right, emerge onto the main floor, and then double back under the balcony to the private room.

"The detainee to see you, Captain," Rook says in a professional tone. "Would you like us to wait outside?"

"Please," says Mombawe, seated at his desk. "Dr. Park is a friend and no threat to me."

"We'll be standing by, sir." Rook exits with the other two Marines, and the doors slide shut.

"It's good to see you, Evelyn," he says at last, gesturing toward one of two leather chairs. Mombawe is like a mountain—stoic and imposing, but never pretentious. "I only wish it was under better conditions."

"As do I, Abraham. I'm sorry to take you away from the emergency. I won't be long."

He doesn't respond verbally, just inclines his head.

"Contrary to what you might suppose, I'm not here to plead my innocence."

"I suppose no such thing. This all seems like a terrible misunderstanding."

"Indeed. I'm here to ask that *Astraea*'s elliptical command authority be restored to the lab."

He looks surprised and produces a holo screen on one side of his oak desk. "It was revoked?"

"Yes. Emergency protocols have locked us out of the flight systems. We've even lost power to the equipment."

After a moment's consideration, he says, "That's to be expected. I'm sure my people are working on it."

I slide forward on my seat. He doesn't know. "Have you… spoken to Lemuel?"

"No." He raises an eyebrow at me. "Why?"

I can barely contain my excitement, but I manage to stay composed. "We got it, Abraham. Parallax delivered a positive ID last night."

The mountain of a man doesn't betray the least bit of surprise. "You're certain?"

"Ninety-nine point seven three one percent."

Mombawe just stares at me. For all I know, he's doing jumping jacks inside.

I'm not sure if I should wait for him to respond or just keep going. I ultimately opt for the latter. "We only captured the first few seconds of the anomaly when the hull ruptured."

"You think there's more?"

"Much more, yes. We have to keep the work going. But I think that Stamos is purposefully keeping us locked out."

"Who?"

I wave my hand. "A chief inspector with an ego trip."

"That'll be the least of your worries now, Evelyn." He nods toward the Marines outside. "Johnson has evidence that this is a terrorist attack, and you've made the top of the list somehow."

"You know I'd never do such a thing."

"I do. But you're no longer under my jurisdiction. My recommendation is that you keep your head down, let the investigation play out, and comply with the people they're sending up."

"Do you know them?"

Mombawe's lips tighten. "One of them, yes."

"That bad?"

"I'm surprised, is all. But the man Johnson tapped is good."

"Meaning…"

"He'll clear you eventually if you're innocent. Just don't push him. He'll be thorough, but fair."

"Fine. Never mind me anyway. What about the lab?"

"I'll do my best to restore power and ellip-co-auth as soon as I can. Your team should be able to resume their work shortly."

"Can you relay that to them?"

"Of course. Can't you get help on this from the other stations?"

"They're not equipped with the same sensor array or else we would have already."

"I see. Well, there you have it."

While this isn't entirely the answer or timing I was hoping for, I still feel as though a significant weight has come off my shoulders. "Thank you, Abraham."

"Certainly." His eyes flutter as he slips into V-cog. A few seconds later, he focuses on my face. "Seems you're in high demand."

"I beg your pardon?"

"The investigating engineer Johnson's sent has just docked and is already asking to see you." He stands and offers his hand. "I wish you the best, Evelyn."

"Thank you."

"And, if I may say, congratulations. I wish the circumstances surrounding your discovery were better, but they don't tarnish the magnitude of the find."

"No, they don't. People may forget me, but they'll never forget this."

"I don't suppose they will." He waves for the sergeant to return. "I'll get word to your team. Stay safe."

SECTION fifteen's main precinct is less than a five minute walk from the command complex. Rook has me back in binders for appearance's sake, and the two minders carry their weapons high across their chests while we cross to the security building. Since this is the hab's busiest area, second only to the main transportation hub on section one, the sight of me being paraded toward the precinct is drawing quite a crowd. I don't know if word has circulated about my alleged involvement or not, but people certainly seem interested in me and my Marine escort.

As soon as we're inside the building—my second time here in less than two days—one of the higher-ups leads Rook down a hall and into an interrogation room. Again, I can't imagine it's been used very much—I'd say never by the looks of it. And I should know. Last time I was in this position on Earth, the room smelled of urine, vomit, and cigarette smoke, so I'll take *Astraea* any day.

"I'm required by military law to stay with you, Dr. Park," Rook says once the door seals shut with the other two locker jockeys standing guard outside.

I catch Rook's reflection in the large mirror that everyone knows isn't a mirror. "I understand. And... thank you, Master Sergeant." I used his rank because I know I'm not supposed to be overly familiar with security, especially when I'm the prisoner, but I feel indebted to him for getting me a meeting with Captain Mombawe. "I appreciate you being here with me."

"Just doing my job."

But we both know it's more than that.

Less than thirty seconds later, an officer opens the

door and lets a man through. The newcomer wears a blue flight uniform and a black and orange *Astraea* Station cap pulled low over his eyes. Then I spot a logo on his shoulder: Solum Terram. Shit.

"Dr. Evelyn Park?" he asks.

"That's me."

He takes a seat. Seems confident enough but out of place at the same time. And why wouldn't he? The whole station is anathema to everything he believes. Which begs the bigger question: why would Johnson ask an ST investigator to spearhead this query?

"My name is… Knight," he says at last.

"Did you forget?"

He furrows his brow. "I'm here by special request of Director Johnson with the Space and Science Administration."

I wave my bound hands toward his shoulder. "I think you got your politicasts mixed up there, Mr. Knight."

"I'm investigating the alleged bombing of *Astraea* Station, as I'm sure you're aware."

"And they sent you? Not exactly an unbiased appraiser." I remember Mombawe's warning, but I just can't help myself.

"My politics do not inform my science, Doctor."

"Is that so? Because the ink on your palm certainly says otherwise." There I go again.

He closes his fingers into a fist. Interesting. Was that shame? Or just him trying to move on? Whatever it is, I'm pushing some buttons here. Sure, I want to treat him with at least some respect if he really is from Johnson's office—don't bite the hand that feeds you. But something feels off. "How can I be of service, Mr. Knight? Or have you already made up your mind?"

"I won't draw any conclusions until I've seen all the evidence. Right now, I'm starting with the person who local authorities have in custody. Your file says you're a damn good astrophysicist. Though, if I'm being honest, I'm not quite sure what you have to gain in rupturing *Astraea*'s hull. Mind filling me in?"

I narrow my gaze. This guy doesn't seem like he's playing me. There's a level of guilelessness behind his eyes—when I can see them under that brim—that's almost impossible to fake. I wasn't the best street rat, but I could usually tell when someone was lying to me. There's just… something in his eyes… something almost… *sad*.

"You want to know what I have to gain, Inspector Knight?"

"Just Knight. And I'm not an inspector."

"The answer is *nothing*, because I didn't do it. Some prick on level thirty has it out for me, and I'm sick and tired of being guilty until proven innocent." I look back at Rook. "No offense."

"None taken."

"You know each other?" Knight asks Rook—funny putting their names together like that. Then Knight's eyes spot something near the Marine's waist. I'm guessing it's his service pistol. But then the sergeant hides his hand with his double rings.

Knight seems to let the connection go and looks back to me. "I'm just here to find the truth and play a hunch."

My conscience tells me to shut up and play along. The sooner I do, the sooner I can get back to the lab. And I was planning on being contrite, just like Mombawe asked. But that was before they introduced me to a Solum Terram agent.

"It doesn't add up," I say at last.

"Excuse me?"

"They sent you, a wolf in wolf's clothing, up here on a hunch? To investigate an act that any of your people would have gladly signed up to do in secret? I don't think so."

"Dr. Park, let me assure you that—"

"The Director of NUESSA doesn't send people out with hunches. Especially not Solum Terram. No, you're somebody special to Johnson, I just can't figure out who."

"Dr. Park, let me conduct my inquiry, and then you'll be free to return to holding until we resolve this."

I narrow my gaze at him. "So what is it about you? Why does Eric trust you so much?"

Knight takes a breath and resumes his line of questioning. "Did you have any involvement with the explosion on section sixteen?"

"No."

"And, assuming your plea of innocence—"

"I was framed."

"—is true, do you have any alibis who can help substantiate your whereabouts leading up to the attack?"

"I do, but if you're like the last inspector, you'll believe the data logs over anything I have for you."

"Data logs can be hacked, Dr. Park."

Is he trying to bait me? I don't remember all the terms Sam used when describing the process of manipulating *Astraea*'s network, but I think I have enough. "Even if they can be hacked, there'll be traces of system kernels and... well... artifacts of... log issues."

He sits back, folds his arms, and smiles at me. "So you're not great with computer code."

"Of course I'm not. I hunt stardust with massive telescopes for a living."

"Alibis?"

"Dr. Sam Collins. And I'll have you know that we were in the detention block of this very precinct together when the explosion occurred. And before that I was under house arrest."

"Which you broke out from via your balcony, if I'm not mistaken, only to be discovered at the precise location where investigators believed Hodges was pushed from in the power level."

I lean forward. "Because we were trying to do the inspector's job for him. The guy's an asshat."

Knight raises an eyebrow at me from under his brim and then looks down. He'd be alright if he wasn't such an asshat himself. Damn Solum Terram. Shame too. He has that familiar timeless baby face. "Listen, inspector."

"I told you, I'm not—"

"I realize that Director Johnson has some sort of special trust in you or something. But you'd save him, yourself, and me a whole lot of time if you'd just let me get back to my lab so we can continue our work."

"You're that dedicated to it?"

I laugh. "You wouldn't understand."

"Try me."

We stare each other down for a moment. I keep thinking he's gonna look away. Most men do. But this guy keeps his eyes locked on mine to the point that it's starting to feel a bit uncomfortable. "I work for SESI."

"I'm aware."

"Annnd…"

"And?"

"And we located an extrasolar anomaly right around

the time of the explosion. I have zero reason to sabotage this station. This is my life's work up here. Then an ST heavy comes in here and accuses me of… " I try to continue but the man's whole countenance has changed to the point that it's distracting.

He leans forward, hands on the table. "What do you mean, extrasolar anomaly?"

I squint at him. "Oh, no you don't. You're not verb-spinning this with your anti-space media juggernauts. No way."

"Parallax?"

That stops me cold. "What?"

"Did Parallax make a positive ID?"

Either this man knows his enemy better than I do, or…

Or he's not who he says he is.

"How do you know about Parallax?" I ask.

"Doesn't everybody?"

"Not some wanker from the Solum Terram. And they definitely don't know what a positive ID means either. Do you?"

The inspector not-inspector licks his lips. He's hiding something. "What star system?"

"Uh-uh. No way. Not until you explain what you know."

He laughs. "You're the one in custody."

I wink. "And you're the one I'm interrogating."

There's a knock on the door.

"Come in," Knight calls.

"Cap, we got something," says a mousey looking kid with wiry hair. He freezes when he sees Rook. "Whoa, locker jockey. Hey, big fella."

"Well who might you be?" I ask.

His eyes snap toward me. He blushes. "Wow. You're *really* pretty."

"Didn't answer my question."

"My name is—"

Knight stands. "We'll continue this later."

"Why put it off?" I reply. "Mind if I tag along?"

"Yes, actually, I do."

"Why?"

Knight squares with me. "Because until I prove you're not guilty—"

"Or guilty," the younger man interjects but thinks better of it when I scowl at him. "Not that you are, of course. I just… It's the alternative outcome, right? Uh… You know what? I'm gonna shut up now and wait outside."

"It's probably best to keep you away from the investigation," Knight concludes.

"That's fair," I reply. "But you do want to know what we found out there, right?"

Knight works his jaw. "I'm curious, yes."

"And the sooner you can vindicate me, the sooner both of us can get on with our lives. So the way I see it, you could use 'a damn good astrophysicist' working your case with you, and I could do without being cooped up again."

After a few more tense few seconds, his eyes soften. "Okay. But you're working with me, not against."

"Deal. That said, being on the same team would be a whole lot easier if I knew about your politicast and why you—"

"With me or against me?" he repeats slowly.

Seeing as this is my best chance to get out of custody and back to the lab, I relent. "With. One request though?" Knight raises an eyebrow at me, but I redirect to Rook. "Any chance I get my multitool back?"

"I'll see what I can do," the master sergeant says. "So long as it's okay with him." He tips his head toward Knight.

"Fine. Just make it fast." He turns to mousey face. "Lead the way, Kit."

20

JERICHO

"Why do you keep checking the time?" Park asks me as we walk toward the lat lift that will carry us to the damaged area of section sixteen.

"Who says I'm checking the time?"

"You've jumped into V-cog three times since we left the precinct, and you just glanced at the clock tower twice—once from the front, once from the back."

I look at Master Sergeant Farooq. "Is she always this persistent?"

He gives me a half smile. Marines. Ever the stoics. I glance at the binders on his hip. I told him to keep them off her for now, but that doesn't mean I won't change my mind later. She's feisty as hell and twice as sharp.

"I want to make sure we catch the culprit, is all," I reply to Park at last.

"Before he or she strikes again."

"Yup."

"You sure it's not you?" she asks.

"Let's just stay focused, okay?"

I'm starting to regret my decision to bring her along. Park's too smart for her own good. But that's also why I want her with us. Big problems are best solved with more than one brain, and hers is one of the biggest I know. I still can't believe some asshole thinks *the* Dr. Evelyn Park of SESI is a conspirator. Lady's a living legend… if not a little crazy in the head. But I can't fault her for being passionate. And curious. It's a wonder she hasn't made me yet. Then again, we did work in two totally different branches of the Infinita program.

And then there's the matter of her alleged discovery. If Park really has received an intentional signal from beyond our solar system, then I want to know about it. Hell, the whole human race is gonna wanna know about it. My Solum Terram affiliation requires that I act pessimistically—uninterested at least. But even Nigel Sallsworth would be curious about extrasolar sentient life, right? So I have Kit working on a few things for me behind the scenes.

"What about you?" she asks Kit.

He snaps out of V-cog and puts a hand on his chest in surprise. "Me?"

She bats her dark eyelashes at him. "You have time for a drink later?"

Kit opens his mouth, but I stop him from saying anything. "Don't answer that."

He does anyway. "I mean, I was gonna say yes, but if we're both too busy then I could always take a rain check and you can call me when—"

"Kit."

"Right. Sorry."

Our escort, Lieutenant Forsythe, waits for us at the lift. As soon as we're all in, he activates the pod, and we accelerate down *Astraea*'s length one klick. I'm thankful that it's a short ride because, just as Dr. Park pointed out, time is of the essence. I'm not telling her that, of course. But that doesn't change the truth of the matter.

In a perfect world, Kit and I solve this case and get Nigel's errand done, then I get accepted back into NUESSA by week's end. Okay, so maybe that's wishful thinking. Point is, I have options again—some control over my destiny. And I'm feeling good. No sense letting anyone ruin my mood.

Of course, they might not have to: the results, or lack thereof, could ruin it all by themselves. My hope is that whatever Kit and the lieutenant have uncovered helps move the investigation forward. Christ knows I'm gonna need way more than the hull breach explanation I gave Johnson to raise eyebrows and prove there's a killer on this station.

Forsythe inputs an override code to open the doors when we stop at sixteen. The entire section's been locked down on account of the disaster. Authorized personnel only. When the doors part, I spot the jagged wound on *Astraea*'s utopian physique about seven klicks up the curve to the east. Where once there were smooth white buildings nestled between rippling trees and blue estuaries, there now hangs a gash whose hemorrhaging was shut down only by the emergency containment systems. This is the closest I've gotten so far, and it definitely seems bigger than it did from *Abigail* or any of the verb coverage.

A sleek nine-seater transport vehicle pulls beside us, and Forsythe directs us to load in. He takes shotgun while Corporal Geller, Kit, and I sit across from Park, the sergeant, and the second corporal, Grabowski.

I pull the cap a little lower over my eyes as the driver passes through several makeshift security gates. We must be quite the sight with three Space Marines, two Solum Terram pilots, and *Astraea*'s chief astrophysicist.

As the cylinder seems to slowly rotate along the

horizon, Park leans across to me. "You're worried that they might make you, is that it?"

"Not sure what you're talking about."

"You're Jericho Fox."

Blood rushes to my face as I see the sergeant raise an eyebrow at me. But I push it all down, stay on my ass, and cross my arms as we pass a white medical tent. "And?" I ask her.

"And I'm just surprised to see you here, is all." She waits a moment, then adds, "Did you really think an ST uniform and a station cap were gonna keep you off people's radar?"

"The thought had crossed my mind."

She lets out a laugh, which kinda pisses me off. "Might want to work on spy craft before your next mission, Fox."

I catch movement from the front row and see Forsythe giving me a half smile too. I ignore it and ask him, "How much farther?"

"Two minutes."

I go back to watching our surroundings whizz by until Park says, "What I don't get is why you'd pick the ST to defect to. Preservationists, at least. But talk about not lying low. Hell, I'm surprised you haven't been thrown out an airlock already."

"I can have Master Sergeant Farooq return you to holding if you don't like the company."

"I didn't say that. Just trying to figure it all out." Park sits back and folds her arms. "I figured you'd have been mad after the trial. Granted, they didn't lock you up, which was a win. But when they didn't exonerate you completely? I can't imagine that made finding work in your field very easy." She taps the end of her nose with a finger. "Which means… the only way you could find a stable job was to switch sides. How am I doing so far?"

Kit leans over to me and whispers, "She's really good."

"Kit."

"Sorry."

The good doctor plays with a few strands of hair at her temple. "So if you're working for the ST, then that means NUESSA *really* wanted you up here. That's a whole lotta red tape. And why wouldn't they? Who better to investigate an explosion than the one and only Jericho Fox? Get it right, and you get reinstated, and Command comes out looking like heroes."

"Yeah," Kit says. "But get it wrong, and the Solum Terram has years of 'I told you so' street cred."

"Kit," I snap.

Park flashes him a pleased smile, then looks back to me. "Quite the gamble they've taken on you."

"Desperate times," I reply, looking away. She's making short work of my position. It's impressive, sure. But I don't like it. And it's dangerous.

"Still," she adds while tapping her nose again. "They'd need a plausible reason besides a terrorist in-vestigation to send you up here… Something benign that would pass inspection and appease the journalists if word ever got out—"

"Okay. You know what? That's enough. Look, I agreed for you to come along because I thought you might be able to help us. In fact, I know we can solve this faster if we work together. Which would also help prove your innocence and get you back to work. And in spite of whatever you think about me, I'm first and fore-most interested in figuring this damn thing out and stopping it from happening again. So, if you're willing to help, then help. But if you're only interested in giving me a hard time, then I'll just send you back to holding right now."

For someone who's not great at comebacks, that felt pretty damn good.

Likewise, Park looks like she's mulling everything over. Finally, her eyes soften. "Alright."

"Alright as in we're good to continue, or alright you wanna go back to holding?"

"Continue." Those same soft eyes dart around a few times while she chews on her lower lip. "Listen, I'm sorry for—"

"Being super pushy?" Kit offers.

She smiles at him. "Yeah, that. I've been treated pretty unfairly lately. I brought some of it on myself. Okay, maybe a lot of it. But regardless, I recognize I might be a bit on edge."

I bark out a laugh. "Ya think?"

She puts a hand on her chest. "I'm being accused of murder, Fox. And acts of terrorism against a mission I'd sooner die for than sabotage. And this... it just... it doesn't make any sense! Makes me so"—she balls her hands into fists—"so mad, ya know?"

"Yeah. Actually, I do know."

Her eyes catch mine and recognition dawns. Then she seems to let her anger melt away like snowflakes—ones *not* in Sallsworth's suite. "I do wanna figure this out with you and get back to my work. So, yes, let's do it."

THE VEHICLE SLOWS to a stop and Forsythe orders everyone out, but I'm not ready for the view of the station's damage when I turn around. I rode with my back facing forward to keep a low profile, and now I wished I hadn't.

A massive hole fifty some meters across yawns in front of us. The edges are rough and upturned, accented by twisted trussing and deck plates that attest to just how much force came from below. Mounds of turf, stonework, and parts of buildings are piled along the perimeter. And everywhere I look, rescue crews are sorting through the rubble and gathering the dead. The survivors have already been found; the rest is left to forensics.

The sight of it all takes me back to the X-10. People dying violently for the sake of space expansion. Only this one is far worse. I catch sight of a human hand in a blackened pile of rubble that rescuers still haven't retrieved.

I need to stay on task, so I turn to Kit and Lieutenant Forsythe before I end up in a state of mind that I don't like. "What did you have to show us?"

We follow them toward an orange station tent filled with gear and executive crew members—specialists mostly. Forsythe stops at a long table piled high with mobile lab equipment and what looks to be shrapnel from the explosion. Two techs stand aside as he gestures to a single fragment of blackened metal in a glass tray.

"A team found this embedded in the hull during your interview with Dr. Park."

I bend down and examine the artifact at the same time that Park does. Her shoulder bumps into mine, but she doesn't seem to notice.

"Looks like titanium," she says after a moment.

"Tungsten," I correct.

"That's right," Forsythe replies.

"What's special about this piece?" she asks the lieutenant.

"Well, for one, it doesn't belong anywhere near where it was found."

"That was a pretty powerful explosion," I say, playing devil's advocate as a means to expedite whatever point he wants to make. "Things get moved around."

"Yeah, but the ship's schematics don't show any tungsten in the blast radius."

"Curious," I admit. "But there are several reasons it could've found its way into the area besides ship composition. Tools, equipment… shoot, I have a tungsten knife back home."

"Expensive knife," Farooq says.

"The techs seem to think it was unusual enough to warrant a closer look," Forsythe adds.

"I appreciate that." Then something catches my eye. I lean in for a second look.

"What is it?" Park asks.

"You see there? Along the inner edge of the curve? It's melted, pretty badly actually." The more I study the artifact, the more my eye sees the deformation. I almost feel stupid that I didn't notice it before.

"It did just survive a massive explosion," she says.

"Yeah, but it's tungsten."

"I don't follow."

I look past Forsythe to one of the nearest techs and tap him on the shoulder. "Excuse me. Do you have a list of the chemical compounds you've picked up so far from the wreckage?"

"You want the whole list?"

"Just the particles that are compatible with things that go boom."

"Right." He nods and sorts through something in V-cog, then sends it to me. I thank him and slip into my lobby, inviting the rest of the team.

"Ummm. I'm still locked out here, people," Park says.

"It's okay, Sergeant," I add. "She can come in."

Farooq unlocks the comms restraint, and a second later Park joins me, Kit, Forsythe, and the three Marines in my V-cog lobby. I'm holding a tablet with the tech's findings on it. In real life, I hear him say, "These are only initial chemical tests. We'll need to get things up to the lab with the spectrometers before we have anything more conclusive. But they—"

"Got it. Thanks."

"Uh. No problem."

I don't mean to be rude with the guy, but we don't have time for a trip to the lab, and I have a hunch that I can find what I need without one anyway.

"Looks like highest concentrations are CH_4 and NH_4NO_3," Park says.

"I... I don't speak algebra too well," Kit says.

"Methane and ammonium nitrate," I reply for him. "Farts and fertilizer."

"Oh. Right."

Park chuckles at Kit, then adds, "If this is sabotage, it looks like the Tantum Terrae finally convinced the cows to revolt."

"Ha," Kit blurts out. "That's hilarious!"

I give him an unimpressed look. "She's kidding."

"I mean, yeah, I know. Sure. It's still funny though."

I scan the list one more time and still don't find what I want. "My guess? Whoever did this wants us to think it was from a system failure."

"Like the station is to blame," Park adds.

Farooq crosses his arms. "And you don't buy it?"

"Nope." I snap out of V-cog and go back to the piece of shrapnel. "Not for a second."

"You sound pretty sure of yourself," he adds.

"Maybe not of myself, but I *am* sure about material science."

"I don't follow."

"According to what the techs have found so far, all evidence points to a dangerous buildup and subsequent detonation of natural gases on the agriculture level exacerbated by fertilizers."

"Correct." Forsythe smooths his uniform. "Though, I should note, all this is extremely unlikely as *Astraea* has time-tested safety procedures to eliminate such risks. That said, in the absence of other evidence, it's… well, the most likely."

"Which is what they want us to think," I reply.

Forsythe squints at me, but it's Dr. Park who picks up my line of thinking first.

"Confirmation bias," she says beside me. "Even though you know it's not likely, it's still the only real solution you can come up with, so you stop looking for other possibilities."

Forsythe bristles. "Dr. Park, I can assure you that we're not ruling out—"

Park snaps her head toward me with a certain twinkle in her eyes. "So it wasn't methane or ammonium nitrate that did this?"

"Nope." I point everyone toward the shrapnel. "Tungsten is one of the toughest metals humanity has. So it would make sense to find it on a legacy hab. Except that, as your engineers have pointed out, Lieutenant, there wasn't any in the vicinity—at least according to the specs. So this piece is an outlier. But that's circumstantial. What's more interesting, however, is that tungsten's melting point is somewhere north of 3,000 degrees Celsius."

"I'm still not following you," Forsythe says. "You'll have to forgive me."

"Ammonium nitrate, even with some methane additives, won't push mercury north of 200 Celsius."

Park jumps in. "So, whatever deformed this piece of metal was a hell of a lot hotter."

"Nearly 3,000 degrees hotter," I add.

"What can do that?" Forsythe asks.

At the same time, Park and I both say, "Nuclear fusion." We share a smile.

I look away first. "My guess is that there's a whole lot more for your mass spectrometers to find on this piece of evidence."

"We can head up there, if you'd like," Forsythe says. "Take us twenty minutes. I just need to arrange—"

"No time, Lieutenant. I can do a quick test here that will tell me what I need to know."

"What kind of test?"

I look around the tent and start gathering the needed items. A wide-mouthed glass, a sponge to lodge in the bottom, a bottle of isopropyl alcohol, some contact cement, and access to the refrigerant on the sample freezer. The last thing I need is a piece of black vinyl. I glance at the tech's uniform, pat myself down for a knife, and then look around the tables.

"What do you need?" Park asks.

"Scissors."

She works at her thigh and then hands me a multitool. "This work?"

"Uh, yeah. Perfect." I take it and turn to the tech. "I'll get you another suit."

Once I have the needed items, I get to work with my science project

"What are you building?" There's a playful curiosity to Park's tone, which is refreshing.

"I'm making a cloud chamber to detect subatomic radiation. A simple particle detector will tell us if this tungsten has been anywhere near a radioactive metal."

"Radioactive?" Forsythe recoils. "Who said anything about that?"

I look up while stuffing the alcohol-soaked sponge into the glass. "I did." I quickly seal the mouth with the vinyl and contact cement. Then I place the glass upside down on the coolant tank and ask Kit for the tungsten in the tray.

"What's this gonna do?" he asks.

"Well, the alcohol just above the coolant should condense and form a supersaturated base layer. Dry ice would be faster, but we're on the clock."

"And then... what?"

"Then we should be able to see subatomic particles. Well, not the actual particles, of course—"

"But their trails through the condensation cloud," Park answers for me.

"Exactly." I stand up from the experiment and look at the lieutenant. "Can we dim the lights in here please? Maybe pull those side flaps shut too?"

He nods and shouts some orders. Next thing I know, we have as dark an environment as we're going to get. I wait for the alcohol to cool and shine a penlight into the chamber at an angle. We watch for a few moments. Then it happens: a tiny vapor trail shoots across the glass's mouth just above the black vinyl.

"There," Kit shouts. "I see one!"

"That's an alpha particle," I say. Two more appear as curves. "And those are electrons."

"So that's it then?"

Park shakes her head. "No. We're in space, kid. Even with *Astraea*'s shielding, we're being bombarded with subatomic particles constantly, mostly gamma and cosmic background radiation, to the tune of tens of thousands of particles per second."

"That sounds like it hurts," Kit replies.

"It does. Messes with DNA like you can't believe. But that's why you got base editing, so there's nothing to worry about."

Kit swallows so loudly I think the whole tent hears him.

"You did get your first-year preventative gene therapy, right?" she asks.

Kit puts two hands over his groin. "Uh. No, ma'am."

"Oh." She inclines her head toward his genitals. "You'll need more than two hands."

I grab the tray with the tungsten in it and bring it closer to the glass. As I do, more condensation trails streak through my improvised cloud detector. I pull it further away and they lessen; back again, and they increase.

Park stands up straight, stuffs her hands in her back pockets, and gives me a genuine smile. "Nice work, Captain Science."

"Thanks."

"So this proves what exactly?" Farooq asks.

"That this tungsten has not only been subject to heat high enough to deform it, but that it's also been blasted with alpha particles, most likely from uranium."

"Why uranium?" Forsythe asks.

"Well, for one, you don't need that much to make a big impact"—I gesture outside the tent—"case in point. For another, any Earth-first faction would have plenty of it at their disposal given their proximity to and relationship with several Solum Terram-supported mining operations."

"The extreme heat would also vaporize all criminal evidence," Farooq adds.

"All, but not *all*." Park gestures to the tungsten.

"Right," I add. "My guess is this was used to support the uranium core, or even help puncture it. Electromagnetic rail system trigger maybe."

"If it's so powerful, why didn't it succeed in taking the whole station out?" Farooq asks. "Better yet, why not just place it in the active plasma fusion generator. Not that I'm complaining."

And that's the twenty-trillion coin question—the thing that's been gnawing away at me since the news first broke. Now that I'm fairly certain I know the compound, everything is starting to make brutal, clinical, and sadistic sense, if there is such a thing. "This blast wasn't meant to kill everyone."

"Then what?" Forsythe asks.

I lift my hat and run a hand over my hair. "Terrorists like to incite fear—desperate need for survival, corporate pandemonium—stuff like that."

"I'm feeling a desperate need for survival." Kit raises a hand. "Anyone else?"

"But this is fear of another kind," I continue. "They're trying to lay low on purpose. Trying to keep their tracks covered."

"What do you mean?" Park asks.

I glance up at her and then pan to the others.

"They're trying to create fear about the station. About its integrity."

Park meets my eyes with a panicked look. "You think this isn't the only bomb?"

Which is exactly what I told Eric, but it was just a hunch then. Now, I'm feeling certain of it. "Lieutenant Forsythe, I recommend we abandon ship."

Forsythe's look of surprise is barely noticeable—a split-second flash suddenly reined in by years of Navy training. "I'll advise the captain."

"Isn't that what they want though?" Farooq adds. "Funnel everyone into a choke point and then detonate a second IED?"

"If this were a standard terrorist attack, yeah," I reply. "But they've got an agenda here that goes beyond shock and awe. These aren't Bemba Militia or Leonidas-X."

"But it could be," Kit says.

The sergeant shakes his head. "They would have claimed responsibility already."

"Then who?" Forsythe asks.

"The Tantum Terrae," Park says with no attempt to hide her disdain.

I give it a second to sink in for everyone and then run with her lead. "The Tantum are smarter than what we tend—than *spacers* tend to think about them." I have to toe the party line. "My bet is that whoever's overseeing this wants the attack to look as accidental as possible. At least for now. And if we want a shot at catching them, I think we'd better play along."

Farooq turns from me to Forsythe. "Sir, while I understand Mr. Fox's logic, I wish to advise the captain about the risks involved with such assumptions. If we order an emergency evacuation, it will make the pre-scribed routes prime targets."

"What if we do both?" Park interjects. All heads turn to her. "We could use the mandatory disembarka-tion alert instead of evacuation procedures. Then we get everyone off the ship in a more relaxed manner, and it would utilize non-official spacecraft, expediting and randomizing the process."

Farooq gives her an approving frown. "Not bad, Doctor."

"It'll also give us a little more time to track down whoever's behind this," I say. "This bomb came on board with someone, and they're clearly good at keeping themselves off the grid. But everyone makes mistakes." I feel all eyes on me with that comment. But I brush the guilt aside and turn to Dr. Park. Her eyes grow distant. No, that's not it. They get... *sad*. Because she won't be able to continue her work.

Damn.

I actually feel sorry for her now. For all of us. While I don't know anything beyond what she alluded to back in the interrogation room, I suspect a person of her cal-iber isn't making stuff up—not when you're one of the faces of the Infinita program. If anything, she's prob-ably shot down more speculation than not. Which I get: nothing screws up legitimate research faster than a litany of bogus claims.

Kit pings me in V-cog and steps into my lobby. "Got what you asked for, Cap." He hands me a manila folder —I like using the construct because it reminds me of the old spy movies. Plus, it's kinda cool to open one up and then play a video on the soft cardboard-like panel. The file is a two-minute montage of everywhere Dr. Evelyn Park was in the thirty-six hours leading up to

Hodges's death and section sixteen's detonation. I watch it at four times normal speed and scan the accompanying time stamps and proximity metadata on potential eyewitnesses. But interviewing them won't be necessary. I close the folder. "And the other thing?"

Kit gives me a thumbs-up and stupid grin. "It's real. At least according to what they know so far."

I thank him for his work and then slip back into the real.

"Did you do it, Dr. Park?" I ask flatly.

"Come again?"

"Did you murder Hodges and Del Toro and then detonate a uranium bomb on *Astraea* Station?" I get ready to wade through her protests, but she squares her shoulders with me instead.

"No," she says just as flatly.

"And did you and your team capture an anomalous signal from Kepler-1649c?"

"We did. Well, we were trying to."

"Then I see no reason to keep you here."

Her eyes get a hope-filled look to them. "You're... serious right now?"

"Based on the evidence we've been able to gather about your whereabouts with subsequent alibis and the testimony of your team, yes. I realize you won't have much time to finish what you started. But if it helps you salvage what you can, you're free to go." I verify with a look to the sergeant that I'm even allowed to do such a thing—all this sudden cross-politicast responsibility is new to me. But the sergeant doesn't protest. If anything, he seems happy, I think. Hard to tell with him.

Farooq says to me, "You're *apparent judicas* in the matter. Judge apparent."

"Well, there you go."

Park looks taken aback. "I'm… uh… Thank you, Mr. Fox."

"It's just Jericho."

She holds her hand out. "Just Evelyn."

We smile and shake.

Evelyn looks at the sergeant. "So does this mean all charges will be dropped, Rook?"

The Marine points at me again. "According to my orders, he's the boss, ma'am."

I give her a shrug. "There's too much exonerating evidence for anyone to keep you locked up for more than an hour, in my opinion. Whoever arrested you at first was being a dick."

Evelyn steps toward me and throws both arms around my neck in a highly unexpected outburst of whatever this is. I'm not complaining. Her hair smells like… well, like prison-grade shampoo. But it's the first time I've been hugged by a woman in a long time, so… Smells fine to me.

"Thank you," she whispers in my ear.

It sends a shiver down my neck. Shit. "You're welcome."

Evelyn seems to remember herself, pulls away, and then smoothes her uniform. Her cool exterior is back. She gives me a professional nod and then looks at Farooq. "Unless you're required to see me back to the lab—"

"Officially, you're no longer under Space Marine jurisdiction," he says.

"Then I recommend you stay with him"—she nods at me—"since it seems like he might need some body-guarding."

"I'm sure my CO will take that into consideration as events unfold."

"Right." Evelyn looks around, almost a bit unsure of herself, which seems unlike what I know of her up 'til now. But her timidness is quickly replaced with a sense of self-assuredness that propels her out of the tent and out of my life. Probably for the best.

"What would you like to do next, sir?" Forsythe asks as I watch Evelyn walk away.

"Let's, uh… start reviewing crew logs for the ag level, as well as the new passenger manifests for the last week."

"Sounds like a plan."

Kit puts one arm around my shoulders. "If she turns me down later, I'll send you her V-rec."

21

NEON

"IT's good to see you up and about," Neon said as Nigel exited his stone hut. She meant it too. While the Tantum Terrae's fierce underground leader had no qualms about killing anyone who stood in her way, Neon recognized that she still needed someone at the top of the Solum Terram, and the budding alliance with Nigel was the closest she'd come yet. Well, "alliance" was such a flimsy word. Maybe it was best termed an "understanding."

The statesman winced at the sunlight and used the provided cane for his right leg. The calf would take the most time to heal; the shoulder injury was less severe, her medical staff said.

After looking her over and no doubt being shocked by her change of clothes, he spat, "Where the fuck have you taken me?"

"Somewhere for you to recuperate. Beautiful, isn't it?"

Nigel sneered at her but eventually relented and looked around. While Neon couldn't read minds, she fancied herself a sage at reading faces. Despite Nigel's grimace, she could tell that he thought the landscape was impressive. And it was—every bit a Monet, Van-Borne, or Torrigarde. This, her secret hideaway from the affairs of leading the revolution, was a humble enclave built into the hills of Calvert Island a short flight from Vancouver. Her lush farmlands and vineyards swept down the west-facing slopes and ran into the Pacific, now catching the full scope of the setting sun. Workers tended the fields while laughing children played in the distance. The air that swept up the rise was moist and smelled of salt.

"Release me," Nigel said flatly.

"Before supper?"

"Yes."

She *tsk*'d him, joined him on the grassy walk outside his hut, and even managed to take his arm. He pulled away at first but eventually complied. He probably feared what would happen if he refused. And he was right to do so. Snipers were always at the ready. But she hoped it wouldn't come to that.

"If you really wish to leave this place, let's at least arrange it for after we eat. I've always found it best not to displease the cooks. Nor do I conduct my best thinking on an empty stomach. Desires, and all. Come."

He limped with the cane in one hand and her sweater-covered arm in the other. "You killed all my men."

"No. *You* killed all your men. I gave you the choice."

After his knee buckled slightly, he managed, "Your violence is shortsighted."

"Is it now."

He nodded. "You limit your influence because of it. Fear only gets your cause so far."

"I thought it was *our* cause."

He nodded again, but less emphatically that time.

"It's also shortsighted and…" He couldn't find his words.

"And what?"

"Evil. Because you're a damn devil, Neon."

"I've been called worse."

"Bitch."

"Warmer. Come now, the name calling serves little purpose. And you and I both know that your hands are just as dirty as mine. I simply don't bother with sneaking around like you do. But enough of this. Let us talk of beauty."

"Beauty?" He touched a hand to his head as if forgetting something. "How… how long was I sedated?"

"Only a few hours. Not to worry."

"And my clothes?"

"You don't like the fisherman's sweater? Hand-knit here on the island. I think it looks rather fetching on you."

"*My clothes*, Neon."

"In your room. Don't be so morose."

He cast a look over his shoulder, but the effort was aborted by a flash of pain.

Her doctors could have healed his bullet wounds within the hour, of course. She ensured that they always had the very best in gene therapy equipment. But for the sake of this trip, Neon decided her staff should use more traditional methods—let the body heal itself, stitched together with needle and thread.

Neon negotiated him toward a wide stone path that wound through Albion, her village, and snuck between more stone homes with thatched roofs. Dinner wasn't ready just then—only because she hadn't said so. Instead, she felt a detour was in order. It was enough for the scent of food to bring the saliva to his mouth. And it did; Neon caught him swallowing as the smells of sea-soned beef, salted potatoes, and fresh lemon on king salmon swirling in the air. It was the waft of warm bread from the boulangerie that put him over the edge —she could tell by the way his shoulders sagged.

Neon pointed him north, out of Albion, toward a part of the vineyard where children pulled grape clusters from bins and dropped them into the mash. They'd made a game of it and barely noticed when she walked into the yard with her guest.

"Hello, Miss Birdie," one little girl cried, which was soon followed by a dozen other enthusiastic greetings. "Who's your friend?"

"This is Nigel, everyone," she replied.

"Hi, Nigel," came in a dozen different tones, many sounding as if the two adults were romantically in-volved. This was answered with immediate sounds of disgust from certain boys. Then there were the few kids who greeted him only out of obligation and seemed more interested in returning to the game they'd been playing.

"Why don't you all prepare for dinner," Neon said. "It's almost ready."

The excited children filed out of the yard, leaving Neon and Nigel alone with the entrance to the grapevine rows ahead. His attention turned toward the sound of ocean waves crashing against the rocky shore far below. But then he just as quickly turned on her. "Am I to be impressed by your benevolence, Neon? Or should I call you Birdie?"

"No to both."

He acted like he was going to say something.

She stopped him. "My benevolence is not done to

summon opinion, and Birdie is what children call me. Unless you fancy yourself a child too?"

He clamped his mouth shut and looked down through the rows of vines to the sea. "Why have you brought me here? And why have you seen to my wounds if you only mean to kill me later?"

"I have no more desire to kill you than an artist destroy his painting, Nigel. But it was necessary to ensure that you gave Jericho the proper orders, which you did, and that he delivers my asset and himself to the proper coordinates, which you provided."

"Then why not let me leave?"

Neon supposed he already knew that answer, but she'd play along. "Come now, love. We both know the deed isn't done until the birds are back in their nests. As I said. Insurance. But don't fear: I'm sure your man will get the job done. This time tomorrow, you'll be on your way home, and my team will be back to hastening your election."

He huffed at the premise. "There were other ways to extort me besides this. Why bring me here?"

"Because I enjoy your company, love. And I wanted to spend some quality time together."

"Your men shot me."

"Means to an end."

He growled but said nothing more.

Neon wasn't lying entirely. She did want to spend time with him. If they were going to have a long working relationship, then she wanted some things to be clear. An understanding, yes, at the very least. And at most? Perhaps he'd come around to see the world as she did, though she was far from holding onto hope there.

Grape leaves brushed Neon's face as they started

down one of the rows. "Are you familiar with John B. Calhoun?"

"The man you abducted and killed before me?"

"Hardly. He's been dead for over 200 years. Calhoun pioneered several experiments in his day, back when the United States had the National Institutes of Health. His most famous, if not most ominous, was called Universe 25. Heard of it?"

"I'm not a fan of twentieth-century science books."

"Clearly." She plucked a grape and crushed it between her teeth, then offered him one.

He declined.

"Universe 25 followed a community of four breeding pairs of laboratory mice in an enclosure that satisfied their every whim. No disease, no conflict, all their needs met. Do you know what happened?"

"They were shot by their overlords?"

"Sex, Nigel. Lots and lots of mouse coitus."

"Charming, I'm sure."

"They thought so. Without the need to forage for food or skirt the violence of nature, they had nothing better to do than procreate. Before long, the community had peeked at 2,200, just shy of its maximum capacity of 3,000."

"And then they all died from overcrowding and food scarcity. I don't need your rhetoric, Neon. I have plenty of my own."

"It's far more interesting than that." She directed him around a break in the rows and traversed the hillside south. "The mice began breaking out into factions, three that Calhoun's research could see: aggressive, asocial, and outcasts. The most competitive attacked the weakest. But infighting also broke out among the lower ranks.

"Interestingly, there was a group who broke off completely that exhibited the most desirable traits of the entire population. Lush fur, clear eyes. The researchers called these the 'beautiful ones' since they spent their entire days preening on the ramparts high above everyone else."

The term "beautiful ones" was common enough, used to describe any human who ventured into orbit, but Neon doubted anyone knew its true origins, including Nigel. So she paused in anticipation of another sharp interjection from him, but none came.

Instead, Nigel filled the silence with, "So what happened? The beautiful ones prevailed while the rest suffered demise below?" He practically recited Solum Terram doctrine, proof they knew not from whence their history cometh.

Neon spit out a grape seed and squeezed his arm a little. He winced. "Oh, Nigel. So predictable. Your secret faith in the spacers betrays you."

"I have no such faith."

"They all died."

Nigel's face went blank. "Pardon me?"

"Some from their injuries, but most from hunger. Even those with all the food eventually died from infection. Sadly, the entire population of Universe 25 went extinct."

"Your point in all this?"

"Isn't it obvious?" She turned them east up the hill toward Albion. His calf would be burning very soon.

Unsatisfied with her question in answer of a question, he changed directions. "My people will be here any minute. They're tracking my location."

"Through V-cog? Mmmm, of course."

His face blanched for a moment, but the statesman

did his best to retain a regal demeanor. But he would frantically check his connection to the grid and realize that while he was still online, *he* was no longer Sir Nigel Sallsworth. Instead, he was a *nobody*. A phantom. Someone who could kick and scream on the verb all they wanted but without so much as provoking the slightest inquiry about his flailing. Any attempts to connect to his people, his businesses, his own family, would be met with instant blocks meant to keep the needy masses from storming the gates. He was, in that moment, just another number in the grid. It wasn't the lack of connectivity that threatened humanity, it was and always would be the lack of power. The terrible vacuum of meaninglessness.

"What have you done to me?"

"Nothing that can't be undone." Ever so subtly, Neon let more of her weight hang on his bad shoulder as they continued up the hill.

Nigel raised the cane and tried using his fingers to probe the small bald spot on the back of his head. More panicked, he asked again, "What did you do?"

"Oh, try not to sound so desperate, Nigel. It's rather unbecoming. Your brain is fine, as are your holdings. After all, we need one another, don't we? And anyone looking for you is engaged in nothing more than a wild goose chase. No harm, no foul."

Nigel didn't laugh. Beads of sweat had formed on his brow. "Universe 25. What is it, some sort of metaphor or something?"

"A lesson from our ancestors."

"We all die in the end. Is that it?"

"Utopia, Nigel. That's what you want, isn't it?"

He hesitated for only a moment before agreeing. "I thought that's what we both wanted."

"Mmmmm, no."

"I'm confused."

"Of course you are, love. That's because you believe that a utopian society here on Earth will solve all of our problems. Divest humanity of the beautiful ones above and release the resources to the ugly ones below."

Nigel's breathing had become more labored, and their pace slowed. She saw the wounds bleeding beneath his clothing and guessed the stitches had ruptured.

"What's the matter?"

"I just… I need a moment."

"Everything okay?"

"I'll be fine." Out of breath and wincing, he added, "If your agenda isn't stopping expansion, then what is it?"

"Resistance," Neon said as she kept constant pressure on his arm by leading him up the hill.

His breathing grew more labored. "I really need to stop for a moment. Please."

But she didn't stop. "Calhoun's supposition of utopia failed to consider Sir Thomas More's satirical undertones."

He sucked air. "Which were?"

"Among others, that utopian life is impossible because humans need pain to survive. Without it—without the struggle, the fight, the contest—we're just mice in a cage with all our needs met. Seeds never sprout, young never hatch, muscles never grow. Atrophy, Nigel. It doesn't matter who we are or what station we have, we all die before our time without the resistance of death's shadow pressing at our backs, propelling us forward to live one more day under the heat of the sun."

"And you bring that death?"

"Only resistance, Nigel."

His guard fell even more as overloaded pain receptors forced his features into tormented shapes. "So you… *don't* want peace and prosperity for all?"

"Of course I do, which is why I need you."

"I… Can we please resume this… another time perhaps?"

"The mice had everything they needed, yet they failed to control the proper flow of resources. Did you know, the year the Migration began, we had enough food on the planet to feed fifteen billion people? A surplus, Nigel, one that existed for almost a hundred years before that time. Not only did we have enough supply to solve world hunger, but we also had enough to save billions of lives during the Hundred Years Migration had we only stored a small percentage of food each year leading up to it. And did we?"

Nigel fell to his knees. Blood streamed down his pant leg and bloomed over his shoulder—a crimson stain saturating the fisherman's bulky weave.

She released his arm and let him catch himself in the grass. "No. We did not. And they died. It was not the lack of food that killed them; it was our inability to solve distribution."

After a few paces of not hearing him reply, she glanced back to find the statesman facedown in the path. Perhaps she had given him too much neurotoxin. Neon made a mental note to double-check her dosage chart later. It was a rather new recipe, after all. Third try's the charm.

The Tantum leader removed the aerosyringe, walked back to Nigel, and knelt by his head. Then she tapped the silver cylinder on her palm a few times. "You will manage distribution for the new epoch, Nigel. And I? I will manage the pain."

She pressed the blunt aerator against his neck and activated the pressure valve. A small *hiss* and the gene treatment was unleashed into his bloodstream. Neon tucked the device into her pocket, started up the hill once more, and slipped into V-cog to ping her head-of-security.

A tall man with deep-set eyes stepped into her lobby. He didn't speak, just loomed.

"Gregor. I have an errand for your team." Neon sent him the file. "Make sure the asset gets off *Astraea*. There's a second ship if the primary becomes a problem. And a bonus for anyone who captures this one alive"—she included a second file photo of Fox. "I expect it to be messy. And if you can't ensure acquisition, then no one else gets to keep him either. Understood?"

"We'll handle it."

The man exited, and then so did Neon.

"Come along, Nigel. Dinner's on."

JERICHO

STATION LIEUTENANT FORSYTHE, Master Sergeant Farooq, Kit, and I hover over a standing workspace, each with different holo screens that are teeming with data. The virtual room we're gathered in is one of *Astraea*'s standard V-cog suites used for small group meetings and presentations. Normally, the room's curved corners and glossy white surfaces reflect light from a solid ceiling emulator. But right now, I need everything dim to help me focus, so Kit's made some mods and turned the space into a darkened warehouse. A touch melodramatic, but I don't really care at this point. I want to keep people safe and catch this asshole—or *assholes*, as I'm not writing off the possibility of a team.

In real life, we're sitting in the transport vehicle with Forsythe's driver behind the controls, ready to speed us on our way whenever inspiration strikes us. And, God, I hope it strikes soon.

At the moment, Forsythe and I are cross-referencing the personnel roster against telemetry patterns in crew behavior, while Farooq and Kit are busy double-checking all new station arrivals over the last week. *Astraea*'s algorithms already oversee this, and with blinding efficiency, but, like humans, machines can still be wrong, even in the twenty-third century. All it takes is one oversight. One bad line of code. One weak rivet. And things fall apart in a hurry.

"Hmmm."

"What is it, Cap?" Kit asks.

"Nothing. Just thinking."

"Okay, cool. 'Cause if you need me, I'm right here."

"Like your own personal Labrador retriever," the master sergeant mumbles.

I worry Kit might take offense to this, but he starts nodding. "Yeah. I've got a pug back home. Well, my folks do. He's the greatest dog, but he gets excited and pees a little bit every time he sees us. I like that. I mean, not the mess part, but... But I can see myself as a yellow lab, right?"

"Keep working, Kit," I say. "Need your sniffer on the hunt."

"Copy that, Cap."

Farooq and I share a smile and then get back to data sifting. I like having the sergeant around. Reminds me of Will. Growing up, he was always so hard-core—the kind of guy you picked first for phase tag and pinged when you got in with the wrong crowd. Always had my back, and no one messed with him more than once. After a few years as a locker jockey, he called me to say he'd finally found his true family. Guy was a Space Marine from the womb, and the solar system is better for it. God knows the settlers on Ganymede sleep a whole lot safer because he's at his post—assuming that's where he's still stationed. I just hope we can offer *Astraea*'s crew the same level of protection before I get summoned for my all-too-important taxi errand.

Speak of the devil. An incoming anonymous ping

code matches the V-rec Sallsworth gave me for the client.

"Hey, guys. I need to take this. Be right back."

They nod, and I step into my suite. Well, not my Amalfi Coast suite—that's invite only. I mean a comms space I fashioned after a pic I saw in a verb mag once. It's a log cabin porch overlooking a lake. Reminded me of some secret hideaway that spies might use as a remote safehouse… just before a sniper opens fire from the pines across the water. Okay, so maybe I have a bit more Marine in me than I give myself credit for. Whatever.

"Fox here," I say as a man appears on the porch.

The client is in his late forties I'd say, with grey firmly entrenched at his temples and crow's feet at the corners of his eyes. He wears a fashionable suit, but nothing over the top. Just like in real life, people use attire to project image, so his choices are intentional and my first clues as to who I'm ferrying back to Earth.

"Mr. Fox, my name is Elroy Faust. Mr. Sallsworth said you'd be expecting me."

"I am. *Abigail*—the *Star Shadow* is docked at bravo ring, bay fourteen. Are you familiar with the area?"

"Yes."

"Good. I just need to wrap up some work, then I can meet you there."

"I would prefer to depart now."

"How about twenty minutes? I'll need at least that long to get—"

"I'm sure you're aware of the situation on the station, Mr. Fox. Considering the fact that my meetings have all been canceled as a result, and that I fear for my safety, I prefer to follow the captain's mandatory disembarkation orders and leave immediately."

"Right. Of course." I feel my body take a frustrated breath—an act that I keep my avatar from mimicking. "I'll meet you there shortly." Before he can protest and define a timeline, I close my suite and hope he doesn't call back.

"Everything okay?" Kit asks as soon as I've returned to the shared workroom. Farooq and Forsythe look up as well.

"I, uh… Can I talk to you for a second, Kit?"

"Sure."

I pull him through into the lakeside porch.

"Whoa. Nice digs. This your suite? Not anywhere to really relax though, unless you rendered out the cabin's inside. But if you did that too, holy biscuits, you have a lot of coin."

"Kit," I say in an effort to stop him before he keeps going. "Our contact wants to meet at the *Shadow* now."

"You mean *Abby*."

"Yeah. Listen, I need you to go stall for me. Help him get settled, maybe pour him a drink, small talk, right?"

"Yeah, yeah, I can do that. But what about the investigation?"

"I'm gonna keep working with Farooq and Forsythe as long as I can. You just try to keep our cargo cool for as long as possible, copy? Name's Elroy Faust. Some ST bureaucrat, looks like."

"Faust. Got it." He squints at me. "Why don't you just ditch him, Cap?"

"Because I like having a job, Kit."

"Yeah, but, seeing you up here? Man, it's like you're a different person. Like you were meant to be in space, ya know? Fighting crime, solving puzzles, catching bad guys, meeting babes—"

"I can't change my ink without a lot of coin—"

"Or power," Kit interjects. "Don't forget power."

"—and I'm not planning on going underground. And neither are you. So I just need you to stall for a few minutes, take care of him, and then I'll be there."

"Fine." He thrusts a finger at me. "But I draw the line at doing sexual favors for him."

"What is wrong with you?"

"I'm just saying."

"I'm pretty sure he's not gonna ask."

"Okay, okay. Good. You think he's the bomber?"

"What? No." So the thought had crossed my mind, but I'm not telling Kit that. I also ruled it out almost as fast as I considered the idea. "Bombing a legacy hab is the Tantum Terrae's MO, not Solum. They're not that stupid."

"You never know," Kit adds. "They could be doing seriously shady hanky panky under the table."

"You just take care of Faust and leave the rest to me."

"But no favors!"

"No favors."

"I'd be sooooo… Then I'd squeeze… Just, ugh. And they would never find the body, ya know?"

I pat his shoulder. "I know."

Forsythe called Kit another transport after I explained that he needed to ready our ship. Fortunately, neither Farooq nor the lieutenant asked any questions. They've picked up that I'm only moonlighting as a NUESSA aide, no small thanks to Evelyn's cross interrogation. Christ, she's intense. And unforgettable. Anyway, I'm glad no one's pressed me further than she did, and I expect everyone's figured out that my Solum Terram employment is grating on my soul. But it got me into space, so, hey, I'm smiling. And if it all ends in me blowing up? Well, that fate is long overdue.

I'm back in the workspace pacing to one side as Farooq and Forsythe scour the mountains of data that *Astraea*'s OS is spitting at them. So far, we still haven't found a thing. But how would we? There's more information than ten teams could sift through in weeks. The system is looking for outliers, but how can it zero in on anything when the whole station is going ballistic? When all the outliers…

…*look the same*!

"That's it," I blurt out and clap my hands once.

"Whadda ya got?" Farooq asks.

"We're looking for the wrong needle."

"I don't follow," Forsythe adds.

"The algorithm. It's cross referencing known users against behavioral habits, right?"

Forsythe scratches the back of his neck. "That's the general idea, yeah. Why?"

"Well, it's referencing behavioral habits during *normal* operating procedures, when everything's going the way it should. So at the moment, *everyone* is an anomaly."

"Because of the explosion," says Farooq.

"Thus the mountain of data," adds the lieutenant.

"Right." I pull up a new holo window and start typing. My brain's doing the data entry on its own, but V-cog maps my avatar with fingers on a holo keyboard so human onlookers, including my own brain, don't freak out when we're all just standing around doing nothing. Some evolutionary expectations are hard to break.

"What are you looking for?" Forsythe asks.

"For people doing normal things."

"How does that help us?"

"Do you frequent a particular restaurant on station, Lieutenant?" I ask as I keep sorting through data.

"Uh, coffee shop."

"Mornings?"

"Like clockwork."

"And if you didn't show up at it, you think that would flag in *Astraea*'s system?"

"I mean, I don't like to think she's watching me that closely, but, sure, I'd say that's anomalous."

"And it is. Which is exactly what *Astraea* is giving us. Almost 400,000 people not doing what they normally do. But what if you showed up to the coffee shop when a bomb had just gone off?"

Forsythe's eyes light up. "*Astraea* wouldn't register it as an anomaly."

"And that's why computer scientists have high anxiety. Humans are just a pain in the ass."

"You can say that again," Farooq replies.

The lieutenant puts his hands on his hips. "So… you want us to look for behavior that would stand out in an emergency scenario because it's too normal?"

I wink at him and keep searching. "Exactly."

Both men give each other what I call the "not bad" frown and start pounding virtual keyboards.

Since my guess is that whoever this terrorist is came in as a recent guest, I decide to start with non-crew new arrivals. The list is surprisingly long. There are extended family members of personnel, celebrities, athletes, verb casters, a few billionaires looking to show off, and then a whole slew of visiting science teams from all three nation states. With such a list, most researchers would roll their eyes and order coffee for the long night ahead. And, yeah, I might too if this were any other situation. But having a bomb go off in a legacy habitation cylinder that's floating in hard vacuum tends to provoke the same kinds of fight or flight responses in all human beings, "Unless you're this guy."

"You get a lead?" Farooq asks and leans toward my screen.

I fold my arms and stare at the name. "Who is Elliot Samson?"

"The Falklands Billionaire?" Forsythe asks as if I'm supposed to know, but both Farooq and I shrug. "He's partnered with us on several projects. Section seven is even named after him. Likes to come up from time to time but doesn't leave his room much."

"I see that." I bring up his file and telemetry. The guy's V-rec is pinging in section one.

Forsythe leans in with Farooq. "That's normal for him."

"To stay in his room?"

"Yeah. He might not leave for days at a time."

"Strange, isn't it? That he's the only person in all of section one's hotels who hasn't opted to use the VIP shuttle and be first off the station? In fact"—I pull up a submenu accessible with my temporary top-level clearance and find what I'm looking for—"according to the sensor suite inside Somnium Lux: Astraea, not only has Mr. Samson not left his room, but he's also been sleeping through the captain's mandatory disembarkation order."

"Son of a bitch," Farooq says. "He's our guy."

"Not necessarily. But whoever's in there is a good place to start."

Farooq turns to Forsythe. "Lieutenant, I want station security to lock down this building and set a perimeter. Evacuate and detain all guests but our target. I want twelve officers on the floors above and below it, but I don't want anyone near Samson's level or room until my team is on site. And quietly. No need to poke the bear."

Between Forsythe's pull and our imposing Space Marine escort, we make it to section one's Somnium Lux: Astraea in record time. Favorite destination for the station's most discerning guests, the luxury hotel offers some of the only windowed views in the entire hab. The complex butts up against the cylinder's endcap, offering rooms presumably priced like those of a coastline hotel jacking up its beachside-facing properties. And guests don't have that far to travel once they arrive on *Astraea*. Three and a half kilometers above is the interior portion of the station's transportation hub, a donut of zero-g buildings circling where the power level meets the cylinder's endcap. Extending into the void is the hub's zero-g docking matrix and traffic control tower whose staff oversees over a thousand arrivals and departures each day.

"So much for being quiet," I say to Farooq softly as

I nod toward the crowd that awaits us outside the hotel. It looks like section one's emptied all four quadrants' precincts and set up security fencing.

Farooq grunts and then waves to a set of security guards manning the last barrier before the hotel's entry. Forsythe outranks the master sergeant on the station, but everyone's watching the thirteen Space Marines in vac armor holding mag assault rifles at the ready in their vehicles. Damn, I might actually enjoy this if it weren't a station-wide emergency.

"My apologies for all this, Master Sergeant," Forsythe says from the driver's seat. "I think everyone's just a little over eager."

"We'll cope. And it's just Rook to you, okay?" He looks over his shoulder at me. "You too."

"Copy that," I reply.

The Space Marine squad spills out of the transports like paper cups dumping lead weights. Rook has his helmet on and, based on what little I can see of his face, is doling out orders over a private V-cog channel. Just as I'm starting to feel like I need a weapon, Rook twists off a sidearm from his Gecko Griptech-covered hip, switches out a blue magazine for a red one, and then spins the pistol in his palm as an offering to me. "Your un-redacted file says that you're pistol trained, Knight," Rook rumbles through his helmet's external speaker.

"I am. The file also has my callsign?"

"That's not the only thing. But you did slip and use it with Dr. Park anyway, so there's that." He pumps the weapon once more until I take it. "Know this one?"

"Hermann & Gruber HG-11 subcompact with an extended amrod—twelve standard-issue rounds for all Space Marines, if I'm not mistaken."

"Let's see if he shoots as good as he talks. Transferring com-auth now."

I feel the tingle in my palm as the weapon bio-locks to my DNA. While I was never as deep into guns as Will, I definitely enjoy the engineering side. Unlike legacy weapons planetside that still use gel accelerant, the HG-11 is a magnetic acceleration weapon, or MAW, that fires variable velocity tungsten projectiles coated in magnetic wafer discharge tech to self-propel down the rail system once initiated by the battery. The pistol's shape, in particular, looks much different than its older and more conventional counterparts. It's basically a rectangle with a hand cutout that boasts a vertical taser bar below the snub-nosed barrel.

Truthfully, I'm not sure I should be carrying a weapon on a NUESSA space station, but I'm not the one who'll be reprimanded for offering my sidearm to a Solum Terram civilian if things go wrong. Plus, if *Rook* thinks there might be a shootout, God knows I'd like to go down having returned some fire. I always felt bad for the soldiers in movies who died on beachheads or entering buildings before ever getting a shot off. That won't be me.

With com-auth bio-locked to me, I press the HUD pairing button on the side and bring up the weapon's menu in V-cog augment. Aside from standard mil-spec items like mag and battery levels, the most notable feature is the projectile selection type, listing needle, core, slug *hi*, and slug *lo* as options. Granted, Rook already removed the standard *core* ammo rod, whose rounds can puncture a ship's hull at high velocity if not aimed properly, and loaded the slower but more energy dispersant slug *lo* rod, so there's little for me to mess up and no possibility of blowing a hole in *Astraea*'s side. Still, it's cool knowing that he has those other mags on his kit as options.

Another of Rook's men offers Forsythe an HG-11, but the lieutenant declines. Instead, he reasserts his position as a NUESSA officer who is content to let the more competent do what needs doing. "I'll observe and direct only as needed. This is your show, Sergeant. Also, the building's been cleared of all staff and guests, save our subject and the security teams you ordered in support."

Rook nods. "Knight, you'll be with Forsythe in the column's middle. Fireteams one and two will lead. Three will pick up the rear. I've sent the picture of the suspect to team HUD. Our team orders are to capture if possible, kill if necessary. My men have their specific orders beyond that."

"Roger that," I say, feeling badass with the weapon in my hand and surrounded by a squad of armored Space Marines.

"Any questions?" Rook asks the unit. Heads shake, including mine, and Rook gives the call to move out.

Here we go.

23

EVELYN

"I'm free, Lemuel."

"Evelyn! Thank God. We were worried sick about you."

"No need anymore. All is well."

Lemuel dabs his forehead with a handkerchief, and it dawns on me that he's doing it in real life too. Avatars don't typically sweat or produce the impulse to wipe it away. "As soon as Johnson signed off on the terrorist notion, it unavoidably bumped you to the top of the list."

"I know, it's okay now."

"He just didn't know. And we couldn't reach you. Then the Marines were given jurisdiction and—"

"Lem. I'm okay. Promise."

He takes two deep breaths. "If anything ever happened to you, your father would kill me."

"Ghosts are powerful beings," I chide.

He points a finger at me. "You know better than to joke about the supernatural with me."

"And *you're* the director of SESI? We're all doomed."

He gives me one of his wide smiles and dabs his forehead one more time. "Where are you now?"

"Aside from reclining in your lovely suite? Heading back to the lab. Two minutes out. Mombawe said he was restoring elliptical command authority soon. From there, assuming Parallax still has sig lock, we'll recall the alpha and be back online in minutes."

"Excellent. And the latest on the explosion? They don't suspect foul play still?"

"No, they suspect it even more. Just not from me."

He scowls. "Evelyn, maybe you and the team need to consider—"

"We will. But there's still time. They're ordering mandatory disembarkation as a precaution."

"So it's… not an emergency then?"

"I think it's a major emergency, but they're worried that funneling the entire station's population to the emergency exits will provide the terrorists the targets they want."

"My God."

"They're taking it slow so as not to raise suspicions. The upside is that it gives us more time to regain the signal and get what we can. I'm not thrilled about it, but at least we won't come out empty-handed."

"How are you this calm right now?"

I chuckle. "You should have seen me earlier. Sam will have some stories to tell." I make a mental note to apologize again.

Lemuel pauses and then gives me a curious look. "So, who exonerated you? The inspector?"

"Hardly. It was Johnson's man. Did you know?"

"Know what?"

"Guess not. He sent Jericho Fox."

Lemuel blinks twice. "Fox?"

"Yeah. In the flesh."

"How was he even allowed off the surface?"

"Oh just you wait. That's not even the craziest part."

Lemuel invites me to continue by raising one eyebrow.

"He re-cast."

"To where?"

"Solum Terram."

"Impossible."

"I thought the same. But he was inked and everything."

A genuinely sad look crosses Lemuel's face. "It's a shame what we did to him. What we allowed. How… How'd he look?"

"Handsome."

He grins. "I meant, health-wise."

"Sure. Healthy, yeah."

"Okay."

"Listen, I'm almost there. I'll update you with our progress now that I'm no longer a mass-murder suspect."

"Sounds good. And don't wait too long on that evacuation. I want the entire team out, and *not* on the last boat."

"Understood, O captain, my captain."

"Cute." Lemuel's library suite fades out and transfers me to my couch. I slip from V-cog and orient myself in the lift as it slows toward the power level. Zero g has my feet off the floor, and I'm ready to push off the back wall as soon as the doors part.

I'm grateful Jericho released me. Granted, I never did anything to warrant arrest in the first place. I suppose it does give me some extra street cred though; who can say they've been in station *and* Space Marine custody in the same day? Still, I would have been better off without the detour, and so would our work.

In a weird way, I'm going to miss collaborating with Rook and Jericho. Sure, even Kit. We had some good chemistry for those few minutes... maybe a little too much in Kit's opinion. I might look them up in the verb once all this settles down. "Hey there. Remember me from that time we investigated a fusion bombing on *Astraea*? Yeah, that was crazy." But who am I kidding: I'm sure they're happy to be rid of me. Most people usually are.

I thrust the notions from my head as I float toward the lab's security hatch. It irises open for me, and I slide through without stopping, aimed right for the central command station, already overlaid with V-cog augmented reality. To my delight, the power is back on and the stations are all filled with specialists. It's go time.

"Howdy, folks."

All heads turn toward me.

"Evelyn," Sam shouts. "It's you!"

"In the flesh."

The lab breaks out into clapping and even a few whoops and whistles. I don't like the attention, but I don't mind the appreciation. Feels good being back.

"How did you...? And then there was the—?"

"Long story. I'll fill you in later, Sam. Right now, we have a signal to catch." I look around the room and smile. "Well? Any word on when we'll have auxiliary nav control again?"

Ramirez smiles. "Mombawe already gave it to us."

"What?"

Sam grabs my shoulder. "He assigned us max vector permission too."

"You're kidding me."

"Nope."

"Said it was the least he could do given all you've been through," Ramirez adds. "We should be back on target in"—he checks a readout—"three minutes."

Stars, I'm gonna need therapy to repair me from having my emotions jerked around so much. I run a hand down my face. "Three minutes?"

"Come on," Sam says, guiding me to the exec chair. "We need you buckled in and ready."

"Yeah. Yeah, of course." I'm elated. Beyond elated. I'm completely freaking out but trying to come off as coolheaded for the team's sake. I grab Sam's arm as she guides me forward. "Thank you, Sam."

"I haven't done anything yet. Let's just see what we can find in the stardust, okay?"

"Right." I buckle myself in, take a deep breath, and start through my checklist. "Celestial trig nav?"

"Go," Ramirez says with a smile.

"Propulsion?"

"I'm a go," Sam replies.

"Parallax matrix?"

"Go," says Cheng.

"Sig capture and archiving?"

"Go," Natalie Mason says.

"Comms?"

"Go," says Bhavna Mishra, our communications specialist who was absent up until now. There are a few other crew members among the late arrivers, but they're standing by as backup and content just watching the show.

"Uplink with St. Johns is five by five," I add with a love tap sent to Lemuel's static avatar. "We are all-systems go for SESI signal capture. Let's make this one count, people."

Another round of applause even more energetic than the one for my arrival fills the bubble. I manage a short whistle between my teeth. Then I call for quiet as the main counter spreads across the bubble's far wall along with a blank semi-transparent window waiting to be filled with data—historical, unprecedented, and, sans melodrama, life-altering data that will change the scope of human history.

My hands are trembling.

Between the shifting numbers counting down from sixty, I look at all the stars and wonder, for the umpteen-millionth time, how many of them hold sentient life. It's been my obsession since I was a child. Whether tucked in by my parents, on a rooftop alone, or across from my college roommate, I always found a way to wish the stars goodnight, and with them, every intelligent being across the galaxies, and the galaxies beyond those galaxies. Where I'd been robbed of the first moments of contact, I would not be robbed of these.

But it's not just me. It's all those people whose shoulders I stand on. The ones in this room, yes. More, the ones going back decades, and then centuries. All those astronomers and astrophysicists who dared believe that we were not alone. Those burned at the stake for believing the world wasn't flat, wasn't the center of the cosmos, and those burned on the verb for channeling trillions in crypto to research what others said was a waste of time. It all comes down to this.

Three...

Two...

One...

Nothing happens.

I hold my breath.

And then the reception window explodes with data. Frequency analysis pegs hard, locked at three times ten to the sixteen, no deviation. Wavelength, one nanometer. Energy, 100 keV. Then the sensors start freaking out.

Cheng swears in Mandarin. "It's breaking up!"

"No!" Mason replies. "Don't touch anything."

"But we're losing focus!"

"No, we're not," she shouts back. "It's not intermittent. It's a pattern! Look."

She throws a second window beside the main data screen. In it, Mason highlights a staccato-looking graph with a complex series of ascending and descending towers, like a stock market trend line that can't decide if it's bearish or bullish. Then she zooms out from the graph and the big picture becomes clear.

"Holiness shits," Kalashnik cries. "Is intentions, yes?"

"Yeah," I reply, barely able to contain myself. "Is definitely intentions."

"There's more," Mason says. The first few seconds of data in her graph auto-segment as a new pattern emerges. It's not that far different from the initial group but enough that Parallax has marked a delineation.

"It's changing," Sam says.

"Please tell me we're capturing and backing up," I say for anyone to answer.

"We're getting it all, Evelyn," Mason says, transfixed on her station. "My God."

"Is like PCM encoding?" Kalashnik asks. Not bad for a medical doctor to know about basic pulse communication, even if it is outdated. Then again, he is on a legacy hab with an advanced SESI team, so I shouldn't be that surprised.

Mason replies for me. "If this is what we all think it is, I'm guessing it will make pulse-code modulation look like cave drawings."

"How's our signal to noise ratio looking, Natalie?" Cheng asks.

"Good. Beyond good." She turns from Cheng to me. "Almost as if it's purposely trying to stay away from FRBs and GRBs. Reading zero reflection."

"This is really it, Eves," Sam says from her chair. "I can't believe it. This is *really* it."

"Cross-checking with SESI Actual now," I say, unable to hide my smile. I open Lemuel's avatar and get a straight line to St. Johns. "SESI Actual, this is *Astraea* Lab One. How do you read?"

"We've got you, ALO," Lemuel replies as he appears standing on a dais superimposed by V-cog in the bubble's middle.

"Roger. Confirm relay reception."

"Relay reception is solid. We're picking up what you're sending down, storing to local."

"Officer Mason is relaying you a package verification request now. Please sign on the dotted line and cross-check, ten-second analysis."

"Stand by." Lemuel looks aside to some non-pictured group of techs. I hear talking in the background and imagine the analysts feeling exactly what we are.

I shouldn't rush them, but I can't help it. "Lem? Can they confirm?"

He waves a hand at me blindly. "Just a moment."

"Copy."

There's a nervous tension in our lab. The signal keeps pouring in, and Mason is looking between multiple screens like a stimmer on hype code. I'm about to ask for an update when Lemuel comes back. His voice sounds official, which makes my heart skip a beat—skips all the beats. He's being recorded. For all time.

"*Astraea* Lab One, this is SESI Actual, Mission Control in St. Johns, Northern Heights, Newfoundland Territory. We confirm Officer Natalie Mason's package analysis of the signal from Kepler-1649c. Alpha signature is a verified anomaly meeting all IPCSI parameters. You've got a live one, Evelyn."

The cheer that erupts from our lab drowns out the celebration coming from St. Johns. I can't see over the zero-g tears obscuring my vision, I just hear everyone yelling. I'm yelling too and can't get my belt unlocked fast enough. On the third try, it pops free, and I push toward the mass of scientists colliding with each other in the bubble. I don't know who I kiss first, but it doesn't matter. I'm squeezing necks and grabbing hands, and I still can't see straight.

"We did it," I keep repeating. "We really did it."

"No," Sam says beside me with tears spiraling off from her eyes. "*You* did it. You led us here, Evelyn." She hugs me hard. "Good job."

"You too. This… this changes things."

She laughs at me. "This changes *everything*!"

I knew it would feel good, but damn if it doesn't feel better than good. Stars beyond, my whole life is… it counts. I count.

Then I realize Lemuel is waiting for a reply beyond sheer pandemonium. I swallow and try calming myself down, but it's no use. Whoever listens back to this recording a thousand years from now will hopefully understand how fresh it all was, no matter how the centuries normalize whatever relationships may come. I had lines prepared. Shoot, I'd imagined this moment my whole life—just, never imagined it would be right now, nor that it would actually be me, a street rat from Bukjeong Village.

"Thank you, Director Brown. On behalf of our whole team, we are"—I accept another high-five from Ramirez—"so grateful for this unique and truly historic moment. We…" The words get stuck in my throat. I can't remember the speech I wrote. I'm a mess. Instead, all I get out is, "Humanity has always wondered if we were the only ones. Well, we're not. We are not alone." Then an idea comes that I hadn't thought of before. It's edgy and political and breaks NUESSA regulations. But it may just ensure that this moment is forever interweaved with the only politicast I believe can lead us forward. "We are forging paths through the darkness."

"We hear that, Dr. Park," Lemuel replies. "Forging paths through the darkness."

He heard it. *And he echoed it.* Stars, he answered the mantra over the global net. As if our discovery wasn't enough, planting the flag for the Sentia Aux will have every talking head breathless for the next decade. It will also have the Solum and Tantum frothing at the mouth. Could even get me fired. But I don't care. It's time we drew the battle lines. Just as Sam said, this changes everything.

When the celebration finally fades, I come back to Lemuel and address both teams at his invite. "Alright, everyone. We've got a lot of work ahead of us. Cel-trig, I want you to coordinate with Captain Mombawe for extended hab control. SESI Actual, we'd love your assistance with sig-proc. And Lab One Crew? Well, somebody better bust out the champagne soon, 'cause damn if this doesn't feel amazing."

This gets a laugh and then another cheer from those in orbit and planetside.

When the new wave of excitement ebbs, Lemuel stares at me. I can tell by the unguarded look in his eyes that they've ceased live transmission. "Congratulations, Evelyn," he says in a non-official tone. There's still plenty of celebrating filling the background, but I'm laser focused on the face of the man who became my surrogate father as soon as I joined SESI. "I'm proud of you."

"Thanks, Lem."

"You just need to know that if your parents were—"

He disappears.

"Comms? What happened?" I double-check my V-cog, hoping that Stamos hadn't sabotaged me again.

"Sat just went down," Mishra says.

"Local?"

She's ripping through code faster than my eyes can track. "Grid's not responding in sections one through four. Up here still looks okay though."

"What would cause such a thing?" Cheng asks.

The lab rattles.

"Evelyn?" Sam asks.

All joy in the room is sucked out. I'm free-floating but notice workstations vibrating from a tremor in the air. Then I spot the stars moving outside. The rest of the crew sees it too. Cheng and Ramirez fight with auxiliary nav control, but correcting this from our end is pointless. We're beyond trying to regain the signal.

"Holy Mother of God," Mason whispers.

The edge of Earth's horizon rolls into view like an intruder creeping into our home.

"We're tumbling," Ramirez says. "Ay Dios mío."

I take a second to get a feel for the new vector's

speed. Fortunately, the end-over-end motion appears to be slow enough that it won't mess with our equilibrium or the ship's artificial gravity too much. Nothing the human body can't adjust for, just as *Astraea* will correct in due course.

"Evelyn?" Sam asks with a rising tone.

"Everyone stay calm." I switch V-cog to my personal suite and punch Jericho's record. It pings him, but there's no reply. "Come on." When that doesn't work, I pull up Rook's V-rec. Same thing. The pings are going out, they're just busy. I try the captain, scolding myself for not thinking of him first. Still nothing. "Dammit."

"Evelyn?" Sam says as she grabs my arm. It startles me, and we slew sideways from her momentum. "What's happening?"

"I don't know. But it's not good." I stop us against a padded support on the far left wall. Instantly, my hand vibrates from the ship, but the intensity is dwindling. It's dissipating resonance, like the aftermath of someone striking a drumhead with a stick. The good news is that energy is fading. The bad news is that I have no idea what caused it or what damage it's done. Strike that. I do think I know what caused it, and my stomach is twisted in a knot. "Can anyone reach the bridge?"

Heads shake. The scent of fear is palpable and takes me back to running away from grifted targets and irate stakeholders. But there's no need to fear the worst yet. The lab has power. But something is definitely wrong, and I can't shake the feeling that another fusion bomb has just been detonated.

"Orders?" Ramirez asks me for what I think is the second time. "Dr. Park?"

"Transfer all lab authority to V-cog. We're evacuating the premises. And Mason, I want the cold storage backup personally."

The words are barely out of my mouth when the station's emergency alarm sounds and Captain Mombawe's voice comes over comms.

"All hands, all hands, this is your captain speaking. Be advised that we have suffered catastrophic damage to section one and have been ordered by the NUE and NUESSA Mission Control to abandon ship. This is not a drill. I say again, this is not a drill. Please proceed calmly to the nearest emergency disembarkation airlock and follow all crew member and posted jettison instructions. I say again, this is an all-hands order to abandon ship. Captain Abraham F. Mombawe out."

Well, shit.

24

JERICHO

IT TAKES us less than two minutes to reach the Somnium Lux's seventh floor where Samson is holed up. I expected some long hotel hallway with dozens of doors on either side. Instead, the elevator doors open on a large square-shaped lobby with high-end furniture and a window boasting a startling view of the void. Out and up, the exterior portion of the station's main zero-g transport hub looms over an Earth and sun that spiral in a disjointed elliptical orbit.

"Damn," one Marine says over his external speakers as the squad files into the lobby from the three elevators.

Another more senior Marine raises a finger to quiet the private.

Fire Team One heads toward the room door that Forsythe has pinged on V-cog and stacks up with Two. Rook leads us forward but directs the lieutenant and me to stand clear. "Bullets eat doors for breakfast."

We both nod, taking the hint.

Rook pulls his pixie from his lower back and cycles it on. Unlike civilian PXSEE's, the Marine iteration of personal exo-sensory environment experience drones has some EM and impact shielding. The defense manufacturer also replaced the fan blades with vectored thrust suitable for vacuum. I wouldn't be surprised if the little device had some weapons or pinchers too. Maybe a laser, who knows. While I might not get permission to keep the gun, I'm definitely asking if I can have that bug.

By the time Rook's pixie is hovering, two of Team Three's Marines have pulled off a nearby vent cover, allowing Rook to steer his drone toward it and disappear inside.

"Sending to team lens now," Rook says.

An invite pings in V-cog. I accept and get an FPV overlay from the pixie's forward camera. The drone navigates two turns through the blackened tunnel before it encounters another cover looking over a spacious vestibule that's three times the size of my apartment— my *new* one. A small arm unfolds above the camera and snakes toward the cover's delicate lattice. A few snips from a scissored hand—*nailed it*—and the pixie has access to the suite.

"I'm in."

The next minute is tense as Rook maneuvers the pixie through the entire apartment—that's what I'm calling it now. This place is way too big to be considered a stateroom or even a suite. I can't even begin to imagine the price tag per night. But if you're Mr. Samson, apparently you can afford it.

With each turn Rook takes into the living room, bedroom, kitchen, entertainment suite, and more bathrooms than any person should ever have in a single property, I feel the tension mount. So far, all Rook has tagged are a clothes bag, some toiletries, and a black gift box on the main king size bed. *Astraea* says Samson is in here. But unless he's hiding in some sort of insulated closet, which thermal imaging can't find any evidence of, then it means one thing…

Astraea is wrong.

From an engineering and computer science standpoint, that's next to impossible. Granted, yeah, *Astraea* could make a mistake; we just proved her algo isn't bulletproof. But this is different. We're talking basic V-cog bio sensors linked over layered grid relays. Even if someone could hack one system, hacking both systems is out of the question. Bottom line, Samson is in the wind.

"Clear," Rook says at last and recalls his pixie.

"I don't understand," Forsythe says. "Where is he?"

"Not here."

"But-but, that's—"

"Highly suspicious?"

Forsythe nods as he's run out of words.

Both men turn to me as if I might offer some critical insight. I shrug and keep my HG-11 pointed down. "Ship's been hacked," is all I can think to say.

Rook doesn't like that answer and orders Teams One and Two to breach the main door while Team Three enters through an additional back door located down a utility entrance. He made sure to double-check all seams and thresholds for sensors and explosives, but there's not so much as a strand of hair to raise alarms.

The breach order goes out, and all units file into the apartment and start clearing every room, knowing the pixie could have missed something. By the time I get to enter with Forsythe, there's a Marine in every main area, scanning for any items of interest.

"Doesn't even look like he's slept here," I say, noting how immaculate everything looks.

"He's a rich snob," Rook adds. "Probably OCD or something."

"Not according to his hospitality complaint file." Both men turn to look at me. "I read up on his past stays out of curiosity. Apparently he has no problem trashing rooms during his many… well, we'll just call them experimental escapades."

"Glad somebody's getting some," Rook says.

The three of us enter the only room that holds anything of interest: the main bedroom bearing the clothes bag and the gift box with thin gold trim.

I reach for the black cube while Forsythe inspects the bag.

"Hold it." Rook grabs my hand before I can make contact.

My heart pounds in my chest. "What is it?"

"I'm detecting something from a seam."

Forsythe backs away. "Radioactive?"

Rook shakes his head. "If I had those sensors, Knight wouldn't have needed to build his cup experiment, now would he." He turns back to the item. "It's thermal. Box is room temp, but there's a faint spike from under the front lid."

"How hot?" I ask.

"Ninety-eight point six."

"Know any bombs that like that temp?"

"No. But I know some triggers that don't like dynamic change."

"You have a bomb tech on your squad?"

"One step ahead."

There's the sound of boots crossing the living room outside, and then another Marine joins us. Corporal Geller, I believe.

"Geller, possible IED."

"On it."

Geller steps to the bed and pulls some fancy hardware from his kit. If Rook's helmet didn't have a Geiger counter sensor in it, I bet this guy's kit does. He starts scanning the box that looks like it should hold some skimpy lingerie or a big corsage and then eventually pulls away. "It's clear. But there's definitely a battery source, some thermal diodes, and... well, some organics."

"Specifics?" Rook presses.

"Hard to say, Sarge. Human tissue? Pretty sure it's safe to open though. Uh, for anyone with headgear, that is." He nods at me at Forsythe. "Might wanna step out."

"You're saying it could be a biological hazard?" Forsythe asks with a tight tone.

"I'm saying that if this billionaire has fetishes, that might be one memento you don't wanna sniff."

The lieutenant absently puts a hand around his throat. "Okay."

He and I step out and close the door, leaving Rook, Geller, and two other Marines to open the box. Rook has the presence of mind to patch me into his team lens to see from his helmet cam. Geller uses a multitool to ease the lid up. Right away, a seal breaks and I see a soft red light inside. But no boom, which is always a bonus.

Geller passes the box to Rook, who gets a good view of the interior. But there's not much to see. The red glow is from a flesh-colored material halfway down with a light source beneath it. Reminds me of when we used to stick flashlights in our mouths as kids to see veins inside each other's cheeks.

"I think I might be sick," Forsthye says.

I ping Rook. "If that's human flesh, why would you want a box of it?"

"Because you're a sick mother fucker who collects skin from your bad dates?" Rook says. "How the hell should I know?"

This isn't adding up, and we're running out of time. But the mystery box is too compelling to dismiss outright. Something's significant about it, I just can't figure out what.

As Rook closes the box and Geller scans the room for contaminants, I pace the lobby and summarize. "We know whoever's doing this has been able to spoof the station's systems, act like he's in his hotel room, and plant a micro fusion bomb in the ag level undetected."

"Assuming it's the same player," Rook interjects as he emerges from the bedroom.

"Could be two different people, right? None of this is conclusive." I rub the back of my neck and start swinging the HG-11 but then think better of it as two Marines jerk away. "Sorry. We also know that he—we'll just call him a *he* for now—has probably been able to blend in with the guests or even the crew."

A private whose name tape I can't see says, "So you don't think it's Samson?"

I shake my head. "The real Samson is probably somewhere back on Earth sipping Mai Tais," I say for Kit's sake but forget he's not here. "Probably isn't even aware of…"

Another thought hits me.

"You good, Knight?"

"What if that's Samson?"

Rook gives me a confused look and then turns back to the bedroom door. "The box?"

"What if that's a sample of his skin or something, and they learned how to… I dunno, keep his V-cog nanos 'on ice,' as it were."

"You can't just yank somebody's nanos," Forsythe says. "Plus, they'd shut down if they didn't have… HOLY GOD."

"Brain tissue." I complete the thought for him.

Rook's face looks like he's staring at a math problem he can't solve. "You don't think that's really possible, do you?"

"I think we're seeing a lot of innovation from a highly capable team of engineers trying to hit a very big target. It might not be probable, but that doesn't mean it isn't possible."

"Hey, Sarge?" says a Marine stepping out the bedroom. He's holding the clothes bag over one arm and offers Rook a small, flat device that he's pulled from a blazer pocket. It's a translucent crypto card, but the illuminated display isn't showing an account balance. It's showing time: fifty-three seconds and counting. Down.

Even before Rook yells an order, I feel my stomach drop to the floor.

"EVERYBODY OUT!"

It takes the Marines, the security detail, and Forsythe and me thirty seconds to backtrack and charge out of the hotel. Had the building not been cleared beforehand, there's no way the staff and patrons would have gotten out in time. Rook yells for everyone to fall back as the final fifteen seconds count down on the Marine's team HUD that I'm linked into.

We follow Rook behind a skywalk support column just past the Somnium Lux's water feature holo sign. It's plenty of distance to survive an IED but not far enough for another uranium bomb. I picture the hundreds of maimed bodies collected by section sixteen's relief workers. A jolt of adrenaline hits me as I consider being sucked into the big black without saying goodbye to my dad or making amends with a few old girlfriends. Yeah, the shit you think about just before you die is weird.

"Three," Geller calls out. "Two… one…"

I wait for the hotel to detonate, for the iridescent glass to blow out the front, and fire to shoot from the roof. But nothing happens.

Nothing at the hotel, at least.

There's a flash of light high overhead from the place where the power level intersects the transportation hub four klicks up. I instinctively cover my head as a loud *boom!* shakes the sky, and wind blasts over my body. It feels like any freak stormfront on Earth, except for the heat that's grilling my exposed skin. A tremor shakes my feet, and the sound of terrified people fills my ears.

I have the presence of mind to glance at the hotel—it's still standing. But high overhead, the torus-shaped transportation hub looks as though it's been hit by an earthquake and set ablaze with lighter fluid from within. Debris shoots through the atmosphere like comets with long tails: pieces of burning metal, chunks of buildings, and small objects shrieking in terror—humans thrown free in zero g. To the north, explosions sound as shrapnel collides with the station's curved walls. Then the shudder underfoot worsens, but it's not from the errant debris field.

It's from something much worse.

My brain connects the flash of light with the traffic

control tower outside: the explosion has blown the main column off-axis. I imagine the docking legs spinning away in a wild melee of twisted steel and colliding ships. More collisions sound outside *Astraea*'s endcap as the station's rotational mass shreds the docks to smithereens, but nothing's as loud as the sound that started the catastrophe: another uranium bomb.

A new wind, one much cooler, rushes at my back and cools my skin. It feels good. And then I realize where it's coming from, or, more importantly, where it's going.

"Hull breach," I shout. My eyes dart around for options as people are starting to scatter.

Even though *Astraea* has enough atmospheric volume to keep her inhabitants alive for several days in the event of low level hull failures, most plans don't account for uranium bombs blowing a hole in the endcap. And based on my glances of the damage above, this munition was substantially larger than the one in section sixteen. Fire around the transportation hub's inner circle bends backward as its oxygen gets sucked toward hard vacuum.

We need to go down.

"The ag level," I yell.

Rook acknowledges my words first and looks at the lieutenant. "Nearest access?"

Forsythe doesn't skip a beat and points to a maintenance outbuilding across a small park. The structure is nestled among some flailing trees. "Stairwell, sixty meters north."

"Let's move!" Rook orders two men to take point, and we follow them across the park.

Above the din, Captain Mombawe's voice cuts through in my auditory cortex and echoes through speakers atop lamp posts. I can't focus on everything he's saying, but I do register the words "abandon ship." Buildings groan overhead as more wreckage gets sucked into the deep black. I imagine the hole widening with each second that passes and hope that *Astraea* will hold long enough for everyone to escape before it's too late…

…before *Astraea*'s executioner does something even worse.

25

JACK

You're almost there, Jack. Two down, one to go. All you need to do is take your time and stay in character.

It's pretty remarkable what you've done too. A few of the architects doubted you, right to your face. So every action of yours now is a testament against those who said you'd fail. You wondered, at first, if the hazing was all part of the training, and perhaps it was. But you know when people are lying, don't you, Jack, because you've spent so much time perfecting it yourself.

Yes, I like your blouse.

No, I don't want to meet today.

Of course I believe extrasolar sentient life will be friendly. Why wouldn't it be?

Soon, you won't have to act any more, Jack. And if the curious decide to go looking under rocks that they shouldn't? Well, you'll be back to truth telling even sooner. But that will be on them for nosing around in Mr. Samson's affairs.

You're still Mr. Leach, a lowly first engineer who won't be missed by anyone but his goldfish and laundry pile. You've got the last of Mr. Samson's flight cases, this the biggest of all, and you're heading north up-station through the power level. A good thing too, isn't it, Jack? Because maneuvering this case around on the main deck without zero g would be one hell of a hassle.

Even still, your palms are sweating. Why, Jack? Are you having second thoughts? Or is this just nerves? Ah, it's the comedown from your recent stim line run. Always a bit jittery after Poor John's opterium jade ride. But it's worth it. As long as you can pull yourself together. Concentrate. And stop thinking about her, would you?

That said, it is difficult when you're this close. To stop thinking about her, that is. Not completing the mission. Like that one time you found yourself on the same flight as Dr. Monahan, you remember? You caught your breath when you saw his face in real life, no longer just a picture framed on your dresser or a playback from the verb, but real life, honest-to-God flesh and blood. You couldn't talk at first—a plague you rid yourself of when mother paid you the first time. But back then you couldn't help yourself. You were face to face with a hero —who wouldn't be overcome? He was kind, if not distant, but still managed to sign your hastily offered backpack. And then you floated to your seat like you were in zero g.

Which, strangely enough, you are now. However, this is not Dr. Monahan who forecasted the end of humanity were you to continue purging money into the void. No, this is about the antithesis, his nemesis. The destroyer of things precious and dear.

The thought of seeing her drags you down. It's as if gravity has grabbed hold of your ankles and rips you from the power level, then pulls you to the ground floor. Down there, you meet your end, struck by the cylinder's rotating circumference, hitting you like a hovertrain.

And from your pulped meat bag of a body, you look up at *Astraea* before your soul departs, and you see this.

All this…

The spinning behemoth of humanity's demise, cloaked in survival but bound for destruction.

It's her fault. *She's* responsible. For the misallocation of trillions of dollars that could be spent to remedy the planet's constant hemorrhaging. She is the doctor who refuses to operate on the patient in need because she'd rather use her surplus of nanoskin to patch a birthday balloon than a dying child's chest. And she smiles, whistling as she goes, oblivious of the death she summons, all for the sake of a frivolous pursuit.

Frivolous, but not preventable.

You've thought of killing her, Jack. Of course you have. She will be one of the hundreds of thousands of deaths that resets humanity's priorities. But is that enough? And, more importantly, is that what Neon would want? Or would she desire to stare into the eyes of the woman who's championed the greatest distraction humanity has ever known? Would she wish to interrogate the devil and then spill her blood back on the land from whence she was born?

"What're you doing in here?" says a man's voice behind you.

You turn to meet him. He's wearing an engineer's uniform like you, only he outranks you. So you lower your head like an underling and take on the tone of a dimwitted drone. "I was just told to check on the EM shielding relays for—"

"By whom? And what the fuck are you doing this far up from section one"—he eyes my nametape—"First Engineer Leach?" Something like recognition dawns on his face. "Wait… you're not Leach."

You press off from the access panel with your feet and rocket toward him. His eyes widen at the speed. And why wouldn't they? He's not expecting an engineer on *Astraea* Station to have batch tweaks installed, not ones that multiply muscle contraction to near dangerous levels and accentuate hand-eye coordination to computer-like precision. So when your hands wrap around his neck in an unbreakable bond, you marvel at his attempts to stop you. He could no more object to deep-sea pressure crushing a balloon than resist you. Hands beat and claw your arms. His nails draw blood. One lucky blow even glances off the edge of your jaw. But none of this dissuades you from your observations as you calculate the seconds remaining until his larynx succumbs.

The man's face turns red and then deathly purple—eyes bulging from their sockets. The blows cease, replaced by the fish-like opening and closing of the mouth as it gasps for air. And then the cartilage and bone snap between your fingers, finally ending their resistance of the inevitable.

You let go, and the diaphragm reflexively pulls in a lung-full of air through a whistling throat. The victim waffles at the edges of consciousness, his eyes moving between your face and the afterlife. You escorted him to the threshold. The natural order of death will take him the rest of the way in time. A minute, maybe less.

A second man floats inside, takes one look at the scene, then starts backing away. But you can't afford for him to leave. So you lunge again, grab the newcomer by the uniform, and let your combined momentum carry you both into the bulkhead. He grunts but manages to unsheathe a tool from his hip. The act harkens back to basic training, a dishonorably discharged Marine perhaps. Something slashes at your gut, but you avoid the blow with ease.

Your hand goes to his wrist, and your opposite arm wraps across his body. You twist the crude tool, still in his hand, and then plunge it into his side. The newcomer cries out, but you end that with one sharp crack of his head against the doorway that leaves him in a state of suspended animation.

It's over.

You pull him into the room and close the hatch behind you. Now you have two bodies to dispose of, Jack. You could leave them here, but cleaning bots will discover them sooner than you wish. So you'll need to be more creative. And you'll need to take care of the cameras too. Perhaps you've been seen already.

Someone opens the access door and floats in.

Your body tightens, ready to lunge again, when a smooth female voice says, "For rain to come…"

You tilt your head at the woman.

She repeats herself, more urgently this time. "For rain to come…?"

"…the parched Earth must call," you answer. This is unexpected. A shadow in the wings. "Who are you?"

She enters all the way and closes the hatch behind her. "Apparently the person who's going to be cleaning up your mess, Jack."

"No names," you reply.

She nods in agreement. "Have you finished?"

The woman's whole presence is disconcerting, isn't it, Jack. You knew there were others acting on your behalf, sent to aid you, but you were never told that they would make contact. The idea that this woman knows of you but not you of her makes you feel exposed. Perhaps even belittled.

"Well?" she asks. "Have you?"

"Everything is in place, yes."

"Then you might wanna get a move on."

You hesitate. "You're going to dispose of the bodies?"

"You think I'm here to give you a pep talk?"

"What about the cameras?"

"Taken care of."

She's resourceful, you give her that. And remarkably calm under pressure. Still, you would have liked for Neon to have told you about her. And you wonder how many more incogs are waiting in the wings. "Were you monitoring my progress?"

"Yes."

"So you planned on meeting me here?"

"I figured how this would end."

"Indeed." You fake a placid face in spite of feeling condescended to. Granted, this event is a small blip in the grand scheme of things. However, you still feel that, as the key contributor to *Astraea*'s downfall, you should have been apprised of all Neon's incogs. Though her concealing the information is not entirely out of the ordinary, she always did hide things from you.

Why, though?

Because you were too young and inexperienced.

Because you weren't ready to take the reins yet.

But now? Now you will prove your capacity to think outside the box. To adapt. To recognize opportunity when it appears and seize it with both hands.

You'll need the right cover, of course. Something plausible. But first, you need to locate your target.

Hands wipe pant legs as you slip into V-cog as Mr. Leach. He pulls up the ship's roster in *Astraea*'s lobby and uses his service clearance to locate the doctor. She's in her operating room, ignoring the suffering to attend to the imaginary. How fitting that you will meet her there, isn't it, Jack? Not only will the hab fall, but the traitorous harlot will be taken alive and brought back to Neon as the spoils of war.

"Are you just going to stand there?" the incog asks as she starts maneuvering the floating bodies toward the hatch. The first man is still making small noises from his mouth in fruitless efforts to be heard, but his energy is waning.

"I have something I need to do before I leave."

"Then you'd better get going, golden boy. Clock's ticking"—an adage from a bygone era, one kept alive by those among the Tantum who still use analog time-pieces. Like the IWC you lifted from Samson. You check it again. With the final bomb in place where it will do the greatest harm, there's still time for you to abduct her, Jack.

"What will you do with the bodies?" you ask the incog.

"Incinerator. Maybe vacuum. I'll need to see what my options are."

A thought hits you like a devastating transfer of inertia, one that you're certain will attract the prey you seek. It connects the dots between the man you'll become and the victim you'll capture. And it makes marvelous sense because it's so obvious. Predictable, even. Like the third bomb, she'll never see it coming. Hidden in plain sight.

"I have an idea for one of the bodies," you tell the incog as you stare into the first man's terrified eyes. "And if you delay it a little, it will buy me just the time I need."

26

JERICHO

WE PLUNGE down the stairs to the sound of air whistling past us. All atmo seeks a vacuum, and *Astraea*'s lungs aren't wasting any time purging themselves. I only hope the station's inhabitants are able to get off in time.

Rook, Forsythe, and the rest of the Marine squad bound down the stairs with me until we reach the ground floor. I'm about to shove open the safety door when Rook steps in front.

"Allow me," he says and then forces the door open with his weapon raised. Two more Marines follow him out before someone calls the all-clear. But that term is relative; the corridor is filled with the masses, all running toward the illuminated exit tunnels, aided by the ship's emergency klaxon. I'm guessing "clear" just means no hostiles, because God knows that is far from a peaceful scene.

As soon as we're all out in the hallway, Forsythe says, "You'll have to forgive me, but I'm being recalled to my post on the bridge. I would stay if I could, please know that."

One more reason to like this guy. "Understood. Thanks for your help, Lieutenant."

"See you on the other side, Fox. Rook."

The Master Sergeant and the Lieutenant exchange quick salutes, and then Forsythe steps into the churning sea of rushing pedestrians.

Rook turns to me. "What'll it be, Knight?"

Yeah, Jericho, what'll it be? Keep pretending like you suddenly work for NUESSA again or face reality and get back to your day job? Everything in me wants to see this thing through to the end. But between the captain's order to abandon ship and the fact that I've probably gone as far as I can with this investigation, it's time to face the music.

I check the time. Dammit. "Listen, I'm scheduled to ferry a VIP off station, so I've gotta go. But please understand that it's not because I don't care about—"

"I know your reason for being up here."

"You do?"

"I said the file was the un-redacted one, remember?"

I give him a half smile. "We all gotta live with the choices we make, and right now, mine means I've gotta stop playing detective and get back to my real job."

"Just glad you have a way off station. Wish we had more civilians like you. Hell, I wish we had more *Marines* like you. Enlist?"

"Let's see how I do at ferry captain first."

He gives me a wink through his helmet's glass. "If you ever do come into a chain, I know a politicast that would love to have you." He offers to shake my hand.

I take it and feel something between our palms. In my palm is a bronze and black metal coin. One side reads "Infinita," the other "Sentia Aux," with the politicast's motto inscribed in English and Latin around the outside edge on either side: "Forging paths through the darkness."

"What's this for?"

"Luck. And a reminder where you'll be appreciated."

"Thanks." Then I remember the HG-11. "Almost forgot."

"Keep it. You might need it."

"Aren't there laws against this?"

"Sure. But I lost my sidearm in the explosion." He winks again. "Take care of yourself, Knight."

"You too." I feel the weight of the coin in one hand and the pistol in the other. "And thanks. For everything."

As the Marine squad merges with the human river, I check my location against *Abigail* and get three proposed routes in V-cog. I settle on the fastest one, stuff the coin in my back pocket, clip the HG-11 to my hip, and then head out. As I push my way toward a people mover headed up to section two, my thoughts turn to Evelyn. Hopefully she's back in her lab and getting what she needs before evacuating. I feel bad for the way things have gone for her and empathize with how it feels to be so close to a major breakthrough only to have it ripped from your hands.

Screw it. I'm checking in with her.

"Virtual cognizance record locator offline," says *Astraea*'s automated voice in my lobby. She sounds far too calm for the implications of such news.

"Last known position?"

"Section thirty, celestial exploration laboratory."

I double-check the timestamp. It was less than ten minutes ago. I decide to reach out to Forsythe.

"Miss me already?" he asks.

"I need a favor."

"Shoot."

"First, are you seeing any damage up in the CEL?"

He gives me a curious look. "Uh, no, not as far as I know. But let me check." Ten seconds later, he comes back. "Everything looks nominal."

"Is there any way you can patch me through to a crew member whose V-cog is reportedly offline?"

"Evelyn's?"

"How'd you know?"

"Let me see what I can do."

Evelyn

"EVELYN! LET'S GO," Sam shouts above the ship's emergency klaxon while red LEDs point toward the circular exit hatch. Her hands try pulling me from the bubble's command terminal. "Evelyn. We've got everything we need. Come on!"

She's right. Parallax was backing up to SESI Actual's firewalled servers at the time of discovery, and I have a backup on cold storage in my pocket. Now it's time to get my crew to safety. I release my grip and let

Sam's hands turn me toward the lab's exit. But we're not five meters away when Cheng turns around from the door with a worried look on his face.

"The hatch won't open," he says.

Sam lands next to him and moves the engineer aside. "Let me try." She snaps into V-cog and then lets out an exasperated growl after a few seconds.

"What's wrong?" I ask.

"Some sort of emergency protocol that's closing off all non-exit compartments."

"But we're still inside," Mishra protests. "Shouldn't it detect our V-cog sigs?"

"Yup," Sam replies. "Clearly a software error."

"Can you fix it?" I ask.

"Trying."

"Tits! This is why I do medicine," Kalashnik says from a bulkhead handhold. "Is no surprises. Human body is much predictable."

Mason gives him an exasperated look. "The human body is predictable? Are you kidding me?"

"Yes. I mean, no, I am no kidding. And yes, is predictable."

"Let's just stay calm," I say to the team. "Sam, is there any sort of manual override maybe?"

"Hard control panel is locked down. So, unless you have a crowbar that we can exert a thousand pounds of pressure on? No."

A few team members glance around the lab, presumably for said crowbar, but Sam sounds like she was being facetious. Plus, I'm pretty sure we won't find anything up to the task. My mind turns toward the very real possibility that we get stuck in the lab for a while. It's not the worst fate. Unless whatever's assailing *Astraea* ends up affecting our module too. Time to make a plan.

"Okay, listen up, everybody. First order of business is getting in vac suits. After that, Mishra, I want you sending out our situation on every command channel you can. They're overwhelmed, no doubt, but eventually they'll get to us. Cheng, I want you to work with Sam to see if you can find an override."

"And I look for crowbar," Kalashnik says.

"Fine, yes. Just everyone keep your wits, and tits, about you. We're going to get out of here in one piece, okay?"

"Is very good," Kalashnik replies at my use of his expletive.

Heads nod, but the group's mood is far from convincing. That's one of the problems with scientists: we tend to be a pessimistic lot by nature, hardwired to doubt our own hypotheses until a peer-reviewed study can validate our findings. And even then, we count the days until someone undoes our findings with a new discovery.

It takes less than five minutes for everyone to don the white nanoprene vacuum space suits bearing the *Astraea* Station logo in orange. Even though the hab still has life support, I order helmets on just in case. Headlamps activate automatically, and soon we look like a school of scuba divers suspended in a spherical tank.

One benefit the helmets provide is diminishing the klaxon's irritating wail. It lets me focus more on the issues in front of us. But even that is short lived when Dr. Igor Kalashnik shouts over the team's V-comm.

"I have crowbar!"

Sure enough, the Russian medical doctor has a hunk of steel that he's unscrewed from the underside of a workstation. Can't fault him for not being resourceful. I doubt we'll be able to generate the pressure necessary in zero-g to get the job done, but anything's worth a shot. Kalashnik glides to the door with his bar as Sam and Cheng move aside.

"Any update?" I ask Sam.

"Not yet. I'll let you know."

"Okay. Everyone else, let's work with Igor."

"Yes. Come, come." The doctor starts ordering everyone into place. We use any part of the doorway and surrounding handholds we can as leverage points. And then, on Kalashnik's command, we push on the makeshift crowbar wedged between the spiraled leaves in the iris-looking hatch. But the bar spins out of position and strikes Ramirez in the leg.

He hollers and lets out a string of expletives in Spanish. Then a stream of small red spheres twirls away from his thigh. There's a puncture in his suit.

"Igor! Get that sealed up," I order.

A sad look crosses his face. Then he nods and pushes away to intercept Ramirez.

I ask Sam, "How's it coming?"

"I told you, I'll let you know," she snaps back. It's deserved.

An incoming call pings my V-cog. I accept without looking and slip into my lobby.

"Evelyn," Jericho says.

"Thank the stars. We're in a tight spot here," I say. "What happened?"

"Explosion in the transportation hub."

"Bad?"

"Bad enough. You okay?"

"We're currently trapped in the lab. Any chance you can get word to someone for us?"

"Word to someone?" His eyes dart back and forth for two seconds. "That explains it."

"Explains what?"

"Why no one can reach you."

"What are you talking about? We've been trying to call out for the last few minutes."

His face grows more concerned. "Evelyn, I'm using an emergency back door for this transmission, care of Lieutenant Forsythe."

"What? You mean, ship-wide comms *aren't* out?"

"Negative. Stand by." His avatar freezes for a moment as he splits his attention elsewhere. An uneasy feeling turns my arms and legs to goose flesh. Jericho reanimates. "Okay. Help is on the way."

"Thank you."

"No problem." But his face tells a different story. "Who said ship comms were down?"

"Uh... Mishra." I shake my head, realizing that name means nothing to him. "Bhavna Mishra, our communications specialist."

"Do you trust her?"

I shoot him a dismayed look. "You think she's lying to me?"

He nods.

"No. No way. Why?" Then the question seems to answer itself in my head. "You think there are multiple collaborators."

"Even if local comms were cut, *Astraea*'s backup system is an offsite sat relay network. She would know that."

In real life, I cast Mishra a sideways look. She's gripping bulkhead handholds, head down and eyes closed, presumably trying all emergency channels. Bhavna couldn't possibly be a collaborator, could she?

Back to Jericho, I ask, "Is there any way I can double-check her work?"

He scratches his jawline. "Not without a whole lot of coaching. You have anyone else with you who's a comms specialist that you trust?"

"Sam Collins. She's a computer scientist."

"Good. Brief her."

"Will do." Just before I end the call, I ask, "Why'd you check in with me?"

"Just wanted to see if you got the data you needed before that last explosion."

I'm a little surprised that he didn't hear the big news over the verb, but I assume he's been preoccupied. Another tremor rumbles the station. "What we could, yes. And it's big."

He smiles, but it fades fast. "Get off *Astraea* and stay safe."

"You too, Jericho. Take care."

27

EVELYN

AFTER JERICHO VANISHES from my lobby, I ping Sam.

"What's up?"

No sense mincing words at a time like this. "Can you spy on Bhavna right now?"

Sam pulls her head back. "On Mishra? Why?"

"Just… can you?"

She narrows her eyes at me. "Sure. I can try a silent mirror exploit that won't raise any alarms. Is something wrong?"

"I need to make sure she's doing what she says she is. And I need you to trust me."

"Do you think she…?" Sam shakes her head. "You know what? Never mind. Gimme a sec."

"Thanks."

While Sam gets to work, I slip back into the real and check on Ramirez. Kalashnik has his bleeding under control, the suit sealed, and nanomeds numbing pain receptors.

"Is doing much better," Kalashnik says. "No problems. Also feels very happy-happy inside, yes?"

"Good work, Igor."

"Is job, eh? Normals."

Cheng calls everyone's attention to the door. "It's opening!"

The metal leaves pull apart slower than normal, but the hatch is indeed opening.

"We're saved," Mishra declares. But I don't share her enthusiasm when I see who awaits. There, floating in a vac suit surrounded by at least half a dozen officers, is the face and figure of one Inspector Alexander Paul Stamos. I'm gonna be sick.

"Are you all okay?" he says in the most conciliatory tone possible.

Furtive glances pass among my team with all eyes eventually landing on me.

"We are," I say after a moment. "Here to arrest me again, Stamos?"

"No. I'm here to get you off *Astraea*. Captain Mombawe's orders." He doesn't look like he's bluffing, and neither do the officers with him. Their stun batons are sheathed, and I don't see any binders out. Still, I don't trust Stamos, and his arrival seems too quick to have originated from Jericho's call to Command. Then again, maybe the inspector was close by already; stars know he was probably trying to think of a new way to detain me. Prick.

"We'll see to our own evacuation," I reply.

"And I'm sure you'd do just fine." The corners of Stamos's lips twitch.

I can't tell if his irritation is directed at me or something else. So I press him. "But?"

"But the Captain has asked me to see to your well-being personally." He looks as if he's swallowed a frog. "Look, we got off on the wrong foot, and I'm sorry about that. I was just doing my job. But I'm trying to help you now, and we're here to ensure that your entire team makes it to your designated shuttles."

"Are you?"

He nods in a way that says he might genuinely want to aid us this time. Or maybe it's just that he was ordered to help even though he still hates me. Probably that. Then, in a somewhat emotionless tone, he says, "If all of you would please follow your respective escorts, we will see to your safe and swift disembarkation." Small tags appear in augmented V-cog overlay atop each officer's head, bearing the first initial and last name of each of my team members. And above Stamos's head? The words "E. Park, Chief Astrophysicist."

"Why are you breaking up my crew?" I ask.

His shoulders slump a little, even in zero-g. "NUESSA insists that your team be dispersed to minimize negative mission impact should anything go wrong."

"And they assigned me to you?"

He chuckles and looks away. "My penance, I suppose. But that's how Command assigned them, and we didn't have time to swap names. And trust me, I don't need another broken nose."

"You sure?"

Stamos gives me a nervous laugh and then holds up his hands in mock defense.

Maybe Jericho was behind this after all. Nothing like rubbing my innocence in the inspector's face. I'll send him a thank you note later. "You heard the inspector," I say to the team.

"If you all wouldn't mind moving as quickly as possible? This way, please."

Stamos turns and pushes down the corridor toward the elevator bank. Likewise, my crew spreads out and follows their designated officers. Sam and I are the last out of the hab.

"Please don't do anything crazy, Eves," Sam says. "I think we need to go along with him this time and just get off the station."

I smile at my friend. "Doesn't mean I have to stop hating the guy."

"I would expect nothing less."

We push out the hatch, and I catch up to Stamos. "I want a roster of all the ships we're being assigned to."

"Sending to V-cog now," he replies.

An incoming message pings in my field of view. In a subwindow, I open the list of crew names and ship assignments. Another helpful bit of information is each vessel's current docking assignment and destination port. Not only are we getting separated on *Astraea*, but we're also being transferred to three different targets: *Calypso*, *Arete*, and *Elpis*—all logical safety stops. I forward the roster to the rest of the team and raise them on our private channel. "Make sure you review your destinations, everyone. Keep your heads down and lines open."

They reply with quick confirmation pings as we line up to board our respective elevators out to *Astraea*'s circumference. From there, we'll take lateral lifts to our designated exit points, each located at a different section of the hab. Mine is furthest south, so Stamos and I take the first available lift and drop toward the power level.

A minute of silence passes as we stay on opposite sides of the space, feeling gravity slowly reclaim us. I look out the glass to the south as a delay tactic against conversation, hoping to spot some evidence of the destruction, but the station's humidity makes it impossible.

"A lot of people lost their lives today," Stamos offers in a barely audible voice. "Hope no more do."

"Never figured you for the caring type." Come on, Evelyn. "Eh, I'm sorry. That was low."

"Nah. I deserve it." He sniffs. "Listen. About the last few days…"

"Yeah. About those."

He shoots me a hard look but then his face softens. "When station security said they had something fishy going on in section thirty and asked for volunteers to investigate, I jumped at the chance."

"What kind of fishy?"

"Some conspiracy bullshit."

"If it was bullshit, then why'd you take it?"

He lets out another of his long sighs. "Tired of dealing with tourists. Everyone wants a section one assignment until you have to argue with entitled rock squatters who think they deserve to see the planet from the heavens and can do whatever the hell they want. Gets old fast."

"And your vendetta against me?"

He looks uncomfortable by the question. "I wasn't on duty for ten minutes before we get the call about Hodges's body being found. You just happened to be first in my sights and fit the profile."

"What profile?"

"Word was that some scientist in the upper echelons was planning to take out some of the crew and even sabotage the station."

"What? Why on earth would any of us do that?"

He shrugs. "Plants for the enemy? How the hell should I know?"

"You mean incognitos? People posing under fake identities?"

"Crazy, right?"

"But plausible. It would take some serious coding to make it happen."

His tone stiffens. "So you're familiar with that stuff?"

There he goes again with his investigative assumptions on overdrive. "Oh no, you don't. You're not going anywhere with that one, Inspector."

He smiles and waves a hand at me. "Sorry. Force of habit."

"If you say so." I settle back down and let my weight lean into the wall.

"I guess I just… got so focused on the mission, on keeping people safe, that I got blinded."

"Sounds like someone else I know."

He laughs. "They all said you were dedicated to your work. Anyway, I'm sorry, Dr. Park. Truly."

I think about it for a second—think about the times I've blown it and misjudged someone. "We all make mistakes, Inspector."

"Eh, it's just Jack."

"I thought it was Alexander?"

"It is, but my friends call me Jack. I'm a second; dad is Alexander the first. So I took my grandfather's name instead."

"Gotcha. Well, Jack, I guess someone should thank you for doing your job, even if you ended up targeting the wrong person."

"My section chief doesn't think so. Getting demoted after this, based on what I'm hearing come down the line."

"Well, we all make mistakes. And plus, I'm a free woman now, so… No harm, no foul."

"Fair enough."

Sensing that there's still lingering regret, I say, "If it helps any, you can buy me a drink when all this is over."

"Just as long as you don't try to headbutt me again."

"Deal."

The elevator slows to a stop. We step into a crowded transportation corridor filled with all kinds of people rushing in different directions. There are families towing kids, adults in half-sealed vac suits trying to jog and work their clothes at the same time, and members of the crew doing their best to point people in the right direction despite looking panicked themselves.

Stamos leads me to the third lat lift and closes the door before anyone else can get on. "VIP," he says as he holds up his badge to a few people protesting on the other side of the glass. Then the pod lurches forward and heads south down the tube.

I take a seat on the forward facing bench across from him. "You could have let them on, ya know. It's no problem with me."

"With a killer still on the loose?" He pulls his lips in tight and shakes his head. "No way. For all I know, you're his target."

"So it's a him now?"

"Why not?"

"It could still be a woman."

"Listen, I didn't mean—"

"Stars! Relax, Jack. I'm just messing with you."

He gives me a half smile and then leans back, arms spread across the front of the car. "Whoever it is, they're certainly smart. And they're definitely not working alone."

"How do you figure?"

He seems to think about it for a second, then leans forward with his elbows on his knees. "You found

Hodges, right? Pushed out of the power level. A cleaning bot finds Del Toro's body stuffed in a machinist's locker a few hours later. Then, when all that's happening, the criminal has time to plant an explosive in section sixteen *and* one in the transportation hub? And all while somehow managing to stay off the grid?" He shakes his head. "No way that's all one person. It's too good. Too clean. Like you said, everyone makes mistakes."

"Well. If it's any consolation, Inspector, I recognize that you were just trying to do your job and"—I swallow the bitter pill—"well, help."

He chuckles and lowers his head. "Like I said, I'm pretty sure I bungled my way back to constable on this one."

"Maybe. But given how diligent you've been with staying after me? Seems like once you get your head wrapped around the numbers, it's hard to dissuade you."

His face flattens. Guess I struck a nerve. "Yeah. Something like that," he says.

We ride for a while without talking, allowing the pod's gentle hum to fill the space between us. We pass several sections before I realize we haven't stopped once, all thanks to his security override. That's a nice perk. I find myself looking up through the pod's skylight and watching *Astraea*'s curved terrain pass overhead. What little I can make out at this speed shows an eerie absence of people—no traffic, pedestrian or vehicular. Everyone is heading down to the ag level. Then it hits me. Is this the last I'll see of *Astraea*? And, if so, how many decades will this set NUESSA back? Surely the investigators will apprehend the culprits before the unimaginable happens.

Right?

"What time you got?" I ask, using his fancy watch as an excuse to break the awkward silence.

"Just after five." He shoots me a puzzled look. "You don't have the time in your head?"

"I just thought if someone's willing to carry around an expensive piece like that, you probably like to use it, right?"

He chuckles and covers the watch with his free hand almost absentmindedly.

"How far down we headed?"

"Section two," he replies.

"Cutting it a little close to the action, aren't we?"

"Eh, they've got things stabilized, and the captain is sending you out on his personal ship."

"You don't say?"

Stamos shrugs. "Don't get too excited. He has three."

"Fair enough."

The car begins to slow and I notice the atmosphere has shifted to something more clear, as if the humidity has been sucked out of the cylinder. *Because it has.* We're passing section four, and I get my first glimpse of the transportation hub's destruction. The inner edge of the massive donut-like terminal looks like it's been erased from existence. Beyond the grotesque gaps is the empty blackness of space along with a sliver of the Earth's horizon passing out of view. Beyond the unnatural state of the station slowly tumbling end over end is the thought of so many souls being lost out that hole.

My eyes move north along the power level. Huge chunks of the light emissions systems have been hewn from the base as if a giant hacked them off with an axe. But the power level column itself is still in place, held aloft by the trussing spars that connect it to the hab's endcap. Were it ever to come free, the results would be catastrophic. As if things aren't bad enough already. Whoever is responsible for this… they need to…

"You okay?" Stamos asks.

I lock eyes with him. "Promise me."

"What?"

"Promise me that you'll catch the son of a bitch who's responsible for this."

He holds my gaze for a few seconds and then gives me an almost imperceptible nod. "You have my word, Dr. Park."

28

JERICHO

I HATE CLOSING the connection with Evelyn. I feel like I need to stay on with her until I'm certain she and her team are clear of the station. Why? Because if she did just confirm the most important discovery in human history, which I'm guessing is what "it's big" means, a person like that needs to survive a situation like this to see it through.

Plus, despite her claims that she'll be okay—and the woman is clearly able to handle herself—I worry about the company she's keeping. Stamos, sure. But he's a jackass more than anything else, not a murderous sociopath. Instead, I want to know who this Bhavna Mishra is and who she's working for. It wouldn't surprise me in the least if the station's destruction served an ulterior purpose besides just setting back the Infinita program, like keeping Park's discovery from ever getting out.

The good news, however, is that the enemy has failed—at least in terms of keeping things under wraps. If the system doesn't know already, I'm guessing it won't be long before SESI releases some sort of statement about Evelyn's discovery. Earth, the moon, and then

Mars, Ceres, and Ganymede will all get the news too before long. No matter what happens to us, there's no stopping Evelyn or her work. Thanks to her, we now know that humanity is not alone in the universe.

I'm less than three minutes from *Abby*, so I turn my attention to Kit and ping him to ready the ship for departure. Elroy Faust should be arriving in ten minutes, assuming he hasn't arrived already. There's just one problem:

Kit isn't appearing in V-cog.

While my natural body walks along a curved corridor heading up to bay fourteen on the bravo ring, my avatar paces Kit's ramshackle lobby that, I think, is supposed to resemble an underground cave in Old Cheyenne—his actual room, if I had to bet. He's a sentimental guy if there ever was one. And, contrary to his ship maintenance habits, a bit of a slob. Maybe it's the whole professional plumber who never gets to fixing his own leaky faucets and broken toilets. I'm just grateful Kit didn't have the coin to render out smells, because God only knows what kind of funk I'd be breathing in right now.

"Kit," I yell one more time, hoping to spike his neural sensors if he's taking a nap. But he doesn't show.

I quicken my pace and instinctively pull the pistol from my hip. I keep the weapon low and to the side; no need to make anyone jumpy. Everyone's adrenaline is pumping enough as it is, including mine. Then again, there are far too many people flooding this corridor to notice my pistol anyway.

A minute later, I turn right from the main corridor and into bay fourteen's cargo hold. The doors are parted. Not how I would have left them, and Kit wouldn't have either. The ten by ten meter room is clear. Just some miscellaneous receptacles, spent fuel containers, and a generic tool chest. The far wall is a pressurized door that opens when cargo needs to come up from a docked ship below, but all personnel access is done through the passenger airlock tunnel in the floor by the left bulkhead. I step toward the hole and then aim the HG-11 down the ladder. I almost squeeze the trigger when I see a person.

"Kit!"

He doesn't move. His body is crumpled in a heap at the bottom of the airlock. He's also bleeding from his head.

"Hold on, buddy," I yell in case he can hear me. "I'm coming."

I press both sides of the metal ladder with my hands and boots and quick-slide to the bottom, stopping just short of Kit's body. I spot check *Abby*'s receiving bay for any threats but see none, and the ship's V-cog lobby shows no one else on board. They could be spoofing the sensors, sure, but I choose to trust the ship's tech because I need to examine Kit.

His hair is matted with blood in the back. I'd say it was a fall, but the blow looks too precise, and I don't see bruising anywhere else. I check his pulse: it's steady but fast. So I gently pat his face to see if I can get him to wake up. "Kit. Can you hear me?" I pat a little harder. "Kit?"

"Get off the ship," he slurs.

"It's me, Jericho."

"I said he's not here." His eyes flutter.

"Buddy. Can you hear me?"

He winces, tries to orient himself, and then finds my face with both hands. "Captain Fox?"

"Yeah, pal. What happened?"

"Holy… holy biscuits, am I glad to see you."

I help ease him up and ask more slowly, "What happened?"

He licks his lips and blinks more, then winces as I accidentally brush the back of his head with my arm.

"Sorry."

Kit pushes himself into a sitting position. "There were two people. Uh, a man and a woman. Black flight suits. Station suits."

"And?"

"They forced their way onto the ship asking for you. I told them you weren't here and that they'd have to come back later, then they came at me, you know? Like thugs. Then we wrestled. I think I hurt one of them. The guy. Hurt him bad."

I raise an eyebrow.

"Okay, so maybe not too bad. But he might have a bruise at least, you know? Could be sore? Maybe he needs to—"

"Did you get a good look at their faces?"

"No."

"V-cog?"

"Oh. Yeah, stand by." He slips into his suite and sends me an invite. Strangely, the private space looks no different than his lobby. And why would it? The kid literally grew up in Old Cheyenne caves. Plus, if someone doesn't have enough coin, it's typical just to duplicate the lobby and use it for a suite.

After a few seconds, Kit creates a window connected to his redundant sensory drive and starts scrolling back in time. I spot my face through his blurry vision, then a whole lot of black, then the two figures walking backward through the *Abigail*'s main corridor away from the airlock.

"There," I say.

He lets it play, and one of the figures shoves Kit aside. It's not a violent action but certainly more than he can handle. Based on the footage, I'd say Kit hit his head on a bulkhead and got knocked out.

I give him a sideways look. "He's gonna have a bruise, huh?"

"Hey! *I'm* the victim here."

"Go back," I say, pointing to the video. "See if you can freeze on their faces."

He reverses a little and then freezes the image. It's as good a frame as we're going to get. "You recognize either of them, Cap?"

"I'm not sure. Could be people I met before… I just… Yeah, not sure. You?"

Kit shakes his head. "Sorry."

"Well. I'm just glad you're okay."

"Thanks. Me too."

"Listen, get your head taken care of, and then I want you suited up and ready to go. Faust should be here in five."

"Yeah, okay. Copy, Cap. What are you gonna do?"

"Get suited up too and then poke around the ship to make sure those bastards didn't do anything to *Abby*."

He smiles at my use of the name. "Smart. I'll join you when I can."

I HAVEN'T GIVEN the ship as thorough an inspection as I'd like by the time Kit rejoins me, but it doesn't look like anything's been tampered with in the cockpit or the engine room—the two places I would have focused on if I was trying to sabotage a ship. For all I know, the thugs were just trying to hijack a fancy shuttle and beat the crowds. Not even the *Abigail*'s own diagnostics show anything anomalous, so I'm leaning toward miscreants who Kit scared away and not terrorists bent on blowing us up. It is weird, however, that they asked for me by name and then decided not to stick around. And there is something familiar about their faces. Maybe they're working with Mishra? Not sure, and I don't have time to run a recall. I wish I could make sense of it all.

"Hello?"

Kit and I look aft and toward the airlock's ladder going up to the docking bay.

"Stay here," I tell him. "I'll get Faust squared away. You get *Abby* ready for departure and keep double-checking systems."

"Aye, Cap."

If anyone can find a needle in a shuttle's haystack, it's Kit.

"Be right there," I yell back to Faust as I move toward the ladder and start climbing. "We'll be just another few minutes until we get the ship ready to disembark."

"The sooner the better," Faust replies.

I get my first good look at the client as I emerge from the airlock. He's dressed in an *Astraea* Station security vac suit with the helmet and gloves clipped to his hip. Faust is younger in real life than in his avatar. Gone is the grey at his temples and crow's feet around his eyes. It's not unusual for people to doll up their V-cog profiles, but usually they want to look less aged, not more. Faust also has a splint over his nose, a clear sign that he's sustained a recent injury.

Then I notice he's got someone behind him.

A woman.

"Jericho?" she says.

"Evelyn?"

She steps forward with a warm smile. "Good to see you."

"Is that Dr. Park up there?" Kit hollers from below. "Hold on, I'm coming."

I redirect to Evelyn. "You got out."

"And with enough to substantiate the claim." She pulls a cold storage drive from her pocket and wiggles in her fingers. "Confirmation that it's an extrasolar signal."

"Jesus, Evelyn. Congratulations. But if something happens to us—"

"Backed up on SESI's local servers too," she says as if reading my mind and stuffs the devices back in her pocket for safe keeping.

Faust looks irritated by all the science talk but doesn't interject.

"This is all great news," I say. "But, uh… what are you doing here? Not that I'm upset or anything, I just figured that—"

"Command wants the team splitting up in order to minimize losses in the event that, like you said, something goes wrong."

"Gotcha." I eye Faust and then look back at Evelyn.

"What's wrong?" she asks me.

"No offense, just seems like an unexpected pairing, the two of you."

"You're telling me," she says with a laugh. "But we've come to an understanding."

Faust nods.

"Well, as long as you can tolerate each other for the ride home, we're good."

"I'm sorry to break up this reunion," the Solum

Terram elite says. "But might we continue aboard your ship?"

"Yeah. Kit's just about ready to—"

"Hey there, Dr. Park!"

"Speak of the devil."

Kit climbs up the ladder, emerges out of the airlock, and then whistles once. "Looking fine."

"You too, Kit," she replies with a smile.

Then he turns to Faust. "Say, you got some bad scrapes on your forearms, sir. They're gonna get infected if you don't get 'em looked at el pronto."

Faust moves his hands behind his back in a stately fashion. "I'll be fine."

"No, seriously." Kit tries reaching for the man's left elbow, but Faust bats the hand away with unnatural speed.

"I said, I'll be fine."

The apprehensive look I get from Evelyn seems to confirm my suspicions: that move was too quick. Granted, licensed tweaks aren't illegal, but there are rules against enabling them while on government property. It wouldn't surprise me if Faust thinks he's above the law. All the more reason to get this over with as fast as possible.

I turn to Kit, who's nursing his hand against his chest. "Let's secure Mr. Faust and Dr. Park below."

"Sure thing, Cap."

"Mr. Faust?" Evelyn asks. "Who's that?"

Faust's eyes dart from me to Evelyn and then to my hip.

I reach for the weapon, but Faust kicks my hand away—so hard that my arm swings back and strikes Kit, who falls down the airlock. Whoever this is, he's definitely code doped, and he's not Mr. Faust.

Shit.

Evelyn yells my name as Faust shoves her back and to the ground. Her helmet pops out of her arm, skitters across the floor, and makes Faust look. I seize the opportunity and pull the HG-11 up, aim, and fire. The gun's hydraulic-like *zzzip-whir* sounds from the muzzle as the projectile whips up a vortex of curled air. But the shot misses Faust and strikes the far bulkhead with a loud *crack* and sparks. The man takes two steps forward before I can get the next shot off and disarms me with lightning speed that sends bolts of pain up my wrists and forearms.

"Get out of my way," he says in a calm tone as he wraps a hand around my neck.

I try to wrestle away, but his grip is like iron and his arm like a truss.

My vision is fading.

Evelyn's face appears beside Faust's head. With arms wrapped around his neck, she sinks her teeth into his earlobe and rips off a chunk. At the same time, she presses a middle finger into his left eye socket. Before she can do more damage, Faust roars, releases my neck, and sheds Evelyn like a discarded coat. She lands on her back and spits out the chunk of ear, mouth covered in blood. The enemy turns on her, giving me another window to retrieve my sidearm that's clattered to the floor. I cough as my throat tries to reopen, then dive for the weapon and bring it to bear on Faust, but he's retrieved Evelyn and uses her as a human shield.

"Put her down, Faust!"

"His name is Stamos." Evelyn strains as the enemy's hand cinches around her neck.

Stamos? *The inspector?* "I'll shoot, Stamos."

"And I'll intercept," he replies, squeezing Evelyn's neck a little tighter as he does.

She gags, and her face is turning purple.

"Dammit! Let her go."

"Can't do that." He backs out of the cargo hold, pays me one last look over Evelyn's shoulder, and then steps into the mass of people rushing to their ships.

"Dammit!" I charge after them and spot Stamos's head moving through the crowd. "Kit," I yell over V-cog. "Launch the ship and get clear."

"What?"

"There's no time. Stay in a holding pattern and be ready to come get us."

"Us?"

"No time to explain. Launch it, Kit!"

"Aye, Cap."

Then I charge into the crowd to chase Stamos and Evelyn through *Astraea*.

29

EVELYN

"One false move, and I'll snap your spine," Stamos says in my ear as he pushes me through the crowd with his fingers in the small of my back. His voice can't be heard above the din of passersby, nor does the look on my face stand out above any other distraught soul in fear for her life. If I was to shout, I doubt a single head would turn and give me a second thought as we all race to abandon ship. The only thing that might serve me is the fresh blood around my mouth or running down the side of Stamos's head.

Still, I need to be ready if Stamos makes a mistake. And I can help speed that up by keeping him off balance. "I always knew you were an asshole."

"And I always knew you were worth killing."

I throw an elbow into his ribs, but he yanks my head back by the hair. "I warned you."

"Then do it."

Stamos hesitates.

"That's what I thought."

He lets go of my neck and shoves me a step forward. "Keep moving."

I use the opportunity to reach Jericho, but Stamos is

jamming V-cog somehow. He seems to notice my effort and prods my back again. "Ah, ah, ah, Dr. Park. No calls. It's just you and me now."

The quad's lat lift hall is coming up at the tunnel's end.

"Dr. Park?" says a man to my left. "What's going on?"

"Julio," I shout. "You need to get help!"

But before my favorite ice cream dolling xenobiologist can do anything, Stamos shoves the man's head away so hard that Julio flies against the corridor wall and collapses. I can't tell if the blood on his head is his own or from Stamos's hand. Either way, my friend will need medical attention. Several people check on Julio while the rest step away from us.

Stamos has us moving again, only faster. "Keep walking," he says in my ear.

I want to ask someone to help Julio get off the station. He's clearly unconscious, maybe worse, and he'll need assistance. But I know Stamos would make others suffer for it.

We cross the hall and board a lateral lift using Stamos's inspector credentials like before, only this time we head north and through the ag level. He's holding his ear with one hand, applying pressure.

"It was you all along," I say after a minute, feeling so stupid for not seeing it sooner. "Sequestering me from everyone else at Hodges's murder scene, arresting me on circumstantial evidence at best… How long have you been dirty, Stamos?"

"You understand so little for one the world thinks is so smart."

"You're… *not* Inspector Stamos, are you."

The corner of his lips twitch, and I catch a faint sparkle in his eye.

"But how did no one else call your bluff?" I snap my fingers. "Because you were transferred from section one, that's why. Stars. The real Stamos is—what?—probably stuffed in a locker somewhere?" Maybe all his tinkering around is what got the techs like Hodges working overtime in the first place. "How did you co-opt their V-cog though?"

"Stop talking," he says in a cold tone that has the desired effect. For now anyway. I have way too many questions that need answering, and I need to find a way to stop him and escape. Part of me wants to lunge across the pod and attack. And if he was a normal person, it might work. But Stamos is tweaked up on some serious batch code that has me scared. When he says he can snap my spine, he's telling the truth; I saw what he did to Kit and Jericho. So, if I can't outfight my adversary…

Then I'll just have to outthink him.

"You're never going to get away with this, Stamos."

He gives me a crooked smile but resumes watching the terrain pass by—long open fields curving up and out of sight beyond the station's sides. Herds of cows and sheep dot the countryside like pieces of patchwork sewn across an emerald-green quilt.

"What are you, Tantum Terrae then?" I ask, hoping to get some response from him. But he just grunts in return. "Stars, on the trip down I couldn't get you to shut up. What, did you use up all your words or something?"

"I said, stop talking."

Well, this is going great. Some old memories resurface in my mind—lessons taught by a visiting hostage negotiator back in Christchurch when I was in school. Hadn't thought about that class in a while, probably because I'd been a hostage when I was thirteen and found myself cursing the instructor for being a few years too late. But life is a funny thing, and cruel. Here I am once again with blood on my face in a room with a man who can kill me, if he wants, or worse, if he needs. Time to dig deep.

"It seems as if you really don't like what we're doing here," I offer, labeling his emotions. Then I wait and hope the pause will work its magic.

The silence stretches on for a few interminably long seconds before Stamos finally looks across at me. "You have damned our entire civilization, Dr. Park."

Is that all? I want to ask but lock down my sarcasm. Instead, I use another technique and mirror his last words in the form of a question, hoping he'll keep talking. "Damned our entire civilization?"

The edges of his mouth curl into a sneer. "You claim to be a scientist. A seeker of truth? But you're nothing more than a traitor to the community."

"Traitor?" I parrot again, hoping he'll go on.

He seems to take notice of my tactics and then looks back out the window. Roadblock.

I try something else. "If you feel I'm that big of a threat, it seems logical that you'd want to kill me."

"I don't want to kill you," he says as if the statement isn't entirely true. There's a black swan in there somewhere—a critical piece of information I can leverage.

"But you do hate me. Why not just satisfy your desire then?"

The question goes unanswered, and Stamos returns to staring out his window. He checks the blood on his hand once and then puts pressure back on his ear. Little does he know that he did answer my question, at least in part. The silence tells me that while he may want to end my life, something else is keeping him from doing it. Which means this man has a deep sense of loyalty to whoever is commanding him.

Or he's just brainwashed. But he doesn't seem the brainwashed sort. Those people always have a certain glaze over their eyes, one that says their actions aren't their own. They're the walking dead, unable to reason for themselves and ever-bound to the will of another. This man is too focused for that. Too ambitious.

Which means he's a true believer.

Admittedly, that's a cousin of brainwashing but retains more autonomy. Despite the blood soaking his palm, I've twice noticed the Viatoribus tattoo before—once when we first met at Hodges's crime scene and another when he transferred me to Rook's care. Both times the tattoo seemed crisp, too new to be the lifelong emblem of a man who'd devoted his life to policing for his politicast. I should have questioned it sooner.

But there's something more to Stamos. He's not just a believer. His words "a traitor to the community" come back to me.

He's a scientist. A vengeful sociopathic killer scientist, sure. But a scientist nonetheless. I just need to prove it.

"You feel like we're wasting precious resources, right?" I say, labeling his emotions again. "And if we would just focus on Earth, we could save it. It's all just simple math and properly allocating resources."

His head snaps toward me.

There we are. *I see you, Stamos—or whoever you are.*

"Why would you say that?" he asks.

Feeling that I've gained some element of control, I ease back in my seat and glance casually toward the passing fields. "Why else would someone risk their life

and career to destroy Earth's first O'Neill-Oberth orbital legacy habitat with 375,000 souls aboard? If it's
terrorism you're after, there are far easier targets planet
side. But I don't think you're a terrorist."

The strangest emotion passes over his face so fast I
almost miss it: a look that says he feels understood. But
the stoic glare replaces it in a flash. So I press on.

"I think you love the planet."

"You're playing politicast propaganda against me,
Dr. Park. Try harder."

"I think you've worked out what the rest of the scientific community hasn't, or what they've decided to ignore. That even if we succeed in reaching the stars, it
will be too little too late."

"Congratulations. You scroll the verb. Now
shut - up."

But I won't shut up. The street rat in me knows
when I'm on the scent of something worth tailing. I fold
my arms and relax my body. Not in a superior way, but
in the leisurely language of someone who is at peace
with their conclusion regardless of what their opponent
thinks. "Lunatics offer themselves to suicide missions.
They're fanatics driven by fantasy, right? Some
grandiose idea fed to them as children that eventually
manifests in a perverse bloodlust. But you're not a lu-
natic. All of this"—I wave a hand around the car—"it's
too calculated. Too precise to be fanatical. It's mathematical."

"Stop talking."

"No one does what you've done unless they're absolutely certain. Unless they've first questioned, re-
searched, hypothesized—"

"Tested, yes, yes. I know the method!"

I raise an eyebrow. So he *is* a scientist. Then he's

also a man of reason, despite whatever extremes he's given himself over to. That, and he's a masterful actor, no small thanks to more batch tweaks, I imagine. Which means he's heavily funded. And why wouldn't he be? If the Tantum Terrae is really behind this, taking down *Astraea* would all but secure their legacy against every other politicast in the system. They'd put everything they have into this. Into *him*.

"You figured out a way to skim V-cog nanos, didn't you," I say after a moment. "That's how you were able to spoof *Astraea* and blend in so well. Probably changed identities a dozen times too."

"Wouldn't you like to know."

"I'll take that as a yes. You sneak uranium bombs onto the station and know just where to place them because your people are smart. Research, right? And then you want me because, well…" I squint at him and study his blank face. The lack of emotion is more disconcerting than all-out rage. "…because someone else wants me."

He blinks.

Time to push his buttons. "Because I'm the prize."

"You," he says through tight lips. "*You* are an afterthought."

"Ouch. That hurt."

"One I am starting to reconsider."

"Double ouch."

He pulls his palm off his ear and balls his hands into fists. "Hodges and Del Toro were afterthoughts too. Merely pieces who got in the way."

"What? I'm not worth killing?"

He scowls at me. "For now."

"Mmmm." This most recent confession piques my curiosity. "So how did you kill Hodges and get down to the power level in time to corner me? Because we both know it's impossible."

He doesn't reply aside from a cold hard stare.

"You had an accomplice. Someone already on station."

"If you're looking for a confession, Dr. Park, you won't get one."

More to myself, I say, "Which would explain how you covered your tracks. And that gave you time to become Stamos. But then there's the issue of the Space Marines." I look up at him as he crosses the lift. "If you already had the perfect front to capture me, why involve the military?"

He grabs my arm and pulls me up. "An unexpected delay. But you got yourself out of that one, didn't you."

"So they weren't in the cards. Interesting."

"Enough." He squeezes my arm until it hurts. "We're done talking."

"No problem. I have what I need."

Stamos's lips turn up to one side. "What is that supposed to mean?"

"It means that unless you call off the rest of your mission, because we both know there's one last bomb, then I'm going to kill myself."

He grimaces. "You may be an esteemed astrophysicist, but you're a very poor negotiator, Dr. Park."

"Am I?" I let the question hang in the air for a few seconds, enough that I catch Stamos's eyes shift. "If you wanted to kill me, there's little doubt I'd be dead; the hate in your eyes tells me that much. So the mission wasn't about me. As you said, I'm an afterthought. Which can only mean that you're bringing me back as the spoils of war. And whoever you're bringing me back to will no doubt be impressed by your assertiveness. Now, if I kill myself—"

"Which you won't."

"—then I destroy your trophy."

"I have *Astraea*."

"Not if they find your bomb first."

His face goes flat again. What an interesting tell.

"Then what do you have, Stamos? A failed mission *and* a trophy who commits suicide?" I hold up both hands empty.

"I've already done more than any before me," he replies. "If it all ends now, it was enough."

"Was it though? The authorities will trace this back to the Tantum Terrae. Your face is already on Jericho's V-cog, and they'll link it to every persona you've taken on. This doesn't do anything but prove how desperate your people have become. The Tantum Terrae can't justify its cause with research so you do it with bombs. Typical."

"It's not typical. They will never find it, and you will come with me."

So there *is* one bomb left. Good to know. "You're right, I will come with you."

He purses his lips and lowers his hand.

I take his body language as an invitation to forge ahead. "If you disarm your bomb and allow me to double-check your work, then I will volunteer to go back to your headquarters with you and suffer whatever meetings I am to bear."

"A worthless offer. I already have you."

"Not really. As I said, suicide."

"I'll knock you out."

I laugh, and not the bluffing kind. It's the tone someone employs when they know they have the upper hand and aren't afraid to throw their cards on the table, all in. "I've already started a countdown of my own." I tap the back of my head with a finger. "A little code that I bought a long time ago, were I ever to be cornered again. I'd rather die than repeat it."

It takes him only a second to parse my meaning. "A dead man's switch? You're bluffing."

"Am I?" I slip into V-cog and send him an invite to my suite.

He releases my arm and hesitates.

"Don't be shy, Stamos."

The killer grits his teeth and then appears in my childhood dining room. Seeing anyone in here unnerves me. But I'm determined to stop him, and this must be done, so I force my emotions to back down.

There, in the middle of the dining room table where I ate my last meal with both my parents as a family, is a black shipping container half-a-meter square with the lid open. Inside glows the rendering of a briefcase-sized neutron bomb that I'd swiped from the verb years ago. It's a placeholder, albeit a dramatic one. But I figured that if I was ever going to kill myself, I might as well do it with some flare.

However, what I really want him to see is the authentication on the case's side. He notices and leans down to read the black market receipt for the unlicensed code I'd used to craft this particular construct. It's the small piece of evidence that screams, "The nanos in her skull will liquify her brain if she loses consciousness or you try tampering with her head, asshole!"

"You're insane," he spits.

"Takes two ta' tango."

"I don't even need you!"

"If your bomb doesn't go off, you will."

We step back into real life where he paces the lift and scoffs at the air. "Listen to you! My God, you're so full of yourself, you and your self-righteous mission to rescue humanity from itself. They can't stop me, and you'll kill yourself for nothing."

In the softest of tones, I say, "You really want to play those odds?"

His lips part to speak, but he thinks twice. Finally, he says, "They'll never find it."

"They got this far."

"And no further!"

"You don't sound so sure."

He spins on me, closes to within mere centimeters of my face, and screams the words, "I am sure!"

"Then I'll flip my switch now."

He glares, red faced, as the pod slows. The bleeding from his ear has resumed as the result of increased pressure breaking through the clot.

"Call it off and I'll go with you. No questions asked, Stamos."

He backhands me across the face and knocks me to the floor. "You bitch!"

The whole left side of my head burns. I manage to push myself up, but then he straddles me. One hand palms the back of my head while the other goes under my chin.

He's not going to wait for my dead man's switch.

He's going to kill me himself.

I try screaming "GET OFF!" but the words only come out as saliva through tight lips. The sensation of being trapped sends a jolt of panic through my body. I struggle against his vice-like grip, but it's no use. I'm pinned. He just sits on my back, cradling my head with some sort of morbid anticipation of snapping my neck.

But I still have power.

I'll be damned if I'm going to let Stamos be the one to take my life. The slender silver switch on the bomb beckons my index finger forward. I comply and rest it gently in place. One point five kilos of pressure and it's all over. I only hope that Sam, Lem, and all the others do what needs doing to make sure our discovery counts. Then some small part of me will be carried on in their work, and that makes me happy. Stamos not winning makes me happy.

So I let out the slow and steady breath of a woman who has made peace with her role in the world.

30

JERICHO

I PUSH my way up the corridor, but I can't keep up with Stamos and Evelyn. The crowd, already antagonized by the fleeing couple, is primed and takes out their anger on me. Shouts for me to slow down and watch where I'm going turn into aggressive threats and more than a few hands trying to shove me back—so much for utopia. It all adds up to me losing sight of my quarry.

"Jericho Fox?" says a commanding female voice behind me.

I turn to face two people who look exactly like those in Kit's V-cog memory. I feel my heart rate increase and, with it, the unavoidable fight or flight instinct brought on by adrenaline. "Sorry. I'm in a hurry."

"You can make time for us," she says. "This way."

Before I can protest, I feel something hard press against my back while a strong hand forces me to give up my HG-11. Any thought of resisting or making a break for it gets dampened by a second pistol pressing into my side and steering me toward docking bay doors ahead.

The pair ushers me into a vacant freight bay easily

three times the size of the one we have *Abigail* docked at. It's stacked high with black crates and enormous shipping containers all bearing various decals and tags for their comings and goings. Likewise, the space has three oversized airlock doors along the back wall used for ferrying cargo with robotic arms.

The two thugs push me forward once we're far enough into the bay, and I instinctually raise my hands since we're free of the crowds. I know what comes next, but I at least want to find out who's killing me and why if I'm going out. "So who wants me dead?"

"Not us," the woman says.

"What?" I turn to face them and risk lowering my arms since both thugs are holstering their weapons. "Somebody mind explaining what the hell is going on here?"

"Our mutual employer sent us to protect you."

"Mutual employ—" It hits me. "You're Sallsworth's headhunters I met at High Top."

"Took him long enough," the muscular man says to his counterpart with that thick old African accent.

"My name's Jones. This is Afumba. And you're in deep shit."

"No kidding. What's all this about?"

"We don't know much. Just that someone high up in the Tantum Terrae is trying to make a play for you."

"Dead?"

"Possibly," says Afumba. "But more likely alive."

Jones nods in agreement. "A person of your fame is a valuable commodity to the right cause if leveraged properly."

"Sounds like another politicast I know."

"They are not a politicast," Afumba interjects.

"They are illegitimate and cold-blooded killers with no moral compass."

"Am I sensing some unresolved childhood aggression there? You might want to see a counselor."

Afumba blinks at me and then turns to Jones. "You sure I can't stun him?"

She smiles. "It's not personal, Mr. Fox. Afumba doesn't like anyone. Especially the TT. They slaughtered his family and left him for dead."

"Sorry to hear that. Listen, I really hate to break this up, but I have someone I need to rescue."

Afumba holds out his large hands to stop me from passing. "I am afraid we cannot let you out of our sight, Mr. Fox."

"Great. The more the merrier. Let's go."

Jones steps in. "And we can't allow you to wander this station. You'll be departing with—"

The left side of her face blows apart and showers me with human debris. Afumba takes several rounds to his back but somehow manages to cover me. I'm guessing reactive gel vest. He uses his massive arms and chest to corral me behind the safety of the closest shipping container. Despite the suppressed muzzle sounds of the mag-acceleration weapons coming from the entrance, people still scream in the corridor outside. The loudest noise comes from the bullets cascading against freight containers and metal crane arms around us.

"You know how to use this?" Afumba says as he pulls my HG-11 from his hip.

I nod and take the pistol back. "Yeah."

"Stay alive."

"Good plan."

"Now go." Afumba leans out, shoots, and gets the enemy's attention while I slip around the far corner and behind the next container, putting distance between me and the enemy. Then I turn and cover him as he drops back. I doubt I hit anyone, but I'm just trying to buy us some margin. MAW projectiles ping around the bay like mad hornets looking for trespassers to sting. Only, without armor like Afumba's, I'll end up like Jones if I'm hit. The sight of her fluids on my uniform sends another wave of adrenaline down my limbs. This is the real deal.

"Keep going," Afumba yells as he points me to the next row. "Move, move, move!"

I lunge behind the last container just as bullets slap against the metal and stitch lines across the far wall. Then I press my back up against the crate and slide over so Afumba can join me.

"Any bright ideas?" I ask him.

A small metallic cylinder clinks its way into view…

Oh shit!

We run right toward the end of the row. I'm not sure if the grenade is the kind that kills or just incapacitates, but neither interests me.

The device detonates just as we slide around the container's far end and hit airlock bay doors. Bits of something lodge themselves in the wall near my head. It's the killing kind. My ears are ringing, and the scent of something sharp stings my nose.

Afumba pulls me behind a solid stack of cargo cases in the corner. "You cover left. I have right," he says.

"Got it."

"Mr. Fox?" I hear someone call above the sound of ringing in my ears. They're near the entrance as far as I can tell.

"He's a little busy right now," I reply despite Afumba's hand motioning me not to.

"Why don't you come and we can discuss this amiably."

"I'm not sure you and I have the same definition for that word, so we're gonna need to… rain check that?" *What?* God, I really suck at comebacks.

The speaker waits, then says, "We'll make your death as painless as possible, Mr. Fox."

Why do bad guys say that, as if it makes the prospect of dying better somehow? *Well, cool. If it's gonna be painless, then sign me up!*

More weapons fire crashes against the nearest bulkhead, forcing me to duck. I spot figures moving through the low light. They've literally cornered us.

"Last chance, Mr. Fox."

"Yeah, still not interested."

Footsteps clomp down my aisle to the left. I ready myself for the confrontation, raise my weapon, then swing out to aim along the back wall. A figure spots me but too late. I squeeze my pistol's trigger first and feel the weapon recoil. The air twists as the projectile zips into the enemy, knocking him sideways. I have to blink twice to register that I've actually hit him—lucky first shot. A sudden burst of weapons fire to my right snaps against the cases near my head, and Afumba hauls me down.

"Watch yourself, Fox."

"Thanks."

Back down my aisle, I spot another figure step into view where the first body lies. But this one pivots fast and fires at me. Driven by instinct, I take a knee, lean out, and shoot back—three rounds this time, as fast as I can squeeze the trigger. The quick *zip-zip-zip-whir* thrums from my pistol, and I'm not even sure if I've hit the target. I just know I'm not dead.

I pull back behind cover again and bump against Afumba as new noises echo near the entrance. There's shouting, heavy footfalls, and faster weapons fire. Then something clatters to the ground on the other side of our crates. I lead with my pistol and find a dark-clothed assailant on his face two meters away. I'm guessing the victim was picked off from a container overhead by Afumba.

The victim's dead hand is stretched toward a mag assault rifle. I squat, reach for the weapon, and pull it back behind cover. I stuff the HG-11 in my uniform and grab the rifle's grip, attempting to pair it with V-cog. But almost as fast I notice that there's no user lock. It's off the books. How they got it on board is for someone else to figure out. Instead, I make sure the amrod still has rounds left in it—twice as many as my pistol—and double-check the battery level. Good to go.

"Jericho?"

My father is in my goddamn V-cog lobby. "Dad! I gotta go!"

"What?" Afumba asks.

Shit. I'm talking in both environments. "Bad time, pops!"

I terminate the connection.

More projectiles continue to throw sparks in our corner, so I wait for a lull in the spray, hoping it's timed for when the enemy is reloading or distracted. I really don't know what the hell I'm doing—just wanna make it out of this alive—and the assault rifle's given me renewed confidence.

A third man squatting behind a square crate sees me and swings his rifle up. Before he can shoot, I squeeze the trigger. The mag rifle kicks my shoulder repeatedly as projectiles zip through the air—too many to count. The target's arms flail and he stumbles backward three steps before dropping out of sight. I release the trigger, realizing the gun was on full auto. Yet another wave of adrenaline hits me so hard I feel like I could run through a wall.

"Knight," a voice yells.

That stops me in my tracks.

Then, from inside my V-cog lobby, "Knight! You back there?"

"Rook?"

"That's Master Sergeant to you," he replies with a smile. "Hold your fire."

"Roger." To Afumba, I say, "Don't shoot. The good guys are here."

He grunts in acknowledgement.

Voices working their way through the rows of shipping containers take turns yelling, "Clear!" as more footfalls move toward us. The weapons fire has stopped. It's over.

A moment later, Rook steps into my aisle in his black and grey combat armor with his darkened face smiling behind his visor. "Good to see you, Knight."

I stand. "You too."

Knowing that the firefight is done, I feel the adrenaline dump hard out of my system. Knees get shaky as I look down the rows and spot the people I've killed. Shit.

"You okay?" Rook asks.

"Yeah," I lie. My stomach starts turning.

Rook thumbs at the bodies. "Good work. First time?"

I nod. The churn in my stomach gets worse. Rook pulls the mag rifle from my hands as I double over and retch on the floor. For all my calm under pressure as a pilot, this is a different animal. It was kill or be killed—I know that logically. And I've seen my share of dead people. But shooting someone is another beast altogether. I take a few seconds to collect myself and wipe my mouth.

"Happens to the best of us," Rook assures me. "It'll wear off."

"I'll take your word for it."

I count thirteen bodies as we exit the bay, plus Jones's. Afumba pulls a few items from her bloody corpse and then joins us. Where all these bad guys came from and why they wanted me dead is playing out in my head like a conspiracy theory on bad code. So far, all I have is that Nigel sent a team to protect me, and the Tantum Terrae countered with a bunch of hitmen with automatic mag weapons. Beyond that, it's a mystery.

The crowd parts for the Space Marine squad as we enter the main corridor. In V-cog, I ask Rook, "Were you able to ID any of the assailants?"

"Negative. All bio sigs were mismatched to bogus IDs."

"Incogs?"

"Your words, not mine."

"You ever encountered it before?"

"Only in training scenarios."

"Right." Neither of us need to expound. Virtual incognito identification mirroring is a theoretical threat, not a known one. But just because no one has ever figured out how to hack the system doesn't mean it's not possible. Samson—or Stamos, who the hell knows— and now all the dead bodies in the cargo hold? Someone got their hands on the tech. Christ, for all I know, no one's ink is real, and they're trying to frame one another.

"So you have Evelyn?" I ask Rook as we hustle down the corridor.

"Negative. Orders are to get you off station ASAP. A Navy transport is—"

I grab his arm in the real. "You didn't grab her?"

"Negative."

I stop. "She's with the goddamn bomber, Rook!"

"What?"

"My client shows up outside our ship, and he's holding her hostage. That's who I was going after when I get sidelined back there."

"Son of a bitch." His avatar freezes, and his real-life head turns slightly as he presumably makes a call. He comes back to me ten seconds later. "Sorry, Knight. Orders stand. We have to get you to transport."

"Like hell you do."

He stops again and glares at me.

"We're going after her now, Sergeant. Copy?" When he doesn't budge, I ask, "Am I still the *apparent judicas* if there's a killer on the loose?"

He seems reluctant. "Technically, yes. But—"

"Then I don't see a problem, do you?" Before he can argue, I grab my contraband rifle out of his hand—an action I know he *let* me do because his mil-spec batch code saw it coming before I did—and head down the tunnel. But when I don't sense them following me, I pause and look back. "You coming? Or am I shooting more bad guys by myself?"

"Not without this." Rook twists off an amrod from his Gecko Griptech vest and tosses it to me. "You're dry. Remember?" Then he holds out a hand, and one of his men puts a pistol in it. "You also dropped your sidearm back there. You're gonna field day the squad bay for the next week."

"Field what?"

He brushes past and hands me the pistol. "Now we can move."

31

EVELYN

I FLIP the detonation switch on my brain.

Nothing happens.

I smack the case sitting on the dining room table. It's just a construct, I know. But it should've triggered. The code is solid.

Stamos pulls his hand off the back of my head, keeping the other under my chin, and then shoves his fingers into my hip pocket. I panic. Swearing.

He grabs something.

The cold storage drive.

Then he lets go of my head and stands. "Get up."

A cold shudder runs through my body as I realize I'm still alive. I don't know how, but I am. I stare at the drive in his hand and reach for it.

"Give that back!" He slaps my hand away, enough that I pull my fist into my chest. I think about wrestling him for the drive but then reconsider. There are more cunning ways. "What did you do to my head?"

He plays with the ring on his finger. "Changed the game."

I don't know how he did it, but Stamos just hacked the hell out of my suite.

Then he holds up the drive. "And took more of what I want."

"You won't be able to do anything with that," I say in an attempt to reason with him. "The encryption is too strong."

"Like the code in your head?"

I open my mouth to reply, but he has a point.

"Oh, don't worry, Dr. Park. I never had any intention of deciphering it. You misunderstand me." Stamos bends down and shows me the device in the flat of his hand like he's offering a dog a treat. Then he curls his fingers over it and produces a series of muffled *snaps* as he makes a fist.

I let out an instinctive "No!" but then scold myself for the outburst. It no doubt provided Stamos the reaction he desired. And it was completely unnecessary: Lemuel has the local backups at SESI Mission Control.

Stamos dumps the drives parts onto the floor and wiggles his fingers like waving fairy dust. Then he blows across his palm and into my face.

I wince and look away.

"Get up, Dr. Park. We have things to do and people to see."

The car slows, and I check the section number as I stand. "Why are we here?"

"Walk." He pushes into the large transportation hall of section thirty's ag level. The area's population seems to have dwindled significantly, which is a good sign. It means people are getting off *Astraea*. Most will have boarded emergency ships, while the rest will head for escape pods. They'll be picked up in space over the next few hours like golf balls collected by a field cart. It makes me wonder if we'll be leaving by escape pod too, which means I might have a better chance of getting away from him.

"Where are we headed?" I ask.

"No more questions. Walk." He prods me forward with stiff fingers in the small of my back. It might as well be a gun.

We pass the last of the quadrant's crew as they rush toward their escape modules. No one pays us any mind. Between the klaxon and *Astraea*'s thirty-second evacuation interval, everyone has tunnel vision. I keep wondering which outer hull access route he'll push me into. It isn't until Stamos turns toward a bank of vert elevators and forces me inside that I start to worry.

"We're headed up?"

The doors close, and I take his silence as agreement.

"But don't you want to get off the station? All the escape pods are located—"

"STOP. TALKING." A fist strikes my face and drops me. Guy hits like a battering ram. I spit blood onto the glossy white floor and then touch a tooth that's screaming in pain. It's loose. That'll need some work. I spit again and feel the ebbing gravity help me stand. Likewise, my blood starts rolling across the floor as centripetal inertia lessens.

We're about one kilometer up *Astraea*'s endcap when I see the light emissions system stutter. In all my time up here, I've never seen that. Not once.

"They've initiated the backup generator," Stamos offers, free of charge. He says it casually, as if...

"You knew they would."

He smiles with nothing behind it but at least refrains from hitting me for speaking again. "All systems are predictable, Dr. Park. Even the basis of chaos theory is pattern and interconnectedness, wouldn't you agree? But predicting the sequence of events during *Astraea*'s breakdown? It's not even challenging. Every NEUSSA article on the subject describes it in vivid detail. All I needed to do was start things moving in the right direction."

Right direction? Those words were intentional.

Then the meaning dawns on me.

"Trigger explosions on either side of the main reactor and, even without hitting it, you divert system needs to the backup in section thirty."

Stamos gives me another flat smile, but this one has a touch more emotion.

"But if you're planning on blowing another hole in the station, why worry about the reactors at all?" The question is barely out of my mouth when the answer presents itself like a shooting star burning a trail across the night sky. "You wouldn't."

"Oh, but I have, Dr. Park."

"You placed a bomb *inside* the reactor?"—something he couldn't have done when that was operational.

"Near enough."

I rub the ache in the back of my neck as I consider the full weight of the revelation. I feel like a complete fool for not thinking of it sooner. But why would I have? No one in their right mind would dream of dropping a legacy hab through the Earth's atmosphere…

No one but a calculating sociopath born into the Tantum Terrae.

The matter of propulsion is what's really in play here. The first bomb gave the station the tiniest nudge, as we witnessed from the lab. The second started Astraea tumbling at a slow rate. And the third? All he needs to do is wait for the section-one end of the station to be pointed at the proper angle, and he has himself a nuclear powered rocket with one short but very powerful burn.

"You're going to destabilize its orbit," I say after a moment. "And send it into the planet." The image plays in my mind like a horror scene. Not only will it kill anyone left on station, but *Astraea* could also kill thousands on the planet depending on where it lands and the environmental impact. "Why risk so many lives on Earth too? I thought you're all about trying to protect them?"

"It's the cost of the message. That abominations like *Astraea* equal lives, not just of those in the heavens above but on the Earth below. The sky is falling, Dr. Park," he says, reciting one of the Tantum's more cliché mantras.

"I thought we had a deal. Me for the station."

"*You* had a deal, Dr. Park. I agreed to nothing. Did you really think I would trade all of this"—he gestures out the lift window to the hab—"for your life?"

"You're insane, Stamos."

"No. No! I'm not insane. I'm *right*. And that is all that matters!"

"Then why keep me alive at all?"

The elevator slows to a stop and the doors open.

"Because I need you to do one last thing for me, Dr. Park." Stamos forces me out of the car and turns me toward the lab. "I need you to corrupt the core data files that you've transmitted to SESI."

"What? That's impossible. They've already been sent. And plus, I don't have that kind of expertise."

"No. You have the command authority. But Dr. Collins has the expertise."

Right on cue, the lab hatch irises open, and I spot Sam floating across the lab with her hands bound behind her back and her mouth gagged. There's a cut over her eye and an ugly bruise to match, but otherwise she looks okay. Behind her, I notice the starscape passing and then Earth's leading edge coming into view.

"Sam!" The outburst gets me a blow to the back of the head. I see stars and fight the pull of unconsciousness. "If you want me to do this, I need to be awake, you bastard!"

"Then you'd better get moving," he says and shoves me toward the hatch.

I COLLIDE with Sam midway through the lab and study her eyes. She's scared. But she looks like a woman who's doing her best to stay composed despite the circumstances. I work the gag off her mouth. "You okay?"

She nods, but the effort is half-hearted. "He's lost his mind, Eves. He put—"

"I know. We're gonna get out of this." I wrap an arm around her waist and use the other to catch us against the bubble's glass wall. Then I remove my multitool and snip off the PlastiCuffs.

Sam rubs at her wrists and works her jaw. "Thanks. But Eves, he—"

"Hit your eye. Nothing some tequila can't fix."

Sam smiles, but we both know a drink is a long way off.

"Enough," Stamos says as he stops himself at the command terminal in the lab's center. "You've got a job to do."

"And if we refuse?" I shoot back.

He lets out a low, mocking laugh. "Dr. Park, do you really think you're the only one who knows how to install unlicensed code in someone's head?"

"What's that supposed to mean?" I check with Sam.

She gives me an innocent shrug. "That's what I was trying to tell you. He did something to me."

"You're a monster, Stamos!"

The maniac grins. "Do as I say, and you'll both live."

"And if we don't?"

"Then I get to pick who watches whom lose their head first. Listen," he says as he beckons me to cross the gap between us. I order Sam to take a seat at her station, and then I push off reluctantly. "I know that you'd sacrifice your life to ensure humanity's greatest discovery, Dr. Park. That's been your MO, hasn't it? The driven astrophysicist who doesn't have time for relationships? Who gets so lost in her work she forgets to eat and sleep? But what the world really wants to know is what Dr. Park will do when it's someone else's life on the line."

His eyelids twitch, and Sam lets out a scream. She's at her station with her hands around her head.

"Stop," I yell. "Let her go!"

"And I will. All you need to do is this one simple thing."

"I need assurances."

"A luxury you're not in a position to bargain for."

"So all I have is your word? You understand that's not enough for me."

"Your loss."

Sam screams again.

"You're a fucking bastard!" I grab a support and swing at his head.

Stamos catches my fist. "*Tsk, tsk, tsk*, bad form, Dr. Park. There's only one way out of this. And I suggest you start playing by the rules."

"Let her go!"

His eyes twitch again, and Sam stops screaming.

"You okay?" I call over my shoulder.

Sam gives a muffled whimper in reply.

I pull my lips back, seething. "I'm going to kill you."

"I don't doubt your desire, Dr. Park. But I do question your abilities. Now"—he releases my hand—"shall we begin?"

"I already told you, it's not possible."

"That's not what Sam had to say."

I turn to her. "It's not?"

She shakes her head sheepishly… as if the job is already done.

"Oh, Sam, you didn't."

"I'm so sorry, Eves. He was going to—"

"I know. And It's okay."

While SESI's local servers backup Parallax's verified findings when we transmit, they're secured by a government firewall, and therein lies the problem: they're cut off from the outside on account of their security level clearance. Meaning *they* aren't also backed up aside from the redundant systems in the same network. You can have ten vaults, but if they're all in the same bank, who cares if the whole building gets leveled? Game over.

So much work will be lost. The results of years, of *decades*, spent scouring the starscape all snuffed out in an instant. Someone else will resume the legacy, I trust. Once they've eased the government's fears, assuaged their doubts, and secured the necessary funding, they'll figure out a way to call the aliens back. It probably won't happen in my lifetime, assuming I survive this, but it will happen, eventually.

However, nothing, *none of it*, is worth Sam's life.

"All I need is your authorization, Dr. Park." Stamos moves away from the main terminal. He has the command screen ready for me. It lists all direct links to SESI's isolated servers, including the onsite backups and secondary ports to team V-cog memory drives in case anyone says something of interest. The world will remember the announcement we made, but there won't be a scrap of hard evidence. My authorization will permanently corrupt everything we've gathered so far, a Humpty-Freaking-Dumpty that we can't put back together again.

"And you'll let her go?" I ask.

"I give you my word."

"As a Tantum?"

He shakes his head. "As a scientist."

"Evelyn, don't… do it," Sam yells above the enemy's strangling grip. Then to Stamos she says, "For… for…"

But she doesn't need to say anything more. I've already made up my mind.

32

NIGEL

THERE WAS a knock at the door followed by a soft voice. "Time to wake up, Nigel."

Sallsworth blinked several times, painfully aware of the early morning light that filtered through his room's single window. The hearth in the cobblestone wall gave up a thin trace of the previous night's fire, and the wooden chair in the far corner still held his clothes. Nigel pushed himself up and groaned as another knock came.

"Nigel?"

"Be right there."

"There's breakfast in the kitchen."

No sooner did Neon say the words than the salty scent of bacon filled his nose and made his stomach tighten. Nigel rotated in bed and landed his feet on the cool hardwood floor. Half a minute later, he had his clothes on despite the pain of his injuries and felt summoned by the animalistic urge to fill his belly instead of to lick his wounds. When the door opened, Neon was gone.

Nigel followed the scent toward the rustic kitchen and found a single pewter plate on the wide board. Red coals in the cooking hearth warmed the room while the sight and smell of warm bread, bacon, eggs, and roasted asparagus compromised his free will. He set into the meal even before he sat, savoring each bite. While he loathed the woman responsible for his captivity, he blessed her at least for this moment of indulgence. He wondered if any meal had ever tasted so good. She had done something to him to make him this ravenous. But he'd figure that out later. Right now, all he could think of was eating. He needed strength to plot his escape.

"It seems you're enjoying yourself."

Nigel looked up. Neon stood in the opposite doorway dressed in a grey knit sweater so long that it swept her lower calves. As before, her orbital fatigues and obnoxious combat boots had been replaced by the humble attire of a lowly villager. Though she still retained her striking beauty—perhaps even more. But he knew better than to let his guard down on account of her appearance, so he ignored the comment and kept eating.

Neon stepped down into the room and sat across from him. "It seems your shuttle has left *Astraea*."

Nigel slowed his chewing.

"Only without my asset, and yours, it would seem."

"Stolen?"

"No. Your *other* pilot. The scrawny one?"

That wasn't right. Jericho shouldn't have left the kid to fly. Something was wrong.

"Oh, don't worry," Neon said with a coy grin. "Our interests are both still alive. But there have been some… *complications*."

Nigel swallowed the half-chewed bite. "What kind of complications?"

"Well, for one, it seems that your man has made mine."

The sweetness with which she said that last line betrayed the phrase's deeper meaning. Nigel stared at her for several seconds, wondering what to do with it. But like a fog rolling through the moors, the weight eventually came upon and pinned him down. "You've put out a kill order on him."

She smiled and picked at one of her painted nails. "He's a liability now."

"And?"

"And you're going to kill him for me."

"What about getting your asset off the station?"

"They'll find another way. But your man will leave in a body bag."

"Impossible."

"Is it?" Neon stretched on the bench and caught a ray of sun on her arms like a feline waking from a midmorning nap. "It's the least you could do to repay me."

Nigel put down the piece of bread he was working on and pointed at her. "We already agreed to terms. No more changes."

"Oh, not that, love. The fact that you ordered your people to protect Jericho behind my back. You're a cagey one, Nigel dear."

"I hardly think that's worthy of—"

"They killed them."

Nigel caught himself. "I beg your pardon?"

More slowly this time, Neon said, "Thirteen of my people on *Astraea* Station are dead. Gunned down in a docking bay."

"Impossible." Jones and Afumba were highly capable, but he doubted they could take on over a dozen Tantum incogs on batch code.

As if sensing his apprehensions, Neon forced a video overlay into his field of view. In it, Nigel watched a few seconds of a bloody firefight between what he assumed were her forces and some assailants behind cover in a back corner. The footage was jumpy, captured from an optic nerve and relayed over V-cog. But Nigel could make out the telltale curled wisps of magnetic acceleration weapons whipping up the air. Sparks dashed across bulkheads, and bodies fell. Then the image froze on a still shot of Afumba's face and, beside him, Jericho's.

"If anything, you should be proud. That's quite a feat." She reached over and grabbed a strip of bacon from his plate.

"What do you want?" he asked flatly.

Neon clenched the meat between her bared teeth and tore the rest of the strip away. "I want Jericho Fox dead, Nigel."

"But I thought this entire abduction was about you wanting him alive?"

"I changed my mind." She gives him a feline-like smile. "If I can't have my toy, neither can you."

Nigel grabbed the table's edge with both hands and felt his face flush. This was madness. No alliance was worth the price of dealing with this… this… *witch*.

"Activate all your dogs and point them at Fox."

"He could be anywhere on the station by now. Even if I had more people—"

"Are you trying to imply that you don't? Oh, come now, love. We both know that you've benefited from our"—she paused as if to think of the perfect word—"innovations, haven't you?"

He narrowed his eyes at her and gave the slightest of nods.

"So surely you must have many operatives on *Astraea* to deploy at your command." It wasn't a question.

"I suppose that some could afford to—"

"Some?" she interrupted.

Nigel noticed a flash of anger in her eyes. There were age lines in her skin that her makeup normally hid. She suddenly looked much older than he'd previously figured. And more determined. Like a mother bear protecting her cub—a maternal instinct Nigel dared not cross. He had the sense to know that he'd never leave this hovel alive if he didn't entertain her. Likewise, he guessed she'd be monitoring his every move until the deed was done.

"I can activate any incogs still on board," he offered at last.

"You see?" She clapped her hands, which sent a wave of pain through Nigel's head. "I love it when a new plan comes together to fix a broken one." The statement sounded like praise but was laced with accusation. Nigel just couldn't fully distinguish the two on account of the new headache he suffered. He needed to leave this island and get away from her *now*.

"On the condition that I go free," Nigel added as soon as he could find his voice.

The demand brought an eerie silence to the room.

Finally, she offered, "If that's what you wish." She said it like a parent who knew the decision her child was making was a poor one.

"Then we have a deal?"

"One more in a long series." Neon pulled his mug of coffee across the table and embraced it with both hands half hidden in the sweater's long sleeves. "There's a rowboat for you on the east shore. It will take you to the mainland where you can summon your search party or what have you."

"A… rowboat?"

She looked over the mug. "Would you rather swim?"

"No, I just…" Then he thought twice. "A rowboat is fine. Thank you." Those last two words stung to say, but he knew he still needed this relationship. At least for the present. "I'll see my way down to the wharf."

"Oh, and take a walking stick, would you, Nigel? It's quite a long way down, and I wouldn't want you to fall."

33

JERICHO

"Captain, I'm gonna need access to station-wide security a little longer," Rook says after patching me into his squad comms.

"It's yours until we leave the bridge, Master Sergeant," Mombawe replies. "Still after the culprit?"

"Yes. And Dr. Park."

If Mombawe is surprised by this news, his face doesn't show it. "I was told security personnel were dispatched to escort her team off station."

"Didn't go as planned, sir. We're trying to pick up her trail now."

The captain lifts his chin. "Do what you can. Then I want your team clear."

"Roger that. Rook out."

Rook's squad of Marines plus Afumba and I halt at quad A's lateral elevator bank, which is where I assume Evelyn and Stamos were headed. Doesn't mean they got on here, but I suspect Stamos was trying to get her clear of the area fast and then find a way off the station. I glance south toward section one and then the opposite way toward section three. "Tell me you got something, Rook."

"Not yet. Her V-cog's still offline. Stamos's too."

"Of course they are."

"Master Sergeant," a Marine says behind us, then offers Rook two standard NUESSA vac helmets with gloves tucked inside.

Rook hands the first helmet to me. "Try not to lose these."

"Roger."

The second set goes to Afumba.

"Don't you have somewhere else to be, big man?" Rook asks.

"Not until Jericho is safe," Afumba replies.

"That's what I thought. Just don't get in the way."

Afumba nods once.

I'm back to picking which way we should head and, more importantly, why. If I were an arrogant asshole posing as a cop and trying to move a hostage off station, how would I do it? I would… what?

I'd leverage my power.

"Search for any lifts with a call stop override," I say.

Rook nods and goes to work in a virtual terminal. He's not five seconds in when he looks up. "Line nine, non-stop, passing section twenty-one now."

"What's of interest that far north?" Corporal Geller, the EOD tech from the hotel, asks.

"They're heading to thirty," I exclaim. "It's where they met. And it wouldn't surprise me if whoever's helping Stamos behind the scenes arranged for another way off the ship there."

Rook agrees and scans all available cars. "Line five has an opening."

The squad dashes up the closest skywalk staircase, sprints over the lat lines until we reach five, and then bounds down the stairs five at time. It's all I can do to keep up with their batch coded bodies. Rook gets his hand between two pod doors as they close and pushes them open. "Sorry, folks. Emergency. Everyone out."

No one protests, and the car empties fast. We load in, and Rook starts the pod forward, entering the same call stop override that Stamos used. Thirteen Marines plus me and Afumba fill almost half the passenger pod. There are plenty of seats for everyone, but I'm too wired to sit.

As we speed past the ag fields, I try to get my mind off Evelyn and familiarize myself with my new rifle. But for all my time shooting at the range, I've never handled something like this.

Rook takes notice and offers a hand. "May I?"

"Be my guest."

He starts double-checking the black-bodied weapon and talking as he goes. "Somebody likes you, Knight. Bronheim 301 MAW medium assault rifle with variable velocity discharge. Stock, they're semi-auto." He taps a mode switch near the pistol grip. "But someone's modded this one with three-round burst and automatic. Plus they've removed the bio lock, as you already discovered. It also has aftermarket mil-spec V-cog-FOV aim integration."

"Damn," a Marine named Bashar says. "Thing's nicer than he deserves."

"I call dibs when he bites it."

"Shut up, Grabowski," Geller says.

"What?"

Rook rolls the weapon over and checks the chamber, presumably to make sure it's clear. "Bronheim's mirror military loadout capabilities. It can fire ten-group flechette rounds, solid core, explosive, magnetic EMP scramblers, and air burst clamor. But I gave you a solid core *lo* for now."

He removes the magazine and then reinserts it slowly a few times to make sure I'm watching. "The next round is always auto-fed. Likewise, quick release jettisons spent mags on empty, which you may not have noticed when you went dry back there. Always keep count—"

"And have the next amrod ready," I finish.

"Somebody knows their basics," Geller says behind me.

Rook hands the rifle back. "Try not to make us look bad, Knight?"

"Just don't slow me down, Rook."

He smiles but it fades quickly. "We're gonna get her, Jericho. And we're gonna get the son of a bitch responsible."

I spend the next few minutes in silence while the Marines speak in low voices amongst themselves in the back of the car. Rook and Afumba, however, haven't left my right and left shoulders the whole time. They just stand there like two unmoving boulders, though Afumba is certainly the bigger rock. Not a half-bad scenario to be in. Granted, both men have very different employers but who, at the moment, happen to have the same goal—protecting me. I can live with that.

"What's on your mind?" Rook asks as we continue north.

"Can't stop thinking about how many people have died today."

So far, the figures are just estimates. Even *Astraea*'s

numbers have to be corroborated, and missing persons will take even longer to verify. That said, it's still bad. The last figures published by Command are 791 from section sixteen and almost 15,000 from the transportation hub, but both numbers are expected to climb. And if the parties responsible have any more surprises up their sleeves, which I have to believe they do, then this is just the beginning.

"You ever been a part of anything this bad?" I ask Rook.

He nods slowly. "I was aboard the *Constellation Five* when the pirates breached it."

"Christ." I turn to face him. "I didn't think anyone got off it."

"They didn't, as far as civilians. No vac suits. But most of the Marines did. It was supposed to be a run of the mill security detail. We still followed procedures and had our helmets on the whole ride. Everyone complains until the air gets sucked out."

"Reports said the hijackers got away clean. Not a single shot fired."

Rook's jawbone pulses. He looks like he wants to say more but doesn't, maybe because of Afumba.

"You're not allowed to say," I conclude.

He clears his throat.

"There had to have been a good reason though?"

The Master Sergeant cleans the front of his teeth with his tongue and then sucks the saliva back like he's gonna snap at someone. "They didn't want to start a war," he says at last.

"You think it would have?"

"No question."

"And you know who," I state rather than ask. I realize I'm treading on thin ice here. Poking at a topic that he's sworn to secrecy on isn't something I take lightly. But his silence answers the question well enough. That and his glimpse at Afumba.

Rook shrugs. "Doesn't matter much anyway, does it."

"It does to me."

He thinks for a second. "Let's just say that if this plays out the way I think it could, that war is right around the corner anyway. All our silence did back then was buy us four more years of peace."

Rook's eyes dart back to Afumba. I think it's about the story, but then I see the ST agent's head tilt like he's listening carefully to someone speaking in a low tone. Old habits die hard. A moment later, the big man's muscles tighten.

I decide to take things head on. "Your mom call?"

Faster than I can think, the entire Marine squad has their weapons trained on Afumba. Very slowly, the giant raises his hands while Geller leans in to disarm him.

"That was a kill order, wasn't it," Rook says to my ST bodyguard.

"Yes."

I back away. What is it with people today? "Sallsworth?"

Afumba doesn't say. But he doesn't have to.

"Why the flip flop?" I ask.

"I do not know."

For some reason, I believe him. But that doesn't mean we're friends.

"Where?" Rook asks.

"Forehead."

"Jesus, you're just gonna shoot him?" I ask.

"Professional courtesy."

I step toward Afumba. The Marines move in too, so

I put my hands out. "Everybody just relax a second, okay?" I glare at Afumba. "Were you gonna do it?"

He sniffs. "No."

"Bullshit," someone says.

I ignore it. "And what would you have told Sallsworth when he inspected your memory?"

"The truth."

"But he'd kill you."

"My choice."

"Then why not just kill me?"

"Because it would dishonor my previous act of saving your life. And it would mean my partner was slain for nothing."

I study Afumba's face. It's stoic, unwavering, and full of resolve. "Stop the lift."

"What?" Rook says.

"Stop the lift!"

Rook nods at someone, and the car slows. We're between section stations when it eventually comes to a halt, and an emergency override order opens the doors.

"Knight, I don't think—"

I cut Rook off. "Go. Get off the ship. And if my Marines see you again, don't expect to walk away."

"I will not." Afumba puts a fist to his heart and inclines his head, which almost gets him shot, but the bullets stay in their barrels. "Thank you, Mr. Fox. I will remember this gift."

Without another word, Afumba turns, leaps from the car, and then disappears around a corner.

"Close it up," Rook orders and then sends the car on its way. "'My Marines,' huh?"

"For a few more hours, anyway."

Rooks shakes his head. "Stupid move, Knight."

"Was it?"

"He could still come back and finish the job."

"He won't. I think your culture and his are probably a lot alike in that regard. Honor and shame?"

Rook doesn't respond.

"Plus, we both know his career is over anyway. He just confessed on V-cog that he wouldn't have followed the order."

"So you let him go."

I shrug. "Professional courtesy."

"I've got three starships yet to leave the docking ring," Corporal Grabowski says as we walk through the ag level's transportation hall in section thirty. The cavernous space is fifteen meters high, boasts several open-air balconies, and has corridors breaking off in the four compass directions. The squad is on high alert after the incident with Afumba. Rook concluded, and rightly so, that my former bodyguard might not be the only ST asset on *Astraea*. We're not planning on hanging around long anyway.

"Locations?" Rook asks.

"Two in quad alpha, bays twelve and fifteen, and one in quad delta, bay four. All Somerset-class. NUESSA registrations."

"That's not right," I say to Rook as we cross the hall. The other Marines have surrounded us, but the space is mostly empty. "He would use private and not government transport now that we've made him."

"Agreed. Grabowski, is there anything else that looks out of spec? A faulty sensor reading, a tripped relay—"

"I've got a main power coupling still feeding an open draw."

"Location?"

"Quad charlie, bay six."

Rook slows and eyes the corporal. "With nothing registered in port?"

"Says it's empty, Master Sergeant."

I nod at Rook. "That's our ship."

"Tag it in squad HUD," Rook says. "Team One with me. Teams Two and Three—"

Incoming fire cuts Rook off and strafes the unit. I hear the *thud-thud-thud* of projectiles sinking into reactive gel armor that hardens as soon as it's hit but softens once the energy dissipates. More rounds strike ceramic armor plating on Marine helmets, chests, and backs. I hit the deck and realize that had the team not been around me, I'd be dead.

As soon as targets are identified, Rook's squad returns fire and starts moving toward cover on the hall's west side by some storefronts. I feel a hand pull me off the ground and start me running toward a stylized nanocrete half-wall. Just then, vector indicators and target reticles overlay in my field of view.

"Mil-spec V-HUD augment courtesy of the NUE Space Marines," Rook says. "Enjoy it while it lasts."

"Roger that." I take two steadying breaths like I would behind a ship's controls and get my heart rate settled. Then I pull the 301 tight into my shoulder and raise the weapon over the half-wall until it aligns with the nearest unselected target in V-cog. The combination of head-up display plus weapon sights is fast and intuitive, and I accept my first target with a subconscious click of the confirmation prompt—kinda like choosing a waypoint in an avionics menu. Presumably, this tells everyone else on the squad that I've confirmed target lock and to look elsewhere.

The man in my sights is firing at our left side from behind a planter in the northeast. Doesn't seem like the greatest cover as I'm fairly certain my 301's tungsten projectiles will make short work of the giant pot. Still, this is only my second firefight, so I wait for him to take his next shot and then squeeze the trigger when he pops up. I miss. So I decide to shoot through the planter rather than wait for him to stand again. The three-round burst mode shatters the clay vessel and hits the target in the chest. He falls backward and gets showered by soil and clay shards.

"Scratch one," I say over comms, unsure if that's proper etiquette. No one corrects me, so I roll with it.

More hostiles are added to the target list as Rook's squad pings them. Within seconds, I count two dozen enemies scattered along the hall's east side. But even as I line up my next shot, the Marines make quick work of the enemy force. Their disciplined staccato MAW fire makes it sound like the guns are talking back and forth.

I zero in on my next target: a woman firing some sort of sniper rifle on the third level. She's lying prone and shooting at Marines to my left. My V-cog targeting reticle shifts colors and confirms acquisition. I squeeze, but the round fails to hit the mark. However, the shot does get the woman's attention. Shit. I line up the reticles again and fire, but the stress and adrenaline throw my aim off. The sniper swings her weapon my way. I shoot three more times, and the last round passes through the sniper's head, snapping it sideways. Her rifle pitches over the edge and drops ten meters to the ground.

"Guns right," someone yells.

I pivot and watch another wave of enemy combatants take positions in the transportation hall's southeast corner. They're interspersed between the elevator cars and charging above and below the skywalks. We're outnumbered three to one, but their lack of coordinated tactics, armament, and experience start to show as Rook's squad picks them off. Two guys in *Astraea* Station uniforms try cutting between elevator cars, but Grabowski nails both in the chest with successive shots. Another hostile vaults a bench in a higher-than-normal leap that betrays batch coding. But his feet never touch down as Sánchez's three-round burst flips him back and onto the ground.

An incoming bullet whizzes past my head so close I feel my helmet's glass vibrate. Adrenaline helps me duck before a second round cracks into the nanocrete half-wall I'm squatting behind.

"You good?" Corporal Korvich asks.

"Roger."

He nods once and then gets back to work.

Rook's voice breaks over comms. "Team Three, assault left. Team One, support. Team Two, eyes up high. Go!"

I don't know what all that means, but Korvich gets my attention again. "Three's gonna extend up our left flank like the tall part of a capital L, then push into the enemy moving right. One is gonna be the bottom part of the L and catch the bad guys in the crossfire. And two is gonna make sure no one surprises us from those balconies."

"Makes sense."

"Makes 'em dead."

Even with my head behind the half-wall, V-cog superimposes digital silhouettes of Team Three stretching out in a line and taking cover behind elevator cars, columns, and generator caps. These mil-spec mods are legit, and I add them to the list of stuff I need to beg, borrow, or steal from Rook when this is all over. Though, I suppose the price will be enlistment, and that's more than I can afford. Better get the most out of these perks now.

I flag Korvich again as he lays down a steady *zip-zip-whir* with his assault rifle. "Which team do I support?"

"Stay where you are, eyes on the ground floor. Pick any bad guys not spoken for. And we call them tangos."

"Roger." I scan the hall and spot an unclaimed *tango* firing on Team One as they stretch out along the north side. He's in a station uniform and has some sort of stubby automatic weapon pulled close to his chest. It's surreal firing at people dressed in NUESSA clothing. If it wasn't for the illegal automatic weapons they've somehow managed to get on board *Astraea*, I'd say we were making a terrible mistake. But they're shooting to kill, and so are we. I fire at my target until the fourth round drops him.

"Getting better," Korvich says.

Another assailant in a security vac suit runs for cover to my right, but I can't get lined up before he joins three tangos behind a set of stairs and a support column.

Geller is way ahead of me. "Frag out," he shouts and then tosses what looks like a military issue dodecahedron EMP. The lemon-sized geodesic sphere lands past the column and then emits a bright blue flash that makes my skin tingle. Yup, that's an EMP. And just like that, their mag weapons are only good as clubs.

"Lie down," Geller yells as he circles the column to cut the angle.

I decide to cover him and move five meters behind.

"I said lie down!" But the hostiles don't seem to be in a lying down kind of mood. Just as Geller swings into firing position, the four combatants rush him. They cross the eight-meter gap as fast as I can blink. The Marine fires on the first and blows the man back. I shoot the second, causing him to slide on his chest, while Geller gets the third. But the fourth leaps over her slain counterparts, lands on the Marine's chest, and wraps her legs around his waist. A ceramic blade comes down on Geller's neck and shoulder in three successive jabs.

I think about shooting her, but I'd be shooting him too. Then again, he does have armor that would—

Never mind.

Geller's pistol punches three holes out the woman's lower back. Her body slides off his chest and lands in a heap. A moment later, incoming fire pelts his side, and the EOD tech backpedals toward me while returning fire. I assist where I can and make sure to keep my weapon pointed away from him.

Back behind the safety of a support column, I check my amrod and see I only have two rounds left. I decide to reload, eject the nearly spent mag, and insert the fresh one. "That knife get you?" I ask Geller, hoping he's okay.

He wraps his gloved knuckles on his shoulder. "Reactive gel only permits things that move slowly. She stabbed too fast. And plating did the rest."

I'm about to say "very cool" when something moves in a small clothing store behind us. My brain works out the likelihood of employees not obeying the captain's minutes-old abandon ship order and concludes that we might be getting outmaneuvered.

"Geller!" I point into the store.

He blinks twice, and suddenly I'm sharing a thermal overlay from his POV. Over the squad channel, he says, "Two tangos, my six o'clock!" Then his weapon lets out its signature *zip-zip-zip-whir* and punches holes through the rack of clothes. I join him and fire as fast as I can on the other hostile, using the thermal overlay as a guide. Both gun-wielding enemies go down amidst a flutter of flaming fabric.

"Thanks for the heads-up," Geller says.

"You owe me a beer."

"Deal."

I check the time and then curse the enemy for holding us up. If Stamos gets off *Astraea* with Evelyn, they'll vanish for good. I can't let that happen.

Even though the bulk of the enemy's westward advance has been minimized by the Marine's L-shaped assault, it seems the position has been compromised by the threat from behind. A new marker appears in my V-HUD, tagged with a text flag.

Over the squad channel, Rook calls out, "Fall back to Hotel One. Go!"

"That's us," Geller says as he helps me up.

We join the rest of the squad heading north and divert left into a west-running corridor. I watch the vector arrow shift as we turn and the distance-to-intercept counter descends. The sound of the enemy fire in the main hall lessens, and Rook's waypoint comes into view ahead. It's superimposed on a stairwell running up to *Astraea*'s main level. The moment the squad reaches it, a second waypoint, Hotel Two, appears higher up and somewhere along section thirty's northernmost edge. By the time I check the stairwell and emerge into the open air of *Astraea*'s curved expanse, I spot Hotel Three: an elevator line headed up the end cap and to the power level. Not exactly the escape route I'd figured on, but it will put distance between us and the enemy, and, now that I think about it, it's the fastest away across the station to quadrant C where Stamos's mystery ship is docked.

The thought's barely through my brain when Grabowski pings the point of interest on the squad's V-HUD. I look straight up through eight klicks of atmosphere to the destination marker labeled Indigo One with the sub text "Hostile: quad charlie, dock six."

"Set perimeter," Rook orders as we close on the elevator bank. "Knight, with me. One team per lift. Go when available."

We race toward the bank of four lifts. Only one pod is ready, doors open. Rook waves me forward, along with Team One's Geller, Bashar, Sánchez, and Grabowski,. As soon as we're loaded in, and it's a tight fit, the doors close and the pod lifts away. We get a perfect aerial view of the other teams as they start to re-engage the enemy pouring up the stairwell some fifty meters up the manicured walkway.

The first hostiles don't make it more than a few steps before withering MAW fire cuts them down. But then several tangos leap from the opening and clear the streams of fire before rolling to cover behind surrounding trees. The jumps are too high for normal people to make, confirming my earlier suspicions.

"They're tweaked," I say to Rook over a private channel.

"Yeah. Good code too."

"No one's snapped their own necks yet," Sánchez

adds. "One time, I was chasing this Radio Ultra dreadlock—a real cabrón, ya know?—through the Beattie IV moon station. He was jumping and sticking to walls like some Rastafarian Spider-Man. But the guy misses one of his jumps, right? And you know where he lands? Headfirst straight into the sewage reclamation processors. Broke his neck. I don't know what's worse: breaking your neck or landing face-first in a pile of human shit."

"Stay focused, Sánchez," Geller says.

We watch in silence as Teams Two and Three continue to engage the enemy. Fewer hostiles emerge from the stairwell, either signaling the end of their forces or that they're regrouping to try a different approach. Either way, Rook's squad seems in the clear, at least for the moment.

An empty pod whizzes past us, summoned to the main level. At the same time, an incoming call pings in V-cog. My father's avatar pops up.

I kill the call.

Ten seconds later, I have a new message. *Now is really not the time, dad.* But then I wonder if maybe he has something to say—knows something about what's going on with all this. Doubtful. He probably just wants to feed me more of his sentimental lines and make sure I'm not getting any "wild fantasies" about switching politicasts.

"Any ideas on who all those tangos are down there?" I ask anyone willing to answer.

"We picked up a lot of ST markers," Grabowski replies.

Rook frowns. "Somebody flipped their switch. Guessing Afumba wasn't the only one who got the call."

"I made their man."

Rook eyes me.

"I made their man," I repeat. "Got a good look at Stamos, or Faust, or whoever the hell he really is. And my guess is somebody didn't like that."

"No kidding. That's a full-on embedded kill team down there, comprised of several squads with smuggled weapons and high-end batch code. Problem is, I'd have thought you were more valuable to Sallsworth alive than dead."

"Same. But we both know how fast things can change in the ivory tower."

"Mmm."

I rub the back of my neck. "Still, I'm getting kinda tired of all the special attention, if I'm being honest." This gets a few chuckles. I watch the gun battle below start to fade away and feel my weight go light in my feet. "Thanks for covering my ass, everyone."

"It's our job."

"And we like your ass," Grabowski says.

"Speak for yourself," adds Sánchez.

We ride the rest of the way checking amrod magazines and battery levels. Then I grab a handhold as we rise into full zero g. Despite all my time in space, these Marines are more relaxed than I am and don't even bother to hold on.

When the lift starts to slow, Rook says, "Bashar, Sánchez, watch the flanks. We cross the corridor and pick up the next available lift. Ready up?"

Heads nod and weapons get pulled into shoulders. I follow suit and hold a hand against the ceiling as the pod comes to a halt. The doors open. Bashar and Sánchez push out first.

"Clear left," Sánchez says toward the power level doors.

"Clear right," echoes Bashar.

Grabowski pushes hard and flies across the corridor.

I'm about to follow him when I stop myself on Sánchez's shoulder. "You hear that?" I point my 301 toward the open hatch at the end of the tunnel to the right.

"Someone's in there," Sánchez adds.

Rook calls for everyone to move quietly and then motions toward the hab's CEL.

A woman screams. And somehow, I know who it is.

34

EVELYN

Stamos can't hurt Sam if he's unconscious.

And nobody's messing with my friend.

While he's busy studying my keystrokes as I enter my command authorization code, I slip a foot under one of the command terminal's floor stirrups. Stamos is still staring intently at the hardware, probably waiting for me to hit the all-important Enter key. Instead, I leverage my mass against the terminal and send a left cross into Stamos's nose. Third time's the charm.

While my fist explodes in pain, he rears back, temporarily disoriented…

But not unconscious.

Dammit.

If I can't knock him out, then I'll just have to keep him busy.

I launch myself off the desk, cradle his head with my left arm, and jam my thumb into his eye socket. We sail across the lab and tumble toward the far wall, but no matter how hard I push, I can't get my thumb past his squinted eyelid.

Stamos yanks my hands off his head with superhuman strength and headbutts my left temple. I have an instant migraine and a head full of stars, but I'm awake.

Then he stretches out my wrists just enough to make my nerves scream. "Do it again, and I'll rip your arms off."

"Alright! Alright."

"And you," he barks at Sam, "don't even think about it."

I look over my shoulder to see Sam halfway out of her chair in some harebrained attempt to assist me. "Sam, just… relax, okay? I've got this."

She nods repeatedly and pulls herself into her seat.

That whole stunt was probably too risky, but I had to try something.

We float back to the central terminal, and I return to entering my command authorization with Stamos staying directly behind me and keeping a hand around my neck this time. I go slow on purpose, hoping something will interrupt us.

"Hurry it, Dr. Park."

"It's complex, okay?"

"I think you know your own security code just fine." For emphasis, he presses a finger into the base of my skull. It hurts. So I finish typing in the rest of my credentials and the alphanumeric override permission string. Then I let my finger hover over the Enter key.

Something moves to my left.

Sam plows into Stamos's shoulder, forcing all three of us to flail across the lab. Our bodies careen toward an exposed section of the bubble where glass meets vacuum. I try to spot the landing, but we're rolling too quickly for me to know who will strike first. It's me, then Stamos, then Sam, then me. The bubble comes around again until Stamos hits first, taking the brunt of the blow.

Sam and I separate in opposite directions, bounce off the glass, and then back toward the middle. I strain to reach a seat back but miss by five centimeters. The free flight makes me feel helpless, especially as Stamos plants his feet and pushes to meet me in midair. His fingers are extended in a diving pose. At the last second, I arch my back to avoid the spear-like strike, but he reaches out and grabs my wrist anyway. Then he whips me forward, transferring all of his momentum into me, and I shoot across the lab to collide with the opposite wall. Something breaks in my arm as I shield my head from the blow. I scream in pain.

Come on, Evelyn! Focus.

Stamos is slowly moving toward me; he put too much inertia into the throw. Doesn't matter how strong someone is, you can't cheat the conservation of energy. This is my chance, but options are limited, and I can't beat him in a hand to hand confrontation. I call out to Sam, hoping she might be able to help, but she looks dazed, presumably from a blow to the head.

Stamos senses my desperation and prepares to meet me. He breathes heavily and coughs once. Blood and saliva fly from his mouth in small spheres. His eyes are locked on mine and filled with such deep animosity that I have trouble reconciling this man to the one who apologized to me in the lift not half an hour ago.

"Come here, you bitch!" he snarls, closing the distance between in agonizingly slow motion.

"Not today."

I push away from the handhold, but something yanks me back into the wall with a jarring blow to my shoulder. The pain in my broken arm worsens, but I hold in the scream so I can focus on whatever's got me stuck. Then I spot it: my vac suit's metal cuff is wedged in the handle's base plate. I tug but it won't budge.

Stamos's outstretched left hand is one meter and closing.

I jerk the cuff again and again. More pain shoots up my arm and robs me of breath.

Half a meter.

My cuff still won't come free.

I remove my multitool, wedge it between my wrist and the handle, and pry with all the leverage I can get from the wall. The skin punctures, but the metal cuff pops clear and my arm with it.

Sam's voice roars behind me. I look over Stamos's shoulder to see her flying in again with wild abandon. He notices my wide eyes and turns to face Sam.

I don't think. I just hold the butt end of the multitool against the wall with my good arm and watch Sam collide with Stamos. His back meets the top of my fist, and the file drives between his ribs somewhere below his left shoulder blade.

Stamos hollers and grabs Sam around the throat. They lock eyes and stare at each other. It's all the time I need to wrap an arm around his neck and lock him in a chokehold.

He thrashes violently, like I've got a bull by the horns. But I'm not about to let this beast go. Worse still, he won't release Sam's neck despite her clawing at his arm and swiping at his face.

One of them pushes off the wall and floats back toward the room's middle. I feel the multitool against my abdomen and consider retrieving it, but that would mean giving up the headlock. Instead, I pull myself higher, clench the tool's handle between my thighs, and then sway back and forth to aggravate the puncture. Stamos yells and throws an elbow at my head. It's enough to dislodge me. Fingers struggle to grab Sam's clothing but in vain. Then I'm free again, and Stamos is choking the life out of Sam.

"No," I scream.

"Let her go, asshole," a familiar voice yells from the hatch. I try to look over my shoulder once, twice, then finally rotate enough to see…

"Jericho?"

He's got an assault rifle pointed at Stamos. "Come to me, Evelyn."

As soon as I touch down on a workstation, I point myself toward the hatch and push away, holding my broken arm to my chest. Jericho takes my free hand and feeds me into the empty seven-meter wide corridor behind him. Only, it's not empty. As soon as I cross the threshold, I notice five Marines hiding against the bulkhead. They've got rifles, pistols, and knives drawn. One raises a finger to his glass-covered mouth in the universal sign of "be quiet." It's Rook.

They're laying a trap.

I divert my eyes to keep from exposing the ruse. Stars, I hope it works.

"Let her go, and I'll take you into custody," Jericho says in a calm and in-control tone. "You have nowhere to go, Stamos."

"Please, Jack," I add, hoping my use of his first name will unnerve him somehow. "Just do what he says."

"Make another move, and I'll kill her," he replies.

"Then you'll lose your leverage," Jericho adds. He's doing his best to end this without bloodshed it seems.

"She's expendable."

My heart skips a beat when I hear Sam yelp. I strain to look past Jericho and see her in Stamos's grip as they linger beside the central command terminal.

Jericho retrains his weapon on Stamos.

"I said, not another move!"

"Okay, okay." Jericho decides to hold up his gun. "I'm not gonna shoot. Just… let her go."

"I want you in the elevators."

Jericho shakes his head. He's really trying to sell it. "I'm afraid I can't do that."

"Then she dies."

"No," Sam cries. "Please, please! Don't kill—"

"Shut up!"

"Alright, Stamos," Jericho says at last. "I'm moving to the elevators. But you have to let the woman go."

Stamos sneers and looks at me. "She goes in too."

"I'm not going," I say, playing the part.

Stamos extends his index finger and hits Enter on the keyboard. Just like that. My heart sinks. The archives, they're gone.

Sam wails from some unseen torture.

"Okay, okay, you bastard. I'll go! I'll go."

"Now," Stamos roars.

Jericho pushes back from the hatch bulkhead and nods at me as he passes. "It's enough."

I use my good arm to follow him down the tunnel and toward the elevator bank. I cast one look over my shoulder and see that Stamos is starting to follow. Stars, if this works—

"I want you both in! Same pod. Leave the weapon outside and then close the damn doors!"

"Stamos, we—"

"FUCKING DO IT NOW OR SHE DIES!"

Sam's crying.

"Alright, easy. Easy," Jericho says in a conciliatory tone. "I need your word that you'll let her go once we're inside. No one else needs to get hurt today, including you."

"My word?" Stamos lets out a weak laugh that stops with a wince. A small trail of blood floats from his back where I've stabbed him. "Here is my word. Get into the lift with that bitch, leave your weapon behind, and I promise not to blow us all to kingdom come." Stamos pulls a palm-sized device from his pocket, holds it up for Jericho to see, and then depresses a button with his thumb. "My hand leaves this switch, and we all die."

Jericho's demeanor changes. Then he releases his rifle. "Get in the lift, Evelyn."

35

JERICHO

I KEEP my eyes locked on Stamos through the glass walls as we back into the elevator car. He hasn't given the slightest inclination that he's going to do what he says, but all we need him to do is come out of the lab.

"He's got a third bomb inside reactor two," Evelyn blurts out as soon as the doors are closed.

"What?" I don't look away from Stamos. "You're sure?"

"He plans to destabilize *Astraea*'s orbit and send it into Earth."

"Can he do that?"

"Yes. At our altitude, orbital decay through natural means would take over a century. But with a nuclear bump on the end?"

"How long?"

"Days? Maybe hours? There are a lot of factors."

"We can't let that happen." Stamos floats toward the hatch. Over the team channel, I say, "Ten meters, Rook."

He doesn't bother replying, even over V-cog. He just gives an ever-so-small nod.

My stomach's tighter now than during a sky-tower touchdown in a lower-pressure storm.

"They're gonna kill him, right?" Evelyn asks in a barely audible voice.

"Yes. But don't stare. Look afraid for Sam. And for the love of God, don't look at Rook."

She nods slightly, and I follow my own advice, hoping this bastard doesn't have some sort of sixth sense. He's got his left hand around Sam's neck, pinning her back to his chest, while his right holds out the dead man's switch at shoulder height.

In V-cog, I tell Rook, "Four meters."

Again, a nearly indiscernible nod.

A hand clutches my bicep. "They won't hit Sam, will they?"

"They'll get the job done. Stay calm."

"Right. But he's capable of—"

"I know." To Rook: "One meter. Here they come."

As soon as Sam crosses the threshold, the five Space Marines close in like spiders racing down a web. Stamos flinches. Whether from his periphery or a sixth sense, he sees the trap and tries to reverse course. But it's too late.

Grabowski seizes Stamos's det-switch hand and pulls it into his chest like a football. I imagine the Marine using all his strength to keep the enemy's thumb from leaving the trigger button—both men have military-grade tweaks in play. At the same time, Rook and Sánchez strip Stamos's hand off Sam's neck and twist her free. Bashar pins Stamos's arm behind him while Geller tries to assist, but the man isn't complying.

I open the elevator doors, push out, and grip a

handhold, hoping to intercept Rook and Sam as they fly our way, but behind them I see Grabowski swinging left, right, and then back again. Despite Stamos's injuries, he's whipping the Corporal around like a rag doll to dislodge his hand, but Grabowski won't let go.

Bashar and Geller get knocked back by the assailant's violent flailing and fight to regain footing on the sidewall and ceiling. Sánchez is still close, however, and capitalizes on the opening by stabbing Stamos in the chest. The Marine has no sooner plunged in his ceramic blade when the enemy punches his helmet, knocking both men apart. Sánchez's head snaps backward. His first limp zero-g backflip reveals a cracked visor and glazed eyes, while Stamos's crushed knuckles pump out a trail of red spheres. My engineer brain balks at the energy needed to crack a visor with human bone.

Rook passes Sam to me and turns in mid-air using thrusters in his armored suit. His assault rifle comes up in a fluid motion, but even I know he doesn't have a shot given the melee. If all his men could get clear, that would be one thing. But right now, everything is hanging on Grabowski not letting go of Stamos's right hand and the other Marines subduing the tweaked out maniac. Without their own military batch code, this would be a one-sided contest; even still, Stamos's tweaks are off the charts.

"You're okay," I say as I catch Sam and then redirect her to Evelyn in the pod. The terrified woman is praying for all she's worth.

Rook repositions on the tunnel's left as Sánchez arches overhead. Bashar drives at Stamos with an HG-11. The stun pad below the barrel is active and connects with the side of the enemy's neck. Telltale voltage arcs cut through the chaos with a *tat-tat-tat-tat* as the capacitor dumps. Even though Stamos's body jerks, he looks more annoyed than paralyzed.

In response to the stun attempt, Stamos grabs hold of Bashar's side and squeezes, making the Marine roar. The enemy's hand is only a claw of broken bones, but he seems to have applied pressure slow enough to get past the reactive gel. Bashar's trying to pull the hand from the injury, but Stamos keeps digging in. More blood pumps into the air forming a red mist. Finally, Geller uses his HG-11 and fires from above, straight into Stamos's shoulder even though I think it was meant for the head.

Stamos roars and kicks away from the bulkhead, clearing himself of the swarming Marine pack, save Grabowski. But with Sánchez presumably dead and Bashar holding both hands over his wound, the task of stopping Stamos is left to Rook and Geller. And then there's me, who's watching the mass murderer fly toward me in zero g, still with Grabowski in tow.

Rook manages to fire twice into Stamos's buttocks and upper leg, but any more and he risks hitting Sam, Evelyn, and me. Then I follow Stamos's eyes up the tunnel and see he's heading toward my rifle.

I have to get there first.

I tell the women to stay inside and then shove myself away from the elevator. I close the three meters to the gun fast, but Stamos snags my ankle with his bloody left claw, and I miss the weapon by centimeters. I'm jerked toward him, and his hand moves from my ankle to my hip to a handful of my uniform at my chest. By the time we're face to face, I punch him in the nose harder than I've hit anyone in my life. The force pushes me away, but his handhold is too tight, so we snap back, which sends my forehead into his face. Wish I'd planned that, but I'll take it. Even if the bastard doesn't feel the pain, the double-blow obscures his vision. God knows it's obscuring mine.

Stamos shuts his eyes and curses while a new splatter of blood flings away from his face. He even loses his grip on my chest, which lets me push clear as he and Grabowski continue to fly toward the power level entrance.

"Coming through," Rook shouts. He and Geller thrust past me, knives and firearms pointed south. A beat later they intercept the target. I hear a muffled *zub-zub-whom* of MAW rounds while Geller joins Grabowski in wrestling for Stamos's right hand.

And then, to my horror, Grabowski flies free.

I shout the word, "No!" but don't hear it.

The bomb must be going off.

A flash of light, and we're all getting consumed. But…

There's nothing. Just a thick river of blood suspended in the air as Grabowski holds up a hand with a severed wrist at the end.

Geller cut the arm.

Holy shit!

Geller cut the arm!

Rook fires his assault rifle into the back of Stamos's head.

And then everything goes silent.

That's it.

For a moment, no one moves. Me, the women in the elevator, the men in the tunnel. We're all just staring at Stamos's corpse and Grabowski holding the hand holding the dead man's switch holding the button.

Rook is first to break the silence and looks at me. "You okay?"

I pat my chest twice. "Yeah. I'm good."

He nods and then looks at his men. "Grabowski, don't even think about letting go of that. Geller, check on that. I'll get Bashar and Sánchez."

I turn back to Sam. "You okay?"

She nods, but fresh tears pool against her corneas. She can't wipe them away fast enough. "Thank you. I don't know what I would have… if he… I just…"

"It's okay, Sam." Evelyn pulls her into an embrace. "It's all over. I've got you."

I turn back to the Marines as they collect their teammates. Bashar's nano systems have already started sealing the hole in his suit, but he's gonna need medical attention. Sánchez, however? I watch with reverence as Rook opens Sánchez's visor to close his eyes. Tiny droplets of blood wobble out of the helmet. I also notice that his suit's armored collar behind his neck is cracked. I'm guessing it gave way during the impact and was part of the sound we all heard.

"I'm sorry, Rook." I don't know what else to say.

"None of us signed up to stay safe. Just to keep others that way."

"Copy." I nod back to Stamos's corpse. It's stopped pumping fluids out but is still surrounded by a shimmering halo of body matter. "Guy was like a raging bull."

"Craziest uppers I've ever encountered."

"Well," Grabowski says. "I held on just fine."

"You held on 'cause you were scared shitless," Geller says.

"Still counts."

"Hold still, dammit."

Rook smiles at his guys like a dad might at his sons after a family wrestling match. That sense of dark humor always stood out to me with Will. The guys I met from his unit always had the ability to crack a joke even at the worst moments. Some people think it's poor taste. Probably is. But for them? I think it's as much a coping mechanism as it is a sign of their calm under fire. Either way, Grabowski held on, and we're all alive for it. He and Geller can bullshit all day long as far as I'm concerned.

"What about the third bomb?" Evelyn asks Rook as she glides out of the elevator. "That your department?"

"Negative. Command is sending in an EOD unit."

"And the conflict down there?" I point below our feet to the main level.

"They're cleaning up now, and a second squad has been assigned to check on the suspected getaway ship. We'll push out and rendezvous with Command momentarily." Then Rook gets a sparkle in his eyes. "Since Stamos did turn out to be a terrorist, I actually need you to sign off, Knight. Officially, that is."

"You mean, I could keep you around as my personal bodyguard for a while?"

"Probably not. But Command likes I's dotted and T's crossed. So they'd rather have your signature than not."

"What about accomplices?" Evelyn adds.

"I just received word that several are in custody."

"Like who?"

"Aside from some of the combatants who survived the firefight, we arrested a member of your team, Dr. Park."

She pulls her head back. "My team?"

Sam looks equally surprised, though probably more panic-stricken. "Who?"

"Your communications specialist, Dr. Bhavna Mishra."

"I still can't believe it," Evelyn says.

Rook nods grimly. "Scrubbers found a treasure trove of secured data on her V-cog stack that links her with time-stamped communications to grey servers on Earth."

"That's hardly conclusive," Sam says suddenly composing herself. "Even we use grey site servers that employ layers of—"

Rook holds up a hand to silence her string of nerd speech. "Our analysts hacked and traced all comms back to sources in Vancouver."

Sam balks. "Well, NUESSA might have—"

"To known Tantum Terrae hosts in Vancouver," Rook clarifies. After giving the news a moment to sink in for the two women, he adds, "I'm sorry."

"But Mishra..." Evelyn shakes her head slowly in bewilderment. "I worked with her for years. I should have noticed. How did I miss it?"

"These undercover incogs are rumored to be experts at what they do," Rook replies. "Wouldn't be too hard on yourself. We believe they've been trained to embed for years before being activated."

Sam seems to be warming to the news. "I mean, I guess it kinda explains how Stamos was able to conceal himself so much. If Mishra had access to *Astraea*'s systems, then..."

"I don't want to think about this right now," Evelyn says and glares at Rook. "Just as long as you think everyone involved is detained."

"I do. A proper investigation will take weeks, of

course. Possibly longer. But for now, I think we have the players in custody or"—he gestures to Stamos—"in body bags. Time to get everyone else off station."

"Whoa. Hey! What's it doing, man?"

"Just hold the fuck still, Grabowski!"

I turn to Geller, and Rook demands, "SITREP."

"It's blinking, Sarge," Grabowski says, holding Stamos's hand between his.

"Geller?"

The EOD tech's got tools in both hands and another in his mouth, trying his best to work on the remote. "Almost done, Master Sergeant. I just need —*would you stop moving, asshole?*"

Rook pushes off to meet them. "Why would it be blinking, Geller?"

"Could be trying to reconnect. Or…"

"Or what?"

"Or it could be…" Just then, Geller stops working on the device. "Oh shit."

36

EVELYN

"Talk to me, Corporal," Rook demands.

Geller pulls his hands away. "It's a timed default relay."

"A what?" Grabowski asks.

"If the user doesn't activate the switch within… Jesus, it doesn't matter. It looks like we've got just over three minutes."

"Until what?" Sam asks.

"Until everything goes nova."

Rook starts barking orders. "Everyone in the lifts! Geller, I want you and Grabowski to—"

Jericho grabs Rook's arm. "There's no time."

"Don't tell me what—"

"He's right," I add. "Three minutes gets us to the main level, but not to a ship. We'll never make it."

"So we're just gonna die here then?" Sam asks in a frantic tone.

"No. We're getting out." I nod at the lab. "Through there."

Jericho eyes me. "Care to enlighten us?"

I shove off from the elevator bank and fly toward

the lab's hatch. "The bubble is an ultra high density CNT reinforced GCM matrix."

"Huh?" Grabowski asks.

Jericho saves me the work of an explanation while he tails me. "Carbon nanotube reinforced glass-ceramic matrix composite. It's basically a blast-proof sphere designed to endure high velocity space debris strikes."

"But a nuclear explosion?" Geller asks.

"Yes," I say as I make sure that everyone's following us into the bubble. "But that's the least of our worries."

When most people think about nuclear bombs, they imagine mushroom clouds and huge shock waves ripping buildings apart. But in space, there's no atmosphere for a shock wave to travel through. There is a fireball, however, depending on the fuel, which has thrust, and then a whole lot of radiation, which, in our bubble, creates a massive amount of heat and cellular damage.

"Rook, I need you to tell the captain that *Astraea* is—"

"Already done," he replies to me.

"Thanks." Another part of my brain kicks in, and I wonder how many people have yet to get off the ship, including Mombawe. "Rook. Can you ask him how many people have yet to—?"

"Do your part, Evelyn, and trust the captain to do his. You get us through this, we'll have a lifetime to mourn our dead and think about what we could have done differently. Roger?"

I nod. "What about the bomb squad?"

Rook gets somber. "They're gonna keep working the problem."

"But in a few seconds—"

"I know. And so do they. Boneheaded sons of bitch-es." He looks away. "They're paid to be badasses, not cowards." Then he gestures for me to keep moving.

I take a deep breath, glide to the main terminal, and freeze when I see the screen with the command authorization and the words "Data Purge: Successful."

Someone touches my shoulder. It's Jericho. "What's the plan?"

I snap out of my daze and bring up the lab's station integration menu. "We have to put a few thousand kilometers between us and *Astraea*."

"This thing is modular," he says as if the thought is dawning on him for the first time.

"Yup," I reply as I type and then forget that I have V-cog again. It's been a day. "We're able to remove it from *Astraea* for refitting and repairs. Even a full station transfer, but that's never happened." Over my shoulder, I yell, "Everyone get buckled in. You too, Jericho."

"How do you expect to generate enough propulsion?" he asks.

"Compressed air along the seal. It should give us enough to—"

"No way. If it's a uni-module pressure seal, even at max discharge, we won't get more than thirty meters per second. And that's not enough."

I know he's right. But I don't have any more ideas. "Well it's better than nothing."

"No. We still fry." Jericho pushes away from me in silence. I can't tell if he's thinking, mad, or just giving up. "Five hundred meters per second. That should give us enough of a margin."

"What, you got rockets stored up your ass, flyboy?"

He gives me a half smile and then thumbs toward the Marines. "No. But *they* do."

I look at Rook and his men. "Their suit thrusters?"

"Nope." Jericho points to Rook's chest rig. "We need all your things that go bump in the night, Master Sergeant."

"Plan?" he asks as he gives the order for everyone to relinquish their fragmentation grenades and then two can-like objects.

Jericho gestures to the hatch. "That tunnel is our chamber, we're the projectile, and these"—he holds up one of the munitions—"are our propellant."

OVER THE NEXT FORTY SECONDS, Jericho, Rook, Geller, and Grabowski secure the spherical hi explosive charges in the tunnel and attach what Rook calls LIMPET mines to the bubble's outer hatch rim as "secondaries." I'm worried they'll just blow the hatch free, but he assures me that they're directional and facing away from the lab. Meanwhile, Sam and I release the lab's station lock with an emergency override. Normal operations would require several layers of permission to achieve bubble separation, activate vectored thrusters, and coordinate transfer with the ferries. Plus, the system won't allow human occupants. The sensors are reading multiple life-forms and putting up numerous system blocks. Fortunately, I have a Sam.

Just one problem. She seems reluctant. About the plan? About our odds of surviving? Who knows. But I've never seen her hesitate like this before either.

"You okay?" I place a hand on her shoulder.

Her face looks stern, eyes hard. Then she turns to me and glares. "We're going to survive," she says after a moment.

"Yeah, okay."

"No." She tightens her lips and seems to swallow her tears. "We make it through this, Eves."

"Yes. Yes, we'll make it through." She had me worried there for a second. I put my helmet on, secure my gloves, and then nod at her screen. "You good?"

She looks down and finishes typing. "Ready."

"Jericho?"

"Hatch sealed, Rook ready, and—"

"*Abigail* standing by for recovery," Kit says over comms.

"Thanks, Kit," I reply.

"No problem, Dr. Park. Anything for you. I mean that, too. Like, all you gotta do is say—"

"Got it." I scan the rest of the lab to find everyone secured, including Sánchez's and Stamos's bodies. I nod at Rook. "Ready?"

"On your go."

And this is the most critical part, because if I fire us toward Earth, then I greatly minimize our odds of being rescued before we enter the atmosphere. Sure, it's 40,000 kilometers to the surface, and that's plenty of time for a ship to match our proposed speed, secure the lab, and get us off. But the pessimist in me requires that I factor in all sorts of unknown variables, including the blast wake acceleration when *Astraea*'s generator ruptures. Plus, while the bubble itself would survive atmospheric reentry, assuming we don't skip off the atmosphere first, the heat would bake us alive in seconds.

I expand the estimated time to detonation clock, which Geller predicts is accurate to within two seconds, and then watch the lab's angular position relative to Earth. We're pointed somewhere over the Pacific with the horizon falling away in agonizingly slow motion. But had we been tumbling any faster, the entire crew would have been pressed into *Astraea*'s endcaps, and no one would have gotten off this station. So I'll take agonizingly slow.

Seventy-six seconds remain on the clock.

"What're you waiting for?" Kit asks over comms.

"She's trying to make sure you don't have to dive toward the planet to fetch us," Jericho replies. "Let her concentrate."

"Oh. Yeah, that's cool."

Fifteen seconds pass by, and we're nearly clear of the horizon.

"Evelyn?" Jericho asks, doing what he told Kit not to. "You good there?"

I nod. Ideally, I'd want us pointed in the total opposite direction from the planet, but that would take time we don't have. So I guess. "Ten seconds to separation."

Everyone gets so quiet over comms it makes me nervous. Sounds like no one's even breathing. Then I hear someone's foot tapping.

"Kit," Jericho says. "Can it."

"Sorry."

We're as good as it's gonna get. "Three, two, one, mark."

The locking clamps disengage, and the station's compressed air valves shove the lab away. I'm thrown back in my seat, and my broken arm screams in pain. We gain even more acceleration from the atmosphere evacuating the connection tube, which I'd forgotten about. But I know the force is nothing compared to what's coming.

The CEL fires a few pulsed thrusts to keep us oriented. I double-check alignment and then give Rook a thumbs-up.

"Fire in the hole," he says and then triggers the devices inside the tunnel.

Orange light flares behind us, and my head whips into the headrest. I grunt against the g forces as we fling away from the station. The agony in my arm multiplies by the second. Then the third and final shove comes from the mines attached to the hatch's exterior rim. The staccato *ba-boom!* startles me, as does the insane pressure on my chest past the point of being able to breathe. For one interminably long second, we endure over fifty g's that tunnels my vision. But when the acceleration dissipates, I'm thrown forward into the harness. It's the worst whiplash I've ever felt. But I'm alive and wide awake now, thanks to the bones in my arm being on fire.

"All munitions spent," Rook announces.

My eyes clear up enough to read the display. "Interior pressure nominal. Distance, 1,700 meters and climbing. Relative speed... seven hundred fifty-five meters per second."

"Alright." Jericho claps once. "That just might do it."

"Whadda ya mean 'just might'?" Grabowski asks. "I thought you said five hundred would do it?"

He shrugs. "I was trying not to scare anyone."

"Oh. Shit. *Oh shit!*"

"That's enough, Corporal," Rook says in a measured tone. The man's a veritable sealed vault of emotions. "Your suit can handle it. Theirs might not. So count your blessings."

I glance at the TTD counter. "Forty seconds."

Our part is over. Now there's nothing to do but wait. I pull my bad arm to my chest and hold it with the other while grabbing a shoulder strap to immobilize it. My brain, however, is far from stationary.

At 755 meters per second, that puts us thirty kilometers from *Astraea* at time of detonation. Without reviewing an intensity degradation graph, I can't be sure how many rads we'll get hit with. Acute radiation syndrome only needs 500 millisieverts, but then again, we all have base editing to offset some of the effects. Well, not Kit, but he's relatively safe in his shielded starship. My guess is that we'll be hit with something more like 5,000 millisieverts. A few days in therapy, and everyone should be okay. But that's a big should, because we still don't know how big Stamos's bomb is or exactly how it will react to an active generator. If the explosion is large enough, and we're not far enough away, then…

"You ready?" Jericho asks me in a private V-cog audio channel.

"Yeah."

"How's your arm?"

"It's fine."

"Liar."

I laugh, but it fades quickly. The Earth appears to rest motionless under our feet even though we're hurtling out to space shy of one kilometer per second. Everything always looks so peaceful from up here despite the turmoil I know that's brewing on the surface below. I can't help but wonder how far all of this loss, all this sadness will set us back.

"You like beer?" he asks after a few seconds.

"I'm a tequila woman actually."

"Shame. I was gonna buy you a round if we get through this."

"No can do."

"What? Why?"

"Kit called dibs."

It's his turn to laugh. "Well, dibs trumps."

"Yes it does. Better luck next time, I guess." I glance at the TTD, then over general V-cog, I say, "Ten seconds."

The tension in the bubble mounts as everyone casts their last looks at each other.

Out of nowhere, Kit yells over comms, "I'm still a virgin!"

And every last one of us bursts into some sort of stifled laughter.

"What?" he asks.

Then, before I know it, *Astraea* Station's backup power unit explodes.

LIGHT from the blast hits us first. If any of us were to look at it without our dimmed visors, the photons would sear our retinas. However, our backs are to the explosion, so the only view we get is from the lab's rear-facing cameras. A massive fireball blooms from *Astraea*'s end, swallowing all of sections twenty-nine and thirty. Just as I suspected, the event was timed for the precise moment that the station was pitched toward the planet to achieve maximum orbital decay. The explosion doesn't stop the hab from tumbling, but it does start it plummeting toward Earth.

"Temp rising," Sam announces. "But we're holding at 480 milligrays."

"You did it," Grabowski exclaims.

"*We* did it," Jericho clarifies and gives me a thumbs-up as our suits work to fight the rising heat.

Any celebration of our survival is cut short by images of *Astraea*'s failing hull. Huge portions of section twenty-eight fly free, blown out by the oxygen burning from within. Smaller segments of the next three sections also break off as fire chews its way across the station's body. But eventually the violence is swallowed by the void to reveal an entirely new horror: the decapitated body of *Astraea* tumbling toward Earth. The cylinder's end has splayed apart as if a firecracker had detonated inside a cigar. Spreading away is an endless debris field of metal, soil, wire, and bodies. I can't make out the crew, of course, but we all know there wasn't enough time for the last wave to get off the hab.

My mind turns toward those who are still inside. Most will have died either by the violent acceleration or extreme radiation. Those who were somehow shielded and buckled in are even now suffocating as the atmosphere flees the cylinder. Perhaps the wind itself shreds them apart before they succumb to the torture of hard vacuum.

It will be years before every bit of wreckage, every piece of human remains is accounted for. And what NUESSA and its private contractors don't find will burn up in the atmosphere, lost forever. But this atrocity is only the beginning. As the dead station races toward the planet, aided by the Earth's gravity, the cylinder will streak across the sky to terrify the inhabitants below. NUESSA will calculate the impact site and do its best to clear anyone unfortunate enough to be near it. But if it's a highly populated area, there won't be much to do. Some will be praying for a miracle while the rest of us prepare for the inevitable. The only hope for those below is that the station breaks up enough to minimize impact while landing in the middle of an ocean or a desert. Stars, help them. Help us all.

"Are you all okay in there?" Kit asks over comms.

"Roger that," Jericho replies. "You?"

"Um, yeah. I'm fine. Headed your way now. It's just… all those people. And then Earth, because, well…"

"I know, buddy. I know. Just focus on coming to get us."

"Right. Yeah. On my way."

I feel helpless as I watch *Astraea* tumble away from us, slowly moving toward the Earth's horizon. Kit's right. All those people.

Sam breaks the sickening silence. "How could he let this happen?"

It takes me a second to realize what she's implying. I forgot that she's religious. "He didn't let it happen, Sam. This is all on us."

37

JERICHO

"FANCY MEETING YOU HERE," says a familiar voice in real life.

"Someone there?" Kit asks me in my Amel 60's V-cog lobby.

"It's Evelyn. I've gotta go, pal."

"Tell her she still owes me a date."

"Sure thing."

"And let me know how things go, okay? If they're buying you back, I have dibs on your apartment. And you better put in a good word for me with Mr. Sallsworth too."

"Promise."

"Okay. Cool. Talk to you later."

I snap out of V-cog as Evelyn takes a seat in the chair across from me. She looks rested and comfortable in her business casual attire—a far cry from the *Astraea* Station vac suit I last saw her in.

It's been five days since we survived the "fall that shook the world," as the pundits are calling it. *Astraea* entered Earth's atmosphere eighteen hours after the final bomb detonated inside the reactor room, forcing the O'Neill-Oberth down through the planet's gravity well. It streaked across the sky in apparent slow motion as the extremists counted down to the apocalypse. Of course, nothing so dramatic happened. The station broke apart and splashed down in sections between the Floridian Desert Strait and the Bahama Shoals. It's hard to see a silver lining in all of the death and destruction surrounding *Astraea*, but if there is one, it's that the only things killed on Earth were aquatic life and the Tantum's dreams of a more significant headline.

Even still, the news has indeed shaken humanity, and my call to report to Director Johnson's office at NUESSA headquarters has only added to my own sense of upheaval. Hopefully it's good, but I'm not counting any chickens just yet.

The sterile waiting room is lined with glossy white chairs and adorned with holographic images from the various stations around the system. I note one particular view of Earth taken from the former legacy hab and wonder if they'll remove it from the rotation out of respect for the dead.

"You excited?"

I look at Evelyn's eyes. "For what?"

She laughs a little and then points at the door to the director's personal conference room. "For what you're going to get in there."

"A mission patch and a photo op?"

"A job."

"Wouldn't count on it."

"After what you did up there?" She folds her arms. "I'll be surprised if they don't offer you *something*."

Sure, an invite back to NUESSA would be the greatest thing I could hope for. But that would take a hundred thousand coins to change my ink. And after the multi-trillion-crypto loss the agency just took, I doubt they have such discretionary income. Moreover, I can't imagine that the Solum Terram wants to let me go. Last I knew, they were looking to ensure I ended up in the Atlantic too.

"My guess?" I say to Evelyn. "It's the last debrief."

"You mean you haven't been in meetings nonstop since we landed?"

I chuckle as I consider just how sore my ass is from sitting. "Oh, I have. Just hoping this is the capstone, ya know?"

She nods and still gives me a look with some sort of knowing twinkle in her eye.

"And anyway," I say as I reach into my pocket. "The Viatoribus isn't the politicast I think I want to join."

"Oh?"

"A certain Marine said I'd make a good addition to the Sentia Aux." I hold up the challenge coin from Rook. "Or maybe I'll just enlist."

"Don't waste your time," she says.

"Why not?"

"I've seen you shoot."

It takes me less than a second to say, "No you haven't."

"Exactly."

Smartass.

We share a smile, and then I ask more to the point, "You really think there's room for me in the SA?"

Evelyn pulls out a coin of her own. "I'd vote for you."

"He gives those to everyone, doesn't he."

She grins and stuffs her marker back in her pocket.

The conference room doors part, and a young man in a suit walks through. He looks between us and then his eyes settle on Evelyn. "Director Johnson will see you now."

"Good luck," I say as she stands.

"Thanks."

"Ah, excuse me. He'll see *both* of you at the same time, please."

Evelyn nods as I join her. "I'm telling you. Get ready."

We're ushered into a wide room with a white conference table stretching the length. An artificial starscape fills the ceiling, giving the environment a space-like quality. To my surprise, every seat is taken but two at the middle and closest to the door.

"Please," Director Eric Johnson says and motions to the chairs. "Have a seat." When we're settled and decline a steward's offer of water or coffee, Johnson says, "Thank you for joining us."

"Did we have a choice?" I ask.

"No."

"Then, you're welcome."

This gets a smattering of laughter.

It also gives me a chance to survey the room. I don't know all of the faces, but several stand out, including SESI Director Lemuel Brown; Manaaki Aihu Mowai Raka, president of the Southlands Nations; Nikolai Vasiliev of Norasia; and Velvet Davis of the American Heights. Also at the table are several NUESSA and SESI executives, some of whom I know well from my days with the agency. Last but not least are Admiral Herman Cohen, Chief of Space Naval Operations, and General J. K. Blackburn, Commandant of the Space Marine Corps.

The fact that this many prominent world leaders are gathered here without a flock of paparazzi pixies or armed excipions upon entering the building means this meeting is as private as they come, and most likely the safest place I could be on the planet right now. I can practically feel the satellites and F-01X fighters circling the airspace outside.

Johnson takes control of the meeting and directs his attention at us. "I know I speak for all those here that, while we are saddened by the loss of *Astraea* Station and those who perished aboard it, we are grateful for your courageous efforts."

This gets a murmur of approval around the table.

"Thank you for your valiant deeds," President Aihu Mowai Raka says with a nod toward Evelyn and me. "Your names will be revered among the Southlands."

"And those in the north," adds Davis.

Vasiliev nods in his predictably stoic fashion, but I know the gesture is worth its weight in Russian vodka.

"We didn't stop the bombs from going off," I add in a somber tone, trying to diffuse what feels like misplaced praise.

"We know," Admiral Blackburn replies. "But we're also aware that the fallout could have been even worse were it not for you. Without your efforts, we may never have known who was behind this, and they would have succeeded in making the attack look like station failure."

"We just did our jobs," Evelyn says. "And there are thousands who are more worthy of this gratitude than us, including the station's Command crew."

Johnson's face grows grim. "We will honor Captain Mombawe, Lieutenant Forsythe, and their staff in planned memorials later in the month."

Evelyn nods and then folds her hands in her lap. "Their loved ones will be grateful."

"And you will both be invited to say words about

them. We understand from your debrief that you worked closely with the Lieutenant in his final hours, Captain Fox?"

Hearing Johnson say my old title feels strange, but I answer the question without hesitation. "We did. He was very helpful in getting us around the station and cutting through any red tape that might otherwise keep me and Master Sergeant Farooq from closing in on the suspect." It dawns on me that the notion of red tape might belittle NUESSA's standard operating procedures meant to keep people safe. "I'm sorry, I didn't mean anything negative by that."

"We all know how cumbersome regulations can be. No offense taken, Jericho."

I nod at Eric, noting his use of my first name. Despite the company present, this is suddenly feeling more casual than I expected.

"As for you both, the work must go on," Eric adds and then turns to Lemuel. "Dr. Brown?"

"Thank you." Lemuel calls for everyone to respond to his V-cog invite. I do and find myself in a darkened theater environment facing a wide holo display. Evelyn is seated beside me, and the rest of the conference room's participants surround us.

"What you are about to see is a matter of international security and is reserved for the members of this room only and those direct reports who you deem need-to-know. This is security clearance level designation top secret.

"As many of you know, the entire data set collected from Parallax on *Astraea* Station was corrupted thanks to a command authorization worm exploit initiated by the Tantum Terrae operative now known as Jack Birdwhistle." The screen fills with an image of the man Evelyn knew as Stamos, and I knew as Faust, along with metadata on every move the terrorist made while on the station.

"Birdwhistle?" Vasiliev asks. "Is not used to call birds?"

"Yes," Brown replies. "But also an old family name from the former United Kingdom. Lancashire, I believe. We have researchers tracing the tree now. We know Birdwhistle co-opted Dr. Collins and Dr. Park to collaborate against their wills in the matter. Both women have been cleared of any charges. Meanwhile, there is strong evidence implicating Dr. Bhavna Mishra in concealing and aiding Birdwhistle's actions."

I sense Evelyn shift in her real-life seat as a file for Mishra replaces Stamos's.

"When will she be brought to trial?" President Davis asks.

"After the prosecution and defense have had ample time to review the evidence. Until then, she'll remain in NUE custody in Oslo."

"Thank you."

Brown continues. "The data loss has certainly hit the SESI community hard as we know that it clearly inferred contact with extra-solar sentient life, something Dr. Park has long championed—in fact, giving her entire career to its pursuit. We are, of course, hopeful that the foreign transmission will continue. As such, NUESSA and SESI have authorized a joint mission to replicate Parallax on not just Calypso, but Arete, Selene, and Persephone." The stations appear behind him and hover over Earth, the moon, and Mars.

"Four stations?" Evelyn exclaims, nearly coming out of both real and virtual seats.

Brown casts her a wide grin. "Humanity can't afford to miss this again."

"I agree, of course. It's... critically important." After she catches her breath, she asks, "Who is in charge of the mission?"

Brown seems to balk here. "Carlson." To the rest of the room, Brown adds, "Dr. Ben Carlson."

Evelyn's enthusiasm evaporates. "He's the right choice."

"He is, yes. Just as you are for deciphering the transmission, Dr. Park."

"I'm honored. But in the meantime?"

"Not the meantime. Now."

Her eyes narrow. "I... don't understand."

Brown holds up the medal around his neck and announces to the room, "Saint Dymphna." Surely aware that no one is familiar with the, I presume, Catholic notable, he continues. "Patron saint of the mentally ill, canonized for her miraculous healings and curing of memory, among other ailments." In real life, Brown lifts the chain over his head and lays the medallion on a lectern, but in V-cog it hovers in front of the holo display. "As we all know, it is against NUESSA/SESI policy to hold any data belonging to the agency offsite. Likewise, cold storage devices are illegal on premises. However, there are certain times that even the saints broke the rules."

"Lemuel?" Evelyn asks. "What are you saying?"

"That while the entire data set and all ancillary network drives were corrupted, the data on my contraband device was not."

The holo display lights up with a three-dimensional array of data that I'm unable to parse. But for Evelyn? It's the greatest treasure in the world. She climbs from her seat in real life, using my shoulder as a cane, and stumbles toward Lemuel, never once taking her eyes from the V-cog display. Her words come out in a choked tone. "You have it? You really have it, Lem? Oh, stars, please tell me this isn't a joke."

"I have it all. I'm only sorry I couldn't let you know sooner."

The scientists embrace in an emotional display of nervous laughter and muffled crying.

While I'm not sure of the data's precise value, it doesn't take a rocket scientist to know that the overall implication represents the most important discovery in human history. So, yeah, there's more than one person getting misty eyed around the table. If anything, I'm moved just by Evelyn's reaction. I can only imagine how much this must mean to her given the loss she's been carrying all week. Brown wipes a tear away too. Then Evelyn appears to remember the room, dries her eyes, and finds her way back to her seat.

Brown continues. "While you'll have your pick of any SESI members you wish, I would recommend Dr. Natalie Mason and Dr. Samantha Collins be among your top choices."

"Yes. Yes, of course. When do we start?"

"Immediately."

Evelyn lets out a small laugh, covers her mouth, and then looks at me. "I can't believe it."

"Congratulations, Dr. Park. You deserve it."

She throws both arms around my real body and squeezes me tight. This time, her hair doesn't smell like prison shampoo.

The moment passes, and Dr. Brown hands the meeting back over to Director Johnson. "In addition to the request put in by the SESI, NUESSA is seeking a new round of emergency funding as well. The present situation has increased pressure on the Infinita program to accelerate exoplanet exploration, and with it comes the primary need to move up the Marquis-class initiative's timeline."

Based on the lack of reaction from the politicians at the table, I get the feeling that this isn't news to them. As if driving that point home, Johnson locks eyes with me.

When he doesn't add anything more, I ask, "Is there… something I can help you with, Director?"

"As a matter of fact there is. How about leading the MCI?"

Now it's my turn to wonder if this is a joke. "Sir?"

"NUESSA unanimously voted to have you reinstated, Jericho. The position is yours if you want it."

Finding words is hard enough for me sometimes, but now I'm just downright speechless. Evelyn, God bless her, was right about the job offer. There are so many questions in my head, I don't even know where to start.

"Whadda you say, Knight?"

"I… I mean…"

"Say yes, Jericho," Evelyn practically shouts and then shoves me with both hands.

"Yes. Hell yes!"

"Good," Johnson replies amidst the soft sounds of laughter coming from the national leaders around the table.

"Eric? If you don't mind me asking?"

"Have at it."

"I'm, uh"—I hold up my palm—"not exactly politically aligned with your cause."

"No. You're not. But we have some funds ear-marked for your transfer."

Some funds? "And the Solum Terram?"

"Obliged without complaint."

"I find that hard to believe. Last I knew, they wanted to kill me." Such a direct statement seems to cool off the room. But it's the truth.

"From my understanding, it was not as black and white as you or we were led to believe."

"The MAW projectiles that missed my head say otherwise. Begging your pardon."

"You have a message from Sir Sallsworth waiting for you when we're done here. Maybe it will provide some needed answers. You're welcome to take it in your new office on the twenty-first floor if you feel so inclined."

New office? They really are wanting to move fast. Which reminds me. "Not trying to push my luck here, but would you happen to have room for one more?"

Johnson eyes me with a guarded measure of curiosity but then seems to pick up where I'm going. "Leslie Smith? Aka Kit? Aka, the young man who hasn't stopped talking about Dr. Park's heroics all week?"

I chuckle. "That's the one."

"We'll see what we can do."

"Thanks. Thank you all."

"Our pleasure. And good to have you back, Jericho."

"Good to be back." Damn, is it ever.

THE FIRST CALL I make from my new office is to my dad. I feel bad for ghosting him twice during my time on *Astraea*, but it was pretty bad timing. Not that he's to blame. Well, for the second call, okay. I can see from my inbox that, in addition to the message he left me while I was riding the lift with Rook and Team One, he's left me twenty-five messages while my system was in mandatory quarantine during debrief and gene therapy. Like the first, the mail wasn't anything life shattering— just my dad. Checking in. And throwing shade on anything *not* related to the Solum Terram.

"Hey, dad," I say from my balcony looking over the Med from the Amalfi Coast.

"Son! Oh, thank God. I've been worried sick."

"Good to see you."

"Good to see you too." He gets choked up. "Are you okay? Where are you? Those bastards aren't probing you, are they?"

"No, dad. I'm fine." I think about telling him my exact location but then remember that I'm not at liberty just yet. "They're treating me well—NUESSA and the Navy alike. Just lots of interviews and questions. Memorials planned for next week."

"Don't let them bully you, son. They're all bastards."

"Dad."

He sniffs. "Okay, well, the Navy aren't bastards. When do you head back to work?"

"Uh, well…"

"Can't discuss it. Got it."

The misunderstanding acts as a suitable stand-in for the truth. For now, anyway. "Yeah. Listen, I've gotta go, but I just wanted you to know that I'm okay and—"

"I miss you."

I bite the inside of my cheek. Half of me is annoyed while the other half wants to give him a hug. I also want to let him know that his politicast damn near killed me, but it feels too much like a cheap shot right now. Plus, the news won't change his mind anyway; probably just add more fuel to the fire. "It's all propaganda" he'll say, and then, "That's just what they want you to think."

"What's wrong?" he asks after a moment.

I take a deep breath. Someone forgot to give me the handbook on how to adult with my father. I decide not to tell him about my politicast change or the new job—what little of it I'm allowed to say so far. I also decide against bringing up the SESI discovery that's gone viral too. He'll just dismiss it and call it "alleged" like all rock squatters would. "I'll reach out to you when I can."

"Understood." He sniffs again, as if clearing tears. "Love you, son."

"Bye, dad."

I close the channel and grab the railing on my balcony.

"Mr. Fox," Sallsworth says. "How good of you to return my call." He and I are back on the mountain-view deck in Davos, and the exquisitely rendered snow is still falling like it did before. But it's still not melting.

"Director Johnson informed me that the Solum Terram has released me."

"He's correct."

I'm not sure whether to thank the man or spit in his face. "Why?"

Sallsworth doesn't blink. "Because your talents are better suited elsewhere, Mr. Fox. And I've already found a new pilot to replace you."

"So it's official?"

"You are, for the moment, a man without a home."

"And you have no claim?"

"None."

"Good. So why were you trying to kill me?"

If the man is put off guard by the direct question, he doesn't show it. "I am sorry for that."

"You admit it?"

"That agents bearing the Solum Terram mark attempted to assassinate you? Yes, of course."

"But they were operating on *your* orders, Sallsworth."

He nods and gives me a frown.

"So, that's it then? You're just… sorry?"

"It was a decision outside of my control, Jericho. Whether or not you choose to believe it is, of course, your prerogative."

I point a finger at him. "And I don't need you telling me what my prerogatives are either."

"Of course. But you are owed the truth, and that is what I give. I did and do not desire you to come to harm."

"I had people shooting at me up there!"

"You have every right to be upset."

"Did you help with the bombing?"

"As you are already aware, I agreed to provide passage for one who turned out to be responsible. It was a debt I had to pay. But no, I did not help with the bombing. That is not the Solum Terram way." He pauses to consider something and searches my face to find it. "You and I are not so different, you know. We both work to see humanity thrive again. We play our different parts and see things from different angles, but we are still very much the same."

Emotionally, I want to come at him with a counter

accusation, not that I've got a snappy comeback ready. Hell, I'd settle for slugging him, but little good that does in V-cog without mutual neurohaptics. Somewhere in my gut, however, I feel like he's... well, like he's actually telling some version of the truth. Even the serpent didn't lie to Adam and Eve about everything.

But if Sallsworth *is* shooting me straight, then it makes me wonder what was happening behind the scenes. If he didn't order the hit against me, then who did? And why was such a thing "outside of my control"? It feels like carefully calculated words to throw me off the scent, but I also can't help believing him somewhat. Damn crows.

"So this is why you wanted to see me? To clear up your conscience?"

"No. I wanted to let you know that the door remains open."

I scoff. "No thanks."

"And not just for asylum," he presses on. "If you ever need anything, anything at all, this V-rec is open."

I narrow my gaze at him. "We done?"

"Yes, Mr. Fox. *We done.*"

"Good."

THE REQUEST CHIME pings from my office door. I rub my face once more and then sit back in my new chair. "Come in."

The panels separate to reveal Evelyn leaning against the frame with her arms crossed. Her face goes from casual to concerned. "You okay?" Then she answers her own question. "You called Sallsworth."

I nod.

"How'd it go?"

"Eh… I don't really wanna talk about it."

"That bad?"

I don't answer.

She doesn't press me. "So, listen. I know I'm already spoken for and all, but you up for a celebratory beer in light of our mutual promotions?"

"I thought you said you were a tequila woman?"

"I am. You ever hear of a Corrido Prohibidos?"

"Sounds like trouble."

She grins. "Only if you can't handle your liquor."

"Game on."

EPILOGUE

Nigel

Nigel Sallsworth sat behind his desk in the Solum Terram's headquarters building, looking over Helsinki. For all the light without, he felt dark within, as if the weight of the world had smothered the sun.

Outside and forty stories below, the transplanted palms swooshed and swayed in the higher than normal winds. Likewise, the foam from the surf carried further than it would have before all of *this*... before humanity had worked in tandem with the planet's natural cycles to produce something altogether...

Artificial.

The word lingered in his brain like the aftertaste of some cheap champagne whose added sweetener attempted to mask the vinedresser's dismal attempts at horticulture. None of this was supposed to be here. The palms. The wave riders. The bikinis and bass drops of whatever the latest cyber-thud had topped the verb that day. But now that artificiality was here, the world clamored for praise of their glorious triumph.

Astraea was supposed to be a triumph too. Not for him, of course. He despised the idea of so much death and destruction. But he understood why it needed to happen, for Neon at least. Hers was chaos, as she so ruefully put it to him on the slopes of her Pacific-facing vineyard. Chaos to keep the world in order. To do what no one else had the stomach to.

Nigel turned from the wraparound windows and took up the framed photograph of his family. He liked seeing the faces printed on paper, liked feeling the wood and glass in his hands. There was something comforting about it all—the legacies of woodworking and glass blowing that had survived a thousand generations, even if this was a mass-made product. It stood for something old.

And then there were the faces of his wife, Esther, son, Malcom, and daughter, Fiona. He wondered afresh what kind of world they would inherit. Sure, he'd known the answer before. Always known—confident of himself, of his advisors, researchers, speech writers. Everyone was confident. Everyone, sure.

"And now?" he asked the faces in the picture frame.

They didn't reply.

Weight pushed down harder, and what little light remained grew even fainter. The numbers didn't lie.

The Joint Session of Nations of United Earth leaders and politicast heads had called for an emergency voting session, one he knew would come. He also knew exactly how he would cast his vote. A war against the Tantum Terrae might as well be a war against the Solum Terram.

But Neon and her recklessness had changed all that.

Of course she was volatile. Violent. Deplorable. Those were precisely the traits that he needed in a black book counterpart. The woman from the west was the poison in his ring, the dart from the shadow in the corner of the room, the nanofilm lining the folded paper message that would kill days after the words were long forgotten.

But then came his time on Calvert Isle.

Then came *Astraea*.

If Neon could bring down a legacy hab with a handful of people, there was no telling what else she was capable of. She commanded her paladins like subjects, ones made all the more willing by the power she wielded over them to distort and destroy. She'd even worked her experiments on her own family, he'd heard. So the whispered title was true after all. She really was the Witch of Calvert Isle. He'd seen it with his own eyes and survived.

But for how long?

And if he changed his vote now, she would come for him. She would feel betrayed.

"All the more reason to act decisively," he said as he poured deep magenta liquid from the decanter. The smell was rich and layered. *"For the betrayed breathe a fire that crashes harmlessly against the shields of the just."*

Unlike the lab rats of Neon's prized two-hundred-year-old histories, humanity would find a way out before the experiment was concluded. They always did. And thanks to the renewed efforts of those in the scientific community, Nigel was beginning to think that the exit was coming sooner rather than later.

No, Neon, he thought. People could not be subdued any more than ocean currents could be thwarted or winds stifled. But power? Power could always be harnessed, could always be redirected to suit the greater good. Like sails atop a ship and a rudder in the stern. And if done well? If the destination be true? The passengers laud the person at the helm.

What the masses truly needed was coaxing. An effective leader had to prove that he knew their wants, understood their desires, and could provide for their needs. Then he could ride the wave of their approval to a new threshold of leadership and ever-growing esteem. That is, after all, how he arrived here, wasn't it?

Nigel swirled the tawny port, studied the legs sliding down the glass, sipped it, and then licked his lips at the end.

The vote to go to war against the Tantum Terrae had to be unanimous, and he knew the council was waiting for him—watching with bated breath to see what he would do. If he voted against the majority, things would proceed as planned. Without war, the council would resume the normal election cycle, and Nigel's Preservationist opponent would be found dead within the week. Nigel would be secretary-general by default, a post he would assume oh so humbly and reluctantly.

But she... *she* would remain the Witch of Calvert Isle and haunt him. So she must be dealt with.

Neon would renege her side of the deal, of course. But Nigel had other ways to overcome his opponent.

And if she came for him?—which she surely would. Then he would be ready. He'd survived worse.

No. *Neon will no longer be my dagger*, he thought as he rolled the port in his snifter. *She must become my foil.*

"Mr. Sallsworth?" said his assistant in V-cog. "They're ready for the vote."

And he knew exactly how he would cast his. For his

wife. For his children's children. And for all those he would lead as the first president of Earth.

To war, Adriana. That they might purge their souls whilst we plunder their storehouses. Ever and always to war.

⁖

Neon

FROM WITHIN V-COG, Neon opened a side door and walked into one of the suites she'd shared with Jack. The molded thatched ceiling and bamboo walls smelled damp, leftovers from an evening rain. A poster of the exact beach outside hung above a mat bed in silent protest of the Southland's economic disparity. Jack grew up in abject poverty not five hundred meters from a tropical luxury resort. There was plenty of money to lift everyone out of the mire, but there wasn't the foresight or generosity of spirit to make it reality.

Neon knelt on the bed and traced the pictured sands with a finger. Then she touched the series of head-shot photographs pinned against it. The one of Evelyn Park had been pulled down, leaving the thumbtack behind. Jack had said he'd bring the women to her as a gift... said he'd even stop to destroy her research.

Neon said it was a distraction… had told him just to leave and come home.

But he hadn't listened.

And now?

Rage. That is what Neon felt. Burning in her bones like a lava flow.

There was only one person in the system she wanted to speak with. Neon pinged Olivia. It took several seconds for the woman to reply. At first Neon worried something was wrong, but her architects had said the incog trace was still at maximum integrity and holding. Delays were normal for deep plants.

"Neon," is all Olivia said when she stepped into the suite. Her eyes communicated the rest.

"Are you okay?" the older woman asked.

"Yes, I'm fine. But… I can only imagine how you're feeling."

"I will have my revenge. Are you still in position?"

Olivia nodded as if confirmation might jinx the whole charade.

"Good. And they suspect…?"

"Nothing."

It was Neon's turn to nod. "I'm proud of you."

"I was trained by the best."

Neon gave her a thin smile, too beset by grief to mean anything more. "What about their discovery?"

Olivia took a steadying breath. "It's real."

"But inconsequential, yes?"

The younger woman hesitated.

"What? What is it?"

"Based on everything I've seen? The signal has all the signs of originating from an advanced civilization. Or at least it was when the transmission left their solar system three hundred years ago."

"And you think this, why?"

"Well, the data they collected looks layered, certainly beyond anything we're able to figure out."

"You mean *they*."

"Right. Sorry. Anyway, the tech needed to generate that beam? Earth has nothing like it."

"And still no verdict on authorial intent?"

"We won't be there for months, I'm guessing. Maybe years." She smiled. "Maybe never."

"That would be the best of outcomes."

"I wonder…" Olivia hesitated for a moment. "We never thought this contact would actually happen. Should it change any of our plans?"

"And why would it?"

"Yes, you're right. Of course. It doesn't." Olivia shook her head as if scolding the wayward thoughts, which they were. "What are my orders?"

"Sabotage the work. Ensure the program will not progress. Then return home."

"But don't you think that if I remain in place I might be able to—"

"You have your orders, Olivia."

"Yes, ma'am."

Neon, sensing that the younger woman was not entirely convinced, redoubled her efforts. "If the project fails from within, there will be no need for you to stay long-term."

"Of course, yes, but—"

Neon snapped. "They killed my son."

Olivia stiffened and then lowered her head.

"Do you hear me?" Neon took a step forward and lifted Olivia's head with the power of her penetrating glare. "They killed - my - *son* on that station!"

"I'm aware."

"Of course you are." Neon checked herself. Her fight was not with Olivia. So she softened her tone and turned away. "Tell me, how did he die? Your report says a firefight, but it leaves out certain… details."

"Like?"

"The last Marine to shoot him in the back of the head."

"Uh, Ishaq al Farooq, Master Sergeant. Goes by Rook."

"Rook." Neon repeated the name several times in her head so that it might find its way into the recesses of her heart. "And then you all escaped via the laboratory?"

"We did."

"Clever." Neon turned on her heel and waved a finger at Olivia. "I don't want these people succeeding."

"Of course."

"And you will stop them?"

"I will."

"There's a great deal riding on you, dear. I can't afford for you to fail me."

"I won't. Dr. Park has asked me to assist her in deciphering the signal."

"Good. Use the opportunity well."

"I will."

"There's another thing I need you to do for me."

"Name it."

"Recover his ring."

Olivia hesitated. "But his body is undergoing an autopsy in a highly secured—"

"And you're a highly regarded public figure now. Use it."

"Yes, of course."

After another strange pause, Neon asked, "Is there a problem, Olivia?"

"No. None at all."

"Only Earth."

"Only Earth," Olivia replied and then stepped out of the suite hastily.

Only Earth forever, should have been Olivia's response. Neon made note of it and returned to walking through her vineyard in the morning mist.

BOOK 2
PARALLAX RISING

What will Evelyn discover in the alien transmission?

How far will Jericho be able to take his new team?

And how will Neon react when she learns that the Solum Terram has turned its back on her?

Find out in Infinita book 2: *Parallax Rising*

Available in trade and mass market paperback, hardcover, audiobook, and ebook at **christopherhopper.com**.

Or your favorite retailers:

Amazon | Apple | Kobo

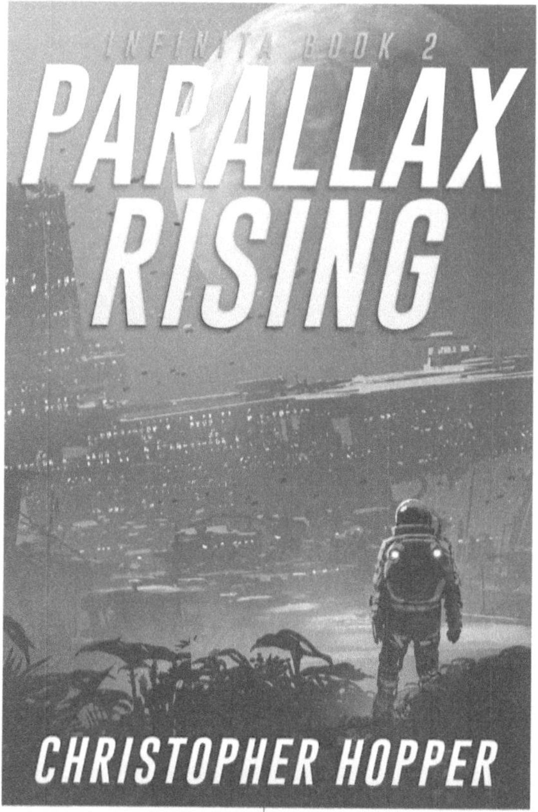

SECURE YOUR COPY NOW!

VIP

Become a VIP club member today!

Membership is free, and you'll receive an official club poker chip, short story, and 10% off Christopher's store for life. Plus, you'll be signed up to get exclusive club perks in the mail and invited to join the private VIP social media group of your choice.

Visit christopherhopper.com to jump on board now.

BECOME A VIP FREE

10 %
OFF
ALL MERCH

VIP
MEMBER
POKER CHIP

SHORT STORY

PLUS
EXCLUSIVE ACCESS TO
PRIVATE SOCIAL MEDIA GROUP

SCAN NOW

GEAR UP IN THE SHOP

Show your spacer spirit by purchasing the officially licensed Infinita t-shirts, hats, and challenge coins. From NUESSA and SESI, to the Tantum Terrae and Sentia Aux, find your factions and choose your sides at christopherhopper.com/shop today!

INFINITA
COLLECTION

FIND YOUR GEAR NOW!

ACKNOWLEDGMENTS

I don't write my books in a vacuum. Some authors like the solitary approach. I never have. Instead, I pursue writing much like video game developers approach creating their masterpieces, with lots of preplanning, designing, and testing, all done in consideration of my readers. Creating this type of "boutique art" takes time and comes down to people, and I'm fortunate to have some of the most talented team players in the industry on my side.

I am grateful for Matthew Titus's masterful work on this story. Without his keen analysis and tireless coaching, I fear my characters would be both stale and lonely, banished to a meaningless trip through the big black.

Jennifer Sell, your editing prowess is unrivaled. Everything you touch shines more brightly and speaks more clearly. Readers and listeners the world over thank you, as do I.

Rebecca Woods and Daniel Wisniewski, thank you for bringing my characters to life for the audio version of this story. Few things delight my heart as much as hearing you use your gifts. You give us a whole new way to enjoy the book, and you're both masters at your craft. I'm lucky to have you.

Lorenz Hideyoshi Ruwwe, thank you for bringing *Astraea* Station to life. Your craftsmanship inspires me deeply. Thanks to my daughter, Evangeline, and my son, Luik, for working behind the scenes on my store and websites. You rock.

To Christie Strahler for keeping my science in check, Gary Guilmette for crafting me yet another robust armory, Steve Janulin for making sure my Space Marines stayed in line, Neil Rubenking for endless autocorrect quips, and Tracey Beattie for ensuring I didn't stray too far from the path—thank you all.

Thank you to my faithful beta readers for sweeping up the sawdust after the lights go out: Nathan Reimer, John Vermillion, Shane Marolf, David Seaman, Mauricio Longo, John Holley Jr., Kevin Zoll, John Walker, Jon Bliss, Mike McDonnell, Sean Ross, Eric Earley, Elijah Cole, George Hain, Dan Wong, and the ever neighborly Christine Spinner. And to Josh Jensen for the computer science tips that are above my pay grade.

Making friends with other authors is a true gift, especially when they're the likes of Ken Lozito, Gerry Riddle, Nicholas Smith, Jonathan Yanez, Nathan Hystad, Jason Anspach, Jeff Chaney, and Wayne Thomas Batson. Thanks for your encouragement and constant belief in my work.

I'm so thankful for my loyal VIPs. Your enthusiasm and immense support in the club communities inspires me to keep writing more great books. Any author lucky enough to have a group of spacers as dedicated as you are to me is twice blessed. Thank you.

Shane Marolf was the first person to tell me that the world needed "science fiction from Hopper's mind." Of all my books, I think that this is the one most faithfully attests to what he first imagined. Thank you for calling it out.

Much thanks also goes to my dear friend Denis Johnson Jr. for his generous consultation on Jericho's family history. Thanks for the honor of seeing life through your eyes. It was fun dreaming about how the world will be when the war on racism is finally over.

I always save the best for last: my wife, Jennifer Lee. I've never met the soul who didn't have a dream, but I've met more than I can count who've never been able to pursue them. You not only saw the spark in me to write, but you also fanned it into flame and kept adding fuel to the fire until the world took notice. Thank you for forging paths through the darkness with me. I love you.

christopherhopper.com/infinitasecrets

intothevoid